D1433506

THE HOUSE

1840's Ireland – When Lord Armstrong builds the house for his bride, Anna, the family is at the climax of its power. But its world is threatened when no heir is born. Anna could restore their fortunes, but it would mean the ultimate betrayal. Then the Great Famine grips the country.

1910's – Clara finds life as lady of the manor is not what she expected when she married Pierce Armstrong. As the First World War rages, she finds solace in artist Johnny Seymour's decadent circle. Then the War of Independence erupts and Clara is caught between two men, deceit and revenge.

THE HOUSE

THE HOUSE

by

A. O'Connor

Magna Large Print Books
Long Preston, North Yorkshire,
BD23 4ND, England.

British Library Cataloguing in Publication Data.

O'Connor, A.
    The house.

    A catalogue record of this book is
    available from the British Library

    ISBN   978-0-7505-4205-0

First published in 2012 by Poolbeg Press Ltd.

Magna Large Print is an imprint of Library Magna Books Ltd.

Printed and bound in Great Britain by
T.J. (International) Ltd., Cornwall, PL28 8RW

Acknowledgements

As ever, my appreciation to everyone at Poolbeg – Paula Campbell, Kieran Devlin, David Prendergast, Sarah Ormston and Ailbhe Hennegan. Thank you Gaye Shortland for your precision editing skills. And continued gratitude to the book buyers, reviewers and you – the readers.

For Mary Kate Browne

Prologue

2007

The divorce should have been a straightforward affair. Both parties wanted out of the marriage. As ever it was in the detail that the problems arose, and so they had gathered with their lawyers to mediate in an attempt to stave off further court proceedings. Nico and Susan Collins sat across a board table from each other in an office at Susan's solicitor's premises, beside their respective legal representatives. Nico's solicitor, Geoffrey Conway, a man in his sixties, had represented his family for thirty years. But as Nico observed Susan's dapper, young and overly confident solicitor, he hoped Geoffrey's experience would outwit his opponent's flair and style.

'To begin with, I think it's good to stress the positive,' began Geoffrey. 'Nico and Susan are in agreement that they should divorce. They are in agreement that they share custody of their daughter Alex.'

'Which leaves just the financial arrangements,' said Susan.

'Indeed,' said Geoffrey. 'There is the family home in Dublin which has a considerable mortgage and two houses in the country, Armstrong House and Hunter's Farm, which have been in Nico's family for many a generation, and which he inherited from his late mother Jacqueline Armstrong Collins.' Geoffrey had a whimsical look as he spoke her name, with fond memories of his old friend, still in his mind a figure of glamour and excitement from their youth at university back in the sixties.

'What my client is proposing,' said Susan's solicitor, Peter, sitting forward, 'is that Armstrong House is sold which would put both Mr and Mrs Collins in a strong financial position to allow them to pay off the mortgage in Dublin and buy Nico a new home in Dublin as well.'

'I've said it before,' said Nico defiantly. 'I'm not selling the house.'

Susan became irritated. 'So, in that case we will have to sell the family home in Dublin, and Alex and I will have to live in some shoebox somewhere, while you will be in that rented flat for the rest of your life. That will be lovely for Alex, shuttled between a shoebox and a rented flat!'

'We both work in good professions – you're a journalist and I'm an architect,' said Nico. 'We can get by.'

'I don't want to "get by",' said Susan. 'We can set ourselves and our daughter up if we sell Armstrong House. My friend Janet Dolan from Dolan Auctioneers viewed the house last week and she said she would be confident of getting well over a million for it.'

'Janet Dolan!' said Nico aghast. 'I can't believe you sent her down to survey my house.'

'Why not? She's the best in the business.'

'The reality is, Nico, you also have considerable

14

debts left over from your parents that you are responsible for,' Peter pointed out.

'Jacqueline did like the high life,' said Susan, smirking over at Nico.

'Indeed she did,' said Geoffrey, smiling at the memory of her.

Nico gave Geoffrey a warning look and the solicitor coughed.

'Nico is adamant he will not sell the house. It's been in the family for one hundred and seventy years. And Jacqueline loved the place.'

'Well, that was Jacqueline all over,' said Susan. 'She was so black or white. Loved something or hated it. She loved French food, hated Italian. Loved yachting, hated dancing. Loved Nico – hated me!'

Nico looked at her challengingly. 'Will we talk about your family's qualities, while we're at it?'

Susan smiled ruefully. 'No – I'd rather not!'

Nico nodded and grinned. 'Wise of you.'

Geoffrey sat back. 'Look, Nico is not disputing the value of Armstrong House or indeed the benefit it would be to you all if it was sold. He merely says he does not wish to sell.'

'We can go to court and force a sale,' Peter pointed out.

Susan sighed loudly and looked sympathetically at Nico. 'Which we would rather not do... I just want you to see this is the right thing to do, Nico, for Alex, for all of us.'

As Geoffrey observed the couple look at each other with obvious affection he said, 'Have we exhausted all possibility of the marriage being salvaged?'

15

'Yes,' said Susan definitely. 'Our marriage was no longer working – there were three of us in this marriage.'

'Three?' said Geoffrey, horrified at the sudden revelation.

'That's right – me, Nico and an architect's drawing board!' She looked at Nico accusingly, and suddenly they both erupted in laughter.

Geoffrey shook his head in exasperation. 'Then we must all agree to differ and let the courts decide.'

Susan sat forward and looked at Nico. 'I know you love Armstrong House, Nico, but it nearly broke your mother and father.'

'Exactly! For me to just to sell it as soon as it comes to me would be a betrayal of my parents and my family. And it would be a betrayal for Alex in the future. It's her legacy as well ... in fact, why don't we ask Alex to decide the fate of the house?'

'Alex is a ten-year-old child – never a good idea to ask them anything more complicated than what topping they want on their pizza,' Geoffrey advised.

'I'm afraid I agree with your lawyer,' said Susan quickly.

'That's because you know Alex doesn't want to sell the house – she loves it as much as I do,' said Nico.

'We have to be realistic,' said Susan. 'What does Alex understand about finances or securing our future – or indeed what's best for her own future?'

Nico sat back, lost in thought.

'I always wanted Alex to have the house one day,' he said then. 'I wanted it to pass to her like it passed down to me – through the generations.'

Book 1

1840–1848

1

The snow was still coming down in a flurry and was gathering on the Georgian windows of the little shops around Grafton Street in Dublin. There had been a light dusting of snow that morning, and as Christmas Eve wore on it had continued to gather on the ground. Anna stood at the counter of a milliner's with her two younger sisters, Florence and Sophia, and her cousin Georgina who was staying with them for the holiday. The shops were full of Christmas shoppers and the young women were making their final purchases.

'It's nearly four, Anna! We need to get home to get ready for the party this evening,' Sophia pointed out.

'This is the last purchase of the day, I promise,' said Anna who exchanged an amused look with Georgina at her sister's irritation. The two older girls had traipsed Florence and Sophia through nearly every shop in Grafton Street.

The shopkeeper tied the ribbon into an elaborate bow on top of the hatbox and handed it over to Anna.

'Now, Miss, will there be anything else?' he asked with a big smile.

'No, I think we've bought enough,' said Anna with a grin. All four girls were laden down with boxes and presents.

'Good day to you then, and a happy Christmas!' said the man.

'Merry Christmas!' sang Anna and Georgina together as they followed the younger girls out on to the street.

'Now, we really have to get back to the carriage in Stephen's Green. Papa will be furious if we are late for tonight's party,' insisted Sophia.

'You go ahead – we'll follow you,' promised Anna.

Sophia gave them a warning look not to delay as she and Florence walked ahead. Georgina and Anna gave each other mischievous glances and giggled as they began to follow.

'Who is the hat for?' asked Georgina.

'Oh, just a friend.'

The two girls had been very close since childhood, even though Georgina lived in the country. Anna often felt she was much closer to Georgina than she ever was to her own sisters, or her brother for that matter. It was like they were born with an ability to always know what the other was thinking. They knew all each other's secrets, and kept nothing from each other. Anna at twenty-one was one year younger than Georgina.

'What time is the party due to start?' asked Georgina, as they passed carol singers under street lamps singing 'God Rest Ye Merry, Gentlemen'.

'Papa said the guests will start to arrive at seven.'

'At what time will Lord Armstrong arrive?' Georgina looked at her knowingly.

'Who's to say he will even come?' asked Anna, but her face was smug.

'You know very well he will.'

'The snow might prevent him. He has to make a very long journey from the west,' said Anna.

'He will make it,' assured Georgina. 'After all, he's coming on very important business, isn't he?'

Anna reached out and grabbed her cousin's gloved hand. 'Georgina, do you think he'll ask Papa tonight?'

'Of course he will. He's said to you he will, hasn't he? And he's already discussed it with your father.'

Anna thought of how her father had taken her into the drawing room the previous week and asked her how she felt about marrying Edward Armstrong. She had nodded enthusiastically, delighted at the prospect. She had fallen in love with Edward on first seeing him three years previously when he had attended their party on Christmas Eve. He had a handsome face, dark-brown hair, sallow skin and hazel eyes, but more importantly he was intelligent, warm and kind. And it was clear from that first meeting that he too had been attracted to her. Since then, he had gone out of his way to visit and become a close friend of the family. Although he lived on his family estate in County Mayo, which he had inherited when his parents passed away, he seemed to have taken every opportunity to stay in Dublin and spend time with Anna's family. Edward was twenty-six years old, and being an only child he seemed to love the hustle and bustle of the large Stratton family.

'Where will you live once you're married?' asked Georgina. 'With his money, you'll have plenty of options. A fabulous townhouse? I saw a house for sale on Leeson Street the other day, but that would be a come-down for you from your family home in Merrion Square.'

'Edward has made it very clear he wants to live on his country estate. He has no interest in living permanently in Dublin.'

Georgina was surprised. 'And how do you feel about that? Leaving your family and all your friends, everyone in Dublin?'

'I don't care where I live as long as I'm with Edward. He doesn't want to be an absentee landlord, he's very progressive. He wants to look after his land and the tenants. He wants to build model villages on the estate and improve farming practices.'

'But won't you miss the dances and parties in Dublin?'

'We can have dozens of parties and dances on the estate.'

'At least you'll be mistress of your own house. Nobody lording it over you.'

Both of them knew she was making reference to her sister-in-law Joanna. Since Georgina's father had died, the family estate where Georgina lived in Westmeath, Tullydere, had been inherited by Georgina's brother Richard and his wife Joanna who Georgina despised.

'Don't worry,' consoled Anna. 'It won't be long until you are married as well, and you can leave Tullydere behind and have your own home as well.'

Georgina's mood changed and she smiled as she thought of her own fiancé.

'Promise me that you'll visit me all the time when I marry Edward,' said Anna.

24

'Of course I will. Your new life sounds like a fairytale.'

'I believe in fairytales, Georgina. I always have.'

As they passed a crowd of children looking in the window of a toy shop, Anna said, 'It won't be long till Edward and I are buying toys for our children, Georgina. He's said he wants a large family. He has six children in mind.'

'Your whole life is mapped out for you, and it's starting tonight.'

'Anna!' shouted Sophia from the top of Grafton Street. 'We are waiting for you! We need time to prepare ourselves for tonight. Not all of us have fiancés waiting for us who own half a county!'

As Anna waved in response, the snow began to fall heavily, and she feared that Edward wouldn't make it for the night.

The carriage made its way into Merrion Square and pulled up outside the Strattons' house, which was one of the rows of four storey townhouses neatly laid out around the square's park. As the young women arrived, the house was already a hive of activity. Maids were scurrying around and delicious smells were escaping from the kitchen. On the ground floor, to the front of the house, were a drawing room and a dining room, and on the first floor was a larger drawing room that stretched from the front of the house through a dividing wall and double doors to the back.

The girls followed Anna up to the first floor and into the drawing room where her father and her brother Cecil were admiring the giant Christmas tree. The tree had been delivered from Georgina's family estate Tullydere, and the baubles bought from Germany.

'Papa, Anna delayed us terribly,' complained Sophia.

'I shouldn't worry,' he said as he put an arm around Anna. 'I don't think your sister is going to be around here for too much longer to cause you annoyance.' He smiled down knowingly at his lovely daughter, with her gleaming chestnut hair and sparkling green eyes.

Four hours later and the drawing room was full of guests dressed in their finery, enjoying John Stratton's traditional Christmas hospitality. A blazing fire crackled in the fireplace and candles lit up the room. The men drank beer and port, while the women drank wine and sherry. Waiters were continually bringing in platters of canapés, followed by an array of pastries and cakes.

Cecil was at the piano playing 'Deck the Halls', while a group of admirers sang around him.

Anna, however, couldn't relax and enjoy herself, as Edward had not arrived. She looked out at the snow and pictured Edward marooned at an inn somewhere in the country. Her stomach felt sick at the thought of her pending engagement being delayed and her Christmas ruined. Every time the front door bell chimed, she raced to the top of the stairs to see who it was that had arrived, only to be disappointed by seeing it was some more jolly revellers.

As the clock struck eleven and she was giving up hope, the bell chimed again. She raced to the top of the landing and peered down. The door opened and in walked Edward, dressed in a suit and cloak, and covered in snow. A butler helped him remove his cloak and dusted off the snow, and then Edward instead of being shown up to the party was shown into the small drawing room downstairs and the doors closed. The butler then made his way upstairs and through the guests, and whispered to her father who nodded and went downstairs.

Anna waited anxiously as nearly an hour passed by. Finally the door of the drawing room downstairs opened and out came a smiling father and Edward. As they began to come up the stairs, Anna quickly turned and raced into the party, where she found Georgina and pretended she had been in conversation with her.

The two men entered the room and looked around. Then her father came over to her and said, 'Anna, would you join Edward and me at the piano, please?'

She managed to look surprised and followed her father over to Edward at the piano. Her father instructed Cecil to stop playing, and gradually a hush descended on the crowd as they all turned to see John Stratton standing between his daughter and Edward Armstrong.

'Ladies and gentlemen, I interrupt the festivities to announce something that is probably of no surprise to any of you: the engagement of my eldest daughter, Anna, to Lord Edward Armstrong.'

The crowd erupted in cheers and clapping.

Two matronly women were sitting by the fireplace, eating mince pies and drinking wine.

'Many a young woman has been trying to land

Edward Armstrong. She's a lucky girl,' said one.

'The fact that her father is one of the country's wealthiest men, and an MP with all that political clout, helped secure the arrangement, I imagine.'

'Edward Armstrong has no need to marry for money, I can assure you, with his estate. I have it on good account that it is a love match. Seemingly they are infatuated with each other.'

The other woman observed them. 'They do make a beautiful couple, and both apparently are kind and generous. Their children will be blessed.'

Edward was a guest in the house that night, but it was three in the morning before the last of the guests left and the family went to bed. The following morning, the snow had stopped falling, and the family walked to church.

Edward walked between Anna and Georgina.

'Thank heaven you managed to reach Dublin last night,' said Georgina.

'I thought I was going to have to take shelter at Carton House, fourteen miles out, for the night. I told the coachman I simply had to get to Dublin and offered him a bribe if he could get me to Merrion Square before midnight.'

'You must have bribed him considerably when he got you here by eleven then,' said Georgina with a smirk.

'I had a very good reason to get here, regardless of the cost,' he smiled at Anna.

When they got back to the house, the aroma of turkey and sage-and-onion stuffing was wafting through the house as they hurried to the Christmas tree and began to give out the presents.

As Anna's father admired the fine walking stick Edward had presented to him, Anna went and took the hat she had bought the previous afternoon, in its attractive box, and handed it to Georgina.

'It was for me?' Georgina said in surprise and delight, and she opened the box quickly and took out the hat.

'I knew you liked it when you admired it in the shop, and I had to get it for you.'

'Thank you!' Georgina squeezed Anna's hand.

'And now I have a present for my fiancée,' said Edward loudly, as he walked to the Christmas tree and took a large rectangular parcel and carried it over to her.

'What is it, a painting?' asked Anna, as she examined it and began to take off the wrapping paper excitedly.

The family gathered around her and stared at the gold-framed painting of a beautiful house.

'Do you like it, Anna?' asked Edward.

'I love it!' said Anna, studying the skilfully painted picture.

'What an unusual thing for a man to give his young bride-to-be! I'd have preferred jewellery if it were me,' said Sophia as Anna stared at the painting, lost in the house's beauty.

'Do you really like it?' Edward asked Anna again.

'I love it.'

'Because this painting isn't your only present,' said Edward. 'This painting is based on the architect's plans I had drawn up for a house that is being built on my estate.'

'A house?' asked Anna, confused.

'I'm having this house built for you, Anna,' Edward said, looking lovingly at her.

'That beats diamonds any day!' Georgina said snidely to Sophia.

There was a general sense of awe as everyone viewed the grandeur of the house's image.

'But what of your present home on the estate, your parents' ancestral home?' asked Anna.

'Pah!' Edward waved his hand dismissively. 'That higgledy-piggledy rambling old fortress. My mother was always nagging my father to knock it down and build a mansion suitable to our position. It's unsafe anyway. I'm having it demolished and extensive stables built on the site. This new house will have every modern convenience, a home worthy of my new bride.' He smiled down at Anna.

Anna's father took the painting and studied it, asking, 'And when did you start building the house?'

'Two years ago ... when I knew we would one day be married. The builders have been working hard to get it ready in time for our wedding. My cousin Sinclair has been overseeing them.'

John smiled sadly. 'I wish your mother had lived, Anna, to see you married in this wonderful house.'

That evening in the drawing room, the family were recovering from the eating and drinking of the day, while Cecil played soothing piano. Anna and Georgina were sitting on the hearthrug together.

'Just think, this time next year, we will both be married women, both be mistresses of our own houses,' said Anna, as she stared at the painting of the house that would be her new home which had found temporary lodging on a sideboard, propped against the wall.

'I'd hoped I'd get a letter from Tom before Christmas,' said Georgina.

'It's probably on its way, delayed in the post from the continent,' said Anna.

'I hope he's all right,' sighed Georgina.

'Of course he is. He'll be back soon and then you can start arranging the final details of your wedding in the summer.' Anna turned and took Georgina's hand. 'I want our children to be every bit as close as we are.'

'I want that too,' said Georgina.

'Let's make a pact then that we'll meet as often as we do now, and not let our lives get in the way of our friendship, or our children's future friendship. Do you promise?'

'I promise,' said Georgina.

2

Lake Geneva
Switzerland
29th April 1841

My Dear Georgina,
I hope you got my last letter. We have been travelling so much, it is impossible to give you an address for you to write back. We arrived in Geneva from Munich

last week, and I can't believe it is the last week of our honeymoon and we are due to return to Ireland on Thursday. The time has gone so quickly.

I love Edward more each day. He spoils me so much. We have had to buy four extra trunks for all the shopping we have done. When we arrive back to Ireland, we will rest a short while at my father's before setting off for Mayo to start life on the estate – in our new house. I am longing to see it.

Please, will you visit us at our new home before your own wedding? And what of the wedding arrangements? Have you and Tom set an actual date yet? I know the detail and planning that needs to go into a wedding, but surely even you do not need this length of time! Please, delay no longer, as I do not want there to be much of an age difference between our children. Remember our pact? Edward is calling me now, we are going out to dinner. But I will be in contact as soon as I arrive back to Ireland, and I will see you at our new house.

Love,
Anna

The carriage made its way through the Irish countryside on the final day of the long journey from Dublin to Edward's estate in County Mayo. Inside the carriage Edward and Anna sat holding hands.

'I can't wait to see the house!' said Anna excitedly.

'Will you calm down!' urged Edward, secretly loving her impatience.

He had been assured by the architects, builders and furnishers that work on the house was completed and it was ready for them to move in. He wanted it to be perfect for when Anna arrived. The building of the house had taken up nearly all of his time over the past three years as he lovingly paid attention to every detail, always mindful of what he thought Anna would like – what colour she would prefer, what fabrics attracted her eye, what rooms would suit her personality. The house was an act of love for his new wife.

The carriage slowed down and entered through a large granite gateway with an arch over it. Anna looked out the window as they made their way through beautifully landscaped parkland.

'How long is the driveway?' she asked as she strained to see the house but there was still no view of it.

They came to a lake and suddenly there was the house high above the lake on the other side, a series of terraces and steps climbing the hill in front of it. It took Anna's breath away.

They rounded the lake and the carriage swept into the forecourt of the house. Edward opened his door and held out his hand to assist Anna as she stepped out. She paused and looked up at the house.

It was a baronial granite stone house, three storeys high. The third storey was tucked just under the roof, with the windows pitched into the black tile roof. A flight of steps led up to the double doors that were open, awaiting the new owners. The windows were tall and gothic. Anna moved away from the carriage, taking in the splendour of the building. Edward didn't look at the house once – he was too intent studying his wife's face for her reaction. She turned and looked at the house's surroundings and gasped. Edward had searched far and wide through the eight thousand acres of the estate for the perfect location to build. He had finally found the perfect spot here. In front of the house, at the edge of the forecourt, a low pillared wall had been built, in the centre of which were steps leading down to the series of terraces she had seen from across the lake. To the left and right of the house were extensive gardens falling gently away from the house, planted with trees and exotic shrubs.

'It's everything I imagined,' said Anna.

Edward went to her, placed his arm around her and smiled. The staff had come out of the house and were standing in line to greet her.

'And here's your welcoming committee,' said Edward as he led Anna past the staff who smiled respectfully and bowed and curtseyed.

Anna and Edward walked up the steps. She reached out and held his hand tightly as they went through the large door and into a great tiled hall. There was a giant fireplace to the left and a majestic staircase at the end of the hall.

Edward led Anna through the rooms. To the right at the front was a large drawing room. It was painted in a deep red and furnished elegantly, with large couches and chaises longues. A hand-carved oak fireplace was on one side of the room and a bow window on the other with a writing desk placed there. The windows in front looked out on the lake. Across the hall from the drawing room was a comfortable parlour, smaller and designed more for the family than to entertain guests.

Behind this room was the dining room, splendidly furnished with mahogany chairs and a table capable of seating twenty-four people. The walls were painted a deep blue, and cabinets and sideboards were laid out around the walls, laden with silver and china. It was hard for Anna to take it all in as she followed Edward. Behind this room was the library, the shelves filled with tomes and volumes. A large writing bureau stood against one wall and other desks stood before the windows. There were wine Chesterfield couches and matching armchairs arranged around the room and in front of the fireplace.

Edward then led her back across the grand hall and down to some double doors beyond the drawing room. He threw open the doors and led her into a ballroom. It was a very grand gold-themed room with French windows down one side leading onto a terrace. It was sparse of furniture with giant gold-leafed mirrors lining the walls, giving the illusion the room was even bigger than its natural size.

Back in the hall, Edward pointed to the doors behind the stairs and said they led to the kitchens.

They walked up the stairs, carved from oak, and followed the turn that brought them to where the bedrooms were laid out on the second floor. Anna followed Edward down to the end of the main corridor and there he took her hand and led her into their bedroom. The room was at the front of the house with a window that looked across the lake. There was a bow window to the side of the room. It was decorated in light blue wallpaper with a fine gold stripe. A couch rested before a white Grecian fireplace, a door beside it leading into the dressing rooms. A four-poster bed was against the fourth wall.

'Well?' he asked.

'It's everything I wanted. Everything. The paintings, the curtains, the furniture, it's all entirely to my taste.'

'I know. I've been an attentive student, listening to your every word, to everything you love. And I built the house to those specifications.'

She almost looked frightened by his dedication. 'How can I ever repay you?'

'You already have. By marrying me,' he said.

3

Anna sat at the desk in their bedroom after breakfast as she wrote a letter to Georgina.

Edward had invited neighbours and friends to the house for dinner that evening to meet his new bride.

Edward walked in and smiled to see her. 'I've just spoken to Cook about tonight's menu for the dinner,' he said. 'She suggested beef?'

'Yes, if you think so.'

He stepped behind her and embraced her. 'You know, that's going to be your role as soon as you settle in some more. Running the house and the staff.'

'I know,' she smiled at him. 'That doesn't worry

me. I'm used to helping run my father's house. But what does worry me is meeting everyone tonight. What if they don't like me?'

'They'll love you! How could they not?'

He released her and went to look out the front window.

'I was thinking today we might go for a walk through the estate. I want to show you around.'

'It's a perfect day for it,' she said as she looked out at the blue skies.

'Who are you writing to?'

'Georgina. I'm worried about her. She still hasn't answered any of my letters, and she's marrying Tom soon but we've heard nothing of the arrangements.'

'They are cutting it fine,' Edward frowned. 'Anyway, I'll meet you downstairs in half an hour for our walk.' He kissed her forehead and left as Anna returned to her letter writing.

As Anna walked down the stairs, fastening the ribbons of her bonnet, she looked around for Edward.

'Sorry, my lady,' said Barton the butler. 'Lord Edward was urgently called away on business in the town. He apologised and said he will see you this evening.'

'Ohh! I see.' Anna was disappointed. 'Very well. Thank you, Barton.'

She went and looked out the window at the sunny day and decided to go exploring the estate anyway on her own.

She made her way through the gardens and out into the country lanes that criss-crossed the estate.

The further she got from the house, the more rugged the landscape became and the more its breathtaking beauty bewitched her. She could see why Edward loved the place so much. She had been very nervous leaving Dublin and everyone behind, just trusting her love for Edward would make everything all right, but now she knew she had made the right decision.

Suddenly from over a hill a horse appeared, ridden by a well-dressed dark-haired man. The horse swept up close beside her, giving her a start.

'What are you doing here?' shouted the man on the horse angrily.

'I – I–' Anna stuttered.

'You're trespassing. You've no right to be here.'

'I – I'm sorry. I must have strayed. I thought I was still on Armstrong land.'

'You are on Armstrong land. And you're trespassing on it. Now get your damned self out of here before I have you thrown off.'

Anna looked at the man, feeling frightened by his anger and hostility.

'But I'm–' she tried to explain.

The man leaned forward, seething. 'Get off this land now! Get off my land!' He then kicked his horse, causing the animal to bolt, leaving Anna in a cloud of dust. She watched as the horse and rider galloped into the distance and disappeared. Anna felt herself tremble from the encounter. She turned immediately and made for the safety of the house as quickly as she could. She had never been spoken to so aggressively before. She wasn't used to hostility in the polite parlours of Dublin. The man was menacing, with his large frame, raven-black hair and dark threatening eyes. Most of all she was confused. If she had unwittingly ventured on to a neighbouring estate maybe she could understand his anger, but he had said it was Armstrong land. Her Edward's land. She would discuss it with Edward later, and hopefully he would shed light on it. She didn't want to upset his neighbours in her first week there.

4

The sunny day transformed into a stormy evening. Anna had anxiously waited for Edward's return and it was nearly eight now and still no sign of him, even though the guests were due to arrive shortly. She felt strangely isolated and vulnerable without him there after her earlier encounter with the horseman. As she heard a carriage pull up outside, she went to the bedroom window and was relieved to see it was Edward returning. She saw him rush from the carriage through the rain to the front door. She quickly checked her appearance in the mirror over the fireplace and a couple of minutes later the bedroom door opened and Edward came in.

'Sorry I'm so late.' He looked strained. 'There was terrible trouble the other side of the estate. An eviction that was ordered and I needed to get down there.'

'An eviction? Why?'

'All a misunderstanding. I'll tell you later. I'd

better rush and get ready before our dinner guests arrive.' He went into the adjoining dressing room.

She went and stood at the door. 'Edward, I wanted to talk to you about something strange that happened today. I think I might have upset one of your neighbours. I strayed on to his land while walking.'

He came out, looking bemused, drying his hair.

'Impossible, darling. Do you know how big this estate is? You couldn't have walked that far!'

'But, I met a man, and he said–'

He quickly came over to her and kissed her forehead. 'You can tell me all about it later. That's our guests arriving. You go down and entertain them while I dress? Apologise for me.'

She nodded and smiled. 'All right.'

She left him drying his hair with a towel and went downstairs.

5

'My lady, Mr and Mrs Foxe are in the drawing room,' announced Barton as Anna walked through the hall downstairs.

'Oh, thank you, Barton,' she nodded. She felt a knot in her stomach. She knew the Foxes were Edward's nearest neighbours and she had a fear Mr Foxe would be the mystery horseman who had threatened her. Barton opened the door for her and she walked in. There sitting down was a kindly-looking couple in their fifties, smiling warmly at her. She felt relief. Mr Foxe was not the horseman.

'Good evening,' she said, smiling back. 'Please excuse my husband. He was detained on business and will join us in a few minutes.'

'You must be Anna,' said Mrs Foxe as she stood and came towards her and kissed her on the cheek. 'I feel it's not my place to be welcoming you in your own house. But you're very welcome here.'

'Thank you,' said Anna.

'I know your father,' said Mr Foxe, smiling. 'I've met him many times. And heard him talk at a few political meetings.'

'Have you?' said Anna, absorbing their warmth.

'And I knew your mother,' said Mrs Foxe, leading Anna to the couch and sitting down with her.

'Did you?' Anna was surprised.

'Yes, when I was much younger my family used to visit her family at their estate in Tullydere.' Mrs Foxe held her hand tightly. 'We were quite close.'

Barton knocked on the door and announced: 'Lord and Lady Fitzherbert, ma'am.'

And another friendly-looking couple entered the room to make a fuss of Anna.

By the time Edward arrived down, the drawing room was full of people and Anna found herself the centre of attention as they acquainted themselves with their new neighbour. She realised she had nothing to worry about. Most of the people were mutual friends of acquaintances and relatives of hers. The others, who did not have any connection with her, were longstanding friends

41

of Edward's family and welcomed her with open arms.

'See, I told you they would love you,' Edward whispered to her, squeezing her hand.

As dinner was announced, Edward and Anna led the party into the dining room.

Edward sat at the top of the table with Anna to his right. Anna observed the guests as the first course was served and wine was poured. She liked the way they all chatted amicably with each other. Her eye was caught by a woman who she had been briefly introduced to earlier in the evening and who now sat at the far end of the table. She was a woman of around thirty, a beautiful blonde with a confident but quiet manner about her.

'Who is that woman there?' whispered Anna to Edward, nodding down the table.

'That's Diana Hunter,' Edward said back. 'She leases Hunter's Farm from us, as she has named it, where she breeds horses. She's an excellent horse-woman, probably the best in the county. She's a widow, I believe. Her husband was in the army and left her well provided for.'

Almost as if sensing she was being spoken about, Diana turned her head and looked directly at Anna. Anna blushed at being caught staring. Diana nodded coolly at her before continuing the conversation she had been engaged in.

The roast beef was served and servants made rounds of the table with serving dishes of vegetables. Anna was pleased to see the guests seemed to relish the food. As more wine was poured and drunk, the volume of conversation and laughter rose.

Then, suddenly, the main door to the dining room swung open, causing everyone to look around. A man strode in, wearing a hat and a cloak, wet from the rain. Anna got a fright as it was the horseman who had attacked her in the afternoon.

'Bloody weather! It delayed me!' snapped the man, taking off his hat and cloak and flinging them at Barton. 'Dry them out for me.'

'I thought you might not make it tonight,' said Edward.

'Try keeping me away from meeting this new bride of yours!' the man smirked as he strode confidently to the table.

Anna looked quickly at Edward as he stood up.

'So – where is she?' said the man as he reached the table.

'Sinclair, this is my wife Anna. Anna, my cousin Sinclair,' said Edward.

Sinclair looked down at Anna and there was a fleeting look of recognition before he smiled broadly.

'Lady Anna,' he said and bowed slightly.

'Come, come. No need for formality. She's your cousin Anna,' urged Edward.

Sinclair smirked slightly and nodded. 'Cousin Anna – in that case.'

Anna nodded back.

Sinclair leaned towards Edward. 'I need to talk to you later, it's fairly urgent.'

'Yes, later, Sinclair. Now don't you think you should join us for dinner?'

Sinclair bowed again to Anna before walking down the room and sitting in a space that had been kept for him beside Diana Hunter.

As the conversation resumed, Anna tried not to look down at her newly revealed relative. But such was her dismay at discovering the identity of the horseman that her eyes were constantly drawn to Sinclair. She saw he was loud and opinionated, quick with a comment and a witty put-down, whoever he was speaking to. He only lowered his voice when drawn into private conversation with Diana Hunter. And Diana and Sinclair were obviously very well acquainted with each other.

She wondered what they were speaking about, and caught Diana's cool eyes inspecting her every so often.

'Tell me, Edward, now you have settled down and are a happily married man, when will you go forward and stand for election?' asked Mrs Foxe.

'I have no intention to stand for election. Not now, not ever. It's too much trouble with no reward.'

'I think you'd make an excellent member of parliament, and could have a great future in politics,' Mrs Foxe pursued.

'Not for me. You'll have to look elsewhere for your candidate.' Edward looked knowingly at her. The Foxes were well-known patrons of different politicians, always on the look-out for a rising star to promote.

'Besides, if he was in parliament,' said Anna, 'he would have to travel to London all the time, and when would I ever see him then?'

'It wouldn't be the best start to a new marriage,' conceded Mr Foxe.

'Maybe when we get the parliament back in

Dublin, you might consider it then,' suggested Mr Foxe.

Sinclair laughed loudly at the other end of the table. 'In that case, you'll be waiting for ever, because that will never happen again.'

Anna's irritation with Sinclair rose and she cleared her throat and spoke up. 'Actually my father says it's only a matter of time before it happens. That Ireland worked best when we had our own parliament in Dublin.'

'And what would *your* father know?' Sinclair dismissed her.

'My father is Lord John Stratton, and has been a member of parliament for twenty years,' Anna said proudly.

Sinclair's face became bemused and he smirked at her as he took up his glass of wine and drank from it. 'I know who your father is, Anna... I merely asked what would he know about politics.'

Anna glared at him, realising he was being insulting.

Sinclair ignored her and looked around the table. 'I think I can speak for *nearly* all here, that Home Rule isn't necessary. We aren't merely a colony needing some local representation. We're part of the United Kingdom, and as such we should be governed from London.'

'My, I didn't want to start a Home Rule debate before pudding is even served. I merely suggested that Edward would look very nice at a political rally,' laughed Mrs Foxe.

'Yes, politics bore me at the best of times,' Edward quickly said. 'I'd much prefer to hear about next month's hunt.'

As the conversation quickly switched to hunting, Anna glanced down at Sinclair who seemed to be giving her a triumphant look before he turned his attention on Diana again.

After dinner the party retired to the drawing room where Diana Hunter played the harpsichord.

'She plays excellently,' Anna remarked to Mrs Foxe who was seated beside her.

'Doesn't she? She has many talents, Mrs Hunter. You should see her with horses.'

'So I've heard... She's very beautiful. How long has she been a widow?'

'Well, she came here after her husband died, and that was about four years ago if I remember correctly. She's originally from Yorkshire and has been leasing Hunter's Farm ever since.'

'I wonder why she chose here, when she has no connection to the place.'

'She's says it's ideal for the horses she raises. Mrs Hunter is from good stock. I believe her father was a wealthy squire in Yorkshire.'

As Diana continued to entrance them at the harpsichord, Anna saw Sinclair walk around the room to where Edward was standing by the fireplace. He put a hand on Edward's shoulder and whispered in his ear. Edward nodded and then the two men left the room.

Anna waited a while and then she excused herself and left too. She needed to know if Sinclair would say anything to her husband about their encounter that day.

As she walked through the hallway, she saw

46

there was nobody in the dining room or the parlour and so headed to the library. She could hear voices inside and carefully went up to the door which was ajar.

'What do you think you were doing today?' asked Sinclair. 'Stopping the eviction I had ordered?'

'I didn't realise you had ordered the eviction of the Doyle family. I would never have allowed it,' Edward insisted.

'They are four months behind with their rent. There was no option but to evict them.'

'Their father was my father's head groom. They've lived and served on this estate for generations. I can't just throw them out.'

'So what do you suggest we do then? Let them live here rent free?'

'Of course not. Just give them some more time. They will come up with the money.'

'In the meantime, their debt gets bigger and the more the chances increase it won't be paid. And we are setting an example to all the other tenant farmers that they don't have to meet their rent deadlines as well. The estate will be in chaos very quickly.'

'It won't come to that. They need time to get back on their feet, that's all.'

'Edward, if we don't get the rents, then we don't have income. The tenants' rents are the only thing that keeps us going. Keeps you in the style you live in. Allowed you to build this palace for your new bride. Pays the mortgages you have! This isn't a charity, it's a business, and you had better remember that!'

'I understand all that... Look, just give them one month. That's all I ask for. One more month for the Doyle family. If they don't come up with the rent by then, then out they go.' Edward sighed loudly.

'One month then, and no more.' Sinclair turned and walked away.

As Anna heard Sinclair's footsteps walk quickly towards the door she hurried down the hallway and hid beneath the stairs. She watched Sinclair stride across the hallway to rejoin the party. A little while later, she saw Edward come out looking dejected and disturbed and he too went back to the drawing room.

6

It was after midnight and most of the guests were departing. Edward and Anna waved goodbye to the Foxes as they hurried to their carriage through the rain and it took off.

Edward turned to see Diana standing there with her cloak on.

'Diana, did you come here alone tonight, or is one of your servants waiting for you here?'

'I came alone in my phaeton,' said Diana.

'Your phaeton? But those carriages are so light and dangerous! Well, you have to stay the night in that case – you can't possibly head back to Hunter's Farm in this weather on your own.'

'Nonsense, I will be absolutely fine,' Diana dismissed his worries.

'I am responsible for you as my guest, and I refuse to allow you to travel alone.'

Just then one of the grooms drove Diana's one-horse carriage up to the front door. Anna was awed and concerned at the thought of this woman travelling alone at night in this weather in such a frail-looking vehicle. But she really didn't want her staying the night with them either, and wanted her gone as quickly as possible.

'In that case I'll send one of my grooms to accompany you,' said Edward.

'Won't be necessary,' Sinclair said as he strode up behind them. 'I will escort Mrs Hunter back to her house, if she permits.'

Diana smiled at Sinclair. 'Well, then everyone will be happy.'

'And it's only a little out of my way anyway.' Sinclair offered his arm and Diana took it.

'But how will you get home in that case, Sinclair?' Edward's concern continued.

'I shall borrow Mrs Hunter's phaeton and have it returned to her tomorrow, if she allows?' smiled Sinclair.

'Of course!' Diana nodded.

'I'll see you tomorrow,' Sinclair said to Edward before turning Anna. 'What can I say? It's been enchanting meeting you.'

Anna nodded. Sinclair and Diana held cloaks over their heads as they dashed out and down the steps to the phaeton.

Edward closed over the door. 'That's the last of them.'

He put his arm around her waist and they

walked back into the drawing room.

'How did you find them?' he smiled at her.

'They were all lovely.' She sat down on the couch. 'That Diana Hunter is the most amazing creature. Imagine just setting off into the night on her own on a night like this!'

'Well, she doesn't have that far to go.'

'But still, I don't know any other woman who would do such a thing.'

'Well, she's very independent. You should see the horses she breeds – magnificent.'

'And she deals with the money and everything?' Anna was astonished.

'I believe she's quite wealthy.'

'Edward – why wasn't Sinclair at our wedding? Him being your cousin?'

'He was too tied up with work here on the estate. He couldn't make it. He's a tremendous worker. The profits have soared since he started managing the estate.'

'Remind me again, how are you related exactly?'

'His father was my father's younger brother. Jamie Armstrong,' explained Edward.

'Ohh, of course!' Anna nodded as all the pieces fitted together.

'You've heard of him?'

'Yes, I certainly heard my father talk about him. He had quite a reputation.'

'Bad Black Jamie, as he was called. He was certainly the black sheep of our family. My grandfather cut him off without a penny because of his antics. He went on and married a large landowner in Meath, and they had a son, Sinclair.'

'And what happened then?'

'You can't change a leopard's spots. He carried on with same antics in Meath as he did here. I think he broke Sinclair's poor mother's heart. He certainly broke her estate. He gambled and drank the estate into oblivion and squandered his money on loose women.'

'I remember hearing the stories. He died owing the Dublin gambling houses a fortune.'

'By the time Sinclair reached adulthood everything was gone. He and I were in Trinity together. He was a fantastic student, excellent mind. He was always my best friend. He agreed to come and manage here when I inherited the estate. I don't know what I'd do without him.' Edward glowed with a look of gratitude and respect.

'Edward – I met Sinclair earlier today when I was out walking.'

'Did you? Neither of you said,' Edward looked surprised.

'Well, I imagine he was too embarrassed to say it, and so was I, for that matter.'

'Is there something you want to tell me?' Edward looked worried.

'I mentioned it to you already – when you were dressing earlier. Well, he just came galloping up to me like he was going into battle and attacked me.'

'Attacked you?' Edward face creased with disbelief.

'Well, not attacked me physically, obviously. He verbally attacked me. He shouted at me and told me I was trespassing and told me to clear off his land.'

'And did you explain who you were?'

'Well, no. But he didn't give me chance.'

'Well, you should have told him you were my wife. That would have put a stop to that. He was just concerned at finding a stranger on the estate.'

Anna indicated the expensive fabric of her dress. 'I hardly look like a thief or a vagabond. He must have guessed who I was, or at least that I was an acquaintance of your new bride.'

Edward looked perplexed but was determined to defend his cousin. 'But you could have been leaving gates open, or anything. Up to mischief.'

'But I wasn't.'

'But he didn't know that.'

'But he said it was *his* land, *his* estate.'

'I'm sure he meant Armstrong land, and you misunderstood him.'

He had used that expression, Anna thought.

'Perhaps,' she sighed.

'I wouldn't give it another thought. He was just trying to protect our land. Sinclair is a good man. The exact opposite of his father.'

7

Anna and Edward were enjoying breakfast in the dining room.

'More coffee, my lady?' asked Barton.

'Eh, yes, thank you, Barton,' agreed Anna as she sorted through the letters that had arrived for her.

Barton poured the coffee from the silver pot.

'I know who this is from!' said Anna excitedly as she singled out a sealed envelope. 'It's Georgina's handwriting! About time she answered me.'

She tore open the envelope eagerly.

'It's probably the details of the wedding,' said Edward.

Anna's face became worried as she began to read. 'No, it's not...' She quickly read down the letter. 'She's asking to come and stay here for a week next month ... but I don't understand ... she's getting married next month.'

'Perhaps she wants to see you and spend some time with you before the wedding.'

'But she doesn't even mention the wedding... Is it all right if she comes?'

'You don't even have to ask,' nodded Edward.

He saw her face had become clouded with worry.

'Now, I have a present for you,' he said, standing up, taking her hand and leading her out into the hallway.

'Another present? What is it?' she asked excitedly.

'Come with me,' he said, leading her out the front door and down the steps to where a young man stood waiting.

Anna looked about, confused.

'This is Seán Hegarty, and I'm giving him to you as your personal servant,' explained Edward. 'Say hello to Lady Anna, Seán.'

Seán bowed his head and smiled.

'But we have a house full of servants! And I have my own personal maid!'

'But they are all house servants with their own duties and cares and your maid is for your needs inside the house. Seán is reserved for you for when you leave the house. Anything you want, just ask and Seán will get it for you. He'll drive you anywhere you want to go any time, deliver or fetch anything for you.'

Anna studied the handsome fair-haired youth with the smiling face and twinkling blue eyes.

'No need to go wandering off across the estate getting lost – Seán will escort you. Isn't that right, Seán?'

'Yes, sir,' Seán nodded.

'But, Edward, I don't think I have any real need for him. Can't you put him to better use elsewhere?' Anna looked at Seán apprehensively. And she wondered whether her run-in with Sinclair had made Edward worried about her getting involved in other situations. She wished she had never told Edward about that.

'Now, if you don't mind I have a lot to do today. Eh, Seán, look after her ladyship.' Edward smiled and walked off back into the house.

Anna looked at Seán, bewildered. 'Well now, I think you're going to be very bored working for me.'

'That's all right, ma'am, I was half-expecting to be,' Seán said.

She got a bit of a start and looked for any sign of insolence, but couldn't spot any. 'Yes, well. I might go into Castlewest in an hour or so, so hitch up the carriage and wait for me.'

She hesitantly turned and went back into the house.

Inside, she hurried to the library where Edward usually wrote his letters and did his accounts. He was there at his desk.

'Edward! I wish you'd asked me about this boy before you thrust him on me. I don't think I want him at my beck and call. I'll be putting pressure on myself trying to think of how to keep him busy all the time.'

Edward laughed. 'Anytime you don't need him, the head groom will keep him occupied. I thought you'd be delighted.'

'I am. He just looks a bit – insolent.'

Edward laughed loudly. 'He is quite spirited and can be amusing, but he's a very good-natured lad. I picked him out especially for you.'

Anna bit her lip. She had better resign herself to making the best of Seán.

8

Seán sat on the driver's seat in front of the small open-topped landau while Anna sat in the back.

'Is it far to the town?' asked Anna.

'About another seven miles,' he said. 'You'll probably be mightily disappointed when you get there.'

'Why?'

'Well, you're used to the big shops and everything in Dublin. The town won't compare at all.'

'Well, to quote yourself – I was half-expecting it to be so.'

The local town, Castlewest, was a large busy market town with one long street coming down a hill at its heart. Anna spent the afternoon investigating the different shops and making some purchases. She was surprised to find that she really enjoyed herself. It certainly wasn't Dublin but it seemed to have most things she might conceivably need, and she was met with friendliness as well as courtesy in the various shops.

Satisfied, at last she returned to the carriage and they set out for home.

'So are you settling in to your new house all right?' asked Seán as he drove.

'Yes, I am.' She looked at him, surprised by a servant asking a question in such a cavalier way.

'That's good. Lord Edward would be mighty upset after all the hard work he put into the house if you didn't end up liking it.'

'Only a fool wouldn't like that house.'

'Well, when I say Lord Edward put the hard work in, he did up to a point. It was really Mr Sinclair who put the real work in.'

'Mr Sinclair?' Anna leaned forward, her interest piqued.

'Yes. But Mr Sinclair made everyone work round the clock to make sure the thing got finished. Lord Edward came up with all the ideas and the designs and the fancy meetings with architects. But, if you don't mind me saying, it was Mr Sinclair that made sure the house got built!'

'I do mind you saying actually,' said Anna. She wanted to think of her house as being lovingly created by her husband, not as a result of slave-driving by Sinclair.

'Sorry, ma'am, I'll say no more.' Seán looked suitably chastised and stared ahead.

They sat in silence as the carriage rode on.

'How long has Mr Sinclair been here?' she asked eventually, her curiosity getting the better of her.

'Oh about five years. Ever since Lord Edward and he finished at university and moved down here.'

'And does Mr Sinclair put in "the real work" into the estate and get things done like he did while building the house?'

'He's a hard worker all right, Mr Sinclair,' said Seán. He quickly looked over his shoulder and looked innocently at Anna. 'Not that I'm saying Lord Edward isn't a hard worker too, of course.'

'Of course.' She looked at him wryly.

They sat in silence for a while as Anna admired the scenery and thought about Sinclair lording over the building of her beautiful house.

'Seán?'

'Yes, ma'am?'

'Do you know a place called Hunter's Farm?'

'Of course, ma'am. It's the place rented out to the Englishwoman.'

'Is it far?'

'Not too far? Why? Do you want to pay Mrs Hunter a visit?'

'No I ... I just heard it's a fine house and wanted to drive past it to take a view of it. Would that be possible?'

'Your wish is my command, ma'am.'

He soon turned the carriage off the main road.

'Do you know much about Mrs Hunter?' Anna ventured. Seán seemed a vessel of local information and didn't seem shy about divulging it.

Seán made a face. 'She's not a kind woman, ma'am. She treats her servants and her workers very badly, that's all I know. She landed in here from England and has been going around as if she's Queen Victoria ever since. Nobody knows anything about her, her dead husband or her family. But I'll tell you one thing, ma'am...'

'And what's that?'

'I don't know where she's from but she's not gentry. She might have pulled the wool over your husband's and everyone's eyes, but not mine. Real gentry don't go on like her. She has airs and graces but no refinement, just a cruel streak.'

'How reassuring to know you are groomed in observing social breeding,' she said mockingly.

Hunter's Farm came into view. It was a small Georgian country house of nice proportions situated up a long avenue from the road. The countryside was rolling and flat. Large trees were to either side of the house, and as the evening was coming in, a mist seemed to be enveloping the building.

'Stop the carriage a minute,' ordered Anna.

Anna studied the house, feeding her curiosity.

Suddenly the front door opened and the unmistakeable figure of Sinclair walked out, followed by Diana Hunter.

Anna got a start to see him and, as she watched

58

Sinclair and Anna speak intimately together at the top of the steps to the house, she became panicked. She did not want Sinclair to see her. Hunter's Farm was out of the way, and it would be clear she was spying.

'Quickly, Seán, get going!' demanded Anna.

The horse began to move forward. Anna saw Sinclair bound down the steps, jump on his horse and gallop down the avenue to the road. In less than a minute, he would be passing them in the carriage.

'Seán! Can you pull the carriage in somewhere and hide for a minute or two?' cried Anna urgently.

Seán turned around and glared at her as if she were mad. 'Hide? What for?'

'Never mind what for! Just do it!' Anna ordered.

'Is it that you don't want to be seeing Mr Sinclair?' asked Seán curiously.

'Seán! Please!' Anna begged.

Seán nodded, snapped the whip at the horse and they took off down the road at great speed and pulled into a small wood. Seán jumped down from the carriage and went to calm and soothe the horse. Anna held her breath as she looked around, seeing they were well hidden by the foliage of the trees. She heard Sinclair's horse tear down the road and storm past the wood and could glimpse Sinclair's black cloak flying in the wind as he rode by.

The very sight of him filled her with a fear she didn't understand. It was her husband's estate. Although Sinclair was a cousin, he was still an employee of hers and her husband. Yet the way he carried himself, the way he had spoken to her, intimidated her.

'Very well,' Anna said to Seán. 'You can take me back to the house now.'

Seán nodded and jumped back up on the carriage.

The evening was coming in when they pulled up in front of the house.

Anna stepped down from the carriage.

'You can bring my purchases to the back of the house and get one of the maids to take them up to my rooms,' she instructed.

'Alright,' said Seán. 'And, tell me, will you be wanting me tomorrow?'

'I'm not sure. See Barton in the morning and he'll inform you of what I am doing for the day.'

'Right so. You know, I don't think it's going to be as boring working for you as I thought,' said Seán with that insolent smile he had.

Anna walked through the main door and into the drawing room where she found Edward sitting, smoking a pipe and reading a book.

She walked over to him taking off her bonnet and kissed him.

'Good day?' he asked, smiling.

'Yes. I went into town, and bought some things.'

'How did you find Seán?' Edward smiled knowingly at her.

'A little impertinent, from what I can see.'

Edward laughed loudly. 'As I said – amusing!'

She walked over to the servants' bell and rang it.

'I'm not sure "amusing" is the right word. I think he might get on my nerves after a short while.'

60

A maid came in.

'Draw the curtains, would you, please,' ordered Anna.

The maid hurried to obey.

'I – eh – I passed by Hunter's Farm today,' said Anna as she took off her gloves.

'Really?' Edward seemed uninterested as he reopened his book.

'Yes. It's a fine house, isn't it?'

'One of the best in the neighbourhood. Probably the best outside our own house.'

'Hmmm. I saw her, Mrs Hunter, outside the house.'

'Did you stop to say hello?'

'No. I was just passing by on the road. She was talking with somebody. I think it was Sinclair.'

Edward looked up and frowned slightly. 'Really? I hope everything's all right. Not a problem with a mare or something.'

'Probably something like that,' mused Anna as she concentrated on the candlelight. 'But please don't mention I saw him. He might think I was spying on him.'

Edward glanced at her curiously. 'Of course I won't.'

9

Anna had counted the days until her cousin Georgina would arrive, each day becoming more and more excited. Georgina was due to arrive from the east by a Bianconi coach, and Anna had got Seán to drive her to the Bianconi stop in Castlewest.

'It's running late, the coach,' stated Anna anxiously as she watched down the street for it.

'Sure isn't it like everything that comes down from Dublin ... always running late!' Seán looked at Anna pointedly, a reference to her bad timekeeping.

She looked at him irritably. 'I'd rather be late than slow, like you!'

'Here she comes!' said Seán loudly as the coach came down the street.

Anna stood up in the carriage, excitedly looking for any sign of Georgina through the coach's windows as it drew to a halt. As the drivers got down and opened the coach door, Anna watched expectantly as people got out and then she saw Georgina step onto the street.

'Georgina!' Anna squealed.

'So that's the cousin you're making all the fuss about! She's looks a little contrary,' said Seán, looking her up and down.

Anna stepped down from the carriage and ran to Georgina. She embraced her cousin warmly and kissed her.

'Oh, it's so good to see you again!' exclaimed Anna.

'And you,' nodded Georgina.

As Anna happily studied Georgina, she realised there was something different about her. She looked the same, but it was her eyes. They had changed and become duller, sadder, the joy gone out of them.

The Bianconi coach drivers were taking the luggage off the top. They placed Georgina's trunk on the ground beside her.

'Seán!' shouted Anna. 'Don't just sit there! Come and take Georgina's trunk!'

Seán raised his eyes to heaven and got down from the carriage. Taking up the trunk, he put it on the back of the carriage and after the two women had settled themselves comfortably they headed back to the Armstrong estate.

Anna clasped Georgina's hands tightly as they made the journey.

'There's been so much going on here, Georgina – I can't wait to tell you everything.'

'How is Edward?'

'Wonderful. Everything is wonderful. It's everything I dreamed of,' smiled Anna.

Georgina smiled, but the smile did not carry to her eyes.

'I was so worried about you,' said Anna. 'I sent letter after letter, and no response. I thought you might be ill, and didn't want me to know.'

'I know, I'm sorry. There has been a lot going on at Tullydere as well.'

'And how's Tom? And the wedding! Tell me –

when is it – the actual date?'

Georgina looked up at Seán. 'I'll tell you all back in the house.'

After Anna had given Georgina the grand tour of the house, she was led to the guest bedroom she was to stay in.

Georgina crossed over to the window and looked out. 'I can see how you love this house. It's exactly the same as the painting of it that Edward gave you last Christmas.'

'It's now hanging in the library.' Anna walked over to Georgina and placed a gentle hand on her shoulder. 'Georgie? What's wrong? What's the matter? You can tell me.'

Georgina's eyes filled with tears. 'The wedding is off, Anna. Tom has jilted me.'

'*What?* But why? He was in love with you!' Anna could not believe it.

Georgina began to cry loudly. 'He met somebody else. Frances Westworth, from King's County.'

'Lady Frances, yes. I met her at several functions and parties.'

'And so did Tom! So many times that he decided he was in love with her and not me!'

Anna led Georgina over to the bed and they sat down.

'They're getting married next month in Cork!'

'No!'

'And honeymooning in Rome.'

'But that's where you were supposed to be honeymooning!'

'I know! He didn't change his itinerary. Just

his bride!'

'Oh, Georgina! But can't you sue him for breach of promise?'

'Oh no, I couldn't face that! Nor could my family. No, there's nothing to be done. My life is over. I'm ruined.'

'Of course you're not! You'll meet somebody else.'

'No, I won't. My name is ruined. Everybody is talking about me being jilted. I'm damaged goods and no man will want to be seen marrying me now. Another man's cast-off. I will never be the mistress of my own house, with my own husband and family. I'll spend the rest of my life at Tullydere, a guest in my brother's house. His wife Joanna makes me feel like an unwelcome visitor in my own family home every day. She enjoys it, my humiliation.'

Anna sighed. She knew Georgina and her sister-in-law never got on.

'Well, come and live here with me and Edward.'

'How can I do that?' snorted Georgina.

'Very easily. There's more than enough room and you'd be so welcome.'

'I can't, Anna. My brother would never allow it. I am his charge and responsibility until I marry. And now that it will never happen I will be his charge and responsibility for the rest of my life. It would reflect badly on him if I came to you, as if he didn't want to be responsible for his sister.'

Anna sighed again. She knew this was true.

'Well, you can be independent. There is this woman who rents a house from Edward, a Mrs Hunter. Quite remarkable, if a little scary. She rents her own farm and runs her own business even. Nothing is stopping you from doing the same.'

'Mrs Hunter. A widow, I take it? No doubt she was left ample means to look after herself by her husband. But I have nothing.' Georgina stood up and walked over to the window again and stared out. 'I have nothing of my own. And you had nothing of your own until you married. Our fortune was to be wives and mothers. Without that, we are nothing.'

10

Anna did her best to comfort Georgina during her stay over the next few days. And she believed the time away from Tullydere did her some good. But nothing worked to stop Georgina from being desolate about her life and future. Her negativity seemed to have crept into all aspects of her personality. She was no longer the carefree girl full of hope. She was now very cynical, hardly having a good word to say about anybody.

As Seán drove the two women through the estate on a sunny afternoon, Anna divulged more information about Diana Hunter to Georgina, telling her she had often seen Sinclair's horse outside Hunter's Farm.

'And do you think they're romantically involved?' asked Georgina.

'I don't know for sure. But he seems to spend a lot of time there, when the only reason he needs to be there is once a month to collect the rent.'

'Sounds like you've almost been spying on them!' Georgina said with a little laugh.

'No, not at all!' Anna's face went red. 'Hunter's Farm is on the way to town, so I always pass it.'

Seán looked back on hearing this lie and gave Anna a withering look. Smirking, he threw his eyes to heaven.

'Keep your eyes on the road, Seán! We don't want to end up in the ditch,' snapped Anna.

'Yes, ma'am.'

'And then when we are entertaining in the house, they monopolise each other's company.'

'And how do you find her?'

'She's cool and distant. I don't think I've ever really had a proper conversation with her. She seems to prefer talking to the men.'

'And they prefer talking to her, I daresay, if she is the beguiling beauty you say she is. I'm quite intrigued to meet this Mrs Hunter. Not to mention your new cousin Sinclair.'

'You mightn't have to wait that long. There he is, up ahead!' said Seán.

'Seán! Do you have to listen in to every private conversation?' scolded Anna, as she sat forward to see Sinclair.

True enough, Sinclair was in a field they were nearing, sitting proudly on his stallion. He seemed to be arguing with some tenants gathered around him. Anna could hear his voice raised in a roar that sent shivers down her back. Then she saw Sinclair raise the riding crop he was holding into the air and bring it down with great force on the head of one of the men he had been talking to.

Georgina cried out in shock as the man fell to the ground.

'Stop the carriage, Seán!' cried Anna.

'No, ma'am, I think it's best we keep going,' advised Seán who kept the horse at a steady trot.

'Seán, I'm not asking you, I'm ordering you! Stop the carriage at once!'

'His lordship will murder me if he hears I stopped,' warned Seán.

'And I will murder you if you *don't* stop!'

Seán pulled on the reins of the horse and the carriage came to a halt.

'Where are you going, Anna?' asked Georgina.

'I'm going to see if that poor man is all right,' said Anna as she stepped out of the carriage.

'You shouldn't get involved in this!' Seán gave a final warning as Anna walked through the gate and into the field.

'Shut up, Seán!'

Sinclair was still shouting at the peasants as Anna made her way over to them.

'What is going on here?' demanded Anna.

Sinclair looked at her, shocked.

'Nothing to do with you, go back to your carriage,' he said.

'This poor man is injured. He needs medical attention,' said Anna as she bent down to look at the man and the bloody wound Sinclair had inflicted on his head.

'He can't pay his rent, so I doubt he'll be able to pay for any medical attention.'

'Sinclair, I saw you hit this man. Why did you

do such a thing?' demanded Anna.

'Anna, go back to your carriage and stay out of my business.'

'But this is not your business. This is my husband's business, which makes it my business.'

Sinclair's face turned red with fury and he pointed his riding crop at Anna.

'You're interfering in things that don't concern you, madam.'

'If this happens on my husband's land, then it does concern me!'

Sinclair and Anna's eyes locked in defiance.

'You'll regret this interference. I guarantee you that,' said Sinclair, then he hit the horse with his stick and galloped out of the field and down the road.

Anna turned around to the other men. 'Take this man in to Dr Robinson in town, and tell him I said he was to tend to him.'

Leaving the men staring after her, astounded, she walked out of the field. It was only when she sat back into the carriage that she realised she was trembling.

'Are you all right?' Georgina put her arms around her.

'I'm feeling quite dizzy after all that.'

'I didn't think you had it in you!' said Georgina.

'Neither did I!' whispered Seán under his breath.

'I just– I didn't even think. The words just blurted out of my mouth, at the cruelty of it!'

'I see what you mean about him. He's larger than life,' said Georgina.

'Seán, take us back to the house,' said Anna.

11

Sinclair took the steps two at a time up to the front door, swung it open and marched through the hall.

'Edward!' he shouted, crossing over to the drawing room. Taking a look and seeing it empty, he checked the parlour across from it, before making his way down the corridor to the library. Opening the door, he found Edward at his desk writing.

Edward looked up, surprised at his cousin's angry face. 'Sinclair, what's wrong?'

'Your wife, Edward, your wife is what troubles me!'

'Anna?' Edward's face creased in bewilderment.

Sinclair began to pace up and down in front of Edward's desk.

'I will not be humiliated by your wife, Edward. I will not be shown up in front of servants and peasants by a slip of a girl who knows nothing about anything!'

Sinclair stopped pacing and slammed his fist down on Edward's desk, giving him a fright.

'Please, Sinclair, calm down and explain to me what happened.'

'There's a tenant farmer I was chastising because of his extreme insolence and non-payment of rent – and she interfered, Edward, she bloody well interfered!'

'Anna?'

'She marched into the field, out of nowhere, and ordered me to stop and that it was her business, her land, and I should mind my place.'

'Sinclair, Anna would not undermine you like that, or insult you.'

Sinclair turned on Edward. 'Am I to be insulted again? Are you now calling me a liar?'

'Of course not. But this must be a simple misunderstanding.'

'Yes, it is, Edward. And it's your wife's misunderstanding. I manage this estate. That is my post, that is my position. I manage it in the most efficient manner possible. I am also your cousin, which makes me your family. And your wife will not ever speak to me like that again, Edward. I won't allow it!'

Sinclair's eyes bored into Edward's.

Georgina and Anna came through the front door of the house, arms linked while they laughed over some story Seán had just told them.

Edward was standing in the doorway of the drawing room, hands behind his back, and a stern look on his face.'

'Edward!' said Anna, surprised to see him waiting for her.

'Anna, I need to speak to you. Georgina, please excuse us.'

'Of course,' nodded Georgina and, giving Anna a supportive look, she went upstairs.

Anna hadn't seen this expression on Edward's face before, and she felt a little nervous as he stepped into the drawing room, waiting for her to enter. She walked in and he closed the door behind them.

'Anna, I've been speaking to Sinclair. What happened between you two? He's outraged.'

'He's outraged! What about me? *I'm* outraged!' she defended herself, as she sat down on a couch.

'Sinclair tells me you interfered with the running of the estate. That you told him off in front of tenants and undermined him. Is that true?'

'He's not telling you the full story, Edward!'

'Did you interfere in his work and criticise him in front of tenants and servants? Yes or no?'

'Well, yes, but I had good cause to!' said Anna.

Edward's face went bright red with anger and he walked over to the front window and stood staring out at the lake.

'Anna, you must never – *ever* – do that again. It is not your place. You are not to interfere with Sinclair's running of the estate again, do you understand me?'

'Edward!' Anna pleaded. 'Sinclair hit a man with his riding crop. Struck him across the head and the poor man fell to the ground, badly injured from what I could see. I – I had to intervene.'

Edward turned around, his eyes slightly softened and his face surprised at hearing the reason for Anna's intervention.

'The man was badly injured?'

'From what I could see, yes. Don't take my word for it, ask Georgina – she was there with me.'

'Georgina!' scoffed Edward. 'She'd say the sky was purple if *you* asked her to.'

'So, not only do you disbelieve me, but my family now as well?' Anna's eyes widened in amazement and hurt.

Edward neared her. 'I'm not saying I don't believe you.'

'Well, it sounds like that to me.'

'I'm saying it still isn't your place to correct Sinclair. An estate like this takes a huge amount of management. It has to be managed with an iron will and fist or else it will quickly fall apart. Sinclair knows this, he understands more than any. His own family estate was lost due to mismanagement.'

'His own family estate was lost due to his father's preoccupations with the public houses, gambling houses and whorehouses of Dublin!'

'*Anna!*' Edward shouted.

'Well, it's true!' Anna snapped back.

'I don't even know where you pick up such thoughts. Georgina, no doubt.'

'You yourself were my informant! Don't you remember?' Anna felt her eyes well up at the injustice of it all.

Edward came and sat down beside her and took her hand. 'What I'm saying is for your own good. Inside the house is your business and outside the house is Sinclair's. Stick to that rule and there will be no more problems.'

She looked at his face and wanted to launch into a tirade of how she despised Sinclair. That she thought him cold and cruel and cunning and didn't trust him. But as she saw the kindness return to Edward's eyes while he begged her to accept the nature of things, she didn't want to upset him any further.

'All right. If you ask me to, I will. But I do not like people being treated badly, Edward.'

'They're peasants, Anna. They don't know any different. And if they were treated differently, they would just take advantage of us. It's the natural order of things, and we can't interfere, otherwise we jeopardise our own position.'

'Well, I don't want to hear any more about it,' said Anna, refusing to allow Sinclair to come between her and Edward any further.

A thought suddenly came to Edward. 'That bloody Seán! Where was he when all this was going on?'

'Sitting in the carriage,' said Anna.

'He's a useless boy! I told him to make sure you didn't get into any trouble!'

So Seán was appointed to keep an eye on me, thought Anna.

'I've a good mind to take a cane to him and give him a beating himself!'

'No, Edward, leave him alone. He tried his best to stop me from interfering, but he couldn't stop me.'

'You can be quite headstrong when you want to be, can't you?' Edward looked amused at her.

'More than you think,' she smiled back.

'Well, soon we'll have the house here filled with children, and you can put all your energy into them.'

12

'Well, you did right to drop the subject,' agreed Georgina, as she and Anna walked through the extensive gardens around the house.

'I've never seen Edward like that before. He seemed angry with me, and not willing to listen to my side of things.'

'I suppose it's not your place to interfere in business.'

'I just thought he would take my side more,' sighed Anna.

'Sinclair obviously holds great sway over him.'

'Sinclair is a liar and twisted the truth. He never told Edward he struck that man.'

'And he made sure to get to Edward first to give his version of events. You need to tread carefully with this man, Anna. He's cunning and, let's face it, brutish.'

'I'll just stay out of his way as Edward said,' mused Anna.

'Look, you and Edward are newly married. You still have to get used to each other's ways and how you do things.'

'He's longing for children,' Anna smiled.

'You'll see, as soon as you have a child, Sinclair won't matter as much to him. Edward is an only child, with not many living relatives. I can see how he's become a little dependant on Sinclair. A house full of children will change that!'

It was evening and a number of friends were visiting the house. They were gathered in the drawing room. Some were playing cards at the table, some were playing charades, while others told stories around the fireplace.

Anna and Georgina sat at a small card table playing poker together. Diana Hunter was playing charades, and both women had one eye on her and one eye on their cards.

'Well, what do you make of her?' asked Anna as she put a card down on the table.

'She's as you said – she certainly stands out from the crowd. Very beautiful and confident. Not in the flush of youth though.'

'Certainly over thirty,' said Anna.

Georgina put her cards down on the table, showing her hand. 'I know some families in Yorkshire. I'll see if they know her.'

The door opened and in walked Sinclair. Anna froze when she saw him.

'Apologies, everyone. I was delayed with estate work,' he said loudly.

'More beatings of defenceless peasants, no doubt,' whispered Georgina to Anna.

Sinclair was holding a bouquet of beautiful mountain flowers.

'Flowers for me, Sinclair? I didn't realise you cared so much,' mocked Edward, and the guests laughed.

Diana Hunter smoothed a hand through her hair and stepped slightly forward, smiling. Sinclair walked straight towards Diana but to her obvious surprise passed her and continued to the table where Anna was seated.

'For you, Anna,' said Sinclair as he bowed to her.

Anna was startled, and she glanced at Georgina who looked equally bowled over.

'Oh, eh, thank you, Sinclair. Very thoughtful of you.' She reached forward and took the bouquet.

Although Sinclair was smiling at her, his eyes were cold and angry and gave her a shiver.

As Anna gave the flowers to Barton, Sinclair went and spoke to Edward and the other men gathered at the fireplace where they laughed and joked.

'What do you make of that?' Anna whispered to Georgina.

'A clever move. He doesn't want to come across as bad to Edward. He wants to pretend there are no bad feelings between you.'

Later that night the fire burned and crackled in the fireplace as everyone sat around listening to Diana Hunter singing. Her singing voice was bewitching and hypnotic, her face lit up by the firelight in the darkened room.

As Diana sang 'She Moves Through the Fair', her eyes seemed focused on the reflection of the flames dancing on the walls of the room. But they weren't. Diana's eyes were trained directly on Sinclair, whose dark eyes stared back at her in equal measure as she concluded the song: *'It will not be long love, till our wedding day.'*

13

Georgina returned to Tullydere, and Anna was lonely for her for a long while. After her argument with Edward, things quickly returned to normal. Edward seemed to think the gesture of the flowers was a wonderful peace offering and that she and Sinclair were now the best of friends. However, although they remained cordial when they met, Anna tried her best to avoid being in Sinclair's company.

Although Seán got on her nerves frequently, she did find herself becoming fond of him. He was a welcome distraction after Georgina left, always at hand to drive her somewhere, always forthcoming with gossip from around the estate. There was a sharp frost throughout the winter, and Anna would often have Seán in the garden directing him to make sure the shrubs and flowers were protected against the weather. She loved the gardens, and was taking a keen interest in them.

'In what part of the estate do you live, Seán?' asked Anna.

'Over by Knockmora,' said Seán, as he trimmed a holly bush that was beside some steps leading up to a fountain. 'I have a lovely cottage and four acres there looking down to the lake. I love it there.'

'Does your family live on the estate here as well? Your parents?'

'No. I'm from the Hamilton estate originally.'

'And why didn't you stay there?'

'Ah, the Hamiltons are a nasty lot. They treat everyone like dirt, and when I got the opportunity to leave, I left quickly. A post came up in the stables here and I grabbed it. And now I'm renting my own land.'

'And is Lord Edward a much kinder landlord than the Hamiltons?'

'Lord Edward is a total gentleman. There isn't a bad bone in his body. He's much loved by everyone on the estate, and in the town.'

'How reassuring to know,' she said, trying not to sound too sarcastic.

'And to be fair to him, he does try to stop Mr Sinclair as much as he can, given the character Mr Sinclair is.'

'How do you mean?'

'Well, Mr Sinclair as you've seen can be very tough. And he shows no mercy for people who cross him. Lord Edward does try to rein him in a bit. Tries to get him to show some compassion. Give people a chance if they are in arrears or can't work as fast as Sinclair demands.'

Anna suddenly felt a great love for her husband, considering how he was trying to steer his domineering cousin to goodness.

'And will you stay on this estate for long, Seán? With your four acres?' she didn't hide the slightly mocking amused tone in her voice.

'Sure isn't it as good as anywhere else? Where else would I be going? I'll marry myself a nice girl from the town, and we'll settle into the cottage and have a big family.'

'As all good Catholic tenants do!' she mocked openly.

'Ah, you can laugh all you want about us Catholic tenants. But if it wasn't for us, you wouldn't have an income to keep this big estate and your big house running. It's our rents that keep you in the style you're used to.'

Anna felt suddenly annoyed by Seán's cockiness. 'I think you'll find that there are many other tenant farmers who would be very happy to take over your four acres any time you feel hard done by, Seán.'

'I'm sure there are, but they'll still be Catholic tenants and you'll still be reliant on their rents, won't ye?'

'Seán, I don't think the Armstrong dynasty will ever be reliant on the likes of you for anything,' she said regally to him. 'Now, cut away that ivy from that wall, once you've finished that holly tree.' She turned and began to walk back towards the house.

'Yes, my lady, anything you say, my lady,' said Seán after her, smirking to himself as he continued to shape the holly tree.

14

As the months passed by and the cold winter turned into a bright fresh spring, Anna and Edward's life swirled by in a series of parties and balls. The social life of their class revolved around the great houses that they owned. And so there were constant invitations to one another's homes. There was a constant competition between the dynastic families as to whose house was more palatial, who could be the most hospitable hosts and have the best balls. Edward always made sure their house lived up to the stiffest competition from their world. And Anna effortlessly turned into a charming and popular hostess. Edward was very proud of her. She was much admired by all their circle. She was relaxed in company, and easily occupied the role she had been born and bred for.

Edward and Anna were making the long journey home in a roofed carriage from the Carton estate in Kildare where they had been guests for the previous week and had attended the most elaborate ball of the year so far.

Anna sat musing beside her husband as he drifted in and out of sleep.

'Edward?'

'Yes, my darling?'

'Why is Diana Hunter never invited to any party or event at any other house but our own?'

Edward opened his eyes and looked at her. 'Don't be naïve, Anna. Many smaller local Protestant farmers get included in the local large house affairs. But they aren't sufficiently "society" to get invited beyond that.'

'I imagine Diana Hunter would very much like to get beyond that,' said Anna.

'You don't like her much, do you?' he asked.

'It's not so much that I don't like her. I just can't

warm to her. Do we have to invite her to every occasion at the house? I'd prefer if we didn't sometimes.'

'It would be rude not to. Besides, I don't think Sinclair would be too happy if we took her off our invitation list.'

'Sinclair?'

'I think he's quite smitten with her.'

'Is there anything going on between them?' she questioned, wondering if her suspicions would be confirmed.

'No, nothing more than a bit of flirting. I think our Sinclair is aiming a little higher than Mrs Hunter.'

'A little higher?' Anna looked at him confused.

'Well, as you said yourself. Diana Hunter is not gentry. But Sinclair is a lord's grandson, when all is said and done. Sinclair is ambitious, and I imagine will want to have his own estate one day – whichever way he can get it... Marriage probably.'

Anna nodded. 'Yes. I'm sure he could do much better than Diana Hunter.'

15

Diana Hunter was sitting on the couch in the drawing room of the house smiling broadly, Sinclair standing beside her, as she held his hand.

'We wanted you to be the first to know,' said Sinclair to Anna and Edward. 'We're engaged to be married.'

'Well, there is a surprise!' said Edward, taken aback but smiling broadly.

'Most unexpected!' added Anna.

Edward shook Sinclair's hand and hugged him tightly, before kissing Diana.

'Congratulations,' said Anna, kissing Sinclair on the cheek.

Diana stood up and, smiling broadly, said to Anna, 'I'm so happy. I want us to be like sisters.' She embraced Anna and kissed her on the cheek.

'Indeed, I'd like nothing more!' said Anna, managing to smile.

'Well, this calls for a celebration!' said Edward, ringing the bell.

Barton appeared almost immediately.

'A bottle of champagne from the cellar, Barton,' said Edward.

Barton withdrew, obviously trying not to look intrigued.

'Where will you live?' asked Anna, curious about the practicalities of the arrangement.

'I will move into Hunter's Farm,' said Sinclair.

'Excellent decision,' said Edward. 'It's a fine house.'

'I've been very happy there, anyway. And hope to continue being,' said Diana, smiling at her fiancé.

Unlike your servants to whom you give a miserable time according to Seán, thought Anna.

Barton came in with a bottle of champagne, popped it open and filled four glasses.

'Thank you, Barton,' said Edward, signalling to him to leave.

As soon as the door closed he handed around the glasses.

'And what about the date?' he asked then.

'We're thinking Monday week,' said Diana decisively.

'*Monday week!*' Anna was astounded.

'Well, there's no point in waiting around, is there?' said Diana, looking at Sinclair with a cool smile.

'We were hoping to use the church on the estate, and could I ask to have the reception here afterwards?' said Sinclair.

'I insist! It's my wedding gift to you,' said Edward as he raised his glass. 'To Sinclair and Diana!'

'Sinclair and Diana!' Anna raised her glass and nodded, discreetly raising her eyes at the thought of it all.

Anna was walking down the street in the town with Seán carrying her shopping.

'According to Jimmy Callan there were massive ructions at Hunter's Farm last week,' said Seán, trying to see above the hatboxes he was holding.

'And who is Jimmy Callan?' questioned Anna.

'He's Diana Hunter's stable boy and a good friend of mine.'

'Have you stable boys nothing better to do than carry gossip all day long about your masters and betters?'

'Sorry, ma'am.' Seán looked suitably ashamed and they walked along the street in silence for a while.

'Well, go on,' said Anna eventually. 'What did this Jimmy Callan have to say for himself?'

'Well, Jimmy says that the parlour maid and the

84

cook at Hunter's Farm said there was a terrible row between Mrs Hunter and Mr Sinclair.'

'When was this?' asked Anna.

'Just at the weekend.'

'At the weekend? But they got engaged at the weekend.'

'Well, that's as may be. But there must have been some negotiating for the engagement because they nearly took the roof off Hunter's Farm with the screaming of the two of them.'

'How very odd!' commented Anna as she mulled over this information.

16

Anna stepped into her gown with the aid of two of her maids the morning of Sinclair's wedding. As she stood while the two maids finished dressing her, she was unhappy at the thought of the day ahead. That Diana Hunter was becoming a close relative and she would be saddled with her for life was bad enough. But that Diana and Sinclair were have their wedding reception in their house, *her* house, was very much annoying her. She didn't like her house being used for their nuptials. Although she had loved her own wedding in Dublin, she now wished she and Edward had it in Armstrong House. Georgina had come down for the wedding, arriving only the day before. With all the wedding preparations afoot, Anna had had no chance to have a proper chat with her cousin but she did notice that the rejection by her fiancé seemed to have become even more entrenched in her, making her even more bitter about life than the last time she had seen her.

'You look beautiful, ma'am,' said her head dresser.

Anna went to the mirror and viewed herself. The ivory satin gown with its scoop neckline and V-waisted bodice was certainly flattering.

Her dresser placed her bonnet on carefully and arranged the curls at the sides of her face. Then the other maid draped her shawl about her shoulders.

'Now, I think you're all ready, Lady Anna,' said her dresser.

Anna smiled and thanked them before leaving her room and going downstairs.

'Lord Edward and your cousin are already in the carriage, my lady,' Barton informed her, as he held the front door open for her.

She stepped into the morning sunshine. Edward and Georgina sat in the open-topped carriage, in all their finery, waiting for her.

Seán, who was driving, jumped down from the carriage and held the door open for her. Even he was all dressed up.

'You look a picture,' complimented Edward as Anna approached the carriage. 'You'll steal all the attention from the bride.'

'No fear of the bride allowing that, from what I recall of Mrs Hunter,' said Georgina.

Anna stepped in and sat beside her husband.

There were villages scattered throughout the estate, but the one nearest Armstrong House was a model village Edward had got an architect to design. The carriage made its way through the countryside towards this little village which was set around a little green, with the church in pride of place. They pulled up alongside the other car-riages and Seán opened the door to let them all out.

'Thank you, Seán,' said Edward as he escorted the two women up the pathway to the church.

'Seán did as he was told and scrubbed up well for the day,' said Edward with a smirk.

Anna glanced over at Seán who was tending to the horses. 'I guess he can do what he's told occa-sionally then.'

Edward gave a small laugh. His wife's irritation with her servant amused him.

'I've heard many a girl has been open to offers from him. Seán is considered quite a catch on the estate.'

'What? Him and his four acres of potatoes?' said Anna dismissively as she smiled at the people gathered outside the church.

Of course Diana Hunter looked stunning on her wedding day, as Anna had expected. The service in the church was pleasant if short with beautiful music chosen by Diana.

'Where are her family seated?' whispered Georg-ina to Anna as everyone stood to sing. Georgina had scoured the church but seemed to recognise most people there as part of the Armstrongs' circle.

'Oh, didn't I mention? They couldn't make it over from Yorkshire in time.'

'Well, why did they have the wedding so quickly in that case?'

'I don't know. Odd, isn't it?'

'What's odder is that no matter how much I checked with people I know in Yorkshire,' said Georgina, 'they have never heard of Diana Hunter socially there or anywhere else for that matter.'

'Really?' Anna's eyes widened, as the music finished and they all sat down.

'Not one person I enquired from had heard of her.'

'She is a bit of a mystery all right,' said Anna as she watched her and Sinclair exchange their wedding vows.

'And one you're now stuck with!' murmured Georgina as Diana said 'I do!'

Back at the house the ballroom had been laid out with long tables as the guests celebrated the wedding. The servants brought in a continual train of glazed ham, roasted duck and pheasant.

'Who is actually paying for all this?' questioned Georgina.

'It's vulgar to talk about money,' snapped Anna.

'It's only vulgar to talk about money if you have plenty of it. I haven't any of my own, so it's not vulgar. I take it from your reaction it is Edward who is paying?'

Anna said nothing as she observed Diana order their servants about, complaining the Claret was not good enough and sending back food to the kitchens that she considered wasn't good enough.

Later, Anna watched Diana and Sinclair take centre stage, dancing in the middle of the ballroom. Although Sinclair had neither property nor fortune, marriage to him had brought Mrs Hunter firmly into their circle. And by the way she was acting, the former Mrs Hunter, present Mrs Armstrong, planned to rise to the very top.

Edward held Anna tightly in bed that night as the reflection of the flames of the fire in the hearth danced around the room. The wedding party was now over and most of the guests had retired to their guest bedrooms in the house or as guests of the Foxes and other neighbouring families.

'It was good to see Sinclair so happy,' said Edward as he caressed his wife.

'I don't think he looked happy. I've never seen Sinclair look happy. He looked as he always does, determined and pleased with himself.'

'Well, if he can't be pleased with himself on his wedding day, when can he be?'

Anna thought before she spoke but decided to voice her concerns. 'I didn't like the way they ordered the servants around for the day, Edward.'

'What do you mean?' Edward sat up, looking confused.

'This is our house, our servants, and Diana and Sinclair spoke to them as if they belonged to them.'

'I didn't see anything wrong with their behaviour.'

'Well, I did, and so did Georgina.'

'Georgina!' Edward said loudly with a cynical

laugh. 'Georgina sees something wrong in everything everyone does since she was jilted by her
fiancé.'

'Don't be cruel about her, Edward!' Anna said
angrily.

'Why? It's the truth! She's welcome here any
time but I don't like how she comes down here
and tries to poison you against things.'

'Against Sinclair, you mean?'

'Yes!' Edward jumped out of the bed and
started pacing up and down.

'She doesn't need to poison me against him,
because I can't stand the man, or his new wife for
that matter.'

'But why?' Edward was aghast.

'Because he's not a nice person.' She was
tempted to tell him all the stories she had heard
about him from Seán, but didn't want to get
Seán into trouble.

'You've no cause to continue this vendetta
against him.'

'I'm not carrying on any vendetta. I stay out of
his way as much as I can. As we agreed, he runs
the estate and I don't get involved in that. But,
Edward, now he is trying to run my house as
well!'

'He was trying to ensure his wedding ran as
smoothly and graciously as possible, so his guests
would enjoy themselves.'

'The wedding we paid for!' spat Anna.

Edward looked at her, slightly disgusted. 'Now
you're just being mean. I think I'll sleep in a
guest bedroom – if I can find any vacant!' He put
on his dressing gown and marched to the door.

'Edward!' she called after him as he slammed the door.

He didn't come back.

'*Ahhh!*' Anna shouted in frustration and fell back onto the pillows angry.

17

News of Diana's pregnancy came soon after the wedding. How quickly Diana had conceived mesmerised Edward. As the months rolled by, and his and Anna's second wedding anniversary came and went, he was puzzled as to why there was no baby for them yet.

Then one day, only eight months after the wedding, Edward and Anna received the news that Diana had gone into premature labour. Riding through the estate that afternoon, on his way to visit Hunter's Farm to lend support to his cousin, Edward gazed across the luscious green fields of cattle and thought about the changes Sinclair had made on the estate. Sinclair had wanted to move into cattle-rearing as he saw it as a good source of income for the future. Sinclair and Edward had rowed over it, as it had meant clearing tenants from large parts of the estate, pushing them into smaller shareholdings. Sinclair had argued that the peasants could cope on smaller acreage with the potato as their main crop which more than fed their large families and allowed them to pay their rent. And as the tenants continued to have larger families, the potato was allowing them to subdivide their farms to their children as well. Sinclair had eventually got his way. Profits were up, which were the main thing, as Sinclair would say.

Edward couldn't wait to have a son of his own. Children and heirs he could spoil and teach to love the estate as much as he did. But now Sinclair was the first to have a child.

As Edward neared the house, he saw Sinclair come galloping down the avenue, his cloak flying behind him.

'Good day, Edward,' said Sinclair.

'I thought you would be back at Hunter's Farm today,' said Edward. Even though Diana Hunter was now Mrs Armstrong, the name Hunter's Farm had stuck.

'The baby probably isn't due for hours. No point in me hanging around there all day, waiting for him to arrive.'

'Him? You seem certain you'll have a son?'

'Of course!' said Sinclair arrogantly. 'The first of many, no doubt. I'm just off to the Miller place. They are being evicted today.'

'Another one?' Edward's face showed his frustration.

'Yes.' Sinclair's voice was sarcastic. 'Do you want to join me?'

'No, thanks. Watching people's misery gives me no pleasure.'

Sinclair smirked at what he saw as his cousin's weakness. 'You need to behave like a man, Edward!'

A maid from Hunter's Farm came rushing

down the road to them.

'Mr Sinclair! Mr Sinclair!' she cried out.

'What?' snapped Sinclair.

'Your wife, Mr Sinclair,' the maid gasped, trying to catch her breath after running. 'She has had a baby boy!'

Sinclair smiled broadly. 'See, I told you!' He winked at Edward.

'Congratulations,' said Edward. 'Let's go to Hunter's Farm to see your son.'

'In time,' said Sinclair. 'You go up. I'll be along a little later. Once I've attended to this business.' Sinclair struck his horse and rode off.

Edward watched him disappear into the distance.

In all her time there, Anna had never been in Hunter's Farm. As she and Edward stood at the front door waiting for it to be answered, she felt wildly curious about the house that harboured her nemesis. A servant answered and they stepped in.

'In here!' called Sinclair from the small drawing room, and the servant showed them in.

Anna was impressed with the inside of Hunter's Farm. It was small compared to the Big House, but beautifully laid out and furnished.

Sinclair looked delighted as he poured them all a glass of wine from a decanter.

'To my son and heir! Harry Armstrong!' declared Sinclair as he raised his glass and they chinked glasses together.

Heir of what exactly, Anna mused as she sipped her drink.

'And how is the baby?' she asked.

'We have to be very careful with him as he's so premature. We have a nurse tending to him day and night.'

'But he'll be all right?' checked Edward, concerned.

'The doctor says he'll be fine once he gets the right attention.'

'And Diana? How is Diana?' asked Anna.

'Diana is in perfect health and delighted with herself, as she should be.' Sinclair raised his glass again.

Anna and Edward were eventually led into the nursery where a nurse was on duty by the baby's cot.

'I'm afraid because he is so fragile you can only stay a brief minute,' warned the nurse.

'And you can't go too close,' added Sinclair, blocking them from getting any nearer the cot.

Anna and Edward just about glimpsed the top of the baby's head in the cot, as he was wrapped up in so many blankets, before being ushered out by Sinclair.

Then, while the men drank a few more toasts to Sinclair's good fortune, Anna made a visit to Diana's bedroom and found her in excellent health and spirits. She stayed but a few minutes, however, for fear she might tire the new mother – and because, in truth, she found Diana as unfriendly as ever and twice as smug as before.

'Did you get to see the baby?' asked Seán, as he drove Anna in the carriage to a visit to the Foxes' house.

Sinclair and Diana's baby had thrown her somewhat. Everybody had been saying it would be her turn next. But surely it should have been her turn first, since she was married so much longer than them?

'I did see the baby,' said Anna.

'Not many have. Visitors aren't welcome at Hunter's Farm for now.'

'Well, with the baby being so premature, they can't risk him picking illness up from visitors. Even Lord Edward and I were only allowed stay a few seconds.'

Seán had that smirk on his face that Anna had grown to dislike and be drawn to simultaneously, as it usually resulted in him divulging some intriguing and secretive news.

'According to anyone who's seen the baby it's the oddest premature baby they've ever seen.'

'And who do *you* know who has seen the baby?' she asked dismissively.

'All the servants who work at Hunter's Farm, of course.'

'And what do you mean an odd-looking baby?' she asked, concerned.

'What I said was an odd *premature* baby,' he smirked again.

'I don't understand. What's odd about him?' She shook her head in bewilderment.

'Well, he's a fine big fat healthy baby. There's nothing premature about him.'

Anna looked at Seán, confused and not knowing what he was meaning.

And then suddenly it all came together in her mind. The reported screaming rows between

95

Sinclair and Diana the weekend they got engaged. The quick marriage within two weeks. The quick announcement of a pregnancy. And then the supposed premature baby. The scandal of what had happened and what Sinclair and Diana had quickly covered up hit her and she felt nauseous. The child had been conceived before the marriage.

18

The months passed by for the Armstrongs in their usual whirlwind of social engagements. Anna looked on as Baby Harry seemed to grow bigger and healthier by the day. And every day more similar to Sinclair. Anna grew more and more to dislike Diana, whose confidence and arrogance seemed to grow by the day as well. She would often visit Anna at the house, and Anna would be forced to endure polite conversation with her as Baby Harry lay beside them in his perambulator.

Diana was also becoming quite the socialite. She obviously had assumed that her marriage to Sinclair had given her full-blown membership of the ascendancy. Hunter's Farm, although small in size, had gained a reputation as being a hospitable house, with Diana presiding over many a celebrated evening. The Foxes were at Hunter's Farm more than they were at the Big House these days, Anna mused. And as Diana's confidence grew, Anna felt her own being diminished. She began to dread hosting parties at the Big House, as inevitably the ladies would discreetly ask her when could they expect an Armstrong heir. A few times she feigned illness to avoid attending weekend parties at other great houses. Herself and Edward remained as close as ever. She loved him more than she'd thought possible, and she knew he returned it. But he too wasn't as carefree and jolly as he used to be. He seemed preoccupied, his mind sometimes drifting. And she guessed only too well what occupied his mind. The unspoken issue between them of wanting but not having a child.

She was sitting in her room one afternoon, writing a letter to her father, when she saw Diana's carriage draw up in front of the house. She sighed to herself as she blotted the paper – she would continue her letter later. Another two hours of afternoon tea with Diana beckoned. She went downstairs and waited in the drawing room. Half an hour later, there was no sign of Diana. Curious, Anna got up and walked out into the hall to see where she was. She checked the drawing room across the way and the library but there was no sign of her. Surprised, she was about to look outside when Barton appeared from the dining room.

'Have you seen Mrs Armstrong, Barton?' Anna asked.

Barton seemed to hesitate, then answered, 'She went into the kitchens, ma'am.'

'Whatever for?'

'I don't know, ma'am.'

Anna walked to the back of the giant staircase and through the doors into the servants' work quarters. She rarely went there. The kitchens, sculleries and servants' dining room were in a large semi-basement that ran along the back of the house. She walked down some steps and headed for the main kitchen. As she approached she heard Diana's voice inside and on reaching the door she peeked in.

The kitchen was a giant, stone-flagged room, with large stoves on one side for cooking, and dressers filled with delph and copper pots and pans against two of the other walls. On the right-hand side was a row of deep stone sinks, above them four tall windows which allowed a lot of light to enter despite the fact that the room was half below ground level.

In the centre of the room was a long wooden table which that day was covered with cooking-apples, rhubarb and blackberries, ready to be made into pies by the cook and kitchen maids. But there were no pies being made at the moment. Instead Diana was inspecting different meats being brought out of the larder by the cook and the maids for her approval.

'That should be thrown out,' said Diana, looking at a side of beef. 'It's not fit to serve.'

'But it only arrived in this morning!' exclaimed the cook, surprised and insulted.

'Don't contradict me,' snapped Diana unpleasantly. 'I said to show me your best meat, not your worst!'

Amazed, Anna walked into the kitchen, giving everyone a start.

'Diana, is there something I can help you with?'

'Oh, em, no, I'm perfectly fine. We're having a dinner party tonight, and Edward insisted I come up and select some meats for it.'

'I see!' said Anna, angry but trying not to show it.

'I do hope you'll be able to come?' asked Diana.

'It's a little short notice,' said Anna. 'I'll check with Edward if we can make it.'

'It's simply not right, Edward!' Anna raged at her husband that evening in the parlour. 'Coming in and helping herself to our kitchen produce and ordering our servants around.'

'Look, what's half a leg of lamb to us?' Edward tried to calm her down.

'That's not the point! We are not that woman's personal larder!'

'I don't know what you have against her.'

'We know nothing of her background, Edward! She's tricked Sinclair into marriage with that child!' She regretted saying it as soon as she had said it.

'What are you talking about?' he demanded.

'I've heard rumours about Baby Harry. That he wasn't premature at all. That she was pregnant before marrying Sinclair.'

Edward looked at her. 'You'll destroy that woman if you spread lies like that, Anna. I'm shocked at you.'

'I'm not spreading lies. I'm confiding the truth to my husband!'

'I don't want any scandal coming near this family, Anna. I won't have my cousin or his child involved in any besmirching because of your jealousy.'

Anna was indignant. 'Jealousy! What do I, with my pedigree and background, have to be jealous of the likes of her for?'

'Her child!' Edward shouted. 'You're jealous because she has a child!'

His words were like a slap across the face.

He lowered his voice. 'A child ... Anna ... a child ... whichever side of the marriage vows he was conceived on.'

Edward turned and stormed out, leaving Anna staring after him.

19

A coolness descended between Anna and Edward after their confrontation. She was very hurt by what he had said. And he seemed in no mood to discuss it or sort it out. His words spun round and round in her head until they brought on persistent headaches.

Anna and Edward began to avoid each other. Finally she decided she needed a holiday and arranged to visit her home in Dublin, before going on to visit Georgina at Tullydere.

Although Edward and Anna expressed pleasantries over breakfast and dinner, they were awkward with each other and she felt they were trying too hard to be nice to one another. Their natural closeness had evaporated. On the day she was leaving for Dublin, Seán brought her trunk down to the carriage and Edward came outside to say goodbye to her. It was the first time they had been separated since their marriage. Edward looked suddenly very sad as she climbed into the carriage and his eyes began to well up. Looking at him like that made her heart melt and she felt her eyes become tearful as well.

'I'll see you in a couple of weeks,' he said. 'Take care, my love.'

She nodded and smiled at him, trying not to show how upset she felt.

She looked at Seán who was standing behind Edward.

'Seán, you're to stay out of trouble until I arrive back, do you hear me?' she said.

'Yes, Lady Anna!' He nodded at her and smirked.

'And you're to look after Lord Armstrong for me in my absence, do you hear me?'

'I'll make sure he hardly misses ya until ya get back,' said Seán.

She smiled at him and the carriage took off. As the carriage headed down the avenue, she looked back at Edward, a lonely solitary figure waving after her.

It took two days and two nights to reach Dublin. She stayed overnight in friends' houses along the way.

Dublin seemed so busy and metropolitan as the she drove home to Merrion Square.

She was delighted to be back home with her

father and family. But she felt so different from the girl who had left there.

The first few days were spent shopping and dining out, but she had made an important appointment on the fourth day that she had told nobody about. And she arrived for that appointment with Dr Malcolm LaSalle full of nerves and apprehension. Dr LaSalle was the one of the finest physicians in the country and had been Anna's mother's doctor before her.

He asked her many questions, all of which she found utterly embarrassing though she realised they were necessary – about her periods, whether she had ever had any infections and even the frequency of her intercourse with Edward.

'Well, that is all satisfactory,' he said then. 'Now let's do a physical examination.'

This was even more embarrassing but Anna gritted her teeth and got on with it. She'd endure anything if it could give her a baby.

After the examinations he said, 'You're a young healthy woman, Anna. There is no apparent reason why you cannot conceive and become a mother.'

She felt relieved at the news and managed to breathe again.

'That is comforting, Doctor, very comforting. I feared there might be a problem.'

'No, you're perfectly fine as far as I can see, Anna.'

'So why am I not pregnant then, Doctor? My husband and I desperately want a child. We need an heir and if there's no problem with me, then why have we not got a baby?'

'There can be many reasons why you haven't conceived. The problem might not necessarily be with you.'

'I don't understand.' She felt bewildered.

'The problem may rest with your husband.'

'With Edward!'

'Yes.'

'Could it really be so?' Such a thing had never occurred to her.

'I've tended some of the best families in Ireland during my long career, including the Armstrongs. And there's one thing I will tell you about the Armstrongs – they are not breeders.'

'What?'

'It was the same for Edward's parents. They only had the one child, Edward. They wanted more. His mother came to me on many occasions. A lot of Edward's relatives have been childless or had just one child.'

Anna's mind raced through Edward's family. It was true what the doctor said. Even Sinclair was an only child. In comparison, her own family and relatives' families were all large.

'I'm not saying this is indicative that there is a problem with Edward fathering a child. I'm just saying in the absence of a problem with you, the problem could rest with Edward.'

Anna walked back to Merrion Square almost in a daze. He had put her mind at rest and in turmoil all at the same time. It had never even dawned on her that there might be a problem with her husband. She had just assumed the problem was with her. She suddenly felt great

103

tenderness and a need to protect Edward. But most of all she felt fearful for the future, for their future.

20

The rest of the days passed merrily at Merrion Square until it was time for her to visit Georgina, and the rest of her cousins at Tullydere. Her carriage left Dublin in the morning and reached Tullydere by early evening. She always felt a warm feeling when visiting Tullydere Castle. As her mother's family home, she felt somehow close to her when she visited there.

Tullydere Castle was situated in the rolling plains of the Irish midlands. With its turrets, towers and castellated roofs, this sprawling building always reminded Anna of something from a fairytale. An unexpected vision rising from the lush green fields and surrounded by numerous sycamore trees.

The carriage drove under a clock tower and into the forecourt in front of the house and the horse had barely come to a halt when the front door flung open and Georgina came rushing out, jumped into the carriage and hugged her tightly.

'Oh, I've missed you!' said Georgina.

Georgina's brother Richard and his wife Joanna came out of the house.

'Welcome to Tullydere!' said Richard, embracing his cousin as she dismounted from the carriage.

'Thank you,' said Anna. 'It's good to be back here.'

'And it's good to have you back here,' smiled Joanna, taking her hand and leading her up the steps and inside.

It was difficult for Anna to have her opinion of Joanna anything but coloured negatively, she had heard so many bad things about her from Georgina. Although she always seemed pleasant and charming to her, Anna was only too well aware the different masks people wore. As she was led through the immense hall at the centre of the house, she looked up at their ancestors on the portraits hanging on the panelled walls. Her mother's family had been in Tullydere since the 1600s and the whole place was rambling, immense and antediluvian, unlike the baronial comfort radiated by her own house. Georgina constantly complained the castle was never warm, no matter how many fires were blazing.

But to Anna the castle brought her back to the holidays of her youth, the freedom and escapism it had always offered. She hoped it would now offer her a temporary release from her marital troubles.

'See how she acts while you are around,' said Georgina to Anna, when they were safely ensconced in her bedroom.

'I've never seen this unkind side to Joanna you complain of,' said Anna.

'That's because she always makes sure to be on

105

her best behaviour when there are guests. Particularly relatives. She's very different when we are alone.'

'And does Richard not intervene?'

'I'm as much of a nuisance around the place to him as to her,' said Georgina.

'Well, at least the place is so vast, you can escape from them.'

'That is not the point, is it? Let's face it, this Diana Hunter lives away from you in another house, and yet she still casts a shadow over you, doesn't she?'

Anna sighed and got up and walked over to the long leaded windows that looked out across the countryside.

'Yes, she does.'

'And how are you and Edward now?'

'We weren't on great terms when I left. Not since the row we had that I wrote to you about.'

'Well, it's the child thing as you said. It's obviously causing him great concern.'

Anna turned around quickly. 'And me! Georgina ... I went to see a doctor when I was in Dublin.'

'And?'

'And he says there is no reason evident why I cannot conceive and have a baby.'

'But that's wonderful news!'

'But he suggests there may be a problem with Edward.' Anna's face creased with worry.

'Oh no!' Georgina eyes widened. 'Have you told Edward?'

'Of course not! I couldn't humiliate him like that.'

106

'So what are you going to do about it?'

'What can I do? I can't do anything, except accept our fate.' Anna collapsed into her cousin's soothing arms.

Anna and Georgina walked through the gently sloping countryside, stopping occasionally to take shade under one of the giant ash trees.

'I think you should tell Edward you saw the doctor,' said Georgina.

'No! I can't!'

'But he will continue to think the problem is with you.'

'I'd prefer him to think that than for him to think he is ... deficient.'

'You love him very much, don't you?'

Anna nodded and smiled sadly. 'I can't wait to see him again. And yet I'm dreading it, knowing there may be no answer to this.'

They walked along in silence for a while.

'There could be an answer to it,' said Georgina eventually.

'What do you mean?' said Anna in surprise.

'A very straightforward and simple answer.'

'Well – tell me!' Anna looked at her cousin sceptically.

'You've been told there is no reason why you can't conceive ... so go ahead and conceive.' Georgina had halted and was gazing intently at Anna.

Anna rounded on her in exasperation. 'Are you not listening to what I've been telling you! It's not happening for me and Edward. It's...' Then she stopped as she examined Georgina's knowing face. 'You're not suggesting what I think you are, are you?' Anna was horrified and disgusted.

'I'm just pointing out you have options. Edward would never know. He would never have to know. Only you would know. The child would never know. The man who fathers your child would never have to know.'

Anna's hand rose in the air and she slapped Georgina hard across the face.

She then lifted up the hem of her dress and began to walk quickly back to the castle.

'Anna! Anna!' Georgina shouted as she raced after her. She caught up with her, grabbed her arm and turned her around to face her.

'Let me go! I don't want to even look at you!' shouted Anna.

'Listen to me! I'm only pointing out your options!'

'Tom abandoning you has obviously affected you far more than any of us have thought. You've obviously gone demented from the whole experience!'

'Not demented, but realistic!' Georgina was shouting back. 'I know now how the world works, Anna, and it doesn't work very nicely. You think that being honourable and respectable and decent brings you the happiness you crave, but it doesn't! It cost me my fiancé – lost to some scheming bitch! And it will cost you your husband and your estate and that fine house you are so proud of!'

'Let go of me!' demanded Anna, trying to shake her cousin's firm grip lose. Georgina held her captive. 'You have no idea what it's like being a guest in your own home like I am. And that is what you will be if you don't produce an heir. You and Edward will be just custodians of your house, while it passes through to the nearest relative who will have all the power. And as a matter of interest who does the estate and title pass to if you don't produce a son?'

'I have no idea! We've never discussed it! Edward has any number of relatives who would be next in line if we were not blessed with children.'

Georgina's eyes bored into her and her voice became a harsh whisper. 'I bet you anything Sinclair is next in line, and his son after him!'

'*No!*' Anna screamed and managed to squirm free of her cousin's clutch. But she didn't run away. She stayed still as a statue staring at her.

'You need to find out,' advised Georgina, her voice now returned to normal. 'But the way you describe how Sinclair and his wife acts suggests to me they know who is next in line, and it is them. They act as if they have that entitlement. And you and Edward are just irritations in the way until they take over. Another few years and it will be confirmed that you and Edward are unlikely to have children and that Sinclair or his son will be the next Lord Armstrong. And then watch how they act. Then you will know what it feels like to be a guest in your own house!'

Anna felt the rest of her time at Tullydere was strained. It was true for Edward, Georgina had become too bitter. For her even to suggest what she had was leading Anna to suspect she really might have gone mad. By the time she set off back home, she couldn't wait to see her husband again. As her carriage pulled in through the main gates of the estate and past the gate lodge, her heart was thumping as she eagerly looked out of the carriage and the house came into view. And there was Edward anxiously awaiting her in the forecourt. She nearly jumped from the carriage and into his waiting arms.

'I'm sorry,' he whispered to her, kissing her. 'I'm sorry for saying what I said.'

'Just hold me,' she whispered back to him.

21

Anna was sitting on the couch in the library, reading. Deciding it was time for afternoon tea, she stood up and tugged the bell-pull to call for Barton and returned to reading her book. After a few minutes, when none of the servants arrived, she pulled the cord again. Another while passed and still nobody arrived. With irritation, she closed over the book, and went out into the hallway.

'Barton!' she called loudly.

The house was in silence as nobody responded.

'Hello! Barton!' she called even louder.

Still there was no response. She checked the different rooms that led off the hall, and there was no sign of anybody. She walked to the back of the staircase and through the doors and down the stairs that led to the servants' quarters. To her amazement everywhere was quiet. Even the kitchen was eerily empty.

'Where is everybody?' she called out loudly and walked to the back door in the passage beside the kitchen. Opening it, she walked into the flagged passageway outside and up the steps to the large yard at the back of the house. Walled kitchen gardens were to the left and the stables and carriage house beyond.

'Is anybody around?' she called loudly.

Suddenly Seán walked out of the stables leading a horse.

'Seán! Where is everyone? There isn't a servant in sight!'

'They've gone down to Hunter's Farm, Lady Anna.'

Anna looked incredulous 'Hunter's Farm! What are they doing down there?'

'I don't know. Mr Sinclair sent for them and they all went down about three hours ago.'

Anna stood, hardly believing what she was hearing.

'Seán, hitch up my carriage and bring it to the front of the house immediately.'

Anna didn't know if she was more consumed with rage or confusion as the carriage pulled up outside Hunter's Farm. She got down from the carriage, marched up to the front door and knocked loudly.

A minute later Barton answered the door.

'Barton!' she exclaimed.

'My lady!' he answered, looking as surprised to see her.

'What on earth are you doing here answering

111

their door?' she demanded.

She looked past him and she saw a number of her servants busy at work inside the house.

'What is going on here?' she demanded, pushing him aside and walking inside.

The inside of the house was a hive of activity with her servants hard at work polishing, cleaning and dusting. Through an open door to the kitchen she could see her cook and kitchen maids busy at work preparing what looked like a sumptuous meal. She walked from room to room in the house, taking it all in, amazed. Walking into the small bow-windowed dining room, she saw Diana supervising servants laying the table, with silver that looked like it came from the dining room at Armstrong House.

'Diana?' is all Anna could think to say.

Diana looked over, unconcerned, at her. 'Oh, hello, Anna. Have you come to lend a hand?'

Anna walked further into the room. 'Diana, what is going on here?'

'We're having the Earl of Kilronin and his party for dinner tonight.'

'So? What has this got to do with *my* servants?' Anna was exasperated.

'Well, I couldn't possibly be expected to manage with my staff, so I borrowed them.'

'You *borrowed* them?'

Diana looked surprised but bored. 'Yes. Is that a problem?'

Anna managed to laugh at the audacity of the woman. 'Of course it's a problem. You can't just borrow our staff without permission and put them to work for some silly dinner party.'

'It's not a silly dinner party actually. Getting the Earl of Kilronin and his wife to come is quite a coup. I've noticed you've never managed to get them to sit at your dining table.'

'*You've mistaken me for somebody who cares!*' Anna suddenly shouted.

The servants all jumped with fright and stopped working.

Diana viewed Anna coolly.

Sinclair suddenly appeared in the doorway and entered the room, giving Anna a start.

'What's all this shouting?' he said.

'It's cousin Anna,' explained Diana. 'She seems somewhat perturbed.'

'I'm not your cousin,' stated Anna. 'You are married to my husband's cousin and that's where our relationship begins and ends.'

'What is your problem, Anna?' demanded Sinclair.

'My problem is you have taken all our servants without so much as a please or thank you. Who do you think you are?'

'I think you'll find Edward gave me permission to take them,' said Sinclair.

'No, he didn't!' Anna challenged him.

'Excuse me?' Sinclair's eyes flashed dangerously.

'There's no way Edward would let you take every last servant and leave the house unattended and without so much as informing me.'

'Calling me a liar is insulting me greatly.' Sinclair voice was low but firm.

'And you have insulted me, Sinclair. Do not take my servants again without *my* express permission... Barton!'

The butler appeared in the doorway. 'Yes, my lady.'

'Barton, you and the other servants return to your duties in the Big House immediately.'

'Yes, my lady,' Barton nodded.

'Do not, Barton!' Sinclair spoke loud and strong. 'Remain here with the work Mrs Armstrong has given you.'

Anna looked at Sinclair disbelievingly. 'Sinclair! They are my servants. You can't overrule me!'

'I can and I do! Barton, the servants will remain at their posts here,' Sinclair pronounced, his dark eyes boring into Anna's.

Anna felt frightened, but was determined not to show it.

The servants were looking very nervously from Anna to Sinclair.

'Barton, I will not repeat myself again. Do as I order. Return to our house,' Anna insisted, her eyes not leaving Sinclair's.

'Very good, madam,' said Barton. He clicked his fingers and the servants left what they were doing and walked quickly from the room, Barton in their wake. Anna could hear him in the hall, giving orders to the others. She felt a wave of relief sweep over her. For a minute she had been sure he would ignore her command.

'How dare you come in here and give orders in my house!' Sinclair snarled at her.

'Your house! I think you'll find Hunter's Farm belongs to my husband. This is *our* house. And those are our servants.' She picked up a silver fork from the table. 'And this is our silver borrowed from our dining room, again without permission. And no doubt the food our cook was preparing for your esteemed guest tonight came from our pantry!'

'What of it?' demanded Sinclair. 'Edward doesn't mind.'

'Well, I do! And I will not be disrespected.'

Sinclair leaned forward to her, his eyes glistening. 'Edward would not deny his heir anything.'

'His heir?' She was taken aback.

'I am Edward's heir and my son after me ... in the absence of Edward having any children.'

'We'll see about that!' Anna said.

'It's the natural line of succession,' said Diana, speaking coolly and in control. 'If anything should happen to Edward, Sinclair is next in line. And after him our Harry.'

'You are being very presumptuous!' said Anna, blinking back tears.

'No, I am not presumptuous – I am *presumptive*,' said Sinclair. 'Because in the absence of you and Edward having a son, the heir apparent, I am the heir presumptive.'

Anna moved towards the door.

'Oh Sinclair!' Diana said sweetly. 'We should be kind to her. It's not her fault that's she's ... barren.'

Anna blinked a few times and quickly left. As she walked out the front door, she could hear Sinclair and Diana laughing loudly behind her. Loud, hollow mocking laughter.

The tears were streaming down her face as she quickly got into the carriage.

'Are you all right, Lady Anna?' asked Seán, full

of concern.

'Just take me home, Seán,' she pleaded as she buried her face in her hands.

Anna went straight to her room, and fell on her bed crying loudly, the scene with Sinclair and Diana replaying in her mind. She cried until she was exhausted and then drifted off to sleep. When she awoke it was dark and she started to cry again, softly this time. The door opened and Edward walked in. He quietly went around the room lighting candles, before coming to sit on the bed.

'Don't try to defend them, Edward. I've had enough!' she said through her tears.

'I'm not going to defend them.'

'Did you give them permission to take all our staff for their stupid dinner party?'

'No, of course I didn't. I wouldn't allow the house to be left unattended like that. You did right to order them home.'

'How dare they!' She sat up and looked him in the face. 'You've let them take over, Edward! Don't you see what you've done? You can't let it continue.'

'I've spoken stern words to Sinclair and told him it must not happen again. He assures me it won't.'

'But they spoke to me so appallingly. You have no idea. I know he is your cousin, and I'm sure he does manage the estate wonderfully for you. But I want them gone, Edward! I want them out of Hunter's Farm. Find a position for them elsewhere away from us and our estate. I can't stand them here any more!'

116

'But I can't, darling.'

'But why?' she was exasperated.

His eyes were filled with desperation. 'Because Sinclair is my heir. Sinclair and his son are next in line if we don't have any children.'

Anna stared at him before giving a low wounded groan that seemed to emerge from the pit of her stomach.

'Why is this happening to us, Edward?'

He shook his head sadly. 'I don't know.'

'Oh, I'm sorry, Edward, I'm so sorry!' She reached out and held him tightly.

'In fact, I'm meeting with our solicitors next week,' he said, 'to ensure everything is in place for the estate and title to pass through to Sinclair and his son, in the event anything should happen to me.'

22

As Christmas 1844 approached, the servants joyfully decorated the house with ivy, mistletoe and holly laden down with red berries. Walking through the house, Anna wished she could reflect their happiness. Georgina amongst others was coming to stay over the Christmas period. Anna would never have believed she would have dreaded a visit from her cousin. But here she was, wishing a letter would arrive from Georgina saying she couldn't make it for one reason or another. Georgina would only hold up a mirror of Anna's unhappiness to her, and magnify it further. Since their last altercation, Sinclair and Diana had kept out of her way. They rarely came to the house at all, let alone arrived in un-announced like they used to. But when she did cross their path, even though they were perfectly civil, they looked at her knowingly. Knowing that they were just playing a waiting game, and one day in the future it would be them and their son who would own and run everything. They were to be guests at the house on Christmas Day and she dreaded that as well.

When Georgina and the others arrived on Christmas Eve, it seemed like a jolly house they were entering. The fires were blazing, the brandy flowing, the parlour games stretched late into the night. Anna avoided being left alone in Georgina's company. She was trying to postpone the inevitable fraught conversations that would ensue. And most importantly she wanted to avoid another confrontation like they'd had at Tullydere. Georgina's solution to her problem made her feel ill and yet, like a nagging distant pain, that solution seemed to gnaw at her.

On Christmas morning there was a light fall of snow. Anna sat up in bed and gazed out at the world outside. Edward was already up and ready. She rang the bell and the servants came in, with hot water in a big pitcher for washing and coal for the fire. With the fire blazing to heat up the room, Anna got up to wash and get ready for the day ahead. The carriages brought everyone down to the church in the estate village.

Inside the church, Anna and Edward sat at the top of the church in the family pew, a family pew that seemed to stretch on for ever in its emptiness. She could see Sinclair and Diana in the congregation with Harry.

As the choir sang 'The Coventry Carol', Anna looked at her husband, who seemed lost in his thoughts. He seemed to have the weight of the world on his shoulders. She looked up at the altar and prayed for forgiveness for what she was contemplating doing.

At the dinner table, Sinclair and Diana made sure to sit at the very end of the table away from Anna. As the roast turkeys and roasted potatoes and vegetables were served, Anna put on an act of being a cheerful hostess, exuding high spirits and vivacity. The well-known philanderer Lord Browne was a guest as well, and tried to flirt with Anna as he always did.

'Is it true what my husband tells me, Lord Browne, that you have engaged a Catholic solicitor?' asked Anna.

'Indeed I have and why not? I wanted the best solicitor in Cork and that is what I have got, regardless of his religion.'

'My father tells me many Catholics have joined the professional classes but I thought they really only tended to their own,' said Anna.

'I've never known a solicitor to turn down money be it from Catholic, Protestant or even Jewish hands!' said Lord Browne, causing everyone at the table to laugh.

'I think that you're treading into dangerous territory, Lord Browne,' advised Sinclair suddenly from the end of the table. 'It might be all very novel having Catholic solicitors or doctors, but we can't concede any control to Catholics. Who knows where it might end if we encourage it?'

Anna looked at Sinclair. 'As ever, you are right, Sinclair. We have to be very careful of people who do not know their place.' She sipped from her red wine.

Sinclair stared down at her. 'And as we know a quirk of fate can change a person's place and position very quickly,' he countered.

Anna raised her glass and smiled broadly at Lord Browne. 'Well, I think it's very progressive of you. In fact, we should do the same and get a Catholic solicitor. What do you think, Edward?'

'I think I'm quite in favour of keeping the status quo, my dear. Catholics should know their place in the order things. Catholics in the professions can only cause problems. Look at what Daniel O'Connell did.'

As the conversation continued Georgina leaned forward and whispered to Anna, 'You've been avoiding me since I arrived.'

Anna looked at her. 'I know. I'm sorry. Let's go for a walk after dinner.'

She looked at Edward who seemed to be staring almost trancelike into the crystal glass containing his burgundy wine.

It was late afternoon on Christmas Day as Anna and Georgina walked out the front door. They were wrapped up in warm coats with bonnets, scarves and gloves. They walked across the fore-court and down the steps to the first terrace. Down the sloping hill, the lake was frozen over near the shore and some of the guests had gone down and were ice-skating, their shouts of excitement carrying through the quiet countryside.

Anna and Georgina turned off the terrace into the gardens and wandered along the pathways there.

'Sinclair and Diana are the doting parents, aren't they?' said Georgina as they walked past a fountain that was frozen over, with robins dancing around it.

'Things have deteriorated considerably between me and Sinclair,' said Anna. 'We hardly speak and he flaunts his power whenever he gets the opportunity. And I am powerless to get them out of our lives. They being our heirs.'

'Without a child of your own.'

Anna nodded. 'Without a child of my own.'

'Anna, you're in a very precarious position, not only for yourself and Edward but for the whole estate in the future. And what if something happens to Edward and Sinclair becomes the new Lord Armstrong? You'll be completely at his mercy.'

'I know. I lie awake at night worried sick about it.'

They walked on in silence for a while before Georgina picked up the courage to speak. 'Have you given any more thought to what I suggested to you at Tullydere? About having a child with someone else?'

Anna didn't speak for a while as they continued

walking. The sun was setting and spreading an orange glow across the Christmas sky.

'Yes, I have given it thought. I've been in turmoil over it. I don't know if I could do it, Georgina.'

Georgina grabbed her cousin and turned her around to face her. 'You must! It's your only way. Have another man's child and pass it off as Edward's.'

'I just don't think I could go through with it.'

'Anna! This is a drastic situation you are in. And a drastic situation calls for drastic action. Sleep with another man and become pregnant.'

'But who would I choose to father my child? Where would I start, how would I even suggest it?'

'You don't suggest it! You just do it!'

'But with whom? Lord Browne? He's ready and willing by the look of him. Is that what you are suggesting? That I wander down to his room tonight and commit adultery with him in my husband's house? Under my husband's roof!'

'I've been thinking about this, and no. You cannot risk having intercourse with Lord Browne, although I did consider him a suitable candidate. If you did that, you would be risking exposure. Men talk, and women get ruined. You can't choose Lord Browne or anybody else from our circles. I hear the rumours and scandals about people. If you were unfaithful to Edward with one of our own, you would live your life in the fear of exposure and ruin.'

'So who do you suggest I choose then?' Anna asked, exasperated.

'You have to look beyond our kind, our class.

You must look to somebody that will never know who you are or who will never come into our circle. It's the only way you and your child will be safe from exposure.'

'I don't understand. Who are you suggesting?'

'A stranger. A Catholic. Somebody with no connection to you and from a different world to yours.'

'A Catholic!' Anna nearly shouted. 'You've definitely lost your mind, Georgina! I can't have a child with a Catholic. Who are you suggesting? One of these doctors or solicitors we were discussing earlier?'

'Not even them. There's always a risk they will meet you one day and your ruse will be discovered. The most important thing is that this deception is never uncovered, because it would mean your ruin and Edward's ruin.'

'So what exactly are you suggesting?' demanded Anna.

'A random man from a random town. Or from the countryside.'

'A peasant!' Anna was horrified.

'This will be your and Edward's child, Anna. The real father is of little importance or consequence.'

23

With Georgina so certain of what had to be done, it was easier for Anna to leave the planning to her. Anna's own mind was a whirlpool of confusion, worry and dread. Georgina was convinced this was the only way she and Edward could be saved. They met and corresponded regularly over the next months, as Georgina put her scheme together.

'Listen to how the servants talk, especially to each other,' she advised. 'Listen in to their conversations. You can't go to a fair and talk in your normal accent as you'll stand out. Learn and practise how the servants talk so you can fit in at the fair and talk to potential suitors.'

'The fair?'

'Yes. A fair. That would be a perfect occasion for you to meet a man. A fair brings people from all over. The town would be packed with strangers. But you'll have to be sure Edward is out of the way, on business.'

Anna felt only dread at the thought.

The perfect opportunity came in April when the Easter Fair was being held in Castlewest. It was one of the biggest fairs of the year. And it happily coincided with Edward being away in Dublin on business. Georgina came to stay in his absence, as she put Anna through the final tutoring.

'If anyone asks, you are a tenant farmer from the other side of the county and you are looking to buy a mare,' she said as they plotted in the drawing room on the eve of the fair. 'The town will be packed with strangers, but do your research, look around. Try and select the most handsome man to ensure your child will have looks.'

'What if the most handsome man has no interest in me?' questioned Anna.

'Pursue him until he does! As the fair goes into the evening, there will be much drinking. From what I hear the inns can become dens of iniquity. Which although normally would be abhorrent, now suits your needs perfectly!'

'Was ever a deception planned so meticulously and coldly?' asked Anna as she sank her head into her hands.

Georgina got up and tugged the bell-pull. When Barton arrived, she instructed him to send in Seán.

'Yes, my lady?' asked Seán when he arrived.

'Seán, myself and Lady Anna are visiting friends tomorrow. Can you ensure a carriage is ready for us for noon?'

'Yes, my lady. I'll be ready.'

'No, we won't be requiring you. I'll drive myself.'

Seán looked uncomfortable. 'But Lord Armstrong insists I drive Lady Anna everywhere and she's not to travel alone.'

'She won't be alone. She'll be with me.'

'But–'

'Will you shut up and get out and do what you're told for once in your life!' snapped Georgina.

Seán looked annoyed but he nodded and left the room.

Anna remained seated on the sofa, staring out the window.

'Really! I don't know how you put up with that boy!' said Georgina. 'He has no manners and thinks he can say what he wants. He's very disobedient.'

'He amuses Edward,' Anna said absent-mindedly as she continued gazing out the window.

'I will drive you to the fair tomorrow, and then we'll organise a time and a place to rendezvous after and I'll drive you home.'

Anna turned and looked at Georgina. 'And you really think it is that simple? That I can just come back here to the house and get on with my life and my marriage as normal after committing the most horrible act of adultery with some horse-trader?'

'Yes. It's as simple as you make it.'

'And what if it doesn't work, Georgina? What if, after having sexual relations with some stranger, I don't end up pregnant?'

'Then you keep going back again and again until you do become pregnant.'

Anna sank her face into her hands. 'I'm to be damned.'

'And you will be damned if you don't.'

24

On the morning of the fair a nervous Anna was surveying herself in the mirror. Georgina had taken a dress that belonged to one of the servants at Tullydere and now Anna was wearing it.

'A perfect fit,' declared Georgina. 'I judged the servant girl to be the same size as you and I was right.'

Anna looked at herself in the attractive but cheap dress, so unlike the embroidered gowns made from silks and satins she normally wore. Georgina had brushed out her usually styled and curled chestnut-brown hair and now it was loose down her back.

Georgina had also brought a black shawl from Tullydere and now she draped it over Anna's head and stepped back.

As she looked at herself in the mirror Anna did not recognise herself.

'You look quite the peasant beauty,' declared Georgina, proud of the transformation she had effected. 'You should attract a lot of attention and suitors at the fair today. Take them off now and we'll hide them again until the time comes.'

It was after lunch when Anna donned the servant's dress again together with her usual bonnet. She and Georgina both wore long cloaks and Anna kept the black shawl hidden underneath hers.

They hurriedly made their way through the house and out to the waiting carriage. Luckily they didn't encounter any servants but Seán looked at them suspiciously as they stepped up into the carriage and Georgina took the reins.

The journey into town seemed to last an eternity and no words passed between the women. Anna's feeling of foreboding reached fever pitch as they reached the town which was indeed packed with people because of the fair. Neither the Armstrongs nor any of their friends came to town on fair day. It was known to be unpleasant with much over-crowding, drinking and fights breaking out. Georgina pulled up outside the main inn.

'I'll come back and collect you at midnight here outside this inn,' she said. 'Now remember every-thing I told you and taught you. This will all be over soon and you will have everything you want. Just keep thinking of that.'

'What have I agreed to?' asked Anna, unable to move.

'Just go!' snapped Georgina.

Anna swapped her bonnet for the black shawl, leaving the bonnet with Georgina who hid it under her own cloak. Then she climbed down from the carriage.

She looked up at Georgina.

'I'm going to be a fallen woman,' she said.

'Better than being a childless one!' said Georg-ina and she napped the reins against the horse and the carriage took off.

As Anna watched the carriage disappear down the street she felt, for the first time in her life, utterly alone.

25

As Anna walked through the bustling streets of Castlewest, it was like she was invisible. She was used to people bowing to her when she went anywhere, moving out of her way as she walked through streets, opening doors for her. But nobody was doing that today. It struck her what a difference wearing some expensive materials made. How differently people acted towards her when they knew she was Lady Armstrong! She had taken it for granted. She was used to it all her life and it had not even crossed her mind before how it would feel to be treated any differently.

She had never seen these people so close up before, wandering through them as one of them. The town was a hive of commercial activity, with everyone trading and selling: a young woman with a tray of oranges; a man with a stall of plucked chickens; a stall further down the road with geese. Everything was available, from ribbons to silks. There were animals being sold all along the street as well – sheep and cattle. She felt frightened but at the same time intrigued, as she watched the people go about their business.

'Soda bread, Miss? Made by myself. You won't get better here today,' coaxed a woman at a baker's stall. Anna smiled and kept on walking. As she looked at the men she shuddered at the very thought of being anywhere near them, let alone having intercourse with them. She continued to search.

It was some hours later that Anna came upon a large field behind the town where the horse-trading was taking place. She was weary, dispirited and frightened. She'd had brief flirtations with some reasonably presentable men but in each case she had soon withdrawn, her nerve failing her.

She walked down through the field through the pens of animals. There was a lot of aggressive bartering going on here, and she could see these-horse dealers were driving hard bargains.

She passed a suckling pig being roasted over a giant fire. Gathered around it was a group that seemed to be drinking heavily and listening to some music being played by a small band.

One of the men suddenly walked up beside her. 'Looking for some company?' he leered at her.

She took one look at his blackened teeth and nearly got sick. She ignored him and kept on walking.

She suddenly saw a very good-looking dark-haired man selling ponies. He looked to be quite a showman, attracting a large crowd around him as he paraded his animals. She spent a long while watching him, as Georgina had advised, before making any decisions. The man seemed very strong and healthy, confident and smart.

'About as good as it gets around here,' she whispered to herself. She couldn't see any sign of a wife or woman around him and she eventually walked up to his compound and started looking at the ponies. There was a stallion kept apart from the others and she went over and began to stroke him.

'See anything that takes your fancy, Miss?' the man asked as he approached her, smiling.

'Em, yes. I like this one,' she said, indicating the stallion.

'That one isn't for sale, ma'am. That's my own,' he said decisively. 'But I've a filly over here that would suit you down to the ground.'

She needed to engage him in conversation, to get his attention.

'No, I've looked at the others, and they are of no use to me. This is the one I want.'

He looked at her, bemused. 'And what would a girl like you need a horse like this for?'

'I've twenty acres rented. And I need a horse that will plough my fields.'

This seemed to get his interest. 'Twenty acres. That's a fairly big holding for a woman. I take it there's no husband, or else he'd be the one buying the horse.'

'I've no husband,' she said determinedly.

'And where's this twenty acres of yours and how did you get it?' he asked.

'It's the other side of the county, and I took over my father's tenancy.'

He was studying her now, taking her in. His expression seemed to show he liked what he saw.

'As I said, ma'am, I can't help ya. The horse isn't for sale.'

'You shouldn't bring something to the fair if it's not for sale,' she said.

He looked at her and smirked. 'I've brought the

shirt on my back to the fair, but I'm not selling that either!' He was leaning towards her now, flirting.

'You look like a man who would sell anything, if the price was right.' She moved closer to him, and smiled. 'I really want that horse.'

'You don't take no for an answer easily, do ya?' he laughed.

'Why don't you let me buy you a drink and we can talk about it further,' she proposed.

'Now that's about the best offer I've had all day,' he smirked at her.

He called a boy to keep an eye on his ponies, then they walked through the field and up into the town. Anna noticed some women were looking at him as they walked by and giving her nasty glares. He was obviously a man with some admirers.

'What's your name?' he asked as they sat down in the inn with two tankards of beer.

'Ann,' she said.

'I'm Clancy,' he said and shook her hand.

Her heart was beating quickly. She had actually managed to get as far as drinking with a man who seemed quite suitable and who definitely was interested. She could hear Georgina's voice in her head pushing her forward and forward.

'So why has a pretty girl like you not got a husband to do her trading for her?' asked Clancy.

'I like to do my own trading. Besides I haven't met a man I wanted to marry yet.'

He was looking her up and down. 'I'm sure you're not short of offers.'

'I'm sure you're not either,' she said. She leaned

closer to him. 'Why don't you tell me all about yourself?'

Clancy was arrogant, in a way a man who knew women came easy to him could be. She could tell he was used to these situations. His life was going from fair to fair trading his horses, and he probably had a woman in every town as well. In Clancy's mind, Anna was just a new addition to his stable of girlfriends. And it all meant he was perfect for what she intended.

They stayed at the inn for a long while, Clancy continuing to drink and order more drink. The inn was filling to capacity, the day's trading was ending and everyone was settling into a night of partying and revelry to celebrate the day's good fortune. Outside in the street Anna could hear music being played and much laughter and shouting. As the dark descended the town was getting a different atmosphere, one of merriment but also disorder. As she looked at the crowd in the inn beginning to fall around drunk, Anna longed for the night to be over and for her to be back in the safety and comfort of her house. Regardless of what Georgina had said, she would not do this again. It either worked this time or not at all. She would remain childless and put up with all that entailed.

Clancy moved closer to her, put his hand on her leg and whispered, 'Will me and you go for a walk?'

She blinked a few times and then nodded. He smiled back at her, took her hand and stood up. They left the inn and walked through the streets of the town, his arm now tightly around her waist. The town was still packed with people. They were drinking in the streets, bonfires were roaring high and people were dancing around them as music was played loudly. There were screams and shouts of laughter and a woman crying loudly somewhere. The whole place was intoxicating and Anna felt her heart beat so fast she was frightened she would faint. Her head was spinning and the smells and atmosphere of the place were crowding in on her as Clancy led her down to the field where the horses were being traded. It was darker there away from the streets.

Suddenly he grabbed her and she felt his mouth roughly descend on hers as he pushed her up against the wall and kissed her hard. One hand grabbed her breast while the other hand roamed roughly over her body and start to pull up her gown.

Anna felt panicked as the reality of the situation hit her. 'Oh, please no!' she begged.

'What's wrong with ya? This is what you were after from the moment you came up to me today!'

He grabbed the back of her head and pulled her towards him, grinding his mouth on hers in his roughness.

'No!' She tried to push him away. 'I've changed my mind!'

'No, you haven't!' He laughed nastily and continued to pull up her dress.

'Hey, Clancy!' There was a sudden shout behind him.

Clancy seemed startled and, releasing Anna, he turned around. There was a group of men standing there looking at them.

'What do you want?' demanded Clancy.

'Hey, Clancy, where did you find the whore?' asked one of the men.

'I found her in the same brothel your sister works in!' Clancy shouted back.

'You've a smart mouth on you, Clancy!' spat the man.

'What do you want?' demanded Clancy.

'I want my money back for that nag you sold me that dropped dead on me the day after you sold it!'

'I told you before. That horse was fine when I sold it to ya. And you won't get a penny out of me.'

'Somebody needs to teach you a lesson, Clancy.'

'Well, it won't be you, now get out of here!' Clancy said menacingly.

The men started walking slowly towards them, and she could see they were holding blackthorn sticks. Anna couldn't believe what was going on. Clancy suddenly let out a loud piercing whistle and within a few seconds there was a group of people rushing over to him. Anna stood behind Clancy, not knowing what else to do, until Clancy and his crowd began to walk cautiously towards the other group. She drew back and watched, mesmerised, as the two groups eyed each other up carefully. Then suddenly they launched at each other and started to fight viciously. Anna looked on in horror as the groups ferociously attacked each other, hitting each other with the sticks. She lost sight of Clancy as he was caught up in the middle of the battle. Suddenly hordes of people began to pour down to the field from the main street, joining in the fight, and a full-scale riot ensued.

Anna realised it was a faction fight. She heard much about faction-fighting. How groups of people were feuding and would fight each other, usually at the end of fairs. She remembered herself and their friends talking in horrified terms about the peasants fighting each other without any regard for injury. Often many deaths resulted, and Anna realised she was in great danger and needed to get away from there as quickly as possible. She walked carefully through the fighters, trying to avoid them as much as possible, to try and get to the main street.

Suddenly a woman appeared in front of Anna, her face a mask of hatred and viciousness.

'You whore!' screamed the woman and smacked Anna across her face with the back of her hand.

The force of the blow knocked Anna to the ground, and she lay there in shock as the fighting continued around her. She struggled to get up but she couldn't. Everything around began to blur in front of her eyes and she felt she was about to pass out.

Then suddenly she felt strong and comforting arms around her and she looked up to see it was Seán.

'Seán,' she whispered. 'Help me, please.'

'It's all right, Anna, I'll get you away from here.'

He picked her up in his arms and carried her quickly out of the field and into the main street.

'You're safe now,' he said, but when he looked down at her he realised she had fainted.

26

Anna opened her eyes and blinked a few times. She sat up quickly and started to panic as the memories of the fight came flooding back to her.

'Hello?' she almost shouted in a panic.

Suddenly Seán appeared beside her and said soothingly, 'It's all right, Lady Anna. You're safe. You're with me.'

She felt relief and solace seeing Seán's face and she remembered how he had rescued her and driven her away from the town in the pony and cart he had the use of to get about the estate. He had wrapped her in some tartan blankets and held her against him as he drove and she had fallen asleep from sheer exhaustion. She didn't remember him carrying her from the cart which he must have done.

She touched her cheek where the woman had hit her.

'You got quite a blow there. I'd say it will come up in a bruise over the next few days.'

She looked around the room, not recognising it.

'I brought you back to my cottage. I didn't know what to do when I found you. I didn't think I should bring you back to your house at that time of night, dressed like that and in the condition you were in. How would I explain it to the servants?'

'Yes, Seán, you did right. Thank you for your

quick thinking and for bringing me here,' she said gratefully. She fleetingly thought of Georgina and the panic she must have felt when Anna hadn't shown up. She felt confident Georgina wouldn't raise the alarm. Who would she tell, how would she explain?

She looked around her surroundings. The room was small. There was a fire blazing in the fireplace, which was lighting the room along with a couple of candles. The furniture was inexpensive but the whole house had a warm homely feeling to it. The smell of the turf fire made her feel secure after her horrible adventure in the riot. She had been lying on a bed that was positioned in the corner by the fire and she swung her legs to the ground now and placed her feet on the flagstone floor. She had never been in a peasant's cottage before. She never imagined what it might be like, it had never even entered her head what it might be like. She had never thought what sort of a home Seán went to after he left work in the Big House. And she could see he had made a cosy home for himself there with not much behind him. And it would be a lovely home for one of those village girls that were rumoured to be chasing him all the time.

Seán went to the table and, taking a mug, he filled it to the brim with a clear liquid from a bottle and came over to her and handed it to her.

'What's this?' she asked, taking the mug and looking at the contents.

'Poteen. Drink it,' he advised.

She took a smell of it. 'No! It smells foul. I couldn't possibly.' She went to hand him back the mug.

'Drink it. You've had a shock and you need it.'

She viewed the contents suspiciously before holding her nose and downing a big gulp of it. Its strength and taste hit her immediately. But he was right, it did settle her nerves.

He sat down on a chair opposite her and stared at her.

'You must find this very strange,' said Anna eventually.

'You can say that again...' He leaned forward, his face confused and almost pleading. 'What were you doing there, Anna?'

She was surprised to hear him address her by her first name, not 'my lady', or 'Lady Anna'. But as she was seated there at his fire, drinking his poteen, it seemed natural.

'I can't explain it. Don't ask me to... How did you manage to spot me?'

'Sure I had been following you the whole day,' said Seán.

'What?' She was horrified.

'When you and your cousin dismissed me yesterday, I followed you into town.'

'You were spying on me?' Anna became angry.

'I was following the orders Lord Edward gave me, that no harm would come to you,' Seán defended himself. 'And just as well I did, because who knows what would have happened to you in that fight. People get killed at those faction fights, you know, all the time.'

'It was appalling! Why don't the authorities do something about it? It's scandalous fighting like that with such viciousness!'

Seán laughed dismissively. 'The authorities! Sure it suits the authorities and you lot, the establishment, for us to be fighting each other. If we're fighting each other, then we can't come together and fight you, and change things that need to be changed.'

'You're saying these fights help keep order? Help keep us in charge?' She looked at him sceptically.

'That's exactly what I'm saying.'

She looked down at her poteen and took another long drink, and they sat in silence for a long while.

'So if you followed me for the afternoon and evening ... then you saw everything? You saw what I was doing?' she asked, fearing the answer.

Seán nodded. 'I saw Miss Georgina leading you off, dressed like – well, not dressed like Lady Armstrong should be. I saw you wander around the fair, talking to strangers. I saw you chatting to that horse-trader and going off drinking with him for the evening. And then I saw you go into the field with him.'

Anna sighed loudly as her heart sank. 'Then you did see everything.'

He looked at her and nodded.

'What must you think of me?' She sighed loudly again.

'Does it matter what your stable boy thinks of you?'

'It shouldn't ... but it does.'

He suddenly leaned forward, demanding answers. 'Were you playing a game or something? You and that cousin of yours, Georgina? Is this

140

how you have fun?'

'No! No, nothing like that!'

'There's plenty of lords who like to go slumming it. Visit a local whore in a local inn, before heading back to their fine wives and their fine living. I haven't heard of too many women up to the same practice, but I wouldn't be one bit surprised what that Miss Georgina would lead you into.'

'Seán! I wasn't in the town today trying to get some kind of thrill. Believe me, I couldn't think of any place less likely to thrill me, or excite me. I didn't want to be there. I didn't want to be with those people. I didn't want to be with ... that man.'

'Well, why were you then?' he asked, exasperated.

She said nothing but stared into the fire.

'You could have got killed. You probably would have got killed. And how would that be explained to your husband? How could he ever understand what you were doing there, dressed like that?'

'I wish my life was as simple as yours, Seán. You would never understand the complexities of my life. I never expected it to be like this. I was so happy and protected growing up. Everything was mapped out for me with Edward, and I believed that I, that we, would be happy and content.'

'So you have a bad marriage with Lord Edward? You always look happy together.'

'We are happy together.'

'Do you know what I think? I think you've been spoilt all your life. I think you know nothing about what we, our people, have to go through.

141

You wish your life was as simple as mine? How? You don't know what it's like to be trying to grow enough potatoes to live on. How you worry sick in case you are late for the rent. Then that bastard Sinclair would turf you out of your home and on to the roadside with nothing. And you'd have nobody to depend on.

'I see you dancing around that giant ballroom. I've seen the bonbons and ice cream you stuff yourselves with. Each bonbon and bowl of ice cream, and cognac, and champagne is put there by the blood, sweat and tears of us – the peasants as you call us. And then that's not enough for you. You still can't be happy with a kind and loving husband like Lord Edward but you go off in to the town, with that tramp of a cousin of yours, looking for some rough fun with a horse-dealer. And you're supposed to be our betters? The upper class? Lady Armstrong, you might have a title, but you've got no class.'

Anna suddenly burst into tears, and sobbing loudly she turned around and buried her face in the pillows.

Seán stared at her for a while as she continued crying.

'Lady Anna?' he asked gently, but she kept on crying and didn't answer.

'Lady Anna... I'm sorry. I didn't mean all that. I shouldn't have said it.'

She didn't stop crying and still said nothing. He was overcome with guilt. He got up and went over to her. He hovered for a long while, not knowing what to do or say. Eventually he sat down on the bed beside her and carefully put a

142

hand on her back.

'I'm sorry, Anna. I don't know the reasons you were there, but it's none of my business... You're a great lady. Everyone says it.'

'No, I'm not,' she said between the sobs. 'You're right. I'm a terrible wife, in every sense of the term. I've made Edward so unhappy. He deserves so much more. I've been easily led by Georgina, and made a mockery of my marriage.'

She sat up and looked at him, her face tear-stained.

'I don't think I can ever bring Edward happiness. I've failed him by what I did today, and I've failed myself.'

He shook his head softly and smiled at her, but his eyes welled up from looking at her unhappiness. 'No, you haven't. He adores you. I see it every time I see you together. His face lights up when he sees you and when he's in your company.'

She looked at him. 'I'd never have thought you'd notice such things.'

'I notice a lot, Anna. I see a lot. And I see you're going through a time of unhappiness. But it'll pass. And you'll move on with your lives, and yesterday at the fair will seem just a bad dream.'

'I hope so,' she whispered. 'Thank you.' She leaned forward and hugged him.

He seemed startled to be in her embrace, and sat there awkwardly. As she gently continued to cry, he put his arms around her and began to soothe her. They stayed like that a long time, until tiredness overcame them and they lay back on the bed and fell asleep.

27

The dawn chorus of birds woke Anna. She opened her eyes and saw the morning light shining through the net curtains. The fire was now smouldering ashes. She looked around and saw Seán fast asleep beside her and the memories of the night came back to her. What had happened between them? The drinking in the town, followed by the poteen, mixed with her anguish and his sweet caring nature had brought them together. And as she stepped out of the bed, leaving his naked form behind her, she didn't regret it. It was like for one night she had been somebody else. She hadn't been Lady Anna Armstrong with all that entailed. She put on her garments and pulled back her hair into a bun. She walked across to the front door and opened it and stepped outside. She got a surprise when she looked around. Seán's cottage was nestled into a hill looking down on the most breathtaking view of the lake. In the nearby woods, the birds were a chorus of different voices.

Anna judged it was about seven in the morning, and the air was crisply cold but so fresh. She stood there, being part of this scene, for a long while.

'You're up early,' a voice suddenly came from behind her.

She turned around and saw Seán there, dressed

in breeches and shirt, looking very sheepish.

'The birds woke me,' she said.

She went over to him and they hugged tightly for a long while, wordlessly.

'It's time you were getting home,' he said.

She nodded.

As he drove the cart through the estate, neither of them mentioned what had happened between them the previous night. It was as if there was an unspoken covenant between them that needed no explanation or apology.

He stopped the cart in a stand of trees some distance from the house.

'Will you be alright from here?' he said. 'It's best I don't land up with you in a pony and cart.'

She nodded. 'I'll creep up to the house and sneak in,' she said, hoping nobody would spot her dressed the way she was.

'Maybe the first opportunity I get, I'll go for a transfer from my duties with you,' said Seán. 'Something away from the Big House – from you.'

Anna nodded. 'It would be for the best.'

'Goodbye, Anna,' he said.

'Goodbye, Seán.'

She got down from the cart and set out towards the house, hiding the black shawl again under her cloak. When she came closer to the house, she slowed her pace and approached the house as if she were coming back from a morning stroll. To her relief she found the door unlocked.

She hurried across the foyer and up the stairs to the safety of her room. She locked the door behind her. She hid her face in her hands as she leaned against the door, thinking about everything that had happened. She moved over to the giant mirror over the fireplace and examined the bruise coming up on her cheek from the woman's blow.

Taking a poker, she quickly stoked up the fire in the hearth and threw some wood on it, watching it turn into a blaze. Then she quickly got out of the dress and other clothes and threw them on top of the fire. Taking the poker again she pushed them into the flames and watched them burn into extinction.

28

Barton poured coffee into Anna's china cup.

'Will there be anything else, my lady?' he enquired.

'No, thank you, Barton,' answered Anna.

'And are you really sure you don't need treatment for that nasty bruise, my lady?'

'I am, Barton,' said Anna firmly.

Barton cleared away her breakfast plate and left.

A minute later Georgina came rushing into the dining room.

'Anna! Where have you been?' she demanded. 'I've been worried sick!'

'I only got back this past hour.'

'Why didn't you immediately come and find me?' Georgina was incredulous as she sat down beside her. 'I waited for you at the inn until well after twelve. And you never came as we had arranged. In the end I had to leave in fear of my life. There was a full-scale riot going on!'

'I know. I was caught up in it.'

Georgina saw the bruise on Anna's face. 'Oh, Anna! What happened to you?'

'A woman struck me during the fight. But I've told Barton I fell over the root of a tree this morning when out for a morning stroll.'

'Oh, Anna! When I think of the danger you were in! I was so worried about you. I didn't know what to do. I knew I dare not tell anyone that you were missing in the town but I thought anything could have happened to you.'

'Anything nearly did happen to me. Only Seán found me and rescued me.'

'Seán! What was he doing there?'

Anna took a deep breath and said, 'I no longer wish to discuss the whole unfortunate affair, Georgina.'

Georgina leaned forward and spoke conspiringly. 'Did you manage to find anybody? Did you go with anybody?'

'As I said Georgina, the subject is closed. I very much regret ever going to the fair. I regret a lot of things.'

'But what about our plan?'

'Our scheme, you mean? Our scheme of deception and folly? Our scheme nearly led to my being killed, and to subsequent great shame being brought on my family and the house of Armstrong.'

Georgina looked at Anna in disgust. 'So you are

147

giving up then? You are standing aside and letting everything go to Sinclair and his wife and son?'

'I no longer care about these matters, Georgina. I feel as if I have been living this past long while in a haze, something that's not real. I feel my desperation for a child has stopped me from looking at life logically. If the estate and title passes through to Sinclair and his son, then that is how fate intends it. If I and Edward are to remain childless, then I accept it, and so will Edward in time.'

'Are you so sure he will?' Georgina asked angrily.

'What choice do we have? I refuse to go along with this plan of yours any more. From now on I will concentrate on making my husband happy in whatever way I can, and trying to make sure I am happy as well ... in whatever way I can.'

'But you've already said you can't be happy the way you are!' Georgina's frustration was bubbling.

'Georgina! Georgina, I love you dearly, but I think it's time you returned to Tullydere.'

'So now I'm to be dismissed!'

'I'm afraid I can't allow myself to listen to your vehemence and bitterness any more. You've changed so much since your engagement was called off, Georgina. You've allowed yourself to become so cynical and unpleasant. All you care about is winning. It no longer matters if what is done is honourable and decent, as long as nothing stands in your way. And you have made me like that too these past few months.'

'Life has made you like that!' Georgina's anger erupted.

'Regardless, I don't think we are good company for each other at the moment... You'll always be welcome here, but maybe leave it some time before your next visit. There's a lot I need to fix, in my head and my life. And I don't need your counsel to deter me.'

'I will leave on the mail coach this afternoon.'

Georgina turned and walked quickly from the room.

29

Anna sat anxiously waiting for Edward at the drawing-room window, sewing. She could not wait to see him, and had been counting the hours until he arrived home from Dublin. Finally she saw his carriage pull up outside the house. She threw down her sewing, raced out through the hall to the front door, swung the door open and ran down the steps. As Edward stepped down from the carriage, she flung her arms around him and kissed him.

'Such a welcome!' he said kissing her back.

'I never want you to leave me again. Not for a single night!' she said.

'Then I won't,' he promised.

In the library, Edward sat at his desk opening letters while Anna lay out on the couch in front of the fire reading a book.

'More bills!' complained Edward as he threw

another piece of correspondence on top of the others.

'Do they ever stop?' asked Anna, not looking up from her book.

'Unfortunately not... And the head groom has left. He's emigrating to America – to make his fortune!' Edward smiled sceptically.

Anna casually looked up from her reading. 'Why don't you consider Seán for the post?'

'Seán?' Edward looked at her, surprised.

'You've always said he's excellent with horses, and full of confidence.'

'He does have the right qualities. But won't you need him?'

'Not really. He was useful when I first came here, as I didn't know my way around. But it's my home now, and he's outlived his usefulness.'

'Well, if you're sure. Though I'll miss him around the house, I'm kind of used to him,' mused Edward.

'It wouldn't be fair to keep him back from an opportunity because of that,' nodded Anna with a smile.

After a while, Anna stopped trying to concentrate on her book and gazed into the fire.

30

'I have some rather wonderful news for you, Lady Armstrong. You are expecting a baby,' said Doctor Cantwell, the local doctor.

Anna's hands shot up to cover her mouth in excitement and disbelief.

'Are you sure?' she demanded.

'As sure as I can be.' He was amused by her reaction, but delighted with the news. The non-arrival of an heir at the Armstrongs' had been the talk of the county and beyond. Lord and Lady Armstrong were such nice people, they deserved this, he thought.

Anna ran through the house from room to room, eventually storming into the library, startling Edward.

'Good heavens, what's the matter with you, Anna?' he asked, looking up from his desk.

'A baby! Edward ... we're expecting a baby!'

Edward sat motionless, staring at her, with his mouth open.

Slowly he rose from his chair. He then rushed to her and grabbed her tightly.

'Anna... I'd given up hope. I'd really given up all hope!' He pulled back from her, staring at her.

She wiped away his tears. 'Are you happy?'

'You've made me the happiest man in the world.'

Anna was astounded with the whole outpouring of goodwill shown to her and Edward with the announcement of the pregnancy. They were inundated with letters from friends and acquaintances from across Ireland and Britain offering congratulations. It was like it had been a given that there would be no direct heir to the mighty Armstrong estate and family, and now this news brought unexpected joy. Anna made sure to answer each and every letter directly.

There was one exception in the chorus of congratulations. Sinclair and Diana had not offered any and had pointedly stayed out of her way. Anna could only imagine their fury and disappointment at being displaced as heirs. She had tried to discuss the matter with Edward but he had been dismissive of the idea that Sinclair would be anything less than happy at the news.

One afternoon Anna was sitting at the desk in the parlour writing her thank-you notes when Barton entered.

'Pardon me, there is somebody requesting to see you,' said Barton.

'Yes, who is it, Barton?' she said, not looking up from her writing.

'Seán Hegarty.'

She looked up, startled. 'Seán?'

'Yes, your former manservant.'

'I know who he is, but what does he want?'

'He wouldn't say, apart from that it was of great urgency,' Barton said.

'Where is he now?'

'Waiting in the kitchen.'

'I'm afraid I can't possibly see him, Barton. Just inform him I'm entertaining guests and am not available.'

'Very good, ma'am.' Barton nodded and went to exit.

'Oh, and Barton ... if he comes to the house again, don't let him in. He no longer works here and so has no business being here.'

'As you wish, Lady Anna.' Barton went out and closed the door after him.

Anna realised her heart was pounding fast. Why on earth did Seán want to see her? She had banished all thoughts of him from her head since he had left, and decided to continue to refuse to think about him. But as she tried to return to writing her thank-you letters, it was hard for her to concentrate.

31

Since she had become pregnant, Edward had a permanent smile on his face. His natural good nature had returned. Gone was the nagging distress he had endured when they were heirless, and Anna and he had the marriage she had always envisaged. So it was unusual to see the stress return to his face one afternoon in the summer, after returning from a trip around the estate.

The summer had been very wet and warm, and Anna was finding it tiresome. She couldn't often go out for a walk because of the rain, and yet there was a humid feel inside the house.

'Is everything all right?' she asked as he came into the drawing room, fanning herself.

'I'm not so sure. The potato crop has failed on a number of the tenant farms on the estate.'

She looked up, concerned. She was well aware of how the tenants had become reliant on the potato for food, and in turn how their rents were reliant on the potato as well.

'What do you mean – failed?'

'The crops are rotten. There's no yield. You can't eat them.'

Anna put down her embroidery. 'And how many farms are affected?'

'I'm not sure yet. Sinclair and his men have set off on a tour of the entire estate to gauge the magnitude of the problem.' Edward went over and poured himself a glass of wine from a crystal decanter and downed it in one.

Sinclair arrived at the house that night. He came straight into the drawing room where Anna and Edward were waiting.

He went over and poured himself a whiskey. His sense of entitlement and familiarity still managed to annoy Anna, even though it didn't have the same impact any more as she fervently believed her baby would be a boy and Sinclair would never be master of her house.

'Well?' demanded Edward.

'It's all over the estate. The crop has failed considerably.'

'It's what we all feared. There's been a blight in Europe, in Belgium and the south of England

during the summer. I feared it would arrive here.'
Edward sat down, looking despondent.

'But how will the tenants eat?' asked Anna.

'Never mind how will they eat, how will they pay their rents?' snapped Sinclair. 'I've sent messengers to the Foxes and the other neighbouring estates to see if they are affected as well. To see exactly what we are dealing with.'

They found out quickly that the blight had affected the farmers in the neighbouring estates and beyond. And it soon became clear how extensive the blight was. It was widespread across the country.

'We've had the crops fail before.' Edward tried to be optimistic. 'There's terrible hardship that year, but the next year things come right.'

'But what do we do for the present? This year?' demanded Sinclair.

Edward pondered a while, then said, 'Evict none of the tenants. Allow them to go into arrears. They can catch up next year.'

'If the rents are allowed to go into arrears then the estate's mortgage will go into arrears!' Sinclair had argued. 'You might not find the banks so kind in their dealings with you as you are with your tenants!'

'And who will we get to replace the tenants if we evict them all? This blight has meant there are no other farmers with money able to come in and take their place,' Edward pointed out.

Anna soon knew her husband was speaking the truth as letters offering congratulations over her pregnancy were replaced with letters from friends who owned other great estates, expressing how difficult things were and how hard it was to see the tenants go hungry. Like Edward, everyone was hoping that the following year's crop would be a success and that the year's hardship would soon be over. The people could endure that year. Most had some food, some resources to get them by through the winter until the following spring.

But as the summer was left behind and the winter arrived, it was the hardest and cruellest winter people could remember. The people, already weary from lack of food and resources, suffered the severe weather in the desperate hope that the following year would be better.

Inside the house, life went on much the same as normal. There were certainly cutbacks in the parties and lavish lifestyle that was normally enjoyed, as there was in all the Big Houses. But as Anna sat in her bedroom in the late stages of pregnancy, looking out at the thick snow across the countryside, she could not help but feel overjoyed at the coming birth of her baby. The suffering of those outside the house, beyond the estate, could not diminish her own happiness.

32

Anna went into labour one evening at the end of January 1846. The doctor was on standby and rushed to the house. When the time arrived. Edward paced anxiously in the drawing room.

'Congratulations, Lord Edward,' said the doctor the next morning as he came in to him. 'You have a son.'

'Can I see them?' Edward asked.

'You can,' consented the doctor.

Edward rushed out of the room, up the stairs and into the bedroom, where he found Anna with the baby nestling in her arms.

'Your son and heir,' said Anna as Edward gently took the baby into his arms.

As Edward cradled the child, he could hardly believe it. After nearly six long years yearning for a child, he finally had a son.

Edward bent over and kissed Anna.

Their son, Viscount Lawrence, was to be christened at the beginning of March in the church in the village on the estate. Invitations went far and wide. Mindful of the hardship people were suffering, Edward and Anna decided that the reception would not be as extravagant as it would normally have been, but they still planned a sumptuous banquet at the house to mark their child's baptism. As Lawrence was christened in the church Anna was overjoyed to see goodwill on everyone's faces. Her thrilled father and brother and sisters and their families were all there from Dublin. All her cousins from Tully-dere were there, including Georgina. Georgina had barely spoken two words to her since she arrived, their once inseparable closeness now gone. Sinclair and Diana did not even bother to try and look happy, their disappointment plainly written across their faces. Anna thought it funny but, now she had her son, she no longer cared about Sinclair and Diana. They were no longer a threat to her.

After the church, the congregation filed out to the carriages waiting on the green. Anna noticed that none of the locals and their children were waiting there to cheer them. But, as she spotted a few children across the green looking thin and dishevelled, she quickly realised they had more to worry about with the failed crops. Everyone quickly made their ways to their carriages. As Anna stepped up to her carriage, she spotted Seán standing alone across the green staring at her. She got a fright to see him there. His stare unnerved her. She quickly got into the carriage and held Lawrence close to her as they took off back to the house.

Anna's father was in conversation with Edward and a group of the other men in the ballroom as the banquet was being served later in the day.

'On the journey from Dublin, I witnessed first-hand what the people are going through,' said Anna's father. 'There seems to be a lot of people begging on the roads. It's very pitiful.'

'Some landlords just evicted their tenants when they couldn't pay their rent,' said Edward.

'They now are destitute. I'm in London next week in Parliament and I'm going to bring the situation up as a matter of urgency. We need funds to supply food to these people.'

'Please do,' said another landlord who had travelled from the south for the christening. 'Things are desperate on our estate. And we have no money, with our mortgage, to give out any charity to the tenants. And the local town is in chaos with displaced people. I've had to forbid my wife to go near the place any more.'

'Any help from London will be much appreciated until the harvest comes in this summer,' agreed Edward.

Anna cut into their circle, smiling. 'Gentlemen, I forbid any more talk of this terrible blight today. This is our son's christening and I want you all to enjoy the day as much as you can. Reality will be there for you all tomorrow, but today is a day for joy.'

Her father leaned forward and kissed her. 'Indeed it is. And where is little Lawrence?'

'He was tired and so I put him to sleep in the nursery. I'd better go and check on him.'

She smiled and walked through the crowd of people out to the hall and up the stairs. Even being parted from her son for an hour was too much. Sometimes she would just sit beside his cot and stare at him for hours as he slept. She opened the nursery door and entered the room, closing the door behind her.

She turned and was shocked to see Georgina standing over the baby's cot.

'Georgina! What are you doing here? Why aren't you down enjoying yourself with everyone else?'

'I just wanted to see him close up. There's been so many people crowded around him that I couldn't get a proper look. Disappointing, considering how close we were, I should be shut out like this.'

'You haven't been shut out, Georgina.'

'I haven't heard from you in months.'

'Well, things have been hectic here what with the pregnancy and then the crops failing.'

'Of course...' Georgina looked down at Lawrence and studied him. 'He doesn't look much like you, does he?'

'I think he has my eyes,' Anna said.

'No, he hasn't ... and he doesn't look much like Edward either.'

'That's a matter of opinion.'

'Babies are always supposed to look like their fathers in the first few months of their lives. It's nature's way of telling the father that this is his child, to form the bond.'

'I don't believe that old wives' tale. As much as every parent thinks their child is remarkable and unique, the reality is they all have two eyes, a nose and a mouth and all look very much the same.'

'Oh, I always see a likeness between the baby and the parent. And as I said there is no likeness between Lawrence and Edward.' She looked up and stared at Anna. 'However, he does look very much like Seán.' She reached into the cot and

160

touched the baby's fine blond hair.

Anna felt sick as she looked at her. 'What are you talking about, Georgina?'

'You can fool everyone else, but you can't fool me. You forget I was a party to all this, it was my suggestion.'

'Georgina, I now think madness can be added to your other liabilities.'

'During the riot at that fair, nine months before you gave birth, you said Seán rescued you. Looking at this child, I think he did more than that. Looking at his child here in front of me.'

Anna became angry. 'I don't think it's such a good idea you visit here again, Georgina. I don't want you in my house any more.'

'Really?'

'No, I have to put up with you today, but I think you should head back to Tullydere tomorrow first thing.'

'Well, I'm reliant on my brother and his wife for transport, so I can only leave when they choose to.'

Anna leaned forward and almost shouted, 'I'll arrange for my own carriage to take you to Tullydere, if it gets rid of you any sooner!'

The baby started to cry.

'Look what you've done now! You've woken Seán's baby,' said Georgina.

'I want you to get out of here!' shouted Anna. 'Get away from my baby. Get out of my house. You're not welcome back here again. And I pity poor Joanna who has to put up with you under her roof!'

'Very well, I'll go,' said Georgina.

Anna reached down for Lawrence and, taking him in her arms, started to soothe him.

As Georgina walked slowly to the door she said, 'You can lie to me, Anna. You can lie to Edward. You can lie to everybody else. But you can't lie to yourself.'

Anna waited until Georgina had left before she broke down crying, holding the baby tightly to her.

33

Edward was holding Lawrence and showing him the new rocking horse that had just been delivered to the nursery that morning. It was the latest in a long line of toys he had bought for Lawrence.

'Edward! He's only a baby, he's much too young for a rocking horse,' Anna pointed out.

'What matter? I want his nursery to be filled with beautiful toys so all his earliest memories are good ones.'

'You'll spoil that child, Edward,' scolded Anna, hiding her delight that he did.

'Isn't that what he's there for? To be spoiled.' Edward cradled Lawrence and kissed his forehead. 'And I'm going to spoil him every day of his life. When it comes to him having his first real horse, he will have the very best one I can find. And when he goes to school, he will have the best education money can buy. Many gentry are sending their sons to England now for school

162

and university, bypassing Dublin altogether.'

'Don't let my father hear you saying that,' warned Anna. 'He would see that as an indication of Ireland being left behind due to direct rule from London, and our class looking more to England for guidance than to ourselves.'

'And when it comes to Lawrence getting married, well, he will marry a real princess, because he is a little prince.'

'You do talk silly, Edward,' said Anna, but couldn't help from smiling broadly at the two of them together.

It was after lunch and Anna had just put Lawrence down for an afternoon sleep and retired to the drawing room to write some letters when she heard shouting in the hall. Edward was out on estate business and, wondering what the commotion was, she headed out to the hall.

She got a fright to see Seán there, at the entrance to the servants' quarters at the back of the hall, being physically restrained by Barton. 'What is going on here?' demanded Anna.

'I'm sorry, my lady, but he asked to see you and when I refused he stormed past me and up here,' Barton said, continuing to try and hold Seán.

'What do you want?' Anna demanded of Seán, appalled.

'I want to speak to you. And I won't stop until I do!' shouted Seán, finally managing to break free of Barton and running into the centre of the hall.

'I've never seen anything like it,' said Barton. 'Have you lost your mind, man? You'll be in serious trouble over this.'

'I either say what I have to say here in front of him and the others when they arrive, or we talk privately,' warned Seán, staring defiantly at Anna.

'Come into the drawing room,' said Anna, turning and re-entering the room.

'But Lady Anna!' objected Barton.

'It's fine, Barton. I will take care of this,' Anna assured him, holding open the door for Seán.

He walked slowly in and she closed the door after them.

'What do you mean by barging in here like this?' demanded Anna, walking past him and sitting down on one of the couches.

'I had to! It's the only way I could get to speak to you! They wouldn't let me see you every time I asked.'

'What could we possibly have to say to each other?'

'Plenty!'

'Well, you have my attention, so say it and stop wasting any more of my time!'

He stared at her for a long time. She couldn't hold his gaze and quickly got up and walked over to the fireplace. 'Well? What do you want?'

'My son!' he shouted.

She felt her whole body shiver with fright. 'What are you talking about?'

'Little Lawrence. He's mine. I know it, and you know it.'

'I don't know what game or prank you are playing, but I'm warning you to stop right now! Goodness, you were always impertinent, but now you are just insane!'

'I've seen him! I've seen our son, I know he's mine.'

She got a further shock with this declaration. 'How have you seen him?'

'You forget I know this house better than you do. I worked on the building of it. I know every back stairs and door in the place. I came through the servants' quarters and made my way up to the nursery without anyone seeing me... I held him and everything.'

Anna was terrified on hearing this, terrified for her son's safety and what could have happened. She was determined not to show her terror.

'You're being ridiculous and I want you to leave.'

'Ridiculous? Nine months to the day that we were together, you give birth to Lawrence and he looks like me?'

'We were together?' Anna said the words derisorily and laughed mockingly.

'Oh, so you pretending that didn't happen as well, are ya? Why not? If you're living in fantasy land, you might as well let your fantasies take over.'

Anna crossed over to the writing desk and sat down. 'I'm rather tired of this charade. But you are being a nuisance.' She fingered the gold locket containing a watch that hung around her neck. It had been a first anniversary present from Edward and he had imported it from Russia. She took it off and held it out to Seán. 'Here take this. It's worth a small fortune. Take it and leave, and I never want to see you again.'

He walked over to her angrily. 'You can't buy

165

me off! Who do you think you are?'

She looked at him sternly but dismissively. 'I'm Lady Armstrong, Seán. Mistress of this house. Mistress of the eight thousand acres that surround this house. Wife of Lord Edward Armstrong. And our child, Lawrence, will one day be master of all this as well. The question is – who do you think you are? You're nothing and nobody. You're a cottier who leases four acres of failed crops from my husband. And you come in here demanding – I don't know, what are you demanding, Seán?'

'I know how important family is. And it doesn't matter what you and your husband have. The child is mine and he deserves to be with his father.'

Anna felt an overwhelming instinct to hit him.

'Seán! Lawrence will be brought up in a different universe from you. You will have nothing in common! You are from different sides of society. See reality for what it is.' She handed out the locket again. 'Take what I'm offering you, Seán. It will be your only chance in life to do something different, to get somewhere. You're intelligent and bright. You don't belong in the town with the people I saw that day, fighting and carousing. You're softer and sensitive. You see people for what they are. You could go to America with what I'm offering you. Start again over there with some money behind you...'

'No!'

'Is it not enough? If you want I'll go right now to my room and get more. I have diamonds and emeralds–'

'The only way I'll take that jewellery ... is if you

and Lawrence come with me. We can start together away from here. Go to America, as you said.'

'Me go with you! Seán, it's you who is living in fantasy land! I wouldn't go across the street with you, let alone across the Atlantic! Leave the husband I love, and my title and position? For what? A peasant boy I have nothing in common with. I feel sick at the thought of it.'

'You didn't feel sick when you came into my bed that night, did ya? I won't take a penny from you! But I will get my son. Whatever it takes. He will know me and I will be a part of his life. Lord Edward is a good man, and he will see the injustice of this when I tell him the truth!'

'He wouldn't believe a word of it, you fool!' she hissed.

'We'll just have to see.' Seán turned and stormed out of the room.

It was only when he was gone that Anna began to shake.

34

Anna viewed herself in the mirror and saw she was frighteningly pale. She had locked herself in her room for the rest of the day to try and think things through.

She had never allowed herself to begin to think of Seán being the father, because she feared all that would entail. She could lie to herself for ever, and never listen to the truth in her heart. But now with Seán rampaging about mouthing off, he was a loose cannon. The reality was that even if he told the world the truth, nobody would ever believe him. It would be unthinkable to everybody. But what put her in danger was that Georgina knew as well. If Georgina her cousin would ever verify that what Seán was saying was true, then Anna would be ruined, and so would her husband and son. And in Georgina she had turned an ally into an enemy.

She could not leave this loose cannon unchecked. Also, it had scared her that he had got to the nursery and held Lawrence. If Seán was so determined to claim his son, what would stop him from one day trying to kidnap her child? She couldn't trust him any more. She needed him off the estate so that he would not be able to access Lawrence, or her, again. She knew what she must do. She would get rid of Seán, so she, Edward and Lawrence could live their lives in happiness and without any fear.

She took off the Russian watch-locket from around her neck and held it tightly.

Anna raced her horse across the estate to the area of Knockmora where Seán's cottage was. It was the afternoon and he was at the stables working. As she approached the cottage she looked around to make sure there was nobody about and then jumped off the horse and walked up to the door. She pushed open the door and stepped into the cottage.

'Hello?' she called out.

When there was no reply she closed the door behind her and quickly checked out a good hiding place. She took a chair and stood on it and reaching up to the top of the dresser, placed the pendent there. Then she quickly left the cottage, mounted her horse and raced back to Armstrong House.

'Are you alright, my dear, you seem quiet this evening?' Edward asked as they sat in the drawing room.

'Yes – well, no. I'm so silly – I appear to have lost my gold locket. The watch-locket from Russia that you gave me.'

'You? Lose a locket? Or anything for that matter! I don't think so!' said Edward, alarmed. He had never known his wife to misplace anything. She was far too exact.

'Well, I must have! I've searched everywhere for it,' she said, distressed.

Edward's face clouded over as he stood up and pulled the bell-pull.

A minute later Barton arrived in.

'Barton, Lady Anna has lost her gold watch-locket. I want you to supervise a search of the whole house – including the servants' rooms in the attic.'

Barton's face clouded over with concern. 'Of course, sir! Straight away.'

'Come on, let's search our room again,' said Edward, taking Anna by the hand.

'I'm afraid we have looked everywhere, Lord Armstrong, and there is no sign of the locket,' said Barton.

'You've searched all the servants' rooms?' said Edward.

'Yes.'

'I'm very pleased it wasn't found there. I'd hate to think one of our trusted house servants would take something. But these are hard times and you can never be too sure.'

'I suppose it's feasible one of them could have smuggled it out already,' Barton said.

Edward turned to Anna. 'Anna, think hard! When did you have it last? Where were you?'

Anna got up and started pacing. 'I definitely had it yesterday as I remember putting it on in the morning... I was writing letters in the afternoon in here...' Suddenly Anna's face lit up. 'And now I remember! I took it off and placed it on the writing desk so I could keep a check of the time as I wrote.'

Edward dashed over to the writing desk. 'Then it must be here somewhere.'

'We've already checked there, Edward.'

Nevertheless, he checked the desk itself and then examined the floor around it, while Barton searched the drapes of the curtains in the nearby window.

'Well, who has been in this room since yesterday, Barton?' Edward asked then, becoming exasperated. He hated to think there might be someone dishonest in the house. 'The bloody thing can't disappear into thin air!'

'Well, nobody – only the usual staff. Me, the under-house parlour maid to do the fires, a very trustworthy girl in my opinion – and...' Barton trailed off and suddenly looked at Anna, full of concern.

'Oh yes, I forgot!' Anna gasped. 'Seán Hegarty was here as well!'

'Seán Hegarty!' said Edward. 'What the blazes was he doing here? He's in the stables now!'

'He arrived in, my lord, and caused quite a commotion, insisting on seeing Lady Anna,' Barton said.

'Anna?' Edward's turned to his wife for answers.

'As Barton says ... he insisted on seeing me and so I received him here in the drawing room.'

'And what did he want? His old position back?'

'No... He told me he has run up gambling debts and with the crops having failed on his land he couldn't pay them back. He was asking, well, demanding, a loan from me to pay off the debts.'

'I cannot believe he would do such a thing!' Edward's temper exploded. 'Why didn't you tell me about this, Anna?'

'I didn't want to worry you, or concern you. I just told him no and that he needed to leave.'

'That he would come here and ask you for money!' Edward was scandalised.

'Could he have taken the opportunity to take the locket?' questioned Barton.

Anna walked over to the writing desk. 'It was resting on the writing table here, so yes, he could have swiped it when I wasn't looking. In fact, I was so taken aback by his intrusion, it was probably why I didn't notice it missing straight away.'

'If you don't mind me saying, my lord, I think

we've found our culprit. He had opportunity, reason and cause,' Barton pointed out.

'Not Seán!' Edward was horrified. 'I'd never believe it of him.'

'Well, we have to investigate it,' urged Anna.

'Of course. Barton, send for Sinclair immediately.'

That night Seán was in his cottage staring into the flames dancing in the fireplace as he thought of his confrontation with Anna.

Suddenly the door burst open and in stormed Sinclair with several of his men.

'What the–?' Seán leapt to his feet in shock.

'You just stay there and be quiet,' commanded Sinclair before turning to his men. 'Search the place!'

'Why are you doing this?' demanded Seán, as the men went to work pulling the place apart.

'You're in enough trouble, so just keep that smart mouth of yours closed,' said Sinclair.

As the dresser was turned over, the locket went flying through the air and Sinclair reached forward and grabbed it.

Sinclair dangled it in front of Seán's face. 'Caught – red-handed!'

Sinclair came marching into the drawing room where Edward and Anna were waiting anxiously.

'Yours – I believe,' said Sinclair, handing the locket to Anna. 'As we thought, it was in Seán Hegarty's cottage. On top of a dresser.'

'I'd never have believed it!' said Edward sitting down, his face a mask of disappointment.

'I would! The whole country is going mental with these crops failing. They'd do anything for money,' said Sinclair.

'But Seán!' said Edward. 'Where is he now?'

'My men locked him up in one of the stables. He won't get out. We'll leave him there till the morning and then bring him into town to the magistrate.'

'Magistrate! You mean he'll end up in court?' Anna looked up, alarmed.

'Of course, what else did you think? He'll be deported to Australia or Van Diemen's land,' said Edward.

Anna had heard so many awful stories of the convicts and the horrors that awaited them in the penal colonies. She had assumed, once the locket was returned, Seán would be thrown off the estate and that would be the end of it.

She had counted on Edward's kindness and his fondness for Seán to prevent him from taking it any further.

'Oh no! I don't want that!' insisted Anna.

'Well, you've no choice. The law has to take its course,' said Sinclair.

'We *do* have a choice, Edward!' said Anna urgently. 'We just won't report the robbery. Just evict him tomorrow and throw him out of the estate. He was obviously desperate when he took the locket. Losing his employment and his home will be punishment enough!'

'Not at all! If it was my Diana who had been robbed, she–' began Sinclair.

'Well, I'm not your Diana!' Anna snapped loudly at Sinclair. 'Luckily! Now, I would like to speak to my husband alone. Please leave us, Sinclair.'

Sinclair nodded curtly and walked out.

Anna rushed to Edward, 'Edward! Please! You were fond of Seán. Show him some mercy!'

Edward nodded and sighed. 'We won't take him to the magistrate. We'll evict him tomorrow. Oh, why did Seán do such a thing?'

Anna gazed into the fire. 'He was desperate. We can do anything – if we're desperate enough.'

Seán sat in the corner of the stable in darkness all night. He remembered Anna holding out the locket to him, bribing him to take it to leave the estate.

He now knew she had set about framing him.

The doors of the stable suddenly opened and in came Sinclair with his men.

'You're a lucky man, Hegarty,' he said. 'Lord Armstrong has a soft heart and a softer wife.'

'What's happening?' demanded Seán.

'You're being evicted from the estate. If it was my decision you would be thrown out of the country to the penal colonies. Come on!'

The men grabbed Seán and placed him on a horse. He was allowed back to his cottage to grab some possessions and then they rode quickly to the edge of the estate where Seán was dumped on the side of the road.

'As you know my men are constantly patrolling the estate, so if I ever catch you around here again, you won't be so lucky the next time!' Sinclair warned, before he and his men rode off.

As Seán looked at his little money and posses-

sions and looked around the forbidding countryside, he didn't feel lucky at all as he made his way
to Castlewest.

Anna felt relief wash over her after that. She was
free from Seán and exposure. Seán was evicted
from the estate and would never be allowed near
her or her baby again.

As the summer months passed by everybody
anxiously and hopefully waited for the potato
crop. When the crop failed even worse than the
previous year, despair and panic set in.

35

The doors into the library were open and Anna
could clearly hear Edward and Sinclair talk as
she came into the hall from the dining room
where she had been having a light luncheon. She
stood and listened.

'People are beginning to die in their hundreds,'
said Sinclair. 'Many were just hanging on till this
crop, but now that it's failed again they can't
survive any longer.'

'What can we do?' Edward sounded desperate.

'We are in a terrible position. We are running
into a second year of non-payment of rents. We
risk financial ruin. We are liable for the rates on the
farms of less than four acres. I say we clear the
land of these farmers and their families, amalga-
mate the farm holdings to make them bigger. We'll

no longer be responsible for their rates payments and we can diversify into more cattle breeding, which is what I've been trying to do here anyway.'

'And what do you suggest we do with all the evicted farmers and their families?' Edward's voice was raised.

'That'll no longer be our problem once they are off the estate. They may emigrate, or go the work-house–'

'Or starve to death!' Edward nearly shouted. 'And while we throw them out on the roadside why don't we have a ball here in the house! A feast, a banquet to entertain ourselves while the poor die!'

Sinclair ignored his sarcasm. 'What do you suggest we do then, dear cousin?'

Edward sat down at his desk. 'I suggest we cope as best we can. I'll write to the banks and tell them we need an extension on mortgage repayments. Even without eviction our tenants will need food provision to get them through this winter which we need to organise.'

'On a practical note, Edward, I strongly suggest we put armed men at the entrances of the estate.'

'Is that necessary?' Edward was shocked.

'Riding through here this morning, I found a few wretched creatures wandering around the place scouring for food. With the amount of people being displaced and desperate we have to protect ourselves from being overrun.'

'I don't want to live in a fortress!' objected Edward.

Sinclair slammed both his hands on the desk in front of Edward and shouted, 'For pity's sake, see sense, man! Do you want a couple of hundred starving peasants storming the front door here? If you have no regard for your wife and child, then have regard for the rest for us! Provide protection for your servants and the rest of us from a desperate starving mob!'

Edward was taken aback. 'Very well.'

'Thank you!' spat Sinclair, before turning and walking out.

Anna waited until she heard the front door slam before she went to Edward who was seated with his face buried in his hands. She put her arms around his shoulders and comforted him.

'Is it as bad as it seems?'

'I'm afraid it very much is. Can you write to your father again and tell him how desperate the situation is here? How we need Parliament's help. Tell him to go to Westminster and beg for help if he has to.'

'Of course I will. But I think he's already aware how things are. I received a letter from him yesterday saying Dublin was being flooded by migrants fleeing the famine in the countryside ... yes, he called it a famine. He said the streets are full of hungry beggars. He asked if the aid was getting through here.'

'Tell him it's not nearly enough. Write to him straight away.'

'Of course I will.'

That night Anna stood at the nursery window cradling Lawrence close to her while looking out at the lake. She tried not to think of the despair outside the haven of the house and estate.

'You're safe here, darling. Nothing can hurt you

here,' she whispered to him.

Anna's covered carriage left the main entrance of the estate and headed towards Castlewest. Edward had advised not going out of the estate as he had warned she would see things that would upset her. But she needed to get materials to be made into clothes for Lawrence. And she was hearing such horrible stories that she needed to see for herself what was going on. As she looked out the carriage window she saw people walking aimlessly down the road. She was struck by their emaciated bodies, dressed in rags, their eyes sunk into their gaunt faces, barely managing to hold out their hands as the carriage drove by in some desperate appeal for help. As she approached the town, she saw a woman lying beside the ditch cradling a baby to her, both wasting away from hunger. And lying in the ditch there were some bodies that she wasn't sure were dead or alive.

The town's streets were surprisingly empty – the town almost looked deserted. It was not the usual bustling market town it was normally, filled with produce and abundance. There was a police presence throughout the town, and a few fragile people stumbling around. The carriage pulled up outside the draper's. Anna stepped down and looked up and down the street and got an eerie feeling. She went up to the draper's door and went to open it, but it was locked, even though there was a sign saying it was open. She knocked loudly on the glass of the door, and a few seconds later the store's owner, Mrs O'Hara, came to the door and unlocked it.

'Oh, Lady Armstrong, it's so good to see you, please come in,' said Mrs O'Hara, beckoning her in, and she quickly closed the door and locked it again.

Mrs O'Hara was a large usually jovial woman who owned and ran the large draper's store with efficiency and politeness. But as Anna looked at her that day, Mrs O'Hara looked distressed and anxious, holding a handkerchief to her face.

Mrs O'Hara looked out the window. 'They didn't see you come in. But they'll spot the carriage quick enough and be out soon.'

'Who, Mrs O'Hara?'

'The people of course.'

'Where is everybody?' Anna asked pleadingly.

'In their houses, if they still have houses. They have no energy to even walk any more. I've never seen anything like it. None of the business people in town have. At least I sell only linen and cotton, they can't eat that. But the food stores can't even stock anything, because they would be rushed and looted by the starving poor.'

Mrs O'Hara went behind the large counter which was stacked with materials.

'How are you coping at the Big House?' asked Mrs O'Hara.

'As best we can.'

'I heard there were to be no evictions there.'

Anna noted that Mrs O'Hara's usual overly respectful manner of address was gone. Clearly, in her stress and panic, Queen Victoria herself could be standing in her draper's shop and she wouldn't care, she was so distracted with what was going on.

'No, Lord Armstrong insists there should be no evictions.'

'Well, that's something. I don't think the town could cope with another influx of people with nowhere to go. The Foxes have started evicting.'

'The Foxes!' Anna thought of kindly Mr and Mrs Foxe. 'I can hardly believe it.'

'Believe it, because it's true! I've heard them saying they need to clear the land of the cottiers to make the estate profitable again as they can't rely on the potato any more. Potato! And I've heard from Mr Byrne in the fishmonger's they are still ordering in salmon and caviar. Caviar! While their tenants starve and we have to suffer it all in the town.' Mrs O'Hara took her handkerchief and started dabbing her eyes. 'They say there will be a breakout of cholera or typhus if it goes on much longer. Typhus! I'll have to go to my sister in Dublin to stay. There's a field behind the town and they are just dumping dead bodies there into a mass grave. I've never seen anything like it.' The tears began to spill down the woman's face and she wiped them away with her handkerchief.

Anna quickly pointed out some cotton and paid for it. Mrs O'Hara wrapped it up and gave it to her.

'Oh no, here they are! I told you they would see the carriage and come out!' said Mrs O'Hara.

At the doors and windows of the shop were gathered a gang of people, dressed in rags. Mrs O'Hara opened the front door and let Anna out before quickly closing the door and bolting it again. Anna saw the ravenous faces in front of her pleading for food. Hands reaching out, they looked as if they barely had energy to stand. She quickly opened her purse, took all the money out and handed it out quickly before hurrying to her carriage.

'Take me home, quickly!' she told the driver.

'Edward! We must do more!' Anna pleaded when she got home.

'What else can we do? The workhouses are already being paid for by the landlords – it's our duty to pay for them. We just don't have enough money to feed everyone.'

Anna made her way to the nursery and rocked Lawrence's cradle slowly. As she looked down at him all she could think about was Seán. How she had thrown him from the security and protection of the estate, and cast him out to the catastrophe that was taking over the land. She had never realised it would be so bad. She hadn't realised she was putting Seán out to that. It broke her heart thinking of him out there alone and hungry like all those people she had seen today. She felt crippled with guilt at the thought that she would probably be the cause of his death.

'I'll find him,' she whispered to Lawrence. 'I'll bring him home to safety.'

36

Anna discreetly enquired from the servants had they heard anything of Seán since he had been put off the estate. Nobody seemed to have heard anything. She asked some trusted servants to enquire in Castlewest if they knew anything of him.

'There's so many people dead or dying, my lady, it's hard to enquire after one man and get a direct answer,' Barton informed Anna, after his enquiries had been unfruitful.

'I realise that, Barton, but I do need to make sure all our estate workers are safe during this terrible time.'

'Even a thief like Seán?'

'Christian duty, Barton.'

Barton's enquiries continued and he finally came back with news. 'Seemingly after Seán was evicted he stayed at the inn in Castlewest for a short time.'

At the first opportunity Anna made her way to the innkeeper.

'Yes, I remember he slept here a few nights. He didn't say he had any plans or where he was going. Then one night he just didn't come back.'

'Didn't come back? And what of his things?'

'He didn't bother collecting them. They weren't worth anything, so I threw them out.'

'I see.' She looked down at the floor.

'Did you try the workhouse, ma'am? He probably ran out of money here and went there.'

'Yes – yes. I'll check there, thank you.'

'We're very honoured to have you visit, Lady Armstrong,' said Doctor Cantwell when she visited the workhouse. The local landlord was obliged under the Poor Act to pay for the local workhouse, but that's where most of their interest began and ended, the doctor knew. This interest from Lady Armstrong was very welcome, and he hoped would result in more funds. She looked up at the gloomy formidable stone building. She looked at the famished people gathered outside.

'Why are they not yet admitted?' she asked.

'We have no room to admit them, Lady Armstrong.'

'No room?'

'We're completely overcrowded as it is.'

He showed her through the front door. She looked around the dark interiors and became depressed at the sight of it and the strong odours circulating.

'Doctor Cantwell, I'm looking for somebody. A man from our estate who we can't find. Seán Hegarty. Have you any record of him here?'

'I'll see,' he said, scratching his head, and led her into his small office where he started taking out the books and going through them.

'No – no Seán Hegarty admitted.'

Her heart sank. 'Could I take a look around?'

He looked amazed. 'If you want.'

He led her through dark corridors. 'We separate

the men from the women, and the children up to fifteen from the adults.'

'So the families are not together?' She was shocked.

'It's the most efficient way to run things,' answered the doctor.

He stood at a door and looked at her for a moment before opening it and waving her in. She walked in. She didn't know what was worse, the famished people outside or the looks on the faces of the people inside. The room was large and long and packed with men. She started to walk through but stopped, unable to go any further.

'Seán! Seán Hegarty – are you here?' she shouted.

Nobody said anything. She turned without saying a word and rushed from the building to her awaiting carriage where she broke down in tears.

37

As she walked through the gardens at the house, alone with her thoughts and reliving the things she had seen outside the estate, she resolved not to give up looking for Seán. She would do whatever it took to find him. She felt weighed down by a horrendous sense of guilt and shame. How could she have done such a thing? Fear had driven her to do it but that was not enough for her to merit forgiveness.

She had to put it right. There were other towns

with other workhouses and she would keep looking until she found Seán.

She would bring him home.

As the months went by she travelled from town to town searching, always bringing money or food from the house and giving it to people as she enquired about Seán. She walked through the towns, looking at each emaciated face to see if it was his. She visited the Hamilton estate where she knew Seán had been born and visited his family. Luckily they were being well cared for by the new landlord there, but they had heard nothing from Seán and were very distressed to hear he had gone missing. As she conversed with his family, she was amazed at the fact that she would be connected to them for ever through Lawrence and they would never know.

She travelled to Dublin and visited all the ship companies to see if there was any record of Seán leaving for Britain. She couldn't find any. She remembered him talking about going to America, so she travelled to Cork to check the records of the ship companies there going to America. But she could find no record. She was haunted by the sights she saw of the people suffering along the way, and wrote tirelessly to her father and his politician friends, giving accounts of what she had witnessed. And when she got back to the house she would sit in the nursery cradling her son close to her.

'I'll find him. I'll bring him home. It doesn't matter how long it takes,' she would whisper over and over before setting off on her journeys again.

She was eating breakfast in the dining room alone when Edward came in holding a copy of *The Times*.

'They've printed another letter from you,' he said, handing her the newspaper. She took it up and quickly read her letter, describing some pitiful sight she had seen and urging the government for more help.

'That should shame them into giving more!' she said, putting down the paper and continuing to eat breakfast.

'Where are you going today?' he asked.

'There's a workhouse down in Galway I've arranged to visit. I've got Cook to prepare food for us to give. And I've raised money from our friends to provide the passage to America for some of the inmates there. I'll be back before dark.'

She got up to go and he grabbed her hand. 'Anna! You can't go.'

She looked at him incredulously. 'Why not?'

'There's been an outbreak of cholera in many workhouses. The doctors and everyone are getting it.'

'Oh no! Well, they will need the food more than ever. I'll just leave it in and won't stay long.'

She went to walk away, but he held on to her hand and pulled her close.

'Anna! No! You can't go!'

'But the people need help!'

'And you can't give any more. If you keep mixing with them you will get cholera. You'll bring it back here and give it to Lawrence, me, the servants. Is that what you want?'

'Of course not! But I can't abandon my work.'

'Anna, you have to. You're wearing yourself down to nothing. Look at you!' He pulled her over to the mirror and made her look at herself.

She got a shock at seeing her reflection. She hadn't had time to view herself for ages. Gone was the bright fresh young girl who worried about what ribbons to wear and who to invite to parties. She seemed to have aged overnight. She touched her own skin.

'You're exhausted, Anna. You need to look after yourself now. There's only so much anyone can do.'

'But you don't understand, Edward. I have to go on. I can't stop.'

He held her tightly. 'But I do understand. And it's now time to stop.'

38

Anna didn't travel after that. She stayed at the house and the estate, minding Lawrence and Edward. Anyone who met her said the sparkle had gone from her. The bright carefree girl was replaced by a sad woman. They said it was all the awful things she had seen while doing all her renowned good works for the famine victims.

At night she would slip out of the house and run through the gardens down to the lakeshore where she stared out at the water whispering, 'I'm sorry. Come home – please come home. We miss you. Lawrence and I miss you.'

Edward sat in the nursery late at night cradling Lawrence close to him as he looked out the window at Anna who was walking through the gardens on her own.

His mind drifted back to a few months ago on the evening he had returned from Dublin having attended a political rally to demand assistance from the government.

He had arrived back to the house in the late evening. Anna had been unwell and had gone to bed early. Edward looked in on her and then the baby and then came down to the library to work on letters to members of parliament. As he wrote at his desk, he heard the door open and he looked up to see Seán standing there.

'What the blazes are you doing here? And how did you get in?' demanded Edward.

Seán closed the door behind him. 'I know this estate better than you – it wasn't so hard for me to slip by Sinclair's guards up to the house.'

Edward jumped to his feet 'I thought it was made clear to you never to enter this estate, let alone the house again?'

'Oh, it was made clear all right. Crystal clear.'

'So you've come back to rob us again, have you?' Edward was confused by Seán's behaviour. If it was a robbery Seán didn't seem panicked to have been discovered.

'No, I haven't come to rob you – I never robbed you in the first place.'

'I think the evidence of finding the locket in

your cottage says otherwise.'

'I didn't rob that locket, it was planted there.'

'And who would do such a thing, and why?'

'Your wife, Lord Edward.'

Edward stared at him in disbelief. 'Have you gone mad, man? I have never encountered such insolence or madness from a tenant!'

'She planted the locket so as to get me off the estate. She wanted me gone because ... because I threatened to tell the truth.'

'What are you talking about for heaven's sakes? The truth about what?'

Seán looked him in the eye and said, 'Lawrence is mine. Ask Anna. That is why she threw me off the estate. But I crept back here tonight to tell you the truth.'

Edward was in such shock he could not speak.

'She thought she could get rid of me just like that. Set me up over the locket and then have me thrown out like a pile of rubbish. I've lost everything over her – my home, my livelihood, my good name – everyone thinks I'm a thief. I've hardly any money left. Nothing left for me but to starve now. While she gets what she wanted, a child, my son, and carries on living here as if I never existed. That's why I had to tell you the truth. To show you what kind of a bitch you're married to.'

'Get out! I want you to leave my house immediately.'

'Are you not listening to me? She's betrayed you, like she's betrayed me! He's my son!'

Edward stood stock still in shock, his head spinning as he heard Seán speak. The filthy lies spilling out of his mouth. Thoughts raced through his head – Anna's sudden request that Seán be given the post of head groom, her insistence she no longer needed his services, the strange incident of the missing locket, Seán's long record of honest service.

He looked into Seán's face and saw the resemblance between him and Lawrence – and he knew he spoke the truth.

Seán's voice was growing louder and louder.

'Are you so stupid you can't see?' he was shouting now, trying to get a reaction from Edward, to make him understand. 'Can't you see he looks like me? He's my son! Lawrence is my son!'

'Shut up! Somebody will hear! I command you to be quiet!'

But this only made Seán more agitated and his voice rose to a scream.

'Lawrence is my son!'

Suddenly Edward reached for the poker beside the fire, raised it high in the air and hit Seán hard across the head. Seán stood swaying as he looked at Edward in disbelief for a few moments while the blood spilled down his face. Then he collapsed to the floor.

Edward stood there for a while, holding the poker, staring down at Seán's prostrate figure. There wasn't a sound from him or a movement.

Edward dropped the poker and bent down beside him. But his body was lifeless.

Edward locked the library door and sat staring at Seán's body for hours. It was only when it was well after midnight and he knew all the servants had gone to bed that he acted.

He fetched a blanket and wrapped Seán's body

in it, then quietly opened the library window and slid the body out. Closing the window, he made his way out of the house and around to the stables where he hitched a horse to the phaeton and led it around to the library window. His heart was hammering and the blood drumming in his ears as he knew the risk of being heard or seen was high. Lifting Seán's body into the carriage, he set off at a gentle pace until he was out of sight and earshot of the house.

Then Edward drove like a madman into town. He knew what he must do. He had committed murder, but nature had given him the perfect opportunity to disguise it. There was a field at the back of the town where victims of the famine were being buried in a mass grave. He checked to see if anyone was looking but there was no one in sight. But even if he was seen, all he was doing was placing another victim of the famine in an unmarked mass grave. He tossed Seán's body in with the others, drove home to the house, and cleared up any evidence.

As he cradled Lawrence now, he knew what he did was wrong. But he knew he did it for Lawrence. Anna was distraught, anguishing over the fate of Seán. She had been on a mission looking for him everywhere, overwhelmed with guilt that she had evicted him and that he might be a victim of famine. She did not know Edward knew the truth of her deception. She did not know Edward knew the fate of Lawrence's true father. But as Edward looked out at her walking through the gardens under the dark sky, he had no doubts of her love for him – her every look and action spoke of it. He knew in his heart why she'd had intercourse with Seán. He knew their own love would survive even though it would never be the same. They had both acted for their own survival, and for their son Lawrence. And now Edward realised they must concentrate on him, that his life will be worthy of their actions.

Book 2

1913–1922

39

It was said that Clara Charter had received twenty-one proposals of marriage from some of London's most eligible men by her twenty-first birthday. When questioned if this was true, Clara would reply that that was nothing in comparison to the amount of less honourable propositions she had received from London's less eligible men. Now, at twenty-four, Clara remained one of the great beauties and most sought-after young women in London society. Hardly a party guestlist was comprised without Clara's name hovering near the top. She was used to this attention, she had received it all her life. Her father's family was Charters' Chocolates & Confectionery, a name whose very mention was as guilty in titillating the taste-buds as Cadbury or Charbonnel et Walker. Her father had gone on to carve out a highly successful career in banking in the city. Her mother was descended from a long line of mill-owners and merchants from the north. And so this generation of Charters had the right background, connections and manners to be correctly placed to take an important role in society. All this, matched with Clara's beauty and fun-loving personality, made her the crème de la crème.

At the annual Charlemont ball, there had been a twelve-course dinner, and Clara had been seated in one of the prime positions. As she chatted amicably and enthusiastically to the people around her, every so often her light laughter would echo down the long tables, prompting other guests to look up and smile. Clara was aware when people looked at her. She could sense eyes watching her admiringly from afar, and she enjoyed it.

Afterwards, she made sure to dance with as many different men as possible around the giant ballroom.

'Will you come this weekend to stay at our country house?' asked a young aristocrat as he danced her around the floor.

'I've told you before I can't. I'd love to but I can't. Your country place is too far away and I've got too many things to do this weekend.'

'But you promised me you would come,' the young man insisted.

'I promised you I would come some time, just not this weekend,' she pointed out to him as the music stopped. Then she smiled at him and quickly walked off the dance floor before he could trap her further. She walked to her seat where a glass of champagne was handed to her by a young captain from the Yorkshire Regiment.

'Thank you, you're a dear,' she said, smiling at him and sipping from the glass.

'Now remember, we're going to the theatre on Tuesday night. Don't forget,' said the captain.

'Darling, how could I forget, when you've reminded me umpteen times since I got here?' Clara said tolerantly.

She felt particularly restless that night. She wasn't sure why, but as the people swarmed around her, she felt agitated. It was then that she saw him. He was standing at the other side of the ballroom. Impeccably dressed in a tuxedo and white bow tie, his brown hair slicked back, a cigarette perched on his lips. She didn't know why he caught her eye. Maybe it was because he looked bored. Maybe it was because whenever she looked at somebody, she was used to finding them already looking at her. And he wasn't, his eyes were gazing off somewhere, beyond the dancing couples that whirled past him.

'And perhaps before the theatre, we'll go for something to eat,' suggested the captain.

'Yes, perhaps ... who is that over there?' Clara discreetly indicated the man who had caught her attention.

The captain looked over and squinted as he studied the man. 'I don't know. I haven't seen him before.'

'*Hmmm.*' Clara turned to the man on the other side of her. 'Tell me, who is that man standing by the pillar?'

'I don't know. Do you want me to find out for you?'

'No, don't bother!' She laughed lightly, picked up her champagne and drank it off. 'This is divine. Did I tell you this story about the bridegroom and the champagne...' And as she continued to tell her story she spoke loudly, in a way calculated to attract the man's attention. Her companions laughed loudly, but the man never looked over once.

Clara's curiosity was burning brightly and she was delighted when she spotted the stranger

talking to an acquaintance of hers, Edbert Bart-
ley. She quickly made her excuses to her friends
and walked with her usual confidence across the
ballroom to the two men.

'Edbert!' she said loudly as she approached
them.

'Oh hello, Clara,' said Edbert, looking happy to
see her.

'I haven't seen you in such a long time, where
have you been hiding?' she mockingly scolded
him.

'I've been in New York, Clara.'

She tutted loudly. 'And not one postcard from
you! You are a bad friend to me, Edbert. You'll
have to take me to lunch to make amends.'

'I'd like that, Clara,' said Edbert, looking chuffed
with himself.

Clara waited for her moment and then turned
to the man standing beside him and gave him a
dazzling smile.

The man did not smile back, but his dark eyes
glanced at her in a disinterested way.

Noticing Clara and the man were not greeting
each other, Edbert said, 'Do you two know each
other?'

'No, I don't think we do, do we?' Clara continued to smile at the man.

'Clara Charter, this is Pierce – Lord Pierce
Armstrong.'

Clara held out her gloved hand and Pierce took
it and said, 'Nice to meet you.'

'And you.' She continued to smile at him.

'Pierce is from Ireland. He's over here attending a few parties.'

'I see,' said Clara, realising this was why she hadn't seen him before, or why her party hadn't known him.

'And are you enjoying yourself, Lord Armstrong?' she asked.

He glanced at her. 'Most of the time.'

Another admirer suddenly appeared by her side. 'Clara, our dance, I believe.'

Clara felt like screaming at his interruption. She wanted to stay and talk to this man who was intriguing her.

'Of course,' she smiled at him and took his hand. She smiled at Edbert and Pierce. 'Edbert, I'm looking forward to our lunch. Lord Armstrong, a pleasure to meet you.'

She was led off to the dance floor.

If she was restless before talking to Pierce, she was twice as restless afterwards. She struggled to find another opportunity to speak to him during the night, but one didn't arise. So she had to be content to try to overhear parts of conversations he was having with other people.

'Heard anything of Robert Keane?' she heard Edbert ask him.

'Yes, he's just back from Scotland. I'm meeting him Tuesday in Fortnum and Mason for lunch.'

That was the little bit of information Clara had been waiting for all night, and she could go home satisfied.

40

Clara's paternal grandmother, Louisa Charter, was coming to have tea with Clara and her mother. Clara's family lived in a Chelsea stucco white townhouse.

Clara had lived there all her life. She loved it there, and her memories were happy ones. She had two brothers, one older who was a doctor, and one younger still at Cambridge.

Clara realised she was running late as the cab left her off outside the house, and she got out and hurried up the steps to the front door. Her grandmother hated lateness, and Clara tried to think of a suitable excuse as she rang the doorbell and waited for the butler to open it – but as she looked down at her hatboxes after a morning of shopping, she realised they wouldn't be providing one.

'Is my grandmother here?' asked Clara as the butler opened the door.

'This past half hour. She's with your mother in the drawing room.'

Clara pulled a face, then removed her coat and hat and handed them and her shopping to the butler before making her way to the drawing room.

'Here you are! We were getting worried about you,' smiled her mother.

'The traffic was terrible from Knightsbridge,' explained Clara.

'Isn't it always?' said her grandmother. 'At any time of day or night, if Clara is going anywhere from anywhere, the traffic is terrible, and that's why she's always late.' She looked knowingly at Clara as she offered her cheek to be kissed.

Clara sat down and looked at her mother who smiled sympathetically at her while she poured her a cup of tea and passed it over.

'None of us can fight our natures, Louisa, and it's in Clara's nature to veer towards the late side of things,' Clara's mother, Milly, defended her.

'This is half your problem, young lady – parents who overindulge you and shoo away any slight to you. I put it down to your having no sisters. I had four sisters and growing up, well, you're just brought up differently from an only girl. No room for indulgence.'

'Well, I will try to be on time in future, Grandmother,' said Clara.

'I think it might be too late to save your reputation at this stage. A society hostess, who shall remain nameless, confided in me that you have the worst reputation in London for showing up to parties late. She says you've often been known to try and fit in two or three parties on the same night, and act as if it's your right to arrive at any time you like.'

'Well, I thought that showed good manners! Rather than declining invitations I make an effort to go to all of them!'

'I do wish people wouldn't talk about my daughter as they do,' said Milly, taking a sip of tea.

'I believe a young lady shouldn't come across as always in a rush ... which is how you come across, Clara. A rush to everywhere except down the aisle, of course. Perhaps your tendency to be late is making you late for your own wedding as well?'

Milly gave Clara another sympathetic look.

'Weddings are not about timing, they are about being with the right person,' said Clara.

'Well, that is where you are wrong, young lady,' said Louisa. 'Weddings *are* all about timing and your timing is decidedly off to me. It's five years since you came out as a debutante. Five years! Most debutantes are married within months – their partner met and married by the time the season is over. That is the point of it all! But you, Clara! You've enjoyed five seasons and not a whiff of an engagement!'

'I just haven't met the right person,' Clara shrugged and drank her tea.

'Met the right person! You've met everybody who there is to meet. If you haven't met the right person after that, then you never will!'

'I haven't met the right person who I can love.'

'Oh dear,' Louisa sighed loudly. 'Let me give you some advice, Clara. Do not marry the man you love – but the man who loves you. Life will be far easier for you that way.'

'Well, she's certainly met plenty who have loved her,' said Milly.

'I would like it to be mutual,' said Clara. 'Mutual love.'

'You see, this is what you get when you have a girl who has been given everything – she thinks she can have everything. Well, you can't, Clara. You can't have everything in life. You've been blessed with looks and charm and you think you can have this love too. But love isn't a given. And you're in danger of ruining your life in the meantime.'

'Ruin my life? I'm only twenty-four.'

'*Only,* she says! Only twenty-four... I was on my second child by your age. They say you don't want to get married. They say you enjoy the whole party circuit far too much ever to settle down. They say you enjoy the season more for the parties than what it is designed for – to find a husband. They say–'

'They say too much!' interrupted Milly.

'But looks fade, Clara, and charm sours alongside it. And you might not always be in such demand. You are in a prime position to elevate yourself to wherever you want, and position this family accordingly. Don't let your time pass and miss your opportunity, Clara.'

'I'm sure Clara knows exactly what she is doing, don't you, Clara?' said her mother, smiling over at her.

'Indeed I do,' said Clara, taking a sip from her tea.

The door opened and Clara's father walked in.

'Ah, Terence, you're home early,' smiled Milly, hoping her husband's entry would put a stop to her mother-in-law's tirade.

'Hello, everyone,' he smiled as he kissed each of the women.

'You'll be staying for dinner, Mother?' he asked.

'If you insist,' answered Louisa.

Clara waited until they were halfway through the

pork dinner before making the enquiries she knew her grandmother would have ready answers to.

'I met a new face at the Charlemont ball last night,' she said.

'A new face or a young one?' asked Louisa.

'Well, both, I suppose,' answered Clara. 'A Pierce Armstrong. Lord Armstrong. Do you know him?'

Clara watched her grandmother's face as the mind behind it flicked through the catalogue of names she stored there.

'Yes, the Armstrongs. Anglo-Irish. I knew his grandfather Lord Lawrence. Absolutely charming man, married a lovely girl from Kildare, and they went on to have six children.'

'Yes?' asked Clara, anxious to know more but not wanting to reveal her interest to her family.

'That's right. The family did extremely well in the last decades of the nineteenth century, during Ireland's boom. They had a house in London and Dublin as well as their main country house on a vast estate in the west of Ireland, which was their base. All the children went on to do very well. One of Lawrence's daughters married the Duke of Batington. A son married into one of those senselessly rich American families with rather Dutch-sounding names who made their money in things like steel.'

'Vanderbilt?' enquired Milly.

'I can't recall,' Louisa paused as she thought. 'The title and the estate passed through to Lawrence's eldest son Charles. And that's when it all got a bit murky.' Louisa reached for her crystal

204

glass and drank some wine.

'Murky?' pushed Clara.

'Lawrence's son Charles inherited his father's estate but none of his charm. He was known for being unpleasant and ruthless. He married some-one like himself, an Anglo-Irish titled lady with not much charm either by all accounts. And they got caught up in that awful land war they had in Ireland in the 1880s. You see, this is the problem with Ireland. You can't just go and live there and work and hunt like one would in Wiltshire or Yorkshire. You get embroiled in their turmoil and politics.'

'What happened?' pushed Clara, trying to head off the beginning of one of her grandmother's political rants.

'They evicted one tenant too many, made too many enemies, and poor Charles was shot one day for his troubles.'

'Goodness, how terrible!' commented Milly.

'Dead?' enquired Clara.

'No, he survived. But he wasn't the same after-wards. And he died a few years later having never fully recovered. The title then passed through to his son.'

'Which would be Pierce?' asked Clara.

'Well, I presume this young man Pierce you met must be his son, yes.'

'How intriguing,' said Clara.

Louisa looked alarmed at her granddaughter's interest. 'It's not really that intriguing at all, Clara. The Armstrongs might have been a force thirty or forty years ago. Now their house in London is gone, their house in Dublin is gone and most of their vast estate is gone as well from what I know. They are a family on the way down, while we are a family on the way up.'

41

Clara entered the tea rooms at Fortnum and Mason, but she wasn't looking for the person she was having lunch with whom she had spotted immediately. She was surveying the room for Pierce Armstrong who should be having lunch there with Robert Keane. She saw them drinking tea at a table and, steadying herself, sauntered over.

'Hello, there!' She stopped at their table and smiled brightly at them.

Pierce looked at her as if he hadn't a clue who she was. Luckily she was saved from embarrassment by the fact she was acquainted with Robert Keane.

'My dear Clara, how are you?' said Robert, standing and smiling, kissing her cheek.

'I'm very well, Robert. And good to see you.'

Robert turned to Pierce. 'Pierce, this is Miss Clara Charter.'

Pierce stood up and shook her hand.

'I think we've already met,' said Clara, smiling at him, before prompting, 'At the Charlemont ball.'

'Oh yes, nice to meet you again,' he said and sat down, leaving Robert and Clara to chat lightly.

Clara felt herself becoming annoyed that Pierce had opted out of the conversation. She couldn't help but glance at him as she talked to Robert, only to find he had picked up a newspaper and was reading through it.

'Well, anyway, I'd better join my friend,' Clara said eventually. 'It's been nice to see you again, Robert, and eh – Lord Armstrong.'

He looked up momentarily at her from his newspaper. 'Yes.'

She smiled and turned and walked across the tearoom to a man who was waiting anxiously for her to join him.

Pierce folded away the newspaper as Robert sat down opposite him.

'You met Clara at the Charlemont ball?' asked Robert, sitting back in his chair.

'Yes, very briefly. I thought her a rather vacuous creature, flirting around the place like a giddy goat. Who is she anyway?'

'Clara Charter ... as in Charters' Chocolates and Confectionery.'

'She's an heiress?' asked Pierce, glancing over at her.

'Not directly. Just part of a wealthy family.' Robert looked over at her. 'And just like one of their chocolates, she's quite delicious, isn't she?'

'Yes.' Pierce took up a chocolate resting on the saucer of his teacup and studied it. 'But the problem with chocolates is, no matter how delectable they look you never know what you're getting – until you bite into it.'

Pierce bit into the chocolate he was holding and chewed. He then tossed the rest of the chocolate back on the saucer, making a displeased face.

Clara hardly listened to a word her male companion was saying over lunch, as she kept one eye on Pierce.

'Clara? Clara – did you hear what I asked?' demanded her companion in irritation.

Clara was jolted out of her dream-like trance. 'Yes! Of course I heard you.'

'Then you will then?'

'Then I will what?' Clara looked at the man, confused.

'Come shooting with me at the weekend?'

'Oh no, I can't possibly. I've already committed to too many engagements. Besides I can't abide shoots.'

'But Clara! You said you would!' he continued to plead, and Clara drifted off again.

Seeing Pierce and Robert Keane get up to leave and then walk towards her to exit, Clara suddenly started laughing and pretended to be enjoying the company of the man with her. As the two men passed her table, Robert nodded and said goodbye. Pierce walked ahead, ignoring her.

Clare cancelled all her appointments for the rest of the day and went home where she sat in silence, thinking about this man and the effect he was having on her. She had never felt like this before. By the end of the day she knew she had met the right man for her. All she had to do was catch him.

42

Clara relentlessly pursued Pierce for the next few weeks. She started checking the guest-lists to all the parties and functions she was invited to and if Pierce wasn't on it, she wouldn't go. Quickly realising he was not to the forefront of London society, she discreetly organised for him to be invited to parties which she could attend and meet him at. She cultivated his friends. She vaguely knew his English cousin Gwen, daughter of the Duke of Batington, and began regularly to call on her for tea.

'I met your cousin, Pierce, at a couple of parties,' said Clara nonchalantly.

'Yes, he's over for a while, I believe,' said Gwen, a very self-assured girl with a strong streak of arrogance. 'He's strikingly handsome, isn't he?'

'I guess he is... Are you two close?'

'No, not really. I don't think anyone is particularly close to Pierce. I'm not that friendly with his sister Prudence either.'

'Did you not visit your mother's home in Ireland much growing up?'

'Only when my grandfather was still alive. Bless him, he was a sweetheart. But then when Uncle Charles took over, we didn't bother any more. Charles could be ... difficult. And the house – well, it's cold and draughty. And it always seemed to be raining when we were there. Awful place, Ireland!'

It didn't seem like that to Clara at all. She had nearly become an expert on Ireland since she had met Pierce, reading every single thing she could get her hands on.

Clara cleared her throat and put down her cup of tea. 'I should think it would be very nice of you to invite your cousin to your garden party on Sunday.'

'Would it?' Gwen looked unconvinced. 'Pierce and I have really nothing in common.'

'Hmmm, regardless ... perhaps in the spirit of Anglo-Irish relations?'

Pierce was invited to the garden party, did attend, and ignored Clara for the day.

Clara spent her afternoon reading up on Ireland. She found herself becoming fascinated with Irish history and she wasn't sure if it was just her fascination with Pierce Armstrong that was causing that. She spent hours going through the books in her father's study, discovering all there was to be discovered.

'Oh hello!' said her father, coming in and being surprised to find her there, head stuck in a book.

'Sorry, I've been using your room to do a bit of research. Hope you don't mind?'

'Of course I don't.' He bent down and kissed her forehead, then looked at the book she was holding. *Ireland in the Nineteenth Century*,' he read out, looking at her curiously.

'Just brushing up on my knowledge for dinner parties. It's quite important, the Irish Question, isn't it?'

He went and sat at his desk, smiling. 'I suppose it is.'

'Ireland is about to be given Home Rule, is it not? Its own parliament with limited powers? So they will remain part of the United Kingdom but will have control of their domestic affairs.'

'Well, yes, it is on the cards, yes. If the Protestants in the north allow it.'

'Well, they can't stop it, can they? I mean if everyone else wants it, how can they stop it? It's like if everyone in a family wants to hold a party, except for one, why should everyone else be dictated to?'

He laughed lightly. 'I don't think it's quite as simple as that, Clara. But it's nice you're taking an interest in current affairs.'

'Isn't it?' She smiled at him as she pretended to continue to read. 'I think I'll join the Suffragette movement next.'

'Clara!' said her father as he sat straight up in shock.

'I'm joking, Father!' She started to laugh. 'Imagine what Grandmother would say if I did though? Imagine what being chained to a railing would do to my marriage prospects!'

'You shouldn't wind your grandmother up, Clara. She only wants what's best for you.'

'I know,' sighed Clara. 'Everyone only wants what's best for me.'

At the library Clara spent hours going through books about the great houses of Ireland. She needed to see a painting or a photo of Armstrong

House in Ireland. She trawled through the books until she found what she was looking for. As soon as she saw the photo she knew it was the house, even before reading the caption below it confirming it. The photo was taken from a boat out on the lake, and showed a series of steps and terraces that led up the hill to the house. She studied the majestic building and it was exactly as she had imagined it. It was almost as if the house was calling to her.

Not only had Clara made sure Pierce had been invited to the Bullingdon dinner before she accepted her own invitation, but she then did some manoeuvring behind the scenes to ensure she was seated next to him. Surely this would be the turning point, she thought. He would be a captive audience all evening. Completely out of character, she arrived at the Bullingdons' early. It was a large dinner party and she knew most of the people there and circulated amongst them, chatting amicably, one eye on the door for Pierce to arrive. By the time dinner was served and they were all seated, there was still no sign of Pierce. She unhappily viewed the empty chair beside her. It was only after the starters were finished and they were halfway through the main course than Pierce arrived. He came in discreetly and had a few words with the host and hostess before being escorted down to his seat.

'I'm sorry. I was travelling up from Surrey and was delayed,' he said to the guests around him as he sat down. He looked surprised but unimpressed to see he was seated beside Clara.

'I always find the trains so bothersome when travelling from Surrey. It is as if they are constantly programmed to run late,' said Clara, smiling broadly.

'I was driving myself, so can't use the railways as an excuse,' said Pierce coolly.

'Can you drive? How wonderful not to be relying on a chauffeur,' Clara said, continuing to smile at him.

'In Ireland, everyone drives,' Pierce said dismissively.

Clara nodded. 'I do like Surrey. Were you down there long?'

'No.'

'And what took you down to Surrey?'

'Private business,' said Pierce, and he began to eat his dinner and communicate with the other guests around him.

Clara did her best to engage Pierce in conversation throughout dinner, but all she received was monosyllabic responses. Although it was obvious from the hum of conversation around the dinner table that Pierce was not one of the world's great conversationalists, he seemed to be reserving his unfriendliness for Clara.

'And when do you return to Ireland, Lord Armstrong?' asked a major who was seated opposite them as the staff cleared away the dessert dishes and people began to move away from the table.

'I'm due to return soon,' said Pierce.

This news panicked Clara.

'I'm looking forward to it,' he added. 'The pace of life in London is far too fast for me.'

'And what an exciting time to be returning to

213

Ireland,' Clara interjected.

'Why?' He glanced at her.

'Well, Home Rule being imminent. It's so exciting to think Ireland will have its own parliament again and control of its own affairs.'

Pierce stared at her. Delighted she had his full attention, Clara continued bravely. 'It must be exciting for you to have the prospect of not being just a part of Britain but controlling your own affairs...'

Pierce leaned forward so not to be heard by the others. 'You have obviously not a clue what you're talking about, and I have no intention of wasting my time explaining it to you.'

Clara blinked a few times as Pierce stood up with the other diners and retired to the next room.

43

Clara's grandmother had called for tea with Clara and her mother.

'What is this I'm hearing back from my sources about you and Lord Armstrong, Clara?' questioned her grandmother.

'I know Lord Armstrong – what of it? I've met him at a few parties, what is wrong with that?'

'I heard you are arranging for him to be invited to places, just so you can show up and meet him.'

'Well, it wasn't long ago that you were criticising Clara for not liking any one particular man,' said Milly. 'So perhaps she's taking your advice.'

'They say you are relentlessly and shamelessly pursuing the man across London,' her grandmother said harshly. 'When I advised she should settle on one man, I didn't mean for her to pick the one man in London who obviously has no interest in her!'

Clara felt her eyes well with tears. She never got upset. She was always in a good mood. She usually didn't give a damn what her grandmother said or thought. And here she was reduced to tears over what she was saying about Pierce.

Seeing she was upset, her mother put down her tea and, rushing over to her, put her arms around her.

'Louisa, now you're upsetting Clara. Please stop!'

'She needs upsetting, if it prevents her from making a further fool of herself. The man is getting a perverse thrill out of you running after him, Clara, and everyone is looking on bemused at the great Clara Charter running around after an Irish farmer!'

'Well, you don't have to worry any more, Grandmother, because it's true Pierce has no interest in me, and so I won't bother him again.' Clara wiped away the tears that were streaming down her face.

'Poor darling!' Milly hugged her tightly.

'Hope may spring eternal,' said Louisa, 'but in this case at least sense has prevailed before you ended up ruining yourself.'

'Hardly ruining herself!' defended Milly.

'You'd be surprised how many other suitors would lose interest in Clara, if word got round

Lord Armstrong had rejected her. People are fickle. And you have played a silly hand, Clara. Not just for yourself, but the Charter family. One hundred and fifty years of making chocolates and toffees, even securing a royal warrant, for you to fall down at the final fence!'

'I – I liked him!' explained Clara through her tears.

'Which is where you made your first mistake,' said her grandmother. Then the expression on her face softened and she crossed the room and sat on the other side of Clara, putting a sympathetic arm around her.

'I have it on very good authority that the young Marquis Wellesley has huge regard for you, Clara.'

'Cosmo Wellesley? We're friends.'

'Well, I've heard he has asked to call on you, and you've never given him permission. Maybe it would be nice to let him call. Do you like him?'

'Cosmo is very charming and kind.'

'There you go! And you really couldn't do better. One of the finest houses in London and estates in England. The Marchioness Wellesley has a nice ring to it, don't you think?' Louisa was practically salivating. 'Why not let him call, Clara?'

Clara wiped away her tears and regained her composure 'All right ... I'll meet him.'

'Excellent!' smiled her grandmother.

Clara got up and left the room.

'Poor Clara! I had no idea she was going through such turmoil over this Armstrong man,' said Milly, distressed.

'You know, I think this might have been the best

thing to happen to her. It's just taught her that life is not always as you want it. There's something about Clara, a rebelliousness, and it's not a good thing.'

'Rebelliousness! Clara? Clara is the most traditional girl you could meet.'

'On the surface, perhaps. But there's something deep down that doesn't want to conform. Her continuous whirl through the season year after year without any thought of settling down demonstrates that. Her falling for Armstrong who doesn't love her back shows it. She thinks that she can live by her own rules, and that's dangerous. She attracts people to talk about her, and then doesn't care what they say. It's not wise to be a person to attract so much attention as she does. Let's hope now she's learned her lesson, makes a match with young Wellesley, and that's an end to it.'

Cosmo Wellesley was charming and kind, as Clara had always found him. He was also delighted to be allowed to call on Clara. She had always known he was very taken with her and he seemed hardly able to believe his luck when she agreed to accompany him to events regularly. He was indeed everything that she should be looking for, and yet her mind frequently drifted to Pierce Armstrong, much as she tried not to dwell on him. People were surprised to see Clara being seen continuously in the same man's company, and rumours abounded there would be an announcement shortly from her and Cosmo. Every so often she would be at the same event as Pierce and she steadfastly avoided him. Still burnt from his rude dismissal of her, and frightened of the emotions stirred by him, she knew it was best to avoid his company. Not that he would seek out her company anyway, she had realised.

She had arranged to meet Cosmo in Claridge's Hotel. Clara loved Claridge's and the new modern interiors, the style of which had originated in Paris.

She sat opposite Cosmo in the centre of the restaurant as he regaled her with stories from the army where he had a high ranking.

When she spotted Pierce walk into the restaurant, she ignored him and also the effect he had on her. He walked across the restaurant and joined Robert Keane who was waiting for him.

'I see your admirer is here,' smirked Robert to Pierce.

Pierce glanced around the restaurant and saw Clara. 'Bloody woman! Does she ever stay home? She seems to be everywhere,' he said dismissively.

'Well, I don't think you'll have to worry about her for too much longer. Seemingly she and Cosmo Wellesley have become quite serious and there might be an announcement soon.'

'Cosmo Wellesley?' Pierce's eyes darted up from the menu. He turned around again and looked at the man dining with her.

He stared at Cosmo, as the memories came flooding back.

Pierce had enjoyed boarding school. Not for him any of those tortured tales of bullying or desperate homesickness. He was always self-reliant, self-composed and when he was sent away to school in England it was as if his position was just waiting for him when he arrived there. The young Viscount was popular, came from a well-respected family, was successful academically and on the sporting field. Pierce took his position for granted.

But when Pierce's father died, he had taken a full year from school. There was so much to be sorted at the estate. His mother and sister needed him there to help with all the legal aspects. At the same time the last of the vast estate was being sold to the tenant farmers under the Wyndham Act, and his board of trustees wanted him there as the new Lord Armstrong and heir to understand and agree to everything that was being done.

By the time he arrived back in school, he was surprised to see a new classmate in his year. Cosmo Wellesley's family had been in India, due to his father's important political position there, and Cosmo had attended school there. Now the family had returned to England and Cosmo had started at Pierce's school. Pierce had never met anybody like Cosmo before. The boy had overflowing charisma, excelled academically, had panther-like prowess on the sports field and was unbelievably popular. By the time Piece arrived back from his sabbatical, Cosmo was the new star of the school, and Pierce had been forgotten. Watching from the sidelines, his resentment of Cosmo grew. Cosmo had stolen his position. Pierce tried to oust Cosmo. He attempted to regain his role, but he could not compete with Cosmo's glamour.

And then it was as if Cosmo knew Pierce resented him. He knew Pierce had been a force before he arrived and, now that he had taken Pierce's position away from him, he would not allow him back. Cosmo's father had been a military strategist on the northwestern frontier in India, and Cosmo had inherited all his cunning. Seeing Pierce was trying to undermine him, his attitude was: fight fire with fire. It started with passing the odd comment about Pierce, or cracking a joke at Pierce's expense. He quickly worked his classmates against Pierce, leaving him an outsider, and there was nothing he could do to fight back. After school, Pierce did not go on to university, but returned to Ireland to manage what was left of the estate and live the life of an Anglo-Irish lord. Cosmo had of course gone on to excel at university and onwards to a brilliant military career.

Now as he watched Cosmo and Clara talk intimately across the table, all the old feelings of resentment and jealousy came bubbling to the surface. Cosmo Wellesley could still drive him insanely jealous.

'An announcement soon?' asked Pierce. 'He is going to marry her?'

'He certainly wants to from what I hear, if she'll accept. By the look of them too, it looks like Clara Charter will accept and finally settle down.'

44

Clara was in the drawing room at home looking through albums of wedding dresses. The style was changing so much recently and she wasn't sure what she should go for, if she and Como set a date soon.

The butler entered. 'Pardon me, Miss Clara, you have a visitor. Lord Armstrong.'

Clara nearly dropped the book, then she stared in silence.

'Miss Clara?' asked the butler.

'Eh, yes, please show him in.' She quickly put the book away, checked her appearance in the mirror and turned to greet Pierce as the butler showed him in.

'I'm terribly sorry for just dropping in like this. It's just that Robert said you lived in this area, and while I was passing, I thought – well, I just thought, why not visit?'

'Em – why not indeed!' Clara smiled and put out her hands in a welcoming gesture. She turned to the butler. 'Eh, could you bring us some tea and refreshments, please?'

'Yes, Miss Clara.'

'Please – eh, take a seat, Lord Armstrong,' urged Clara.

They sat opposite each other and fell silent for a while.

'Nice weather we're having – for the time of

year,' said Clara at last.

She felt she was walking on eggshells as she conversed with Pierce, rigidly sticking to mundane topics. She did not want to ask too many questions as it might appear she was nosy, and she had seen how he did not like intrusion. She did not want to express any opinions as she had seen how he had dismissed her opinions as uninformed. At least they could remain on safe territory and discuss their mutual friend Robert Keane, and continue to agree on his merits.

'A marvellous fellow,' said Pierce.

'A champion chap,' agreed Clara.

'Good-natured,' declared Pierce.

'With a kind heart,' confirmed Clara.

'Stoic and steady,' Pierce pointed out.

'And yet entertaining company,' Clara added.

They lapsed into a silence.

'Tea?' smiled Clara as she raised the teapot.

And yet, as strained as the conversation was, she felt completely captivated. He seemed to be seeing her for the first time. It was the first time he had paid her attention, and she saw him study her.

'Your father works in the city?' said Pierce as his eyes took in the opulent drawing room.

'Yes.'

'And you have two brothers, Keane tells me?'

'Yes, an elder who is a doctor and a younger, who is my pet,' she smiled. 'Do you come from a large family?' She already knew the answer.

'Just one sister. Older than me.'

'She's married?'

'No, she still lives in the family house in Ireland.'

'Not for long, I imagine. I'm sure she is not short of suitors.' As Clara studied Pierce's fine features she imagined his sister must be very beautiful. She did wonder how she had managed to stay single for so long, without being pressurised into a union.

'I really wouldn't know,' said Pierce, suddenly dismissive, and she could have kicked herself, because he looked somehow irritated with her, and she wished she had remained on the neutral ground of discussing Robert Keane.

'I hear you like the theatre,' said Pierce.

'Oh yes, I love it,' she smiled.

'I have tickets to the Palladium. I was wondering if you would like to accompany me next Thursday?'

She blinked several times, unsure she had heard him right.

'Y-y-yes. I think I would like to.'

Clara hardly paid any attention to what was on the stage at the Palladium. She was far too distracted by being so close to Pierce.

She had given up on ever attracting his attention, and she wondered why he seemed to be showing an interest. She had half-hoped that once she had spent some time in his company, the strange spell he had over her would be broken, but it wasn't.

He dropped her back home in a cab and walked her to the door.

'I wonder if you are free next week?' he asked. 'We might meet for lunch at Fortnum and Mason.'

'Well, yes, I would like to ... but I thought you

were due to return home to Ireland?'

'I think I'll delay my return for a while.' He smiled at her and returned to the cab.

Over the next three weeks, Clara and Pierce met regularly. They would meet for lunch or dinner, or for a walk in Hyde Park. She never found him easy company. She never acted in the carefree way she did with others. He was very serious, she found. His looks gave the impression he would be a party boy. But he wasn't. He was the very opposite to her. He never tried to impress her like the others. Maybe it was the fact that he was so unlike the others that she found captivating.

'Are your family out?' Pierce asked Clara as he had tea with her in the dining room.

'Yes, they are visiting with my grandmother.'

Pierce stared at her intently and then suddenly lunged forward, grabbed her and kissed her.

'Pierce!' she said.

He pulled back and looked at her coolly. 'Yes?'

She leaned towards him and kissed him back.

Pierce left Clara's house and was walking down the street when he saw a car pull up outside her home. He watched as he saw Cosmo Wellesley get out of the car and bound up the steps, holding a big box of chocolates and flowers. He looked on in irritation as Cosmo disappeared into the house.

Clara and Pierce were in Covent Garden, walking along the balcony of the arcaded building. Classical street musicians were playing below them and they stopped and leaned on the railing to listen.

'Clara, you know the Keanes' party is on next Thursday?'

'Yes.' She looked at him.

'I wondered would you attend it with me?'

She thought hard for a minute and decided she needed to be honest. 'I can't, I'm afraid, Pierce. I'm attending the party with Cosmo Wellesley.'

'I see.'

'Do you know him?'

'Vaguely.'

'Pierce – I've very much enjoyed our time together. But I need to tell you that myself and Cosmo have an understanding.'

'An understanding?'

'We've discussed marriage.'

'I see.'

'It would be unfair to both you and Cosmo if I continue to see you.'

'And do you want to stop seeing me?'

She looked at him. 'No.'

'And what if I asked you to marry me. What would you say?'

'I would say – yes.'

There was a family summit with Clara's parents and her grandmother when she announced her engagement.

'But what of poor Cosmo?' demanded her grandmother.

'I'm very fond of Cosmo, but the feelings are not right.'

'And they are for Pierce Armstrong?' Her

grandmother was incredulous. 'But you could have anybody, Clara. Why settle for him?'

'But I'm not settling for Pierce. I am in love with him.'

'Oh dear. I have told you so often – in my experience the worst marriages are the ones where love is involved. Clara, all that's left of the Armstrongs is a huge crumbling house, a small farm, a cold man and an odd sister!'

'Pierce isn't cold. He's just reserved,' defended Clara. 'And we don't know his sister Prudence, so it's unkind to speak of her in that way.'

'But Clara, have you thought this through?' pleaded her mother. 'You'll be leaving London. Leaving your family and all your many friends to go and live in the countryside of Ireland. There will be no stores, no theatres, no restaurants, no Claridge's!'

'From what I hear the house is beautiful, the countryside breathtaking and the local town Castlewest will provide everything I need. And Dublin isn't that far away, and you've always said it's a fine city, the second city of the empire.'

'Second city of the empire for now, but for how long!' interjected her father. 'Darling Clara, the situation in Ireland is unstable to say the least. It looks like they will get their own parliament in Dublin. But this might cause a war with the northerners who don't want it. You haven't thought this through. Ireland is changing rapidly, and the Armstrongs' days of being a powerful family could be numbered. You would be in a vulnerable position.'

'Nonsense, if Dublin gets its parliament, it will

226

be a peaceful parliament and run by families just like the Armstrongs. Families like the Armstrongs have always run Ireland and they always will, that's what Pierce says.'

'He would say that, of course, being part of the gentry,' dismissed her father.

'There's no talking to her,' sighed her grandmother. 'She's made her mind up. I suppose at least she gets the title. Lady Armstrong,' she sighed.

45

The wedding was to be in the Dorchester, and Clara, her mother and grandmother set about its organisation with military precision.

'There are really only six hundred families in society in London, so concentrate on having as many representatives from those as possible,' advised her grandmother one afternoon in the drawing room with Clara and her mother.

Pierce was there as well, sitting in an armchair in the corner reading the newspaper.

'Whether we know them or not?' queried her mother.

'Well, if we don't, it will be an excellent opportunity to get to know them!' said Louisa.

Clara was sitting at a desk making lists of names.

'But that will be too many,' she said. 'There are all our relatives as well, not to mention Pierce's Irish set.'

'Your father has insisted that no expense is spared, Clara, so don't fret about numbers,' said her mother.

Pierce gently looked up, his interest piqued.

'And then there are all my friends,' said Clara.

Milly looked at Pierce. 'Though you have many relatives, Pierce, your immediate family is just your sister, am I correct?'

'That is correct, Mrs Charter.'

'And when will she be coming over?' asked Clara. 'The week before?'

'I imagine she'll arrive the morning of the wedding,' said Pierce.

'The morning!' Clara was shocked.

'Well, I imagine she can only spare a day or two away from the farm. Who's going to look after it in her absence?'

Her grandmother stared at Pierce. 'This sister assists in running your farm? Most extraordinary!'

'I can't wait to meet her,' smiled Clara, who returned to making her list of names. She suddenly looked up. 'I wonder – I wonder, Pierce...?'

'What is it Clara? Spit it out,' said Pierce irritably.

'I'd like to invite Cosmo, Pierce. Would that be intolerable for you?'

Pierce smirked at her. 'Not in the least. In fact, I insist on his being at our wedding.'

Finally the wedding day arrived, and with nothing left to chance by the Charter family it passed off smoothly. It was only when Clara was at the top of the church and heard Pierce say 'I do' that she felt her breathing return to normal. It was as if over the past months she was terrified he would break off the engagement, have second thoughts, maybe even not show up on the day. For although they were committed to each other, and her whole being was wrapped around him, she had the strangest feeling that she'd never really had him. She felt she never really had his attention. He seemed distracted. And that almost made her panic. So as she walked down the aisle on his arm, she felt incredible relief and was the happiest girl in the world.

Then, as she smiled broadly and kissed the swarms of guests congratulating her on the steps of the church, Pierce suddenly presented a woman to her.

'Clara, this is my sister Prudence.'

Clara felt a shock at seeing the woman in front of her. She had expected Pierce's sister to be a raving beauty, a female mirror of Pierce's looks. Prudence looked nothing like her brother. She looked much older than him, strong-looking and dressed in a slightly dowdy fashion.

'I'm so glad to meet you!' She embraced Prudence and kissed her on the cheek. 'Pierce has told me all about you!' This wasn't true, as Pierce had barely mentioned her. 'I just know we're going to be the best of friends.'

'Of course,' Prudence smiled back.

The day seemed to last an eternity, and there were so many people for Clara to talk to and greet at the Dorchester.

'Has anyone seen Pierce?' her father asked.

Clara had been so distracted by everyone she'd hardly noticed that Pierce was missing. He had disappeared after dinner and she hadn't seen him since.

'He's mingling and there are so many people here, it's hard to spot him,' said Clara as her eyes scanned the room, searching for him.

She sought out Cosmo and found him sitting in a corner. She sat down beside him.

'Poor Cosmo!' She pushed the hair back from his forehead. 'Can you ever forgive me?'

He managed a smile at her. 'I could never be angry with you, Clara. I just hope you've made the right decision.'

'I have.'

'Look after yourself, Clara, over there, with him... If you ever need somebody, I'll always be here for you.'

She smiled at him, reached forward and kissed his cheek.

46

The train hugged the coastline as it chuffed along the Riviera. Clara was sitting opposite Pierce in their compartment.

'I think the seating at the wedding was perfect,' said Clara. 'All that work paid off. Even my grandmother said it went off without a hitch.'

'*Hmmm.*' Pierce continued to gaze out at the blue sea through the window.

'I must write to the Dorchester immediately and compliment them on the service.'

'Indeed.

'And the flowers! They were so–'

'Clara!' interrupted Pierce, turning his eyes from the window to his wife. 'Are you going to prattle on about that wedding for the whole honeymoon? I can't enjoy the scenery from the constant commentary. If you insist on continuing, I'll have to go into the next compartment.'

Clara sat back and smiled, embarrassed. 'I'm sorry, Pierce. I'm going on about it a bit. I'm just very happy it went as well as it did.'

'I think we have well and truly established that fact. Now could we move on?' And he returned to gazing out the window.

'I'm sorry, of course... A full week in Monte Carlo to relax. I'm going to enjoy it.'

'You might as well – after all, your father is paying for it.'

Clara and Pierce were staying at the Hotel de Paris in Monte Carlo. They booked in and were shown to their suite.

Clara looked out the window towards the sea. 'Oh, I can't wait to explore!' she said. 'Will we go for a walk along the sea and up to the palace?'

Pierce was in the bathroom inspecting the hot water flowing from the taps.

'Pierce?'

'We were hoping to get new plumbing into the house as good as this,' said Pierce. He sighed and turned off the taps. 'Not much chance of that now.'

'Why?' asked Clara.

Pierce ignored her question as he came out of the bathroom, put on his jacket and headed to the door.

'Wait a minute, Pierce, I want to change my clothes before we set off!'

'Set off where?'

'Walking to the palace, as I was saying.'

'You can set off walking to the palace if you wish. I am going to the casino.'

'The casino? But why?'

'To gamble, of course, what else is there to do in Monaco? I'll see you for dinner this evening.' Pierce walked out of the room, closing the door after him.

Clara spent the rest of the day strolling along the seafront by herself.

That evening they ate at the restaurant in the Hotel de Paris.

'Did you enjoy the casino?' questioned Clara.

'Amazing building. Had a good game of roulette.'

'Did you win?'

'Of course.'

'What would you like to do tomorrow?' she asked, not wanting to push him in to doing something he might not enjoy.

'I haven't decided yet,' said Pierce.

After breakfast the following morning, they returned to their room.

'I'm just going out for a stroll. Shouldn't be too long,' said Pierce as he headed towards the door.

'Wait – I'll come with you.'

He yawned. 'No need, I'm going for a brisk walk and you'll only-slow me down. We'll do something when I get back.' He left the room.

Clara sat down on the couch in the room. She had hoped he would be a little more excited about the start of married life with her. A little more inclusive of her. But he was the opposite of her. He didn't get excited about things. He remained cool and in control. And she had been twittering on about the wedding non-stop from London. No wonder he was bored listening to it by now.

By nine o'clock that night she stood at the window of their room looking out at Monte Carlo twinkling under the night sky. Pierce had not returned and she was beginning to feel worried. When he hadn't returned by afternoon, she went out walking by herself. There was no sign of him on her return to their suite.

She left the room and took the lift down to the ground floor. She walked through the marbled foyer and into the bar to see if he was there, and then on to the restaurant. But there was still no sign of him.

She went to the reception.

'Good evening, Lady Armstrong, can I be of assistance?' asked the receptionist.

'Yes – has Lord Armstrong left a message for me here?'

'One moment, and I will check,' he said.

Clara waited anxiously.

'No message from Lord Armstrong,' he said on his return.

'I see, thank you.' She turned and walked

across the hall slowly to return to their room and wait for Pierce.

She sat at the open window waiting nervously until midnight came and went. Finally, at three in the morning, exhausted, she lay on the bed and drifted off to sleep immediately.

When she woke the next morning, she fully expected to find Pierce there, with some excuse that would make sense of his disappearance. But as she checked the suite, it was apparent he had not returned all night. Full of anxiety, she quickly bathed and dressed and hurried downstairs, praying she would find him in the foyer or restaurant.

But he was nowhere to be found in the hotel.

Monte Carlo was small and so it would surely to be easy to find him, she reasoned.

She walked across the square outside the Hotel de Paris and up the steps into the casino. She walked across the giant hallway and, after checking through the massive building for him, made enquiries at the reception.

'Lord Armstrong was here the day before last, but has not returned,' said the manager.

Clara spent the rest of the day visiting every restaurant, bar, hotel and the hospital searching for her husband but in vain.

As she returned to the hotel that evening, panic set in.

She could hardly sleep that night from worry. She didn't know what to do.

She couldn't ring home and ask her family for help. They would be horrified that the groom had gone missing on his honeymoon. She couldn't contact any of her friends as it would cause a scandal.

Pierce couldn't have had an accident because the place was so small she would have been notified immediately. Unless he had taken a boat and gone out sailing, and had a sailing accident, she suddenly thought, causing her to have a blind panic.

The following morning she dashed down to the harbour and checked with all the boat-hire companies. But no man of his description had rented a boat, and none of the boats was missing. As she wearily returned to the hotel, she felt completely vulnerable and alone.

She hurried to the suite, hope rising again in her breast. But Pierce had not returned. She braced herself and lifted the phone. Her whole life had been one of protection and comfort, she had never had a moment's discomfort, let alone the sheer terror she was now experiencing. She imagined the headlines in the British papers: *Earl Missing on Riviera Honeymoon*.

She dialled reception and her voice was shaking as she spoke. 'Could you fetch the police for me, please?'

Clara sat on the couch in her room as the police viewed her suspiciously.

'So what you are saying, Lady Armstrong, is that your husband went for walk in the morning three days ago, and you have not seen him since?'

'That's right.'

'And why did you not contact us before?'

'I – I didn't want to anger him if he showed up.'

'Anger him? So you had an argument?'

'No, of course not. We'd gone out to the dinner the previous night–'

'The first night of your honeymoon?'

'Yes.'

'And he went missing the next day?'

'Well, that's why I think he's had an accident, went climbing, perhaps fallen–'

'Did he say he was going climbing?'

'No.'

'Was he dressed to go climbing?'

'No – but – I'm just trying to think of every possibility.' Clara stood up and started to pace frantically.

At that moment the door opened and Pierce walked in, looking causal and nonchalant.

Pierce looked at the two policemen. 'Hello there – is there a problem?'

Clara stared at him in disbelief then sat down quickly, a sudden migraine overcoming her.

Clara was lying on the bed in the hotel room. She could hear Pierce's voice in the distance as he talked to the policemen.

'It's all just a silly misunderstanding. I decided to hire a car and go for a drive into Italy. I was distracted by the scenery and ended up going much further than I intended. I got completely lost in an isolated hilly area. Next thing the car breaks down and I'm stranded in this backwater village with no phone, no transport, no nothing. It took them all this time to find a mechanic and fix the damned car.'

'Perhaps it's not advisable to go off without telling your wife for the rest of your stay here,' said one of the policemen.

'Perhaps you're right,' agreed Pierce and gave a little laugh. 'So, sorry for wasting your time.'

He showed them to the door and then turned to look at Clara who was stretched out on the bed.

He came and sat down beside her.

She sat up and hugged him tightly, crying. 'I was so worried! I thought you were dead!'

'No, alive and well, I'm delighted to say. There was nothing I could do – stranded, you see.'

She pulled back and glared at him accusingly. 'But you should have told me you were driving into Italy.'

'Hindsight is a great thing. I thought you'd be all right.' He smiled at her. 'I didn't realise you were such a worrier. I'm used to dealing with women like my sister Prudence, you see. The world could come crashing down and it wouldn't knock a feather off good old Pru – she would still manage to have her gin and tonic at the normal time.'

She hugged him tightly. 'I'm just glad you're back.'

47

From the train window Clara studied the beautiful landscapes of her new country, getting more excited with every mile as they neared her new home.

'Are you excited about arriving home?' she asked.

'Not particularly,' answered Pierce.

It was a lovely May morning as the train pulled into the station in Castlewest.

'Here we are,' said Pierce, standing up and taking hold of their hand-luggage. They climbed down onto the platform.

Pierce stood scanning the crowd for his chauffeur. Many people were disembarking from the train and the platform was busy.

'Joe!' Pierce shouted across the crowd and a young man who seemed to have nodded off on a bench jumped up and ran across to them.

'Sleeping on the job?'

'Not at all, sir, just closing my eyes from the sun.' Joe grabbed the luggage.

'Hello, Joe,' Clara said, smiling warmly at him.

Joe looked at her as if she came from another planet before managing to stutter 'My Lady.'

'Come on, quick sharp to the car. Did the rest of our luggage arrive from London yet?' said Pierce.

'Yes, sir, it arrived last week,' answered Joe.

Outside, Joe loaded the luggage into the back of the car, before opening the door for them.

'Thank you,' smiled Clara, sitting in.

Joe started the engine and drove away from the station. As they drove through the town's main street Clara thought it a large prosperous town. The streets were busy with people going about their business. There was an abundance of shops – grocers, drapers, butchers, bakeries and all seemed to be filled with happy customers. The extravagances of Harrods and Selfridges might become special treats in future, but she was sure she could get everything she needed here. The car continued out of the town and through the country roads towards the house. Clara marvelled at the rolling countryside, the hills on one side of the road and glistening blue inlets of the lake on the other.

'It's everything I imagined. I can't wait to paint it,' she said.

'We used to own all the land here for miles around,' said Pierce, as the car drove through the local picturesque village. 'Even this village used to be ours. It was built by my great-grandfather, Edward, for the workers on the estate.'

She heard a note of loss in his voice.

They drove through a large stone gateway and up a winding driveway. As they reached a lake and began to circle it, she saw the house on its hill on the far side.

At last they arrived.

Clara stared up at the house, its majesty taking her breath away.

Joe jumped out and, taking the cases, carried them up the steps and through the front door.

Clara stepped out of the car and gazed around her, then walked eagerly over to the balustrades at the edge of the forecourt. The view was magnificent. The lake seemed to stretch for miles to the hills on the other side and below her was the series of lovely terraces she had seen in the photo she had found in the book in London, with extensive gardens spreading to the left and right. In the gardens to the right, on the same level as the first terrace, she could glimpse tennis courts behind some trees.

'Clara!'

She hurried back to Pierce.

'So – you're back!' said a loud voice.

Clara was startled to see Prudence standing in the open doorway looking down at them.

'Just about,' said Pierce as he walked up the steps to the front door.

Clara walked towards the steps and smiled up at her. 'Hello there.'

'You're late, aren't you? I was expecting you a couple of hours ago,' stated Prudence.

'We were delayed in Longford. The train broke down, don't you know,' explained Pierce.

Prudence raised her eyes in a resigned way and repeated, 'Don't you know!'

Clara walked up the steps and, smiling, walked past Prudence and into the house. She stood still while she took in the huge hallway, savouring the atmosphere. She looked at the gallery of portraits that hung on the walls.

'Well, come into the drawing room and I'll order

240

tea. I suppose you're starving,' said Prudence.

Clara and Pierce followed her into the drawing room to the right of the hall. It was a bright large room luxuriantly furnished with antiques. Prudence summoned the butler by the bell pull.

Clara took off her hat and coat and sat down. A minute later a butler arrived in, a man in his fifties.

'Fennell, bring tea and a round of sandwiches,' instructed Prudence. 'Make them up out of the pheasant left over from last night's dinner.'

'Very good,' said Fennell and he withdrew.

Clara thought it strange she wasn't introduced to Fennell, and on the whole she was very much being made to feel like a visitor in her husband's house.

'Fennell is getting worse,' Prudence said to Pierce. 'I don't know if it's age or insolence, but he almost seems resentful when you tell him what to do these days. I'd change him in an instant, but trained butlers are hard to come by.'

'Especially with what we're offering in wages,' added Pierce.

'Oh, he'll have to do, I suppose. Compared to the younger servants he's positively enthusiastic in his duties,' said Prudence.

A parlour maid came in with a tray of sandwiches while Fennell brought in the tea and left it on the table in front of them. The parlour maid poured the tea into three delicate china cups. As she was pouring Clara caught the girl staring at her.

Prudence sat back with her cup of tea and viewed Clara. 'Well, I don't know what you're going to do around here all day without being bored out of your mind.'

'Oh, I don't need much to entertain me.'

'That's not what I've heard,' said Prudence.

Clara wondered what she had heard.

'I'm very much looking forward to my new life here,' said Clara.

'Are you much of a horsewoman?' asked Prudence.

'I'm afraid not.'

'You do hunt though?'

'No. I've never been on one.'

'You've never been on a hunt!' Prudence was incredulous.

'I'm afraid not.'

'Well, that's a big part of the social life here excluded for you in that case.'

'I don't like blood sports.'

'Don't like blood sports!'

'I always think it's cruel chasing the poor fox like that.'

'The fox, the scourge of the countryside! I would keep my opinions to myself if I were you and not share them with our friends and neighbours – it might make you unpopular. It's all fishing, shooting, hunting around here, you know.'

Clara looked down and took a sip of her tea.

'And how do you expect to fill your days here then?'

'By being a wife to Pierce, running the house here, entertaining–'

'I see!'

'And I paint. I love painting. I look forward to painting the countryside around here.'

Prudence looked at Clara as if she were mad, before saying 'Painting? Indeed!'

Clara was delighted to see all her trunks sent from London waiting for her when Pierce showed her into their bedroom. She walked around the huge bedroom and went and stood by the front window and gazed out across to the lake.

She turned and looked at the four-poster bed. Pierce lit up a cigarette and sat on the bed. She went over to him and, smiling, put her arms around him.

'This is what I dreamed about – being here in your house with you,' she confided to him.

'Did you?' He looked at her, puzzled. 'When you had London at your feet?'

'I didn't care about that. All I cared about was being with you. In your company. And when I thought you weren't interested in me, I was heartbroken.'

'Heartbroken!' Pierce gave a snide laugh. 'Why does everything have to be exaggerated these days? One can't be merely sad or unhappy, one has to be ... heartbroken!'

Her face dropped and she felt like a fool and pulled back from him. She turned away from him quickly and went to a trunk and opened it.

'It'll take me ages to sort out all my things,' she said, making sure he couldn't see how he had upset her.

He got up and sauntered to the door. 'Well, it'll give you something to do in that case.'

She spent the next few days exploring the house

and grounds. She was fascinated by the portraits hanging in the hall and on the staircase, and asked Pierce to explain to her who everyone was.

'That's my Great-grandfather Edward and his wife Anna. He built this house for her before they married.'

'Really? How very romantic,' said Clara.

'He showed the tenants incredible benevolence during the Famine. As did my Great-grandmother, Anna, who worked tirelessly for the locals all her life. And how do they repay all that generosity? They shot my father Charles – Edward and Anna's grandson.'

She could sense the real bitterness in his voice. She wanted to ask him about the shooting, to find out more, but he was so closed up she didn't want to upset him by arousing such a frightening memory.

'They look kind, they have kind faces,' said Clara as she studied them. 'But she looks sad as well. There's a sadness in her face ... her eyes.'

'For goodness sake, it's only an artist's impression of her ... she was probably sad from having to pose for the damned painting for so long!'

Clara smiled at him and they moved on to the next portrait of a fair-haired man with hazel eyes.

'That's their son Lawrence, my grandfather.'

'A very handsome man.'

'I suppose.'

'You look like him, despite your dark eyes.'

'Do I?' He seemed unconcerned. 'He was Anna and Edward's only child. He was a great businessman. Exceptionally intelligent. Ran the estate like clockwork and built up the family fortune.'

They moved on and looked at a painting of a ballroom with many elegantly dressed couples swirling around dancing. She looked at the caption which read *'The ballroom at Armstrong House 1888'*.

'Oh, this is the ballroom here!'

'Yes, at one of the great functions held in this house back then.'

They moved on to a portrait of six young adults, all looking happy and cosseted.

'And these are Lawrence's children. He always hated being an only child so wanted a large family. These are my aunts and uncles and this–' he pointed to a defiant-looking boy in the centre of them, '–is my father Charles. They were a very popular and in-demand group of young people, and they all went on to marry exceptionally well.'

Clara thought of her friend Gwen, Pierce's cousin, whose mother was one of these children and had gone on to marry a duke.

'They all moved away when they married – to Dublin, London, one to Newport in America. Just my father was left.'

They moved on to the next portrait of a young man with unforgiving dark eyes and a challenging look. 'My father Charles again. He inherited the title and estate and tried his best to keep things as they were and they shot him for it.'

'Did they – did they ever catch whoever shot him?'

'No. One of the disgruntled tenants who resented our wealth and power.' Pierce turned quickly away from the portrait. 'Now, you've had our family history.'

'And where is your portrait, Pierce? Why is your portrait not adorning the walls here?' She smiled at him.

'A portrait?' He looked at her as if she were mad. 'In the long list of things we need to spend money on, a portrait is at the very bottom of the list.'

'I suppose our own children's portraits will hang here one day. How many children would you like, Pierce?'

'I hadn't given it much thought – the obligatory heir, one presumes.'

'Oh, I'd like a lot more than that!'

He looked at her warily. 'I don't think Prudence's nerves could stand a house full of children. I'm not sure mine could either for that matter.'

'You'll feel differently when they arrive.'

'Besides, we're over-budget on staff as it is – we couldn't afford a nursemaid and what not at the moment.'

Clara continued browsing through the house, getting acquainted with it.

She was in the library and when the doorbell kept incessantly ringing and it was obvious Fennell or one of the other servants wasn't going to answer it she went out through the hall and opened the front door. There stood a young lad with a box of groceries.

'Delivery, ma'am, from Casey's Grocer's.'

'Oh, there doesn't seem to be anybody about. Maybe just leave them on the sideboard there.' Clara stepped out of the way to let him in.

'You there!' came a shrill voice from Prudence as she walked down the stairs, giving both Clara and the boy a fright. 'What do you think you're doing?'

'Delivering from Casey's,' explained the boy.

'I've never seen anything like it! Coming up to the front door indeed! Now you can just turn around and take yourself to the back door where you and your sort always go.'

The boy, embarrassed, turned around.

'Did Casey not tell you where to go?' demanded Prudence.

'No, ma'am.'

'Idiot of a man!' Prudence slammed the door shut and looked accusingly at Clara. 'And you letting him in as if he were the Prince of Wales!'

'I didn't know,' explained Clara, thinking it was all a fuss over nothing.

'You know, that Casey is really getting above himself. I'm going to give him a piece of my mind.' Prudence went over to the side table, lifted the phone and asked for a connection from the operator.

'Casey? It's Lady Prudence here,' she said when she was finally put through. 'Now listen here, you sent some twit of a boy out here with our groceries and he had the audacity to come up to the front door. In future make sure all deliveries go to the back door. Thank you... Our bill?... What about our bill?... Only six months overdue?... Mr Casey, my family have been shopping at your store for over a century and you have the appalling im- pudence to bring up something as vulgar as com- merce with me?... And so you should be... There's many other shops who would only be too delighted with our patronage, and so I think you should remember who you are speaking to in future.'

Prudence slammed down the phone.

'Can you believe it! He starts talking about his bill! That's the trouble, you see, nobody knows their place any more. It's become a nation of grubby shopkeepers, to paraphrase Napoleon. If it's like this now, can you imagine what it will be like if they get their own parliament in Dublin?'

Prudence turned and walked past Clara, leaving her staring after her.

48

The butler poured coffee into Clara's cup and left the room. It was breakfast time and she and Pierce were finishing their meal in the dining room.

'Pierce, does Prudence have any suitors?' asked Clara.

'Suitors? I really wouldn't know. You'll have to ask her yourself.'

'It's just – I wonder what her plans are for the future?'

'Plans? Future?'

'Well, her living arrangements?'

'The same as they are now, I suspect.'

'What? To live here ... forever?' Clara was amazed.

'Why not? You lived in your family home, as she

lives in hers.'

'I know but I always intended, or hoped, to get married and be mistress of my own house one day. Surely Prudence hopes for the same?'

'Well, she's never expressed any unhappiness living here. She's invaluable around the farm – in fact, she practically runs the place.'

'But ... it's just when I married you, I didn't expect to be living with your sister for ever more.'

'So what do you suggest I do?' Pierce became irritated and impatient.

'Well, I don't know.'

'Put her out on the street? That would be nice for her, wouldn't it?'

'Well, of course not! You're being silly.'

'Well then, what are you talking about?'

'I don't know, I'm just saying–'

'Well, there's no point in you talking about something if you don't know what you're even talking about, is there?'

'Pierce!'

'I'm afraid you're just going to have to get used to it, living with Prudence.' Pierce finished his coffee and stood up to leave. 'Let's face it, she's far more useful around here than you'll ever be.'

Clara came down the stairs and as she walked through the hall she could hear voices from the library. The door was ajar and she recognised the voices as Pierce and Prudence talking.

'So,' said Prudence. 'Let's talk pounds, shillings and pence. What's she worth and what's she brought with her?'

'Nothing,' said Pierce.

'I'm sorry?'

'She hasn't any money.'

'I'm in no mood for jokes, Pierce. She's one of the Charters' Chocolate family, she must be worth a fortune.'

'She's one of them, but she's not an heiress.'

'But that wedding cost a packet!'

'Her parents are wealthy, but I imagine most of their money will go to their eldest son, as things do. Clara will probably get something eventually, but not the bulk of it. I think she gets a small allowance from her family.'

'You're not teasing me, are you?' Prudence sounded horrified.

'No.'

'Well, why the hell did you marry her then?' Prudence's voice rose to a shout.

'I had my reasons.'

'Pierce! We packed you off to London in order to meet an heiress!'

'And I met many – but married none. Things don't go according to plans always, Prudence. I didn't find any millionairess to marry. They aren't like apples on trees, waiting to be picked, you know.'

'I don't believe that for a second. With your looks, a title, our family connections, they would be queuing up to snare you. I've seen the way women look at you.'

'Well, there's no point in going over it now. What's done is done. And I married Clara.'

'But for what purpose? She's about as useful around here as a broken teapot! With her airs and graces! That girl was brought up to marry someone who could look after her financially and in every other way. Don't you see, you and her getting married means neither of you can supply the other with what you both need. You both needed the same type.'

'Somebody with money?' he asked cynically.

'Somebody with money and somebody bloody capable in life!'

'I'm not a prostitute, Prudence.'

'I don't know what we're going to do now. A correct marriage would have secured our future. Now we're going to have to keep struggling on. And who knows what's coming if they get their Dublin parliament here? I can't imagine their new government being kind to the likes of us with taxes and whatnot.' Sighing again, Prudence started to march out of the room. 'I'll have to get rid of one of the parlour maids. And the chauffeur is a luxury we can no longer afford. And we can kiss goodbye to the new plumbing system as well!'

Hearing Prudence come her way, Clara raced behind the staircase and hid there, watching as Prudence marched through the hall and out the front door.

Clara escaped from the house and down the steps in front of the house to the gardens. She fled down the next flight of steps that brought her to the next level and kept going until she arrived at the shore of the lake. She began to walk with a quick ferocity down the rocky shoreline, nearly falling a couple of times as she replayed the conversation she had overheard between her husband and sister-in-law. She finally stopped walking and sat down on a large boulder staring out across the lake, catching her breath.

Things now made sense to her. He was in London to make a financial match – maybe that was why he feigned disinterest at the beginning. She thought of the words Pierce had used when Prudence asked why he had married Clara knowing she had no money of her own: '*I had my reasons.*' What other reasons could he possibly have other than he was in love with her?

She felt suddenly overjoyed at thinking he had married her even though she couldn't provide for him financially. It was the confirmation that she had hoped for and was beginning to be frightened she would never receive. Remembering their tour of the portraits and his brief history of his family, she remembered the bitterness when he described his father's shooting. Something had obviously shut down in Pierce because of that, something that stopped him from being able to express his emotions and made him appear cold. But now she knew he loved her, and that was all she needed.

That night Clara came into their bedroom. The fire was still blazing in the fireplace, casting the room in a warm orange glow. In the bed Pierce lay on his back, fast asleep. She walked over and sat down on the side of the bed, gazing down at him, his features lit by the firelight. She placed a hand on his shoulder and his eyes flickered open. He turned around and looked at her.

'What is it?' he asked.

She smiled lovingly down at him. 'It's all right, you don't have to say a word. I understand now.

You've experienced so much pain in life that you can't open up and show the real love that is in your heart.' She nodded earnestly at him as she spoke. 'But now I know that love is there, I don't need you to say anything any more.'

He glared at her in confusion. 'I don't know what you're talking about. Are you suffering from some mental illness?'

She continued to smile at him. 'It's all right, I understand. You need to hide your feelings, that's just you.'

He shook his head in a bewildered boredom.

She bent forward and kissed him lovingly.

'It's very late, Clara, go to sleep,' said Pierce as he closed his eyes.

49

The garden party was meant as an introduction for Clara to meet the Armstrongs' neighbours and friends, many of whom had not made it to London for the wedding.

Clara sat at her dressing table, adjusting her hair. Outside she could hear much talking and jollity and she knew the party had already started. She hoped she could fit in with them. Their world seemed so different from the one she came from. She hoped they wouldn't all be like Prudence who seemed to be a different species from her. She sighed and stood up, taking a final look in the mirror before turning and leaving the room.

The gardens to the right of the house had been set up with a series of round tables with white linen tablecloths on them that reached to the ground. In the tennis courts beyond couples were playing, while most of the visitors sat around the tables drinking tea and having sandwiches and being waited on by Fennell and the other servants.

Prudence and Pierce sat at a central table with their neighbours the Foxes and some other friends.

'So how is the new Lady Armstrong settling in?' asked Emily Foxe, a kind-looking woman in her forties, who lived in the nearest Big House.

'Judging from the ridiculous smile she seems to constantly have, quite well,' said Prudence, sitting back in the early summer sunshine with her cup of tea.

'You must be doing something right, Pierce, that she's so happy,' Emily said.

Pierce lit up a cigarette.

'I can't wait to meet her,' said Emily's husband, George. 'I hear she's quite a looker.'

'That she is, I suppose,' said Prudence. 'She has a refined beauty. Of course wouldn't we all if we had never done a day's work all our lives or even ever been on a horse?'

'Never been on a horse!' Emily was aghast.

'Or been on a shoot,' continued Prudence.

'What does she do in that case?' asked George.

'She paints. She finds the countryside so – *inspiring!*' Prudence laughed out loud. '*Shhh,* here she is.'

The party looked up towards the house and

Clara was standing there at the top of the steps, a vision in a cream cotton dress that came down to her ankles, tied at the waist with a silk band, her pale blonde hair gleaming in the sun.

'Here you are!' said Prudence as Clara descended the steps and walked across the lawn to them. 'Everybody – Clara, Lady Armstrong.'

There was a chorus of good-natured hellos from the crowd.

'We were just hearing all about you,' said Emily Foxe.

'All good, I hope?' said Clara, smiling at Prudence.

'Of course!' said Prudence. 'Fennell, bring over an extra chair.'

Fennell did so and Clara joined the party.

Clara spent the day circulating among the guests. One thing she was well trained in and had an abundance of experience in was socialising, and she smiled and charmed her way through the afternoon. The people were friendly and polite to her, making her feel welcome, but she feared she had very little in common with them. She felt a simmering resentment from the numerous young women there, and by the way they vied for Pierce's attention she felt they were put out that she had married him.

'Will you be coming to the regatta next weekend, Clara?' asked Mrs Foxe.

'I'm not sure...' Clara looked to Pierce for guidance but none was forthcoming. 'I'm sure I'd like to if–'

She broke off speaking as she heard a car come

roaring up in front of the house, blowing the horn loudly all the way.

'Johnny Seymour is obviously back from Dublin,' said Prudence with a disapproving sigh.

Curious to see these latecomers, Clara hurried on to the terrace and climbed the steps to where the motor car had parked. A glamorous blonde in a silk cocktail dress was getting out of the car on the driver's side while a good-looking man in a white tennis outfit, long white flannel trousers and a short-sleeved white shirt, got out of the passenger seat. Clara could see that they were very drunk.

Clara retreated down the steps and went to fetch Fennell to deal with the situation.

The couple stumbled down the steps and across the terrace into the gardens where the man had managed to take only a few steps towards the party when he fell to the ground, and lay out flat on the grass, causing everyone to gasp.

'Johnny!' screeched the blonde as Fennell came rushing to his assistance and tried to get him back up on his feet.

'He's drunk!' stated Prudence. 'He's really too much, he has no manners whatsoever. Thinks he can get away with anything.'

As Johnny got back on his feet he roared with laughter. The girl with him started laughing too and they fell into each other's arms and kissed.

'And I wonder who this new tart is?' said Prudence.

'Well, she won't be around for long, I imagine. They never are,' said another.

'Who is he exactly?' asked Clara, her eyes wide

at the spectacle of it all.

'Johnny Seymour, he's an artist – a neighbour of ours,' Pierce said.

Clara was realising when they mentioned 'neighbours', they were usually referring to the next Big House which could be miles away.

'The Seymours have been around here as long as the Armstrongs,' Prudence said. 'They live in Seymour Hall. They were a very respectable family and very wealthy in their day. I don't know where they got Johnny from – but he inherited the house or whatever else there was left to inherit, but none of their manners.'

'He spends most of his time in Dublin,' said Mrs Foxe.

'Luckily for the rest of us,' said Prudence. 'Because when he's down here he fills Seymour Hall up with Fenians and bohemians. The antics I've heard go on there would make you blush.'

'Hello, everybody!' said Johnny loudly as he approached their table, his arm around the blonde.

There was a collective 'Good afternoon, Johnny!' from everyone as they all smiled fake smiles at him.

'When did you get back from Dublin, Johnny?' asked Prudence.

'Last weekend,' said Johnny, grinning down at his blonde companion.

'We drove all the way down,' the blonde said proudly.

'Got stopped by the police in Longford for – what was the charge again, Dorothy?' Johnny asked.

'Driving without due care and injuring livestock – geese!' said Dorothy with the naughty expression of a schoolgirl.

'Tea, Johnny?' asked Prudence, raising the tea-pot.

'No, thanks.' He turned to Fennell. 'I'd prefer a bottle of that fine gin Patience keeps stashed in your pantry, Fennell.'

'It's Prudence!' corrected Prudence, annoyed.

'Yes, very prudent of you to keep it there. Come on, Dors – game of tennis, I think.'

Johnny and Dorothy headed over to the tennis courts. 'Fennell, bring the gin over to us at the court!' Johnny called over his shoulder as they went.

'He never changes,' said Mrs Foxe, looking on as Johnny and Dorothy tried to play tennis, but were too busy laughing and falling down to take the game seriously.

'She's ruining the court with those heels!' Prudence pointed out as Dorothy ran around after the ball.

Clara found it hard to keep her eyes off Johnny and Dorothy's high jinks for the rest of the afternoon, but managed to concentrate when Home Rule was being discussed around the table.

'It would already be through and the Dublin parliament would be set up if it weren't for the Ulster people refusing to allow it,' said George Foxe.

'Well, I for one hope they keep protesting and it never comes to pass,' said Prudence. 'I mean, the people are bad enough as they are – could you imagine what they'll be like if they get their own parliament? You know, I remember as a girl being

258

in town with Papa, and when we walked down the street people would automatically nod to us when we walked past. None of it now. They've lost all respect.'

'But if Dublin gets its own parliament it would empower the country,' said Clara, 'and it would be like when it had Home Rule before. It would be very good for people like you.'

Everyone looked at Clara in surprise.

'That was when the peasantry knew their place and allowed their betters to run the country. Now, they're taking over!' said Prudence. 'They own all the shops and businesses in town. We've even had to engage a Catholic solicitor now since old Mr Brompton passed away.'

'Who have you employed?' enquired Emily Foxe.

'Conway. Very good, but one generation from tilling the fields, I imagine.'

Johnny Seymour suddenly appeared at the table.

'You can't stop what's going to happen so you might as well accept the inevitable,' he said.

'Are you in favour of Home Rule, Johnny?' asked Mrs Foxe.

'I'm in favour of what is unstoppable, and that's Home Rule.'

Dorothy suddenly appeared. 'Darling, isn't it time we went home?'

'I suppose it is. We've an early rise in the morning. A court appearance for reckless driving involving geese!' He laughed. 'Come along, Dors!' He put his arm around her and they set off for their car.

'He knows that many subversives, I wouldn't be

surprised what his politics are,' said Prudence.

The evening was one of banter and chat. Clara enjoyed it, but felt the whole occasion, apart from Johnny Seymour's input, was subdued and it was so different from the glittering social occasions she was used to in London.

In her room that night after the party was over, she wondered where Pierce was and went over to the window and looked out. She saw him walking up from the gardens with one of the young women who had been a guest. She watched as they walked across the forecourt to a car. Pierce stood there smoking with one hand in his trouser pocket, as the girl chatted away happily, giggling all the time. The girl's hand regularly touched his chest. Finally the girl got into the car, blew him a kiss and drove off.

Clara was brushing her hair when Pierce came in to the room. 'Where were you?' she asked breezily.

'Just out for a walk.'

'On your own?'

'No, with one of the girls from the party,' he answered. 'Clara, in future it's not advisable for you to give your opinions on politics.'

'I wasn't giving my opinions. I was asking some questions.'

'Well, in future I think you'd better refrain from mentioning politics at all. It's really not your place.'

'But if there's to be a war between the northerners and the southerners over Home Rule, I think that will very much be my business!' Clara said forcefully.

'No, it won't. It will have nothing to do with you.'

'Pierce, I spent the day hostessing your garden party without fault. I charmed your neighbours and friends and you pick fault because I expressed concerns over a political question?'

'I'm going out again.' He turned to go.

'At this time of night?' Clara called out after him.

'I need some air.' Pierce left the room.

Clara was left staring at her image in the dressing-table mirror.

50

Joe drove out of the main entrance to the house, Clara and Pierce sitting in the back. Pierce had business in town and Clara had some shopping to do.

Clara could see a small Georgian house down the fields that seemed to be their nearest neighbour.

'Who lives there?' asked Clara.

'That's Hunter's Farm. It still belongs to us, part of the estate that wasn't lost.'

'Really?' Clara was excited by this news of this pretty property still belonging to them. 'Hunter's Farm... I wonder why it's called that?'

'Obviously because it was used by huntsmen during hunts in the past.'

Clara sat back, thinking. 'And what do we do with the house?'

'It's rented out to anglers in the summer months.'

'Pierce – perhaps Prudence would like to move there?' Clara asked excitedly. 'I mean, it's so close she could still run the farm, and yet have her own home – and give us some privacy.'

He looked at her dismissively. 'Don't be ridiculous. Firstly, we can't afford to lose the income from the anglers who rent it. Secondly, we can hardly afford to run our house on the estate, let alone a second one. Thirdly, Prudence would never agree to move out of the house to be relocated to Hunter's Farm.'

Clara sat back and nodded. It was worth a try, but she had to admit there was no getting rid of Prudence.

Clara found Joe polishing the car in front of the house.

'Good afternoon, Lady Armstrong,' he greeted her.

'Afternoon!' She opened the front door of the car and sat in front of the wheel.

The key was in the ignition and she turned it on.

'Lady Armstrong! What are you doing?' asked Joe, concerned.

'I'm going to learn to drive, and you're going to teach me. Sit in!'

'But – but has Lord Pierce giving permission.'

'I don't need permission.'

'No, but I do!'

'Well, I've just given it to you.' She smiled at him. 'I believe everyone can drive in Ireland and I'm going to learn.'

'But – but–'

'If you don't teach me, I'll learn myself!' warned Clara as she put her feet on the pedals and the car jerked forward.

'Wait! All right!' conceded Joe as he jumped in beside her.

After a few preliminary instructions, Clara announced she was ready and the car took off down the driveway.

'See – I'm a natural!' said Clara as the car veered between the driveway and the grass verge.

'Have you ever driven before?' asked Joe.

'Of course not!' laughed Clara as they drove through the entrance and down the country road.

'Giddy-up! I said – giddy-up!' demanded Clara as she tapped her riding boots against the horse's flanks. The horse remained stubbornly still in front of the stables at the back of the house. The head groom and two stable boys stood staring in puzzlement.

'Oh come on!' Clara demanded of the horse.

The groom, leaning forward, suggested, 'If you don't mind me saying – maybe if the lady spoke with more authority, the horse might heed her.'

'Show him who's boss,' added the stable boy.

Clara glanced down at the men and nodded.

Clara deepened her voice and spoke loudly: 'Right, you – do as I say and – *move!*' She dug her heels into the horse's flanks.

The horse neighed loudly and took off, causing

Clara to scream and pull on the reins. This action resulted in the horse stopping suddenly and Clara was flung through the air screaming until she landed in a pile of hay.

The men came running over to her.

'Lady Armstrong – are you all right?' demanded the groom, horrified.

Clara turned over and sat up, bewildered, hay all over her.

'Quite all right, thank you.' She pulled the hay out of her hair. As she looked at the three men and their shocked expressions she suddenly started giggling.

'She might have hit her head,' one of the stable boys pointed-out.

'Will we fetch the doctor?' asked the groom.

'No need for that,' said Clara as she scrambled to her feet.

She looked at the horse as it trotted unconcerned around the courtyard.

'I don't think he likes me much... Have you any Shetland ponies I could start on?'

They all laughed.

Clara had spent the afternoon shopping in Castlewest and walked down the busy pavement towards the car where Joe was waiting for her. He jumped out of the car and taking her shopping put it in the boot.

'You know, I think I've been ripped off in Harrods all these years. I've found some perfectly beautiful dresses here at a fraction of the price they charge in London.'

'Yes, ma'am,' nodded Joe with that bewildered

look he always seemed to have when he was out with Clara. He opened the door for her. 'Back home, ma'am?'

Clara took off her gloves and looked around the busy street.

'No – I think I fancy a drink first. What's that bar like over there, Joe? Cassidy's?'

Joe's eyes grew wide in horror. 'Not for your type, Lady Armstrong.'

'Oh good!' Clara winked at him and smiled mischievously. 'Come along, and I'll buy you a lemonade.'

Clara set off to the pub with Joe in quick pursuit.

She marched through the door and looked around the traditional pub. There were a few men sitting around drinking stout who all turned around and stared at Clara in surprise. Clara walked up to the bar and sat up on one of the bar stools. The publican was a man in his fifties. He was drying glasses behind the bar, behind him was a big mirror with the engraved caption 'Guinness is Good for You'.

'I wonder if it is?' asked Clara.

'I'm sorry?' asked the publican.

Clara nodded at the mirror. 'Good for you?'

'Well, it's never done me any harm,' answered the publican.

'A fine endorsement. I'll have a glass, and a lemonade for my driver.' She smiled around the pub.

An hour later Clara was drinking brandy while the publican leaned across the bar talking to her. The other men had gathered around her.

'Ah, it was tragic at the time when your husband's father was shot, the late Lord Charles. They lay in wait for him as his carriage came out of the main gates in the estate and out comes the gun and shoots him – *bang* – right in the chest.'

All the men shook their heads in sorrow.

'But, to be fair,' the publican continued, 'there's some that said he was asking for it.'

All the men nodded in agreement.

'You can't put widows and children out on the street like he was doing and not expect somebody some day is going to lose his head and try to kill you. Not that I'm condoning it or anything.'

'Of course not,' nodded Clara. 'Go on.'

'Ah sure, he survived, but he didn't leave the bed for months, and he was only a half a man after that. The kids were young at the time.'

'Shocking behaviour,' said one of the men who stood around her.

Clara looked at her empty glass. 'Another brandy, please. And a drink for everyone as well.'

There was a chorus of thank-yous.

The publican came to the door to see her off when she left.

'Lovely to meet you, Lady Armstrong,' he said.

'And you!'

'Visit us any time! You'll always be welcome!' called one of the customers.

51

Clara walked around to the back of the stairs and through the door that led down to the servants' quarters which were in a semi-basement that stretched along the back of the house.

In the kitchen she found the cook, Mrs Fennell, and her kitchen maid Katie busy at work rolling pastry and cutting apples to make apple-pie.

'Hello there!' said Clara as she walked in.

The two women looked up and got a shock to see her there.

'Lady Armstrong! Is everything all right? We didn't hear the bell ring,' said Mrs Fennell.

'Oh, I didn't ring it,' said Clara.

'Well, can we get you something?'

'No, thank you. I just wanted to draw.'

'Draw what? Water?'

'No, I mean sketch. Sketch you and the kitchen, if that's all right?' She indicated her drawing paper and pencils.

'Draw us and the kitchen?' Mrs Fennell was confused.

'Yes, I want to do a sketch of every room in the house, and I thought I'd start here. I want to send them to my family, you see, in London, so they can get a full picture of the place.'

Mrs Fennell looked at Katie, concerned. 'Well, as you wish, my lady. But it's most peculiar. Lady Prudence comes down here occasionally, but I don't think I remember Lord Pierce being in the kitchens or servants' quarters ever – and I've been coming here since I was girl, as my mother was a kitchen maid here before me.'

'How very fascinating. You must have grown up in the little village that was for the estate workers then?'

'That's right. Though we live here at the Big House now.'

The cook began to roll her pastry again as Clara sat up on a high stool and started sketching.

Clara managed to get Mrs Fennell to relax and open up after a while.

'Oh, there were such parties here in the house back in the 1880s, Lady Armstrong! I remember sneaking up the servants' stairs and creeping over to the ballroom and hiding so I could look at them dance all night! And the food that would be served here!' Mrs Fennell paused and her eyes got a faraway look as she remembered. 'That was when money was no object around here – unlike now!' She gave Katie a knowing look and Katie nodded her head in resigned agreement. She started cutting her pastry again.

'And who would be coming here to the parties? Who were the guests?' probed Clara.

'Well, all the gentry of course, from near and far. Big shots from Dublin and London, million-aires from America. That ballroom upstairs would be full of the dignitaries.'

'It sounds marvellous,' said Clara dreamily.

'It was marvellous,' Mrs Fennell confirmed. 'Lord Lawrence was a magnificent host, and a finer gentleman you would not meet. All his children met their husbands and wives at balls upstairs here. Including Lord Pierce's father Charles – he met their mother at a ball here.' She gave Katie a wary look and Katie bit her lower lip.

'Arabella? She was very beautiful from what I can see in the paintings.'

'Eh – that she was,' Mrs Fennell's voice took on a cautious tone.

'What was she like – as a person?' Clara put down her drawing paper and, folding her arms, smiled over at the two women.

'Well, Lady Arabella came from very good stock. She was quiet – not what you'd call a big socialite like the Armstrongs we were used to. And when Lord Lawrence passed away, bless him, and Lord Pierce's father Charles took over–' Mrs Fennell started working on her pie very quickly. 'You don't want to be hearing all this from me. Sure what do I know? I know nothing.'

Clara leaned forward imploringly. 'Oh, but I do, Mrs Fennell. Please go on.'

'Well, there's nothing more to say really. After Charles' accident...'

'The shooting?'

'Well, he found it hard to get around, and poor Lady Arabella's nerves gave way. Her nerves were bad. The days of the big parties here were more or less over. It was hard on their children, Master Pierce and Miss Prudence.'

The back door suddenly opened giving everyone a start as Prudence marched in, holding two dead rabbits in one hand. Prudence hadn't spotted Clara in the corner and Clara winced as Prudence flung the dead animals on the kitchen table.

'There, Rory shot them down by the river. Put them in a stew or something, will you?' instructed Prudence.

She got a start when she spotted Clara.

'What are you doing down here?' she asked.

'I'm sketching,' said Clara, feeling like a bold child having been caught.

Prudence glanced around the kitchen. 'Sketching what, in God's name?'

'Just Mrs Fennell at work,' explained Clara.

Mrs Fennell went bright red with embarrassment.

'Mrs Fennell!' Prudence shrieked in disbelief. 'And when, Mrs Fennell – pray tell – when will you be departing the kitchens here to embark on your new career in Paris as a model?'

Mrs Fennell coughed loudly and taking up the rabbits headed to the larder with them.

Glaring at Clara, Prudence left.

That evening Pierce was in the drawing room reading the newspaper when Prudence came in, closing the door behind her.

'Where's Clara?'

'I haven't a clue.' Pierce did not look up from the newspaper.

'Pierce, you're going to have to do something with her. She's running amok!'

'Amok?'

'I caught the silly cow down in the kitchens today drawing the cook!'

'Hardly running amok.'

'That's not all she's doing. She's driving through the countryside at high speed, causing chaos, trying to learn to drive. It's a wonder she hasn't killed somebody and herself along with them. Then she was spotted drinking stout in Cassidy's bar in town in the afternoon last Thursday! Stout! She's made a spectacle of herself in front of the stable boys displaying her wares as she's thrown through the air by horse after horse. You just simply need to do something with her!'

Pierce glanced up from the paper. 'What – exactly?'

'Tell the fool that as Lady Armstrong she needs to behave in a certain way. That she can't just go around gallivanting wild through the countryside as she wants in front of the peasantry.'

'Well, you see, the problem is I don't actually give a damn,' said Pierce coolly.

'Don't give a damn about what exactly?'

'I'm just not that interested in anything she does.'

'Obviously!' Prudence looked at her brother in exasperation. 'Well, in that case I wish you'd had the good sense to pick a rich wife that you didn't give a damn about. At least then we could have had new plumbing and a proper heating system installed while we put up with her daft antics!'

Pierce returned to his newspaper. 'I think the killing of an Archduke the other side of Europe is really going to put everything in perspective very soon.'

Prudence glanced at the newspaper headline which said that Franz Ferdinand of Austria had been assassinated.

'What's that got to do with us?' Prudence demanded.

271

'A war. We're all going to war.'

Prudence sat down thoughtfully. 'At least it might save on the expense of servants, if half of them are drafted into the army. It will save me from having to get rid of them. I do hate firing people.'

Clara walked into the room, dressed in a glamorous gown.

'Isn't it a lovely summer's evening?' she smiled. 'Will I tell Fennell we are ready for dinner?' She went over to the bell pull.

'I was wondering would you like to do something tomorrow?' asked Clara that evening to Pierce as he came into the room.

'Can't, I'm afraid. I told Philly Scott I'd go over to her place to take a look at a mare that's giving her trouble.'

Clara remembered Philly as one of the flirtatious girls from the garden party who spent the day fluttering her eyelashes at Pierce and giving her dagger looks.

'Philly Scott?' Clara looked at him annoyed. 'Why does she need you to look at her mare?'

He looked at her disparagingly. 'Why not? She's a great girl, Philly. We grew up together ... pity she hadn't a pot to piss in, really.'

As Clara heard this she burned with jealousy, wondering if Philly would have been a marriage prospect, had she been wealthy.

'If she hasn't a pot to piss in, how come she can afford to keep a mare?' asked Clara.

'You ask the most tiresome of questions,' snapped Pierce as he turned to leave the room.

'I'm going out for a cigar. No doubt you'll find some way to amuse yourself tomorrow, from what I hear.'

Clara awoke at four in morning. She turned around and saw she was alone in the bed.

52

Clara was sitting at a table in Cassidy's bar writing a letter to her mother one afternoon when the door of the bar opened and she looked up to see Johnny Seymour walk in.

He was carrying a suitcase and marched up to the bar. Clara studied him intently. She had made enquiries about him and seemingly he had become very well recognised in the Dublin art and literary circle. The Dublin scene had acquired quite a reputation, producing amazing characters like the poet William Butler Yeats and his brother Jack the artist, Lady Gregory and James Joyce. It seemed to her a dazzling world, a million miles away from the cucumber sandwiches, afternoon tea and set rules of the Anglo-Irish.

'Get me a whiskey, Cassidy, the damned train for Dublin is late,' Johnny said, throwing his suitcase to the floor.

'Ah, sure that train hasn't run on time since Victoria was on the throne, Mr Johnny,' said Cassidy, putting the glass of whiskey in front of him.

'Well, it's a damned shame.'

'That it is. And why are you not driving yourself up as you usually do?'

'I got a six-month ban from driving, Cassidy,' Johnny said mockingly.

'Why? What happened?' Cassidy was aghast.

'My car had an argument with a flock of geese in County Longford.'

'That's an awful pity.'

'A pity for the flock of geese anyway, Cassidy!' Johnny turned around and surveyed the bar.

Clara quickly dropped her eyes and concentrated on the letter she was writing. Johnny saw Clara and then bent over the bar and had a whispered conversation with Cassidy.

A minute later the glass of whiskey was slammed loudly on her table, causing her to look up with a start.

'Hello, there. You must be Pierce's wife?'

'That's right.'

'Hmmm, I think I met you at the garden party up at your house, but to be honest I can't remember.'

'You were in a fairly inebriated condition as I recall.'

'Oh dear!' He pulled up a chair and sat in front of her. 'Did I disgrace myself?'

'Not overly.'

'It was all Dors' fault. My companion?'

'I remember her.'

'Dors is a kind of cocktails-at-dawn kind of gal. She's a terrible bad influence on me, you see.'

'Really?'

'Yes. And I'm so easily led.'

'I'm sure.'

He causally lit up a cigarette. 'Smoke?' He offered his packet.

She was horrified. 'No – no, thank you.'

He sat and looked at her. 'I think I should let you know from the start, I don't believe in titles. So do you want to be called Clara or Mrs Armstrong?'

She looked at him, surprised. 'Em – Clara will do, I suppose.'

'Good, I hoped you'd say that,' he looked her up and down. 'I have to say – you look like awfully good fun.'

'Do I?'

'Yes. Pierce has done very well for himself. I always thought he was a bit of a stick in the mud, to be honest. Does he know you're frequenting the local public houses on your own?'

'I haven't hidden the fact from him.'

'Or advertised it to him either, I imagine. You'll get yourself a reputation if you're not careful. And once you get a reputation around here it's very hard to lose it. I should know... I'm returning to Dublin for a while.'

'So I overheard.'

'I'm showing in an exhibition.'

She longed to ask him about his art and the world he occupied, but didn't want to come across as that interested.

'But you must call on me next time I'm down,' he said. 'We're neighbours – Seymour Hall is just across the lake. At night I can see the lights on in your house, I'm sure you can see mine too.'

'I haven't looked.'

'I'm sure with a pair of binoculars I could see

right into your room.'

'Doubtful, but I'd better keep my curtains drawn then, hadn't I?'

'Well – do call in to me.'

'I'm sure my husband and I would be enchanted to call on you.'

He smiled knowingly at her. 'Indeed.'

A train's whistle suddenly blew.

'Oh, there's my train! Better rush! I hate travelling by train, you can get lumbered with the most tedious company and there's no escape! Till next time!' He suddenly got up, grabbed his case, threw some coins on the bar top and rushed out the door.

Cassidy looked after him, smiling. 'Ah, sure he's great crack, Mr Johnny. Always was since he was a boy, not a bit like the rest of the gentry.' He suddenly looked over at Clara, embarrassed. 'If you'll pardon me saying, Lady Armstrong.'

'The Dasdales have arrived to Hunter's Farm from Paris,' Prudence informed them over breakfast.

'The Dasdales?' enquired Clara.

'This couple who rent Hunter's Farm for a month or so every year,' said Pierce.

'He comes for the fishing, an accomplished angler,' said Prudence, 'and she's – well, she's half mad in my opinion.'

'They say she reads fortunes, can see the future,' said Pierce.

'You stay away from them, Clara,' said Prudence. 'Bad enough you mixing with the locals – you don't need the tourists as well.'

Clara actively sought out the Dasdales and came across them fishing along the lake shore.

'Hello, I'm Clara, Lady Armstrong. I do hope you're enjoying your stay?'

'Very much,' said the woman.

They were a couple in their fifties. They introduced themselves without ceremony as Velma and Thierry. It wasn't long before they had invited her to accompany them back to Hunter's Farm for tea.

'We get great peace here,' said Velma as they sat in the drawing room over tea. 'Paris is so rushed and here we can just relax.'

'Yes, it's very relaxing all right,' agreed Clara. 'You must come to dinner in the house some evening.'

'Perhaps we will.' Velma was studying her intently.

Clara took to dropping into the Dasdales regularly. She liked their easy welcoming ways.

'Is it true what they say – that you can read the future?' Clara asked one day.

'Yes – she's psychic,' confirmed Thierry.

'Only sometimes,' said Velma, sitting back in a dismissive fashion.

'Oh please, read my future. I need to know – me and Pierce – will we be all right?'

Velma sat forward and took her hands and held them.

'You are easy to read, you speak as you find it. You don't hide things well – perhaps this is not so good sometimes. Pierce, your husband, I've met him several times.'

'What will happen to him in the future?'

She shook her head. 'Your husband is impossible to read. I can't get anything from him. He's – blocked – a wall around him. All I can see is that someday you will save the House of Armstrong.'

'I? But how could I save anything?' Clara smiled, puzzled.

Velma folded Clara's fingers against her palms and drew away smiling.

'That's all I know.'

53

July was a frantic period of diplomacy, failed diplomacy and rapid mobilisation as Europe prepared for war. The summer in Ireland continued to pass in a lazy haze of garden parties, cocktail parties, tennis and regattas, as Clara continued to struggle to fit in. It was the Armstrongs' turn to have a cocktail party at the house the night the United Kingdom of Great Britain and Ireland declared war.

'We'll have to postpone the grouse-shooting season,' moaned Prudence.

The war had taken Clara by surprise, but it seemed so far from them in the house that it was hard to see how it could involve them until Pierce arrived home and announced he had enlisted in the army.

'Enlisted!' Clara was horrified. 'But you have no military experience or background. What use will you be?'

'What use will any of them be,' said Prudence. 'Joe the chauffeur and the stable lads have enlisted as well.'

They were in the drawing room and they were waiting for the guests to arrive.

'Why so soon, Pierce? War was declared only today.' Clara felt panicked at the thought of him going.

'I knew the war was coming so I enlisted last month.'

'But why didn't you discuss it with me?' demanded Clara. 'Tell me what you were planning.'

'For what purpose?' Pierce, dressed in a tuxedo, stood at the array of drink decanters laid out on the side table and poured whiskey into a crystal glass.

'For what purpose? Because I'm your wife!'

Fennell walked in, announcing, 'Mr and Mrs Foxe.'

'It's a pity we can't pack Fennell off to Flanders with you,' said Prudence under her breath to Pierce.

'You're slipping into being cruel after being good all day,' observed Pierce to his sister.

'Well, I must have just passed my watershed of being good.'

The Foxes arrived with their son Felix who was dressed in his new officer's uniform.

'Look at you!' exclaimed Prudence. 'It makes a change to see you out of tweed.'

'I-I-I-I got it this a-a-a-afternoon,' said Felix who had a bad stutter, and whose rosy cheeks made him look far too young for the rank he had been given. As in the case of Pierce, he was automatically allowed entry into the officer rank due to his class.

'You look very handsome,' said Clara, giving him a kiss on the cheek, disguising her stress at the whole situation.

'T-t-t-hank you, Clara. I-I-I t-t-t-t...' stammered Felix.

'Oh for goodness sake, Felix!' snapped Prudence. 'Stop! Take a deep breath and try again!'

Felix went bright red.

Clara walked over to Prudence and whispered to her, 'There was no need for that. You're drawing everyone's attention to his stutter.'

'Drawing attention to it! But sure everyone knows about it – he can go on forever!'

The other guests arrived, most of the younger men already proudly wearing officer uniforms.

Clara circulated amongst them, ensuring their cocktail glasses were at all times full. Clara felt there was a heady sense of excitement rushing around the room as the war talk took over. The warm evening seemed to mix with the excitement and Clara instructed that the French windows that led to the terrace at the side of the room be opened to allow air to circulate.

'Who invited *them?*' asked Prudence.

Clara looked across towards the door and saw that Velma and Thierry Dasdale had entered the room.

'I did actually,' she responded.

'Why?' Prudence looked perplexed.

'Because they have been good tenants over the past month and I happen to like them.'

Clara went over to them, greeted them warmly and asked Fennell to get them a drink.

'How good of you to come,' she said.

'Well, it is a distraction after all this bad news about the war,' said Velma.

'Will you delay your return to Paris until the war is over?' asked Clara.

'I'm afraid we can't. Who knows how long it will last?' said Thierry.

Clara spotted Pierce strolling through the French windows and out onto the terrace. She excused herself and followed him. She found him resting against the balustrade, gazing out across the lake while he smoked a cigarette.

The sun was beginning to set and the sky had turned a red glowing hue that reflected in the still lake.

Clara walked over to him and stood beside him.

'When are you leaving?'

'Next week.'

'Next week!' She turned and stared at him in shock. 'So soon?'

'Yes – unless I ring up the Kaiser and ask him to halt their advance until my wife feels the time is right for me to go.' He took a drag from his cigarette.

'You don't have to be so – so bloody sarcastic all the time.'

'Don't I?'

'No! Or so – cold. You're heading off to war. I need to hear reassurance from you, that everything will be all right. That you'll be back quickly and we can get back to our normal life.'

'Our normal life? And what exactly is our

281

normal life? You doing whatever you do – I doing whatever I do. Passing each other with a few inconsequential words.'

'I want more than that. You know I do. I want to spend every moment with you and for us to be inseparable. I just accept it's not easy for you. But in time...'

'In time ... what exactly? You want me to reassure you. I can't. I can't reassure you about anything. Not now. Not ever. Not with this war. Everything is going to change. And do you know something? I can't wait for it to. I want everything to change. I want everything to be turned upside down, so we feel, I don't know – alive, I guess.'

She stared at him, trying to understand him, but she couldn't.

She turned and walked back inside.

To her dismay, she noticed that Velma was in an agitated state, and shaking.

'Velma, what's wrong?' asked Clara.

'I'm sorry, I need to leave.' Looking down at the floor, she rushed from the room followed by Thierry and Clara. They waited in the hall outside as Fennell went to get their coats.

'What was it?' asked Clara.

Velma was shivering despite the night's warmth. 'I just saw so much tragedy ready to unfold with the people in that room. It terrified me. They don't know what is ahead of them.'

'The men going to war?'

'Yes, and more.'

'Pierce? Did you see anything for Pierce?' Clara was nearly terrified to ask.

'He's impossible to read, I'm sorry. As I said

before, he's blocked.'

'But you didn't see him being injured?' Clara was shivering as well.

'I can't read him. I'm sorry.'

Thierry and Velma left the house.

Clara returned to the drawing room where the cocktail party had returned to full swing.

'What a remarkable woman, that Velma!' commented Emily Foxe.

'That's one word for her,' said Prudence.

54

Prudence drove the car to the station with Pierce and Clara in the back.

'I suppose we'd better get used to driving ourselves now Joe has headed off to the front,' said Prudence as she pulled up in front of the station.

Pierce and Clara got out of the car.

'There's no need to come any further,' said Pierce. 'I don't like goodbyes.'

'But Pierce, I want to,' pleaded Clara who was desperately trying to hold back the tears.

'If you insist,' sighed Pierce, then turned to Prudence and said, 'I'll write.'

Prudence nodded. 'Do that.'

Clara slipped her arm through his and they walked through onto the platform and the first-class carriage. The last of the men were boarding and the platform was crowded with their families saying goodbye.

'I'll write to you every day. Every single day,' promised Clara.

'There will probably be delays with the post.'

'I don't care. I'll write anyway.'

'If you must.' He reached the door of the carriage and turned to her.

'Please be careful,' Clara pleaded, refusing to cry because she knew it would annoy him.

'I will.' He reached forward awkwardly and kissed her cheek before stepping into the carriage and closing the door.

She watched him take his seat. He didn't look at her again.

At last the whistle blew and the train began to move.

Clara waved but he continued to look straight ahead as the train pulled away. She walked through the crowd and out to the car and sat into the front beside Prudence. It was only when she was there that she allowed the tears to flow freely. She took out her handkerchief and clutched it to her face to stifle the sobs.

Prudence started up the engine and raised her eyes to heaven as she said, 'Not in front of the peasantry, Clara. Can you not wait until you're back at the house before you start squawking?'

And so, suddenly he was gone without Clara having the time to prepare or even think about it. Leaving her alone in the house with just Prudence and the servants. The war had seemed to come from nowhere and whisk Pierce and all the other men away. Everyone said they would be back shortly, back by Christmas, but that was no consolation to Clara for being parted from Pierce and left at the mercy of Prudence.

At dinner that evening, Clara sat at one end of the table and Prudence at the other, only breaking the silence to talk about something mundane or comment on the food.

'I wonder if you're using the motor car tomorrow?' asked Clara.

'No. I imagine I'll be far too busy running this place to go on any jaunts.'

'In that case, I might drive myself into Castlewest to do a spot of shopping.'

Prudence looked at her displeased. 'Well do try not to cavort with the locals, will you?'

'I don't cavort with them,' defended Clara. 'I stop to chat to them. I find them all very friendly and welcoming.'

'You would! But you should never forget that you are not one of them. We used to be the owners of thousands of acres around here and we should maintain our position.'

'Johnny Seymour's family was very important too, and he is very friendly with all the locals from what I hear.'

'Johnny Seymour! Hardly an example of how to live your life!'

Clara was on the telephone to her grandmother in London.

'Well, it's like the entire city has been mobilised. Everyone who is anyone has gone off to the front.' Her grandmother started listing friend after friend of Clara's.

'I hope they'll be safe. I worry about Pierce. I

haven't heard a thing from him. And I've written to him every day.'

'Perhaps he's not a big letter-writer. I can't imagine he is.'

'A simple "I'm fine" would suffice. I'm so anxious and I've nothing to do all day but let my imagination run away with me.'

'Well, your whole life isn't Pierce Armstrong. You have many friends at the front whom you should be writing to and keeping their morale up. A letter would make all the difference to them. I bumped into poor Cosmo Wellesley's mother the other day and he's off to the front, and his brothers.'

'You're right. I've been so wrapped up in Pierce, I haven't given a thought to my friends. It's just when you're here in Ireland, it sort of takes over. The war, France, seem a million miles away.'

'It may as well be from where you are.'

Clara chatted some more before saying her goodbyes and putting down the phone. She turned around to see Prudence standing there.

'Just on the phone to my grandmother,' smiled Clara.

'In London? I hope she called you – our phone bills have hit the roof since you landed in on us.'

55

Clara came down the stairs and went to one of the sideboards in the hall. She picked up the morning's paper that was waiting there. She walked into the small drawing room and sat down to read about the digging of trenches by the troops for security, to block the German advance.

Prudence walked in and saw Clara with her hand over her mouth, looking shocked as she read.

'Did you see Fennell anywhere?'

'No – Prudence, have you read today's paper?'

'No, but I read yesterday's and the day before. I imagine it's more of the same.'

'But I never imagined it would be like this.'

'What did you think it was going to be like then – a tea party?'

'I'm desperately worried about Pierce. I haven't heard anything from him.'

'Haven't you?'

'The mail mustn't be coming through from the front.'

'Oh it's coming through all right. I've received post from Pierce.'

'*You have?*' Clara was incredulous as she dropped the newspaper on the coffee table.

'Yes, three letters.'

'Well, why didn't you say? I've been worried sick.'

'Well, you didn't ask. Besides, I didn't know he wasn't writing to you as well.'

Clara stood up anxiously. 'Well – how is he? What did he have to say? Is he all right?'

'Quite all right ... well, as all right as one can be when one is mired in trench warfare, I imagine.'

'Can I read the letters?' Clara's eyes lit with hope.

'Certainly not! They are private letters between a sister and a brother, not for your eyes.'

Clara, exasperated and fed up, went to march past her. 'Well, thank you very much!'

'I'll ask him to write to you,' said Prudence after her.

Clara stormed out and Prudence picked up the newspaper from the coffee table, frowning at the headline.

Prudence was shown into their solicitor Rory Conway's office in Castlewest.

'Ah, Lady Prudence, a pleasure as always,' he greeted her. He was a man in his thirties who managed to look both boyish and bookish at the same time.

'Isn't it?' said Prudence as she took a seat in front of him.

'Any news of Lord Armstrong from the front?'

'Yes, he's still warring away. In fact, that's what I wanted to see you about, Conway.'

'Really?'

'This war seems to be bigger than they all predicted. Who knows what it may bring? I want to know what would happen in the event of my brother being killed?'

Conway's smile dropped. 'Killed?'

'Let's be pragmatic, Conway, I always am. If the worst came to the worst where would that leave the estate and everything else?'

It amused Conway that Prudence always still referred to it as an estate, even though it had been very much cut down to farm status by several government land acts.

'Well – em,' Conway sat forward and put his fingers together, 'Lord Armstrong hasn't made a will.'

'I know.'

'Without a will, with the custom of primogeniture, the title and estate and money would pass to your nearest male relative among your Dublin or London cousins.'

'My London cousins already have enough titles and my Dublin ones have enough money. If Pierce was killed, leave them to me, I can handle them, they wouldn't dare cross me. But if my brother's wife had a male child, everything would pass to her son?'

'Of course. I've met Clara on a few occasions, and she's a most charming woman.'

'I've yet to meet a man who has thought otherwise. But what of me, Mr Conway, where would it leave me?'

'Ah – to use that unfortunate term they use to describe the area between the German and Allied trenches – in no man's land.'

'As I imagined… Mr Conway, I would like you to draft divorce papers.'

Conway's face dropped. 'Divorce papers! For whom exactly?'

'For my brother and his wife.'

Conway was taken aback. 'But Lord Armstrong hasn't given me any instructions about divorce.'

'I am giving you instructions now.'

'But why hasn't he written to me directly?'

'Perhaps the letter didn't make it through from the front?' said Prudence, fixing him with a steely look.

Conway dropped his gaze. He was not about to challenge Prudence Armstrong. 'And ... and is Lady Armstrong aware of her impending divorce?' he asked.

'Not as yet, and of course we must keep it like that for now. I can rely on your absolute discretion, I'm sure. I don't know why my brother married Clara – it's plain to see it wasn't out of love. But I think the sooner we get rid of her the better. The next thing that will happen is they'll get this Dublin parliament and the first thing your lot will do is outlaw divorce, and then we'll never get rid of her.'

Conway shook his head in a bewildered fashion.

'You just leave everything to me, Conway, and I'll sort it out. Once we have Clara out of the way, I think it is important for Pierce to draw up a will and name me as his beneficiary of the estate, as Mama and Papa would have intended.'

He sat back. 'I'll await your instructions.'

Prudence stood up and nodded. 'Thank you and good day, Mr Conway.' She turned to walk out. She liked Conway. He always showed deference to the Armstrongs, aware of the privilege of having aristocracy as his clients, she mused.

56

Clara anxiously awaited the post every morning, sifting through it in a frenzy to see if there was a letter from Pierce for her. There never was. But there was a regular letter to Prudence. Clara would stand in the hall holding the letter and staring at his handwriting.

'Is that for me?' Prudence would say, seizing her letter and fanning herself with it. 'I'll read it later.'

She would replace the letter on the ornate side table, resting against the mirror. Often she would leave it there a couple of days, taunting Clara. Taking Pierce's letters for granted.

Clara took her grandmother's advice and wrote to the families of all the service men at the front who were her friends, requesting contact details. They all answered promptly and she then wrote to all the men. She kept the letters light, jovial, good-humoured – asking how they were getting on, sending her regards, telling them she was thinking of them and hoping they would keep themselves safe. She hardly expected to hear back from any of them. They had a war to fight, and she Clara Charter was just a distant memory of a girl who used to flirt with them at parties. If Pierce could not find the time to write to her, then these men obviously wouldn't. So she was astounded when she started getting responses from them.

It started as a trickle when she received a couple of letters back. She took the letters from the side table and sauntered into the parlour. She preferred it to the grander room across the hall. It was cosy, more private. As the autumn of 1914 led into winter, the fire would be blazing there, filling the room with a sweet scent of wood and turf burning.

She sat on the couch, carefully opened the letter and saw it was from Rupert Davenport.

'Rupert!' She smiled delightedly as the good memories came flooding back.

'Clara, I was so happy to hear from you. I thought when you married that chap and went off to live the life of a country lady in Ireland that it would be the last I'd ever hear from you. It meant a lot to get your letter. It's bleak here and reading your letter brought me back to happier times. Remember playing poker over at the Evertons'? You trashed us all! I teased you that you had missed your way, and should have been a professional card player...'

She nestled back to read the two letters.

The next day there were more replies from her letters, and the day after that even more. She immediately started writing back to them all. It made her feel as if she was doing something for the war effort. If she could make them feel the slightest bit happier, that was something, wasn't it? It also made her feel closer to Pierce. It was having regular contact with the front, and that was the nearest thing to having regular contact with Pierce.

Prudence was in her bedroom. She took an old envelope from Pierce, put in a blank sheet of paper and resealed it, smudging the post-date so it was illegible. She then went down to the hall and, seeing the post that Fennell had left on the sideboard, she quickly slipped the envelope in with the others. She had been doing this for a while, making out that Pierce was writing to her much more than he actually was.

Prudence walked into the hall a few moments after she heard Clara coming down the stairs.

'My, my! We are popular, aren't we?' said Prudence, looking at the stack of letters Clara was sifting through. 'Anything from Pierce though?'

Clara shook her head.

'Anything for me?'

'Yes, here.' Clara handed over the envelope Prudence had earlier placed there.

'I did tell him to write to you. Practically insisted he did,' said Prudence, sighing and taking the envelope. 'It's worrying why he isn't writing to you, isn't it?' She smiled. 'But, I wouldn't dwell on it.'

Clara came into the library a few days later where Prudence sat at the table going through the accounts.

'Yes?' asked Prudence, looking up from her paperwork.

'I've received an invitation to a party at the Bramwells'.' Clara was surprised. Nobody seemed to be having parties since the war started.

'Oh, how lovely for you. Major Bramwell must be back on leave from the front.'

'Yes. Did you receive an invitation?'

'No. They probably realised I wouldn't be inter-

293

ested in going. But don't mind me, you should go.'

'Oh no, I don't think so.' Clara shook her head and put the invitation down on the desk. 'I don't really know them, and I wouldn't feel right going without Pierce.'

'Well, I wouldn't let that stop you. Let's face it, I wouldn't say he would mind one way or the other if you went.'

Clara accepted this was the truth as she studied the invitation. 'You don't think it would be inappropriate?'

'Of course not. The Bramwells are old friends of ours, and you should go and represent us.'

'It would be nice to get out for an evening.'

'Then off you go. They don't live too close, mind you. About forty miles away. But you're a dab hand with the car now, and Fennell can give you instructions so you don't get lost.'

Clara dressed in one of her most exquisite dresses and put on her diamonds and styled her pale blonde hair. It was good to be going to a party. She was looking forward to it.

She walked down the stairs and into the drawing room where Prudence was sitting.

'You look very glamorous, Clara,' Prudence complimented her.

'Not too much?' Clara patted her hair self-consciously.

'No, of course not. What time are you to be there?'

'The invitation said ten.'

'A little bit late, isn't it? The Bramwells were always "early to bed, early to rise" types. Nell

Bramwell was renowned for it.'

'Maybe the war has changed them. Anyway – goodnight.'

'Enjoy!'

Clara had received detailed instructions from Fennell and as she drove along the country roads towards the Bramwells', she felt invigorated. She felt independent, driving herself to a party. Fennell's instructions were perfect, she thought as she turned in to the entrance of Bramwells' and up the drive. As she parked in front of the house there didn't seem to be much evidence of a party. There were no cars there, and the house looked in relative darkness. She checked her watch and saw it was a little after ten. She imagined the party might be at the back of the house. The government was warning everyone about wastage, so maybe that was why there were no lights on. Her shoes crunched across the gravel driveway as she walked to the front door and pulled the giant doorbell that let out an enormous chime that she could hear echo around the house. There was no reply and so she pulled the bell again. A minute later she, could hear several large locks being undone on the other side of the door.

The door eventually opened and an elderly butler in his nightgown stood there, looking Clara up and down in horror as she pulled her furs close around her neck.

'Ma'am?' asked the butler eventually.

'I'm here for the party,' Clara said, realising all was not right from the deathly silence in the house.

'Who's that, John?' demanded a woman's voice and Clara looked over his shoulder to see Nell Bramwell coming down the stairs, also dressed in a nightgown.

'It's a woman, Mrs Bramwell, enquiring about a party.'

'A party?' asked an amazed Nell, squinting to see who it was. 'Is that you, Lady Armstrong?'

'Yes. I'm here for the party.'

Mrs Bramwell stared at her. 'But dear ... there is no party. Major Bramwell is at the front, leaving me in no mood for parties, I can assure you.'

'But I received your invitation...' Clara's voice trailed off as realisation dawned.

'Oh dear! You must be mistaken. I sent no invitation.'

'But I assure you I got one.'

'In that case, my dear, I'm afraid you've been the victim of a practical joke.' Nell looked Clara, dressed in fur and diamonds and a silk dress, up and down.

Clara was mortified. 'I see – apologies, Mrs Bramwell.'

'Well, won't you come in for tea? You poor thing, you've come miles.'

'No, I've disturbed you enough. I'm sorry.' Clara turned and rushed down the steps and over to the car, trying to escape the excruciating embarrassment and Nell Bramwell's sympathy.

Clara drove home at top speed over the bumpy roads, trying to keep the tears of embarrassment from flowing. She arrived home well after midnight. She parked outside the house, hurried up the front steps, opened the door with her key, and trudged exhausted upstairs to bed.

'Nell Bramwell rang here this morning,' said Prudence the next day. 'Wanting to check you got home all right.'

Clara was sitting in the library, writing letters to her friends at the front.

'I got home very well,' said Clara, hardly looking up from her writing.

'She said you were the victim of an appalling practical joke.'

'I'd rather not talk about it.'

'It'll be the locals. They'll do anything to try and wind us up. Very cruel, really. And Nell Bramwell has such a big mouth, the story will have gone far and wide by the end of the day. She went into avid detail of how you stood there at her door in your diamonds and furs, all dressed up and nowhere to go. It's so bad! People love to laugh at other people's stupidity, don't they?'

Clara didn't look up but concentrated on her writing.

57

The constant muffled pounding vibrated through the air as Pierce made his way into the local head-quarters. There was a freezing cold rain and he shook the water out of his hair as he entered the small chateau that was being used by the army as offices. He removed his raincoat, entering the officers' den where his superiors were gathered around a table with maps.

'Armstrong, we want you to look at these maps to verify positions on the ground,' said Major Dorkley.

'Yes, sir.' Pierce approached the board and began to answer their questions. He spent an hour there going over the maps.

'Right, that's about it for tonight,' Dorkley said. 'We'll reconvene tomorrow morning.'

The officers started to leave the room.

'Armstrong, hold back a minute, will you?' said Dorkley.

Pierce waited and closed the door when the others had left.

Dorkley went and sat behind his large desk, indicating that Pierce should sit down opposite. He opened a cigar box and took one for himself before offering Pierce one. Dorkley then lit both their cigars.

'May as well have a smoke before you head back to the trenches,' said Dorkley.

'Thank you,' said Pierce.

'How're conditions there?'

'The rain has made things much worse. There's quite a bit of flooding and the freezing weather has made conditions fairly appalling, to be honest. The rats are a major problem as well.'

'I see.' Dorkley sighed and drew heavily on his cigar.

'But if it's bad for us, then it's bad for them as well.'

Dorkley nodded. It was nearly inconceivable for

Dorkley to imagine Pierce had no previous military experience or background. He seemed to glide into the role. Dorkley had expected the young Lord Armstrong to be pampered and the whole front to be a shock to his system. But Pierce seemed to be immune to the conditions and the tension that was weighing heavy on everybody else. He intrigued Dorkley. He intrigued everyone.

'Armstrong, I notice you haven't applied for leave to go home yet like everyone else. You've been exemplary since you arrived here, and I just want you to know I'll rubber-stamp your leave once you've applied.'

Pierce didn't blink. 'That won't be necessary.'

'Pardon?'

'I won't be applying for leave, Major.'

'I see. But, I thought you had been just recently married – is that true?'

'That's true.'

'Would it not be nice to go home and see your bride?'

'As I said, that won't be necessary.'

Dorkley nodded, bemused. 'As you wish, Armstrong.'

58

Clara was walking down the street in Castlewest after posting a letter to Pierce when she heard the hooting of a car as it sped down the main street. She immediately spotted that the driver was Johnny Seymour, with an older incredibly well-groomed woman beside him. Clara could just about count four people crammed in the back of the car who were making much noise and screaming with laughter. One of the women in the back of the car was swigging from what looked like a bottle of gin. The car suddenly pulled over and Johnny jumped out of the car and ran into the wine merchant's, emerging a couple of minutes later with a big box of bottles of alcohol which he threw in the boot of the car before jumping back into the driver's seat and tearing away.

'I thought I saw Johnny Seymour this afternoon in town,' said Clara matter of factly that night as she and Prudence sat in the parlour reading.

'Yes, I've heard he's been back from Dublin up at Seymour Hall.'

'They were creating quite a racket... Why isn't he at the front?' Clara was curious.

'Why is Johnny Seymour not doing anything he should be doing? He excuses himself from the normalities of life, which I imagine includes the war. From what I hear he's holding all-night parties up at Seymour Hall with a gang of well-dressed degenerates.'

Clara's eyes opened wide with the thought of the antics that must be going on, judging by the company he was keeping in the car that afternoon.

Prudence sat giggling while she read the most recent letter from Pierce as they ate lunch. Clara couldn't imagine Pierce ever writing anything that would cause anybody to giggle, let alone Prudence.

'Amazing!' said Prudence as she closed over the letter and folded it back into the envelope. 'Pierce has received another promotion. He seems to be jumping up the ranks there. He never showed any such ability before.'

'Perhaps war is providing change for him ... that's what he wanted.'

'Hmmm – anyway, the bad news is, he won't be home for Christmas.'

'*What?*' Clara's heart sank. 'I don't believe it!'

'Believe it, because it's true.'

'But some of my friends in London who are officers in the army are getting leave to return to their families!'

'Well – lucky them!'

Prudence returned to eating her lunch. Clara sat looking at the cold chicken salad, her appetite gone. She couldn't bear the idea of not seeing Pierce over Christmas. Of being stuck with just Prudence in the house.

'I think I'll go home to London for Christmas.' The words were said before she had even thought about it.

'Splendid idea!' said Prudence happily.

After Prudence had dropped Clara off at the train station for her to make the long journey back to London for Christmas she returned to the house and arranged to meet the local dressmaker, Mrs Carter.

She led Mrs Carter upstairs, into Clara and Pierce's bedroom, and into the adjoining dressing room.

'These are the garments,' announced Prudence, pointing to the rows of exquisite dresses belonging to Clara. 'I want them all taken in a size.'

'All of them?' checked Mrs Carter.

'Yes, and you've two weeks to do it.'

59

London had changed in the few months she had been away and Clara was taken aback. Even though she knew things had to change with the war going on, she still expected it all to be the same somehow. It was true for her grandmother and family's reports, the whole country did revolve around the war now. It was all anybody talked about. Her brother as a doctor had been run off his feet working in a hospital treating wounded soldiers. There were many friends back from the front for Christmas and she tried to meet as many as possible. They all seemed to be thrilled that she was writing to them. She felt embarrassed when everyone asked her how Pierce was doing. She had no news to give them.

She was out having tea with her friend Captain Daniel Miller.

'I met your husband, Pierce, over there,' said Daniel.

Clara's face lit up. 'Really? Where?'

'In a little village called Amiens, just near the trenches. We had a night off and a few of us were in a local hostelry. He was there.'

Clara sat forward anxious. 'How was he?'

'He seemed fine. Very much in control.'

'I'm so worried about him.'

'I shouldn't worry about Pierce Armstrong. He's built a reputation for himself. He's fairly fearless, from what I hear. Doesn't say much, but doesn't need to.'

She sighed and sat back. 'When do you return to the front?'

'Day after tomorrow... Can't say I'm looking forward to it.' Daniel smiled, embarrassed. 'We're not all as brave as your husband.'

She reached forward and clutched his hand tightly.

Clara was walking through the back gardens of her family home in Chelsea, deep in thought. There was a hard frost and the fountain had frozen over.

She started to break the ice to allow the robins perched around have some water.

'I'm off home, Clara!' her grandmother called to her from the house and Clara walked through the gardens towards her.

303

'All right, grandmother. I'll phone you tomorrow.'

Louisa looked at her granddaughter. 'When do you return to Ireland?'

'Next week – if I return.'

Louisa looked perplexed. 'And why wouldn't you return?'

'Because I'm not happy there.'

'Of course you're not happy. You've got a husband fighting at the front. There's a war going on. There would be something wrong with you if you were happy.'

'A husband fighting at the front who never writes to me. Ever. Not once. Not since he left. He writes to his sister all the time. But not so much as a card to me!' Clara's voice broke with emotion.

Louisa looked shocked. 'And you write to him?'

'Of course! All the time! I'm at my wits' end.'

'Well Pierce Armstrong was never going to be an emotional type, Clara. You knew that when you got engaged to him.'

'I don't want an emotional type. But I don't want a block of ice either... I can't stand any of it. I feel like an unwanted guest in the house. Prudence goes out of her way to make me feel unwelcome.'

'It's not her house. It's yours. You are the mistress of the house.'

'You trying telling Prudence that.'

'No! *You* tell her.'

'I can't tell her anything. I've nobody there. I've no friends. I chat to the locals and the servants, otherwise I'd go mad.'

'You were warned by us all before you married, Clara, about the problems you were facing.'

'I know. All of it wouldn't matter if I had Pierce. But because of this damned war I don't have him any more.'

Louisa grabbed her shoulders. 'Everyone is suffering because of the war, Clara, and we all must just get on with it. There are many people in far worse situations than you. What of your poor brother? Imagine the horrors he's seeing every day arriving back from the front to the hospital! Now, I didn't approve of this marriage, but you've made your decision and you can't come running back home just because the going gets tough. You are now Clara, Lady Armstrong, with a husband who is being very brave on the front from all the accounts I've heard. Think of how it would look if you didn't go home! It would be scandalous. It would look like you were abandoning your husband while he fights the enemy. It's out of the question. You need to go back to the house, be mistress of the house, and establish your new life there, in whatever guise it takes. Do you understand me?'

'Yes, Grandmother.'

60

When Clara arrived back at Armstrong House in January 1916, she was determined to take her grandmother's words to heart. She looked up at the house, beautiful in the snow.

'This is my home,' she whispered to herself. *'My home.'*

She walked up the steps and let herself in the front door. The hall felt chilly and she walked into the drawing room where she saw Prudence sitting in front of the fire.

'Ah you're back! How was it?'

'It was nice seeing everyone again. There were soldiers everywhere back on leave. London, Dublin. The trains full of them.'

'Goodness! The food must have been good in London by the look of you!' declared Prudence in a shocked tone.

'I'm sorry?'

'You must have done nothing except eat. You've piled on the weight.'

'Have I?' Clara said, concerned, as she went to the mirror and checked out her appearance.

'You'd want to watch that. Pierce simply cannot stand overweight women.'

'I'd hardly call myself overweight,' Clara looked down at her svelte figure.

'Well, you mightn't. But everyone else will. Of course they're too polite to say it.'

'Unlike you,' said Clara as she left the room.

Later in her dressing room, she struggled into a dress which would not close. Certainly, the dresses she had taken with her to London had begun to feel a little snug – she really had indulged in all the wonderful food, to say nothing of chocolates – but she'd had no idea of the extent of the problem! Prudence must be right, thought Clara. She had put on weight. She resolved to go on a strict diet.

Clara sat combing her hair in the mirror while a young housemaid Molly hung up her clothes.

'Is there anything else, my lady?' asked Molly.

'Thank you, no.'

Molly opened the door and stepped out.

'Oh!' called Clara. 'Can you make sure the water is heated? I'll be having a bath this evening.'

'Certainly, ma'am,' Molly said, closing the door behind her.

Prudence had been coming down the corridor and overheard this exchange.

'Molly, leave the heating system alone and do not put on the hot water,' instructed Prudence.

'But the bath will be cold for Lady Armstrong,' objected Molly.

'So?'

'So – what'll I say when she asks why it's cold.'

'You tell her the system is on the blink, you silly girl,' answered Prudence. 'And do the same in future if she asks for hot water for the bath.'

Clara turned off the hot tap and stepped into the bath she had filled. She gasped with shock as she found the water was freezing. She quickly climbed out and, putting on her dressing gown, walked into the main bedroom and rang for the maid. A minute later Molly arrived.

'Molly, I thought I asked you to put on the hot water?'

'Yes, my lady. Sorry, my lady. It's just the system is on the ... blink!' Molly said the word as if she didn't understand what it meant.

'I see. Oh dear! Well, have some water heated in pots and brought up to warm the bath somewhat in that case,' sighed Clara.

'What seems to be the problem with the water? It never seems to be hot when I want a bath?' asked Clara as she stopped Prudence in the hall.

Prudence was dressed in her hunting outfit having just returned from a day out with the local hunt.

'Yes, it's not working very well at the moment. That happens periodically unfortunately,' said Prudence, taking off her hat and throwing it on the sideboard. 'It's tiresome, especially in the winter.'

'And how long has it been like that?'

'Since around ... 1896, I'd say.'

'1896! Well, why don't you have the wretched thing fixed!'

'All that costs money, Clara. And since you didn't bring any dowry with you, you'll have to continue to suffer like the rest of us. Think of the poor soldiers at the front, and what they would give to have the luxury of even a cold bath.' Prudence walked on and up the stairs.

Before going to bed Prudence put on the heating system to ensure she had a hot bath in the morning, and made sure she had all the hot water used up before Clara woke.

61

Clara walked down Castlewest's main street after leaving the post office where she had posted another letter to Pierce. She was contemplating a quick drink in Cassidy's before returning to the house when she heard her name being called. She looked across the street to see Emily Foxe waving over to her. Clara waved back and waited for a moment between the cars and horses so that she could cross the street to her.

'Hello there, stranger!' smiled Emily, kissing her cheek.

'Nice to see you again.'

'Any news from the front? I hear from our Felix Pierce is quite the hero.'

'Yes, so I believe,' Clara smiled, trying not to show her real feelings. 'How is Felix getting on over there?'

'As well as can be expected,' Emily looked worried and lowered her voice. 'Goodness, if his stammer was bad before you should hear it now! The constant shelling has made his stutter horrendous. He was desperately disappointed you didn't come to his homecoming dinner. He wanted to talk to you all about Pierce and the great job he's been doing.'

Clara was confused. 'What homecoming dinner?'

'The dinner party we threw for Felix of course. You know, it really isn't good for you to stay up at the house all the time being a recluse. You need to get out and mix with us all. You've a patriotic duty to keep the home fires burning–'

'Emily, what are you talking about? How could I go to Felix's dinner if I wasn't invited or informed about it?'

'But you were invited, Clara. I sent my footman to your house with the invite especially. Others have sent you invitations too. We all know what pressure you're under with Pierce being away but, forgive me for saying it, a response is expected when people leave messages or phone the house or send invitations. You shouldn't just ignore us. People will try to be friendly only for so long and then they'll give up.'

'Emily, I'm very sorry, I didn't get Felix's invitation or any others. Please apologise on my behalf to anybody who may have sent me an invitation. Now, if you'll excuse me, I need to get home.'

Clara turned and headed back to her car, feeling a mixture of confusion and anger.

Fennell stood before Clara in the drawing room.

'It's been brought to my attention that messages have not been passed on to me. I am not being told when there are phone calls for me. And messages delivered to the door are not being given to me.'

Fennell looked uncomfortable and embarrassed.

'Well?' asked Clara.

'I'm very sorry, Lady Armstrong. I don't know what to say if this has been happening.'

'Well, who has been answering the phone and who has been taking in the messages? Which one of the servants? Would it not be you? Is that not your job?'

'I do not know.'

'It's simply not acceptable for this to happen and I'm extremely annoyed. In future ensure that all messages are given directly and promptly to me, do I make myself clear?'

'Very good, my lady.'

Clara was visibly upset. 'Then you may go.'

Clara marched into the library where Prudence was at work at the desk.

'Prudence, I'm very angry with Fennell. Phone messages and invitations have been coming here and I've not been given them.'

'What a shame.'

'Well, it's more than a shame. It's scandalous that the servants have been falling down with their duties.'

'Scandalous? Dear Clara – the war in the Flanders is scandalous. The Rape of Belgium is scandalous. Food shortages are scandalous. Indeed, the cost of living and the price of a loaf of bread are scandalous. But a few messages not being passed on hardly constitutes scandal. Pierce said you had a predisposition for exaggerating.'

Clara felt shocked to hear of Pierce using this description of her. Shocked to hear he had used any description of her. She was angered. 'Regardless of my choice of adjectives, Prudence, I expect the servants to do their job, war or no war.'

Prudence sat back in her chair, a smug smile on her face. 'Oh what a spoilt little thing you are! In case you hadn't realised we are considerably down on servants as half of them have gone off to war. This has meant the workload of each servant has increased considerably. And I'm sure nobody has time to play at being your social secretary.'

'I understand that – but–'

'Good, then we'll say no more about it.' Prudence took up her fountain pen and began to concentrate on the work in front of her again.

Clara was opening her letters in the parlour. She tore open one letter and saw the Chelsea address. As she read the letter she saw it was from the father of her friend Daniel Miller. He was writing to her to inform her that Daniel had been killed in action. He thanked her for the friendship she had shown Daniel over the years and wished her the best. She stared at the letter in disbelief as she remembered having lunch with him at his club at Christmas. She crumpled the letter in a ball and held it tightly, thinking of such a young life full of vitality wiped out in a second. As time wore on she became very agitated every day as she waited for the post. If she hadn't heard from a soldier for a while she became anxious that something had happened to him. Then when she finally received a letter and there was a logical reason that there was delay in the post or he'd had his position moved she felt such relief. But with others she would receive a letter from his relative or a friend or her own family telling her the unfortunate man had been killed. It was as if reality was suspended as the roll call of her friends being killed kept coming.

62

Dear Clara,
I do hope you're feeling better since Christmas, and you're settling in back at the house. I still have to give you a wedding present and I've decided what it is. You talked about all the portraits hanging in the house of Pierce's family. And I think it would be fitting for your portrait as the new Lady Armstrong to be hanging amongst them, pride of place. This should make you realise you have as much right to be there as any of them before you.
I've made enquiries and I've commissioned an up-and-coming local artist called Johnny Seymour who lives locally to you to do your portrait. I have it on excellent authority that he is magnificent. Your beauty deserves to be captured for eternity in art, and at the same time it will give you something to do until this dreadful war is over. I'll be in contact with the details shortly.
Your loving grandmother,
Louisa

'Johnny Seymour!' Clara gasped loudly.

It was very appropriate of her grandmother to be arranging Clara's position on a wall among the other Lady Armstrongs that came before her.

Louisa knew Clara's love of painting and that this would mean a great deal to her. Louisa was obviously trying to cheer her up. But to employ Johnny Seymour of all artists! She thought about the man and was nervous about him painting her and nervous to be in his company for any length of time. Yet the thought elated her as well. She had always wanted her portrait to be done, and Johnny seemed fascinating company.

'We may be having somebody spending some time at the house here,' Clara informed Prudence.

'May? Please be definite.'

'My grandmother has arranged for an artist to paint my portrait as a wedding present.'

Prudence stared at Clara with a disbelieving smirk. 'A portrait! There's many a thing this house needs, but one thing it doesn't need is a painting of you!'

'Well, my grandmother begs to differ.'

'Your grandmother doesn't have to live with the faulty heating system. Why not get her to give you a plumber for a wedding present rather than an artist? Far more practical.'

Clara smiled dreamily at Prudence. 'Ah but, you see, it's not "our" wedding present, it's mine. And I was never practical, not in the least.'

'The mind boggles, it really does!' Prudence shook her head, bewildered.

'The artist is...' Clara coughed lightly. 'Johnny Seymour.'

'*Johnny Seymour!*' Prudence's screech could be heard all the way down to the kitchen.

Fennell entered the drawing room.

'Em, Mr Johnny Seymour here to see you, my lady.'

'Oh!' Clara got a start. 'Give me a minute, then show him in.'

Clara ran to the mirror over the fireplace and had just enough time to fix her hair and check her appearance before Johnny walked in.

'Hello there!' he said, smiling broadly.

'Mr Seymour,' she nodded and stretched out her hand for him to shake.

'Well, this is a pleasant surprise,' said Johnny. 'Unexpected money coming my way is always a pleasant surprise, so I was delighted to get the commission from your grandmother. I spoke to her on the phone – most charming woman.'

Clara wondered how much he was getting paid.

'I hear you're very good,' she smiled.

'At many things! Pierce is at the front, I heard?'

'Yes, it's just me and my sister-in-law here, and the servants of course – those who haven't enlisted.'

'Of course!' There was a note of sarcasm in his voice. He went over and studied some portraits on the wall. 'And it is here you are to hang, metaphorically speaking of course.' He went from portrait to portrait.

'Yes,' she smiled at him.

Prudence came into the drawing room.

'Afternoon, Johnny.' She looked him up and down. 'Johnny, how old are you?'

'Old enough to know better, and young enough not to care.'

'But you're a young man.'

Johnny made a sweeping bow. 'So good of you

to say.'

'But why aren't you at the front?'

'The front of what?'

'The war front!'

'Oh, that front! Because I don't want to be there, Prudence.'

'It's Lady Prudence.'

'If you say so, then who am I to contradict?'

'Have you been to the front?'

'No.'

'And you have no intention of going to the front?'

Johnny looked at Clara. 'She learns quickly, doesn't she? I have no intention of being at the front, back or side of any war, dear lady.'

'Well, I think it's scandalous, I really do. A man in his prime–'

'You're too kind.'

'Ignoring his patriotic duty to – to paint pictures!'

'Guilty as charged, Patience.'

'It's Prudence!'

'I'm so glad you insist on ridding me of the formalities of calling you "Lady".'

Prudence gave them both a withering look and marched out.

Clara was trying not to laugh. 'You shouldn't have provoked her. She'll make your life difficult.'

'Oh, what could she ever do to me?' he said, smirking at her.

Clara showed Johnny around the house to see what room he wanted to use to paint her in. He walked around the giant ballroom with the row of French windows that looked out on the gardens to the side of the house.

'This room is never really used any more. I believe there used to be great parties here. I had hoped when I married Pierce we could hold parties here again. But finances dictate otherwise, and of course the war came.' She looked sad.

'Well, I think this room would suit us just fine,' he declared.

'Really?'

'Yes. It's a beautiful room, excellent light from the windows, and if it's not used then we won't be disturbed.'

He went to the side of the room where there were gilded chairs lined up, and selecting one he brought it over to the centre of the room.

'Come here, sit down,' he ordered.

Clara came over and did as he asked.

He stood back and looked at her and then, approaching her, he took her chin in his hand and started tilting her head at different angles.

'You've never sat for a portrait before?' he asked.

'No.'

He studied her posture. 'It shows.'

His words made her self-conscious.

He studied her face before letting it go and walking around the room.

'I'll be coming and going somewhat. I'm trying to organise an art exhibition of up-and-coming artists in Dublin so I'll be returning to Dublin on business a bit.'

'I understand,' said Clara, thinking how exciting the exhibition would be and how she would love to hear all about it.

He stood and looked at her. 'We'll start work tomorrow. So, come on. Let's get into that car of yours and go for a ride.'

'I'm afraid I can't! I have to–' She stopped as she realised she couldn't think of one thing she had to do.

Clara sped through the country roads around the lake.

'You drive nearly as badly as me!' he shouted.

'Do I? The chauffeur is fighting at the front unfortunately.'

'Unfortunate for him anyway.' Johnny lit up a cigarette and sat back. 'It's a beautiful day, isn't it? The scenery looks amazing. I can see why Jack Butler Yeats insists on painting it all the time.'

Clara glanced at him. 'Have you met him?'

'Of course. His brother William as well.'

'I love both their work. They both grew up near here, I understand?'

'Yes.'

'I suppose you know them all, in Dublin. The literati?'

He dragged on his cigarette and smiled at her. 'Those worth knowing I do... I fancy a drink. Cassidy's?'

'I shouldn't!' She shook her head.

Clara parked the car in Castlewest and the two of them walked into Cassidy's bar.

'Good evening, Lady Armstrong, and Mr Johnny,' welcomed the publican warmly.

'Hello, Mr Cassidy.' Clara walked through the

318

pub to the large open fire and sat at a table beside it.

'The usual?' asked Cassidy.

'Times two!' she replied.

Johnny was bemused as he sat down opposite her.

'I take it you're a regular here?' he asked.

'I often sneak in for a quick one,' she said, looking naughty.

'Whatever would Prudence say?'

'Oh, I think she knows and I don't think she's too impressed.' Clara paused as Cassidy placed two glasses of Guinness in front of them, then continued, 'I get on with all the townspeople. They are very warm. I chat away to them all the time.'

'Another thing that doesn't impress Prudence, I imagine?'

'No, she likes to set herself apart.'

'And what of Lord Armstrong? Does he disapprove of his wife mixing with the locals.'

Clara looked into the rich creamy top on top of the glass of stout. 'He hasn't said if it bothers him, so I guess it doesn't.'

He observed her looking lost for a few seconds and then suddenly she was smiling at him.

'Please tell me all about your world in Dublin. I want to hear all about the writers, the poets, the artists. Everything!'

Three hours later Johnny was standing by the fire in the bar with all the customers gathered around him as he finished a song.

'You're pretty and charming and that's all I know...

I've a wife and six children back in old Ballyroe!'
The customers erupted in laughter and clapping as Johnny winked at Clara.

63

'Good morning, Pittance!' said Johnny cheerily, as he passed Prudence in the hall the next morning.

'Prudence!' she snapped back.

'Yes, very wise to be so in war time,' said Johnny with a smirk.

In irritation Prudence stormed off.

Johnny started laughing.

'You shouldn't tease her,' admonished Clara, coming down the stairs to greet him.

'Why? She needs teasing. I'd say she's got away with everything all her life.'

'You're being unfair. Prudence and my husband have known a lot of hardship in their lives, as children. If they are both the way they are, there are reasons for it.'

'Both?' asked Johnny curiously.

Clara looked away, realising she had said too much and revealed something about Pierce she wished she hadn't.

'Is that the attire you have chosen for the portrait?' Johnny asked, looking her up, and down, clearly unimpressed by her plain dark-grey skirt and white blouse.

'Oh, no, no – I'll go up and change now – I was

waiting for you to arrive first.'

Johnny proceeded to the ballroom while Clara returned to her room to dress for the portrait.

She had spent much time deliberating what to wear and she had finally decided on a glamorous bejewelled gown with a train. Her predecessors in their portraits were dressed luxuriantly and she wanted to fit into the same mould. She put on the dress and was relieved to find it fit – her new diet was certainly having its effect. She walked down the stairs and into the ballroom where she found Johnny setting up a giant easel. He took one look at her and his mouth dropped open.

'Is this all right?' she asked, knowing she looked wonderful.

'No! You look terrible!'

'What?' she said disbelievingly as she looked down at her gown.

'Too much, Clara, it's just too much!'

Her eyes widened in surprise. He marched towards her, grabbed her hand and led her quickly out into the hall and up the stairs.

At the top of the landing he said, 'Which room is yours?'

'The one at the end.' She nodded down a corridor and he marched her down towards it and swung open the door and led her into her bedroom.

'Maybe I should call a maid,' suggested Clara quickly, uncomfortable about being alone in the bedroom with him.

'No need. I can dress you myself.' He stopped and smirked at her. 'Don't worry, I won't ravish you. Where are your dresses kept?' He opened a door and seeing it was the bathroom closed it again. Opening another door he saw it was a dressing room and marched in and started riffling through her dresses.

'What are you doing?' snapped Clara as she walked into the room.

'Looking for something that makes you look human, less like a mannequin.'

He started taking the dresses and flinging them to the floor as he dismissed them.

'No – no – no – awful!' he declared as he threw dress after dress to the floor.

She watched him, getting agitated.

'You're creating a lot of work for my maid to hang up all the dresses after you,' she said loudly.

'Here's a thought, why don't *you* hang them up. It will give you something to do!'

She continued to watch him and then her temper snapped and she marched up to him and shouted, 'Will you stop, *please!* They might be just props for a portrait to you, but they are my clothes, expensive clothes–'

'Goes without saying!'

'And you're mishandling them.'

He suddenly stared at her and shouted, 'Yes! There! That's the look I want! The defiance in your eyes. The face flushed with life. I don't want you sitting there like a porcelain doll in a perfect dress. I want you sitting there *alive!*'

She was breathing heavily as she stared at him.

He picked out a simple silver-grey silk dress and handed it to her. 'Here, this will do. Put it on and come back down and we can start work. And don't be long primping and preening! Five minutes!' He leaned forward and whispered, 'And don't lose that look on your face.'

He walked out, leaving her clutching the dress.

Johnny was painting Clara in the ballroom when the door opened and Prudence walked in. She marched across the floorboards and stood right in front of Johnny.

'May I help you?' he asked, shaking his head in confusion.

Her hand came from behind her back and she held a white feather out to him.

'For me?' he asked, his eyebrows arched.

'Yes.'

Johnny reached forward and took the white feather. 'You're too kind. I will put it in my feather pillow along with the rest of them.'

She marched to the door and turned to look at the two of them. 'Children play while men die.'

Johnny nodded at her. 'Very profound. May I say something profound in retaliation?'

'By all means.'

'Shut up!'

Prudence slammed the door after her.

'I imagine the Germans would be far more terrified of her at the front than they ever would be of me. Perhaps she should go in my stead? Is she always so aggressive?'

'Yes.'

'How do you stand living with her all the time?'

'I manage.'

Johnny threw the feather away and continued to paint.

Clara looked at him curiously. 'Doesn't it

bother you? Being handed a white feather? Told you're a coward?'

'Not in the least. I don't give a damn. That war is just a waste of time, and is utterly pointless. If others want to throw their lives away on a muddy foreign field, that's their problem. But I'm not doing it.'

Clara felt herself getting angry. 'You mustn't call the war pointless, Johnny. My husband is fighting it. Many of my friends are fighting it.'

Johnny stopped painting and observed her. 'That's it! Hold that look on your face!'

His words made her more angry. 'I wish you wouldn't say things just to provoke me so you can get your damned painting correct!'

'Oh, it's my damned painting now, is it?' he laughed. 'I thought it was *your* damned painting. Anyway, I'm not saying it just to get a reaction from you. I really don't believe in this war.'

'But why?'

'Because what's it about?'

'Because the Germans invaded Belgium—'

'No, that's a consequence of the war not the cause of it.' He adopted a bored voice. 'It was all about a lot of chest-thumping in my opinion. And that was then and this is now. Nobody expected it to turn into this deadlock of slaughter, and I don't think anybody really remembers what it was all about in the first place. So no, I don't agree with it one little bit.' He continued painting.

'I think you're being very disrespectful – under the roof of an officer in the army and talking like that.'

'I've never shown much respect for anything, so

324

I don't think I will now. Now keep quiet – I need to concentrate.'

Clara's mouth dropped open and she was about to chastise him, when one look at the intensity of his face at work stopped her.

64

'What are you doing next Saturday night?' questioned Johnny.

'Well, I have no plans,' answered Clara.

'You do now. A gang of friends of mine are down from Dublin and we're having a bit of a get-together in my house. Be there no later than ten.'

Clara sat across from Prudence on Thursday evening as dinner was being served.

'Chicken again!' Clara was exasperated. She had expressed her dislike of chicken continuously but it made no difference – it was still served regularly.

'There is a war going on, Clara. Let's be grateful for what we have,' said Prudence as she happily tucked in.

Clara sighed but tackled the chicken, hoping to put Prudence in good form before she broke her news. Eventually she chose her moment.

'Oh, and I'm going to a get-together at Johnny Seymour's on Saturday night.'

'Johnny Seymour's!'

'Yes.'

'A get-together! A get-together of what?'

'I don't know – a get-together of his artist friends and writers, I imagine.'

'A get-together of his well-heeled vagabond motley crew I imagine... There's something smacking of very bad taste about attending a party when your husband is fighting a war. Indecent even.'

'You didn't say that when you encouraged me to go to the Bramwells' party that turned out to be a practical joke. You nearly pushed me out the door to it.'

'Yes – well, I thought you'd learn your lesson from that experience.'

'I have. I've learned to ring ahead to make sure I have the details correct. I have and they are.'

'I can't imagine what Pierce would say.'

'Like anything I do, not much, I imagine. Why don't you inform him and if he has any issue with it, he can write and tell me. That would be a novelty.'

'But – what will you wear?' asked Prudence. 'You can't fit into any of your frocks since you put on all that weight.'

'You'll be glad to know my diet has worked, and I can now fit into them all again,' assured Clara. 'The continuous serving of chicken helped my diet a lot.'

As Prudence studied Clara she realised she had lost weight, and the weight loss suited her and made her more beautiful than ever.

'Perhaps you've gone too thin?' Prudence commented. 'If there's one thing Pierce hates, it's a skinny woman.'

Prudence was with one of the stable boys, who

had a bucket in his hand and a piece of hose stuck into the petrol tank of the car.

'Will I stop yet, Lady Prudence?'

'Yes, that should do it,' said Prudence, smiling.

Later, Clara came into the drawing room with her silk shawl over her glamorous dress. 'I'm going now. I'll see you later,' said Clara.

'Yes, enjoy!' Prudence hardly looked up from her reading.

'You're sure you don't want to come as well?'

'No, thank you. Not my cup of tea.'

'I won't be late.'

Clara left, feeling it was lovely to get away from the house and Prudence for a night.

65

She drove the several miles to Johnny's house and turned the corner into his gateway. Although smaller than Armstrong House, Seymour Hall was an impressive manor house perched on a hill looking out over the lake. A number of cars were parked outside the front of the house and she felt nervous as she sat in the car waiting to go in.

What's wrong with you? she scolded herself. You're Clara Charter, doyenne of London society – you're able for any social occasion.

But for her even to have to say that to herself made her realise how much she must have changed from before she married Pierce. She got out of the car. There was loud music blaring from the house and as she approached the front door she could see through the windows lots of elegantly dressed people inside dancing, laughing, having fun. She rang the doorbell but nobody came. She tried it again and still nobody came. Realising the bell couldn't be heard over the din of the music, she pushed the door open and walked into the hallway. All the doors inside the house were open and people were drifting in and out.

She went through the rooms searching for Johnny. Finally she spotted him deep in conversation with a woman in her forties who was wearing a diamond tiara and earrings. She recognised the woman from seeing her driving around beside Johnny in his car in town.

'Ah hello!' Johnny called over. 'There you are! Thought you weren't coming!'

'Sorry I'm late,' she said and went over to them.

'Never a problem being late here, as long as you're not early to leave.'

He kissed her on both cheeks, giving her a start.

The woman beside him was looking at Clara quizzically.

'Countess Alice Kavinsky, may I introduce Clara, the Lady Armstrong.'

Clara immediately recognised the name. Countess Kavinsky was a famous actress of the Dublin stage.

Clara smiled at her. 'I thought you didn't believe in using titles, Johnny.'

'He doesn't!' said Alice, before looking at Johnny knowingly. 'Only if he is trying to impress one aristocrat with another.'

'Anyway, come along, Clara. I need to introduce you to people,' said Johnny. 'Excuse us, Countess.'

He led her away through the crowd.

'Aristocrat indeed!' he whispered to Clara. 'She's actually from a small farm somewhere. Married a Hungarian Count who later committed suicide.' He waved a hand at a long buffet table. 'Help yourself to some food if you feel peckish.'

As Clara looked at the feast of food laid out on various tables she realised that the government's call to conserve rations had obviously fallen on deaf ears in these quarters.

Clara smiled at everybody as Johnny introduced her. They were all writers, poets, artists, actors and playwrights and Clara recognised some of them as being very famous.

They eventually circled back and joined a group which included the Countess Kavinsky where the topic of discussion was inevitably the war, to Clara's disappointment – she had imagined that these intellectuals would have other subjects to discuss. However, as she listened she realised that they had their own take on the matter.

'What you have going on is wholesale slaughter. We're not even hearing the magnitude of what's been happening because the press is gagged by the government,' said a playwright whose play had just been a triumph in Dublin.

'Poor fools are being marched to their deaths and don't even know it – there hasn't been anything like it since the Dark Ages.'

'The war will mean the collapse of empires everywhere. All these outdated empires will collapse and be replaced by working democracies that look after what the people want, not what an outdated elite want,' said a man in his thirties with intense blue eyes and blond hair whom Johnny had introduced as the poet Thomas Geraghty.

'Like America – that's the future,' said Alice Kavinsky.

'Starting right here in Dublin, in Ireland – why not? A revolution here would lead by example. This war is an opportunity to get rid of the old order and in with a new republic!' continued Thomas.

'Where we can protect people's rights,' put forward another guest.

'A society based on culture and the arts,' offered another.

'But no bloodshed! There's enough of that going on on the continent,' Johnny said firmly.

'A society based on giving everyone the same opportunity regardless of their circumstances.'

Johnny had drifted off and Clara was left standing there at the edge of the group feeling awkward.

Suddenly one man turned to Clara and said, 'Clara Armstrong? As in Lady Armstrong, I presume?'

'Yes,' nodded Clara.

'The Armstrongs have a reputation for hosting elaborate hunts. I hope you aren't part of it?'

'No – I hate hunting!'

'Good!'

Clara edged away only to be cornered by an elegant woman in pearls and a short haircut. 'You see, my dear, it's only a matter of time before women get the vote. I mean, how can they stop us now? We're doing all the work while the men are at war. I'm training as a mechanic myself. You should try it – fascinating.'

The evening sped by and Clara met one eccentric person after another.

She eventually found herself back with Countess Alice who was intent on explaining her personal philosophy to her. 'I believe there won't be contentment in this world till we have complete equal division of personal property. I mean why should just one person live in a big house while a huge family is crammed in a one-room flat? Darling, you must accompany me to the slums of Dublin. They are the worst in Europe without doubt. And you know this country has one of the highest average incomes. It's just not being distributed properly.'

Johnny slipped over to her and whispered, 'How are you enjoying it?'

'I don't know! I've never encountered anything like it.'

'Good!'

'They are all bursting with ideas of how the world should be run. They all want change and quickly.'

'I know.'

'They scare me.'

'Good!'

Clara got a shock when she looked at her watch and saw it was three in the morning.

'I have to go!' she said suddenly.

'So soon? But it's only getting started,' said Johnny.

'For you maybe. But Prudence is timing me, I can assure you.'

Clara smiled at Countess Alice as she said goodbye. 'I hear you're a great actress. I'd love to see you on stage one day.'

'So kind. And I'm so delighted to have met you at last. I've heard so much about you.'

'Have you?' Clara was confused.

'So much. You must be quite special for Johnny to endorse you like that. He doesn't endorse all his girls, you know.'

Johnny suddenly appeared at Clara's elbow. 'Right, shall I show you to your car?'

Outside she sat into her car and smiled up at Johnny.

'Are you sure you're all right driving back on your own,' he asked. 'You're more than welcome to stay here.'

As she looked up at the comfortable grandiose building, she was half tempted.

'Are you trying to ruin me? I don't think so. Thanks, Johnny, it was fascinating.'

She started the engine and set off. It was a nice moonlit night and she was enjoying the drive back through the country roads when the engine cut out and the car came to a halt. She tried the key again and again, but the engine would not get past the revving stage.

She sat there wondering what to do. She was stranded and still quite a distance from Armstrong House.

'This can't be happening!' she shouted loudly as she got out of the car and, grabbing her purse, set off walking. She looked an unusual figure as she walked through the countryside, her blonde hair, pale skin, cream satin dress and shawl luminous in the moonlight. She seemed to be walking for hours and was exhausted as she finally turned through the gateway of the house and began to walk up the long driveway.

Prudence stood at the window of her bedroom as she saw Clara walk across the forecourt and wearily climb the steps up to the front door, her shawl trailing behind her.

'Really, Clara, you really must check if the tank has petrol before you set off on one of your jaunts in the future,' said Prudence.

'The car has always had petrol in it before.'

'You see, this is the problem with you, Clara. The petrol doesn't just magic itself into the car, it is arranged. And you rely on other people to arrange it.'

'Well, I won't in future!'

'Good! I wasted the labour of two stable boys today to go fetch the bloody car. I sometimes wonder should we cut costs and get rid of the car altogether.'

'Never!' Clara nearly shouted at the idea.

'Isn't the car just a waste? I mean, everyone else can ride horses perfectly except for you.'

Clara stood up, appalled. 'The car is not going, Prudence! Or I go with it!'

'Oh, don't give me an ultimatum, Clara. I hate ultimata.'

Clara marched out of the room leaving Prudence to laugh to herself.

66

If her grandmother had intended having her portrait painted to act as a kind of therapy for Clara, she had judged well. Clara enjoyed the experience immensely.

To be associated with art was something she had always wanted, and now her image was becoming enshrined for ever in Johnny's work. She didn't know what to make of Johnny. He could be hilariously funny, terribly insulting, incredibly moody. Some days he maddened her so that she felt like slapping him, other days he made her laugh so she felt like embracing him. He would work intently on the portrait and then without warning throw down his paintbrushes and declare they were going off to Cassidy's bar for the rest of the day to get drunk, or off to take a boat and go rowing on the lake. He was exciting. And he was the polar opposite of Pierce. After getting so used to Pierce's evenness, his coolness, his aloof removal from the everyday world, Johnny's expansive personality was intoxicating.

The Easter Rising in Dublin exploded without any warning. Days of shootings and carnage wrecked the prosperous city centre in a short time, much to citizens' fury.

'Scandalous, if I may say,' said Fennell as he served Clara breakfast while she read the front-page report of the Rising.

'Honest decent people unable to get about their lives and go to work over a few silly men playing soldiers!' He finished pouring the tea into Clara's cup.

'Quite right, Fennell! It's seldom one hears you speaking any sense!' It was Prudence at the door of the room.

Fennell pursed his lips and walked out.

Prudence took the newspaper out of Clara's hand to her annoyance and studied the front page.

'Silly arses! Do you know they copied the warfare in Flanders and built a series of trenches in the park in Stephen's Green, planning on holding out there for months. But all the British troops did was go up on the roof of the buildings around the park and shoot down at them!'

The Easter Rising was quickly suppressed and the republicans who fought it arrested. They left behind a city in ruins and an angry public. However, as the authorities put the leaders on trial and sentenced them to execution for treason the public mood shifted from anger at the rebels to fury at the authorities for such severe sentences.

Clara sat at the bar in Cassidy's, the newspaper in front of her, while she had a glass of wine in the afternoon.

'Ah, it's shocking, just shocking!' said the publican. 'Sure them brave lads didn't deserve to be shot. All they were doing was trying to bring about independence which is what we all want anyway.'

'Shocking!' said a chorus of customers around

the bar as they nodded.

She supposed it was shocking. Death was always shocking when it came swift and unexpected. The whole world had become brutalised, and this was just another arm of it. The brutality of the war seemed to be so far away, but now with the Rising in Dublin it seemed to be edging closer. The public was becoming aware of just how ferocious the Great War was and the extent of the casualties. The Battle of the Somme had been a bloodbath and the newspapers could no longer suppress the facts with the excuse of keeping the public mood positive. She sighed and folded over the newspaper, bade goodbye to Mr Cassidy and the others and went out to the car.

As she drove out of Castlewest she thought about Pierce who had made no contact with her since she had seen him last.

Johnny rowed them across the still water of the lake in the small boat. Clara sat opposite him, looking at the house up on its hill.

'I should warn you, I'm not an experienced rower, so I hope we don't get in trouble,' he said.

'I think you should have warned me of that before we left the shore, as I am not an experienced swimmer,' she said lightly.

'I will try not to sink us then.'

'Please do.'

He stopped rowing and looked back at the house and the surrounding countryside.

'You see, this is what we write about and paint about in Dublin. Trying to capture the real Ireland. The whole Irish revival in the arts.'

She looked at him curiously. 'And politics.'

He nodded. 'Yes.'

'You believe in Home Rule.'

'I believe in it because it will happen. I only believe in things that are certain to happen.'

'Prudence says–'

'Prudence! She's the old Ireland. There won't be a place for her in the new country if she doesn't change her ways and move with the times. She wants to hang on to the past. But you can't. You can only move forward. If you take this county, the power used to be centred around the Big House, the epicentre of the estate. It's not any more. The power has shifted to Castlewest and it's in the hands of the shopkeepers, publicans, solicitors, doctors who function there. And not before bloody time!'

'But you're from a Big House family. Don't you mind losing all your power?'

'I've moved with the times.'

He started rowing again. 'I have to return to Dublin next week. I'm behind with my work. I need to get this exhibition organised. Which is going to be hard since most galleries in Dublin are smashed after the Rising. And I have to attend a meeting at the Abbey.'

She nodded. He was on the board of directors at the Abbey Theatre. She suddenly felt a terrible dread of him going. He was the only bit of fun she had. The only excitement outside the house.

'How I would love to go to a play!' she sighed.

'Why don't you? Come to Dublin and I'll bring you to the theatre.'

She blinked a few times. 'I can't! It wouldn't be

337

right. Attending the theatre with a man while my husband is at war.'

Johnny roared with laughter as he began to row back to shore.

'What's so funny?'

'You! You don't mind going drinking in a local bar with me, but you couldn't be seen out in society with me. There's a rebel in you. But it's a rebel very concerned with her reputation!'

67

As Clara came down the stairs Fennell approached her.

'Oh, my lady, Mr Seymour is here for you. He's in the library.'

'The library?'

Clara walked across to the library and opened the door. She saw Johnny standing there holding up one of her paintings to the light. She stored them in a folder there.

'What do you think you're doing?' she demanded as she walked over to him.

'I found them over there and decided to take a look. You never said you painted.'

Clara snatched her work from him. 'You've no right to snoop around poking your nose into things that don't concern you.'

'But art always concerns me.'

'This isn't art, it's a few sketches. You're so intrusive! You march into my dressing room and throw my dresses around. You march into the library and go nosing through my sketches. The world doesn't revolve around Johnny Seymour, you know!'

'Oh, stop getting worked up over nothing.'

'My drawings are private and I don't want you looking at them.'

'But all artists have to show their work to others. It's what we do.'

'I'm not an artist.'

'I beg to differ!' He grabbed the painting from her. 'These are bloody good.'

'Give it back to me!' She tried to take it but he wouldn't let it go.

'It shows real talent. Certainly potential. I could show it to some critics in Dublin.'

She reached forward, grabbed the painting and ripped it up. Then she crossed over to the fireplace, flung it in and watched it evaporate into ashes.

'That was stupid of you,' he said.

She turned and viewed him coldly. 'I'm Clara Armstrong, wife of Lord Armstrong, an officer in the army. I do not show drawings to critics. I think you forget my position and who I am.'

He walked slowly to her and put his hand under her chin. 'No, Clara, I think it's you who is forgetting who you are.' He dropped his hand. 'I just dropped in to say goodbye before I headed to Dublin. Can you give me a lift to the station?'

She drove him to the station in silence and parked the car.

'I'm not sure how long it will take me to organise my exhibition in Dublin, but it will probably be a couple of months before I can resume the portrait.'

She nodded as she looked ahead. 'That's fine.'

'That's if you want me to resume your portrait?'

'It's as you wish. Let me know if you're coming back.'

He leaned towards her and whispered into her ear. 'Don't be angry with me. I didn't mean to snoop on your paintings. I'll write to you.'

She turned and looked at him, smiling cynically. 'I don't think so.'

He leaned forward and kissed her cheek. 'See you in a couple of months.'

He got out of the car but she stayed put.

As he ran to catch his train he shouted, 'I hope I didn't ruin your reputation kissing you in public!'

'No,' she yelled after him. 'But you might have ruined it by then shouting you had to the whole town!'

Laughing, he waved to her as he jumped on the train.

68

Pierce looked down the trench at the soldiers lined up there. He looked up at the clear night sky. He looked at his watch and saw the second hand tick towards the designated time. As the second hand ticked past twelve he knew he should give the signal and yet he paused. He reached into his pocket and took out two photos. The first was a photo of his house in Ireland. Then he looked at the other photo which was of Clara who was smiling beautifully.

'Sir?' asked the private beside him.

Pierce looked down the line of men anxiously waiting. He quickly stuffed the photos back in his pocket, placed the whistle in his mouth and blew hard. At the sound of the piercing whistle, the soldiers quickly climbed up the trenches and spilled over the top. Pierce clambered over and along with the men began to race across the darkened landscape towards the enemy line. The rat-a-tat-tat of the machine guns cut into the night and began to spray bullets at them. Pierce faltered as the first of his soldiers were cut down by the bullets screaming into the night. He stood still and looked to his right and left seeing the casualties everywhere. He thought about sounding the retreat, but then he saw some soldiers racing on. He joined them and continued to run towards the enemy trenches. He ran as fast as he could. As the machine guns continued to gun down the troops his heart was pounding and he was gasping for breath as he expected to be shot any second.

He suddenly remembered growing up in Ireland. His father bringing him out shooting one sunny afternoon.

They stood at the top of a rolling field.

'Fire the gun into the air to get the rabbits running,' said his father.

Pierce aimed the gun into the air and fired a shot. Suddenly a rabbit jumped up from some long grass and started running across the field.

'There he is! Shoot him!' ordered his father.

Pierce aimed the gun at the rabbit and fired, but missed him. He aimed again and fired but missed him again.

'You'll lose him! Hit him!' ordered his father.

But as Pierce tried to get an aim on the rabbit, the rabbit wasn't running in a normal fashion, he was zig-zagging across the field making it impossible to get him in the direct line of fire.

As Pierce remembered this, he started to run in a zig-zag fashion across the no man's land. As the others ran in a direct line, he manoeuvred quickly from left to right. He kept doing this for what seemed like an eternity and suddenly he was at the enemy trenches.

'We're here! We've made it!' Pierce screamed at the others. But as he turned to look he saw there were no others. They had all been gunned down and he was on his own.

Gasping, he jumped down into the trench. He could see the German soldiers at their machines gun positions shouting at each other.

He held up his gun and aimed it at them. Suddenly a soldier appeared from nowhere and knocked the gun out of his hand. He reached down to get it, but was knocked over on to the ground. He turned and looked up where ten soldiers stood around him, pointing their guns at him.

Pierce was marched into the small room and

pushed down on a chair. He looked around the room and it seemed to be a high-ranking officer's room. Looking up, he saw a group of German soldiers staring at him.

An officer came in and started speaking to the soldiers. The officer came up to Pierce and studied him.

'Name?' demanded the officer in English.

Pierce said nothing but stared back. The officer reached into Pierce's pockets and took out his wallet and photos. He looked at the photos of the house and Clara before putting them in his pocket and then he riffled through the wallet.

'Captain Pierce Armstrong,' read the officer. He turned to the soldiers and said, 'Leave us.'

The officer went to a table and took up a cigarette box and lit a cigarette.

'So, Armstrong, you got inside our trench and didn't shoot anybody, or set off any grenade. All you did was hand yourself to us... Cigarette?'

Pierce nodded and the officer handed him a cigarette and a light.

'You're quite a coup. A high-ranking officer. Tell me, what are you planning to do next?'

Pierce dragged on the cigarette but said nothing.

'Be silent then. You'll be transported to a prisoner-of-war camp where you'll be questioned. I'm sure you have a lot of information that will be helpful to us.'

'Questioned? You mean interrogated,' Pierce said.

'Make it easy on yourself and give the information freely.'

'What'll happen then?'

The officer took out the photos and looked at the house. 'Your home?'

Pierce nodded.

'And your wife?'

Pierce nodded. 'Clara.'

'A privileged man. It's going to be a long time before you see either again.'

Pierce watched the man intently. The German officer found Pierce's dark eyes unsettling, his cool unconcerned behaviour strange.

'Let me go,' Pierce suddenly said.

'What?'

'Let me go free. Bring me to the edge of the trenches and I'll find my way back to our side.'

'Are you crazy?' The German officer started laughing.

'Please. I won't be able to stand being captured. Anything but that.'

'You're a prisoner of war, now shut up.'

'Please. I've never asked for anything in my life from anyone. I've never needed anything from anyone. But I need this from you. Let me go free. Please. I'm begging you.' Pierce's stare bored into the German's eyes.

The German officer returned his stare for a long time, and then he got up and walked out of the room.

Pierce heard the officer giving orders to the men outside and then there was silence. He eventually got up and walked to the door. He peeped out and saw nobody about. His heart started to pound. He stepped back into the room and saw the German officer's clothes stretched out on the bed. He quickly changed into them. He slipped out of the small building and started walking down through the trenches. He kept his head down as he walked past some soldiers. He got to a quiet area and then he jumped up over the trench into no man's land. He fell to the ground and began to drag himself along the ground towards the British lines.

After the earlier onslaught nobody was expecting any more advances and so the artillery were not on the alert. But Pierce didn't raise his head as he continued to drag himself through the mud. When he was halfway over he wriggled out of the German clothes and continued on his journey until he finally reached the British trenches where he collapsed.

69

Clara took up her letters and looked through them. She stopped suddenly when she saw Pierce's handwriting on an envelope. Her hands started shaking as she carefully tore open the envelope and unfolded the paper inside.

I'll be home on leave on the 19th, Pierce.

As she read and reread the note she started crying. She stood up and started running through the house shouting, 'He's coming home! He'll be home next week!'

Tossing and turning the whole night before

Pierce was to arrive home, Clara was consumed with nerves. All she had wanted over the months was to see Pierce back. But now he was due she was consumed with worry. Would he be changed? Would he be different to her? She hoped he would have missed her so much that the barriers would have come down. Maybe he would have changed. Clara decided it might be better for Pierce not to see all the letters she got from the front, in case he got the wrong idea. She managed to find a loose floorboard in one of the guest bedrooms and, taking it up, she hid the letters in a couple of bags under it. The letters had been her little way of helping her friends in the war, but now she must concentrate on her husband.

Prudence sat at the steering wheel outside the station, Clara standing up in the car beside her so she could see over the station fence onto the platform. There were a lot of soldiers coming home on leave that day and the station was packed.

'Oh, sit down, won't you, you're giving me vertigo!' pleaded Prudence.

Clara reluctantly sat down.

'Here it is!' she shouted, jumping up again.

'For goodness' sake!'

The train was pulling into the station. As soldiers started spilling out on to the platform there was a rush of people to their loved ones.

'I can't see him, I can't see him!' said Clara, standing on her tiptoes.

'Everything comes to those who wait,' said Prudence.

'There he is!' said Clara as she spotted him

cutting through the crowd.

She jumped from the car and made for the station entrance. She pushed through the emerging crowd until she got to him, flung her arms around him and held him tightly.

'Clara, there are people looking,' he said irritably as he drew back from her.

'I don't care!' she said happily, gazing into his face. 'You haven't changed. I thought you would have changed.'

'Let's get to the car and back to the house,' he said. He turned to the corporal who was carrying his bag. 'This way.'

They reached the car. Prudence was sitting back, a cynical smile on her face.

'Welcome, dear brother,' she said.

He smiled and nodded at her.

The corporal put the bag into the back of the car. 'Is that everything, Colonel?'

'Yes, you can go. Enjoy your leave.'

The corporal nodded and dashed off to his family.

'Colonel?' said Clara, amazed. 'You've been promoted?'

They got into the back of the car. 'Yes, last in a long line of promotions.'

Clara sat holding his hand tightly in the back of the car, gazing into his face.

Pierce was lying in a hot bath filled to the top of the tub, his eyes closed. Clara walked in, holding some fresh towels.

'You're in luck. The plumbing is actually working today and there's hot water,' she smiled down at him.

He opened his eyes.

'Can I get you anything?' she asked.

'No, I have everything I need,' he said, reaching for the tumbler of whiskey resting on the edge of the bath and downing it in one.

'I'll leave these for you,' she said, putting the towels on the chair and retreating into their bedroom. 'We've organised a gathering for you on Saturday night,' she called from there. 'Just some close friends and neighbours. All desperate to see you.' She sat down on the couch in the room.

A minute later Pierce came out with a towel around his waist, and proceeded to dry his hair with another towel in front of the fire.

'We didn't know what to do for the best. Whether you wanted to see people or just wanted to relax,' said Clara.

'Whatever you think.'

'Well, it's your leave, your decision,' she smiled. 'Perhaps if you had written and said what you would like to do.'

'It wasn't really high on my list of priorities.'

'I can imagine.' She thought hard before speaking but decided to blurt it out. 'I mean, perhaps if you had written at all while you were away. Not one letter, a postcard even. Just to let me know that you were all right, thinking of me. Alive even.'

'I did write. I wrote you a card at Christmas.'

She looked at him, surprised. 'I never received it.'

'Pity.'

'But even that, one card, Pierce, to your wife!'

'I had a war to fight, in case you had forgotten.'

348

'You still managed to write to Prudence all the time!'

He turned around and faced her. 'I didn't write to her that much. From time to time, maybe. Besides, I had to deal with business with Prudence.'

Clara looked down at the floor before looking up at him. 'But Pierce! I'm your wife! I wrote to you non-stop. Did you get my letters?'

'All of them.'

'Well, why in God's name didn't you write back?' she demanded angrily.

He walked over to her. 'Can you even imagine what's it's like over there? The flooded trenches, the vermin, the stench of dead bodies, the disease?'

She drew back. 'I'm sorry – I know it hasn't been easy for you. But if you'd only written to me, shared your experiences with me. I could have–'

Pierce went over to his dressing room. 'Let's dress for dinner.'

70

It wasn't as if Clara saw much of Pierce over the next few days. He went off riding on his own, or went walking for miles along the lakeshore. He would stand on the shingled beach at the lake, looking out at the still water, not a sound for miles except a bird and it seemed impossible to imagine the trenches being on the same planet.

349

Clara realised he needed time to recuperate and tried to understand what he had been going through. She was careful not to push him too far.

On the Saturday night he dressed in his uniform and he and Clara descended the stairs together to greet the guests as they arrived for the dinner party. She held his arm tightly. Many of the guests were already waiting in the parlour and they rushed to Pierce when he arrived in the room.

'Welcome home!' they cried.

The girls and women kissed him while the men grabbed his arm to shake hands or clapped him on the back.

Watching, Clara realised he was acutely uncomfortable.

'Come on, everybody, give him some space,' she said loudly with a big smile.

'But he actually escaped from the Germans!' said Mrs Foxe. 'They had taken him prisoner and he got away somehow. How did you do it, Pierce?'

Clara looked at Pierce in amazement. Why was this the first she had heard of it? Why hadn't he told her? She felt panicked at the thought of him being captured and held his arm tightly.

'It was nothing. Really it wasn't.' Pierce's obvious discomfort indicated it was no false modesty on his part.

'That's not what my husband said,' said Nell Bramwell. 'He said your escape was the talk of the ranks.'

'Shall we all go to dinner?' coaxed Clara. 'Mrs Fennell has done a marvellous spread for us, and all made with the war effort in mind, so no waste!'

She linked her arm through Pierce's and they turned and headed towards the dining room.

'I meant to tell you, the Cantwells send their apologies, but they can't make it. Their nephew was killed in France. Shot dead,' said Prudence in a matter-of-fact voice as they ate dinner.

'That's young Timothy Cantwell, isn't it?' said Mrs Foxe.

Clara saw she had gone ashen-faced.

'I'm afraid so,' said Prudence. 'Excellent shot himself as I remember. I'd been on many a hunt with him.'

Everyone became subdued.

'I wish it would just all stop!' said Emily Foxe, grasping her husband's hand. 'They said it would only last a few weeks.'

'It's bound to be stopped soon,' said Clara encouragingly. 'That's what all my friends at the front say. And this war, the Great War, will be the last war. No more wars ever again. Imagine!'

Pierce gave a dismissive laugh. 'It's not nearly over. And it won't be the last war. It's only the start of wars the likes of which we've never seen before.'

'Pierce, you're upsetting Mrs Foxe,' said Clara quietly.

'I'm not upsetting her. The war is,' said Pierce.

There was silence for a while, broken by Clara smiling and talking cheerily. 'Has anyone seen these moving pictures from America? Movies? I can't wait to see one. Seemingly it's like watching a play on a screen. Isn't that exciting?'

News of young Timothy Cantwell's death

dampened the spirits for the rest of the night. They gathered in the drawing room for drinks after dinner. Clara saw Mrs Foxe go over to Pierce and talk quietly to him. She strained to listen in.

'Pierce, could I ask a huge favour?'

'You can certainly ask.'

'I'm so worried about Felix out there. He's not like you, Pierce, he isn't built from the same material. He could never be a war hero like you. I just wonder could you look out for him?'

'He's not in the same regiment as me.'

'I know, but you're a high-ranking officer now and maybe you could – I don't know – just seek him out and talk to him. See if he needs anything.'

'Everyone has to fight his own war, I'm sorry,' Pierce said and moved away from her.

Clara tried hard to concentrate on the conversation she was involved in but couldn't take her eyes off Mrs Foxe's upset face.

Finally, the last of the guests left. Prudence had gone to bed early. Clara waved goodbye at the door, then walked back into the drawing room where Pierce was sitting staring into the fire with a glass of port.

She closed the door and went and sat on the couch.

'Pierce, I overheard your conversation with Mrs Foxe. Did you have to be so cold to her?'

'I wasn't being cold. I was just stating the facts.'

'The woman's son is off fighting the war and she's worried sick. She didn't want facts, she wanted some comforting words.'

'Well, she came to the wrong place to find them.'

'Isn't that a bloody fact!' she said angrily, causing him to look up at her. She bit her lower lip before continuing. 'I just think you could have said you'll do your best for him.'

'But it would be a lie. I don't have the time to do my best for him.'

'Then lie to her! Damn it, lie to her!'

'Where did you learn such language?'

'From your sister!'

Pierce looked into the fire. 'So if I lied to her, when Felix Foxe is killed and buried forever out there, she will think I didn't do my best for him and hold me somehow responsible. No – best to be straight up and honest.'

'Pierce! Don't say such things about poor Felix.'

'Why? It's the truth. It's a wonder "poor Felix" has got to this stage without being obliterated. The lifespan of junior officers is very short – most get mown down first. All that excellent breeding snuffed out in a second.'

'Well, you didn't!'

'I'm different.'

She stared at him, then stood up. 'I'm going to bed. Are you coming?'

'I'll be up after I've finished this.' He nodded at his glass.

71

Rory Conway took back the legal documents Pierce had been called into his office to sign.

'And that completes all the estates affairs and puts it in running order,' said Conway with a smile. 'Thank you, Lord Armstrong.'

Pierce nodded.

'So when are you due back to France?'

'In a couple of days.'

'I don't envy you. Ah, but sure you'll be home again in no time.'

'Doubtful.'

Rory Conway thought about Prudence's visit to him and her instructions to draft divorce papers for Pierce and Clara. He had delayed doing so as he wanted to be sure it was Pierce's wish. He decided now was as good a time as any to find out Pierce's intentions for the future regarding his wife, his sister, his house and his estate.

Pierce reached into the pocket of his uniform and, taking out a silver cigarette case, took a cigarette out and lit it. He offered one to Conway who declined.

'I've given up – bad for the health,' smiled Conway, before his face went serious. 'As is this war, by all accounts...' He paused, seemed to hesitate. 'I wonder, Lord Armstrong, if I could raise a delicate matter with you? Have you given any thought while you're home on leave to put your own affairs in order?'

'I thought that's what we've just been doing.'

'That's just the day-to-day running of the estate. I'm talking specifically about you. I mean in the unlikely and tragic circumstances of you being killed.'

Pierce's eyes widened in surprise.

Seeing his reaction, Conway sat forward quickly. 'I mean, I'm sure you would want your wishes carried out and your loved ones taken care of.'

Pierce said nothing but continued to stare and say nothing. Pierce Armstrong always had a strange almost hypnotic way of looking at you that Conway found very unnerving.

By way of an explanation Conway continued quickly, 'I mean, I know your sister is very concerned about what would happen to the house and farm – eh, estate, in the aftermath of your untimely and tragic death.'

Pierce blinked and sat forward slowly. 'My sister? How do you know? She has been in to see you about my untimely – and tragic – death?'

Conway gulped, realising the situation he had put himself in.

Fennell closed the door as he came into the drawing room.

'Lady Armstrong, if I could have a word?'

'Yes, Fennell?' She looked up and saw he looked upset and his eyes were teary.

'We received some bad news today. Joe, you might remember the chauffeur, was killed in action at the front.'

'Oh, Fennell!' Her hands shot up to cover her mouth. 'The poor boy! His poor family... He taught me to drive...' Her voice trailed off as she remembered his pleasant disposition.

'I know. Also, myself and Mrs Fennell are tendering our notices as of today.'

'What? But why? You can't just leave us in the lurch like this. Where are you going to? Mrs Fennell has lived on the estate all her life!'

'I'm afraid there is a situation in the house that has made our position untenable.'

'Which is?' Clara was perplexed.

'Lady Prudence.'

Clara walked into the drawing room where Prudence and Pierce were in conversation.

'I've something important to discuss with both of you,' said Clara, steadying her nerves.

Prudence viewed her warily. 'Good, I hate discussing mundane matters.'

Clara looked at her husband. 'Pierce, I will not live under the same roof as Prudence any longer.'

'In that case, when do you pack?' questioned Prudence.

'I'm not joking here. We have to make alternative arrangements for Prudence. Otherwise...' She faltered for a second. 'Otherwise, I return to London.'

Pierce said nothing as he stared at Clara.

'A woman should test her husband's love only if she is sure of her husband's love, Clara.' Prudence sat back in her gilded chair and crossed her legs.

'I am sure of Pierce's love. And I know he will

back me in my decision that you must leave, Prudence.'

'I can have Fennell arrange a Dublin train ticket for you – just in case,' said Prudence.

'It will not be needed.'

'You hope. And why – pray tell – do you want me to leave my own home?'

'Because you have been mounting a campaign against me since I arrived. You have done everything from keeping a Christmas card from Pierce from me, to bad-mouthing me in town. And I simply won't stand for it any more.'

'They say the war is having a terrible effect on wives being left at home. Here is a case in point. Clara, you are out of your pea-sized mind. I haven't a clue what you're talking about.'

Clara marched over to the bell pull and yanked it hard. A minute later Fennell arrived.

'Hardly a time to be ordering tea, whilst you are attempting to evict me,' said Prudence in her normal assured fashion.

'Fennell will back me up. Pierce, he will tell you everything she has done. Everything from emptying the car of petrol, leaving me stranded at night, to taking in my dresses to make me lose weight. To serving chicken all the time, which I detest. To pretending the hot-water system wasn't working when I wanted to have a bath... It's been a campaign of mental cruelty. Hasn't it, Fennell?'

'Lady Armstrong speaks the truth,' said Fennell.

Prudence viewed Fennell coolly. 'I always say you can't get the staff any more.'

'That will be all, Fennell,' said Pierce.

Fennell turned and left.

Pierce turned and looked at Prudence. 'Well?'

'Well, what can I say?' She spoke in a cheery non-concerned voice. 'Snared like a rabbit in a trap. Never rely on the discretion of servants or underestimate a woman, that's my advice to you.'

'Pity for you that you didn't advise yourself the same,' said Clara.

'You're such a snitch, Clara. I hate telling tales out of school. But then I didn't go to school, I was taught by a series of governesses here at the house.'

'I pity them with you as a charge.'

'Mama used to complain I went through them with alarming speed, in fairness. I was smarter than most of them. Anyway, my tricks are in the past, and I promise to behave in the future, scout's honour!' She put her hand on her heart.

'I'm afraid it's too late for that, Prudence,' said Pierce.

'Too late for what exactly?'

'I can't go back to the war front and leave you two at war here. I think it's time you moved on.'

'Moved on? To where exactly?' Prudence's face creased with horror.

'You can move to Hunter's Farm for now. Still run the estate if you care to.'

'Hunter's Farm! I will not leave my home. I was born and bred here and I'm not going down to that bloody farmhouse.'

'You have no choice,' said Clara, feeling elated.

'This house is every bit as much mine as it is yours, Pierce.'

'That's not what the deeds say.'

'I don't give a damn what the deeds say! I was the one who stayed here while you were off at school. I nursed Papa back after the shooting, and minded Mother when she became desolate and her nerves gave way. I oversaw this place as the estate was dismantled under government act after government act. You were too young, or away in that posh school, or had your head filled with air!'

'That's enough, Prudence!' snapped Clara.

'Damn you!' shouted Prudence. 'I never liked you, I don't mind telling you. I sent him to London to snare a fortune, and he came back with you. Useless, beyond compare. And now you want to exile me to Hunter's Farm!'

'It will do you good.' Pierce lit up his cigarette. 'You need to realise you are not the mistress of this house, and you need to start a new life outside that role. Perhaps you should consider Gregory Hamilton's wedding proposal. It's been hovering for long enough.'

'That old fool! Damned if I will!'

They sat in silence for a while.

'When am I to go?' Prudence looked down at the floor.

'Before I leave for the front again,' said Pierce.

'So soon?' Prudence smiled though her eyes were welling with tears. She stood up and began to walk to the door. She turned and said, 'I've never asked for anything in my life–'

'Then please don't start now,' Pierce cut in.

Prudence closed the door after her and Clara ran to Pierce and put her arms around him.

'I knew you would back me. I just knew it,' she

kissed him.

'Isn't it a husband's place to back his wife?'

'Of course, but, I knew you would anyway. Because you love me.'

He looked at her curiously.

Prudence came into the library where Pierce sat at the desk. She had her coat and gloves on.

'Well, I'm off to my exile. I've packed my bags. Fennell has kindly agreed to drive me down. Just to make sure I'm gone, I suppose.'

'Very well.' Pierce sat back and looked at her. 'You'll still run the farm and draw a salary. I've set it up with Conway. You'll have all the use of the estate and food from the kitchen.'

'You're making a terrible mistake, Pierce. Leaving her in charge.'

'If it is a terrible mistake, it's *my* terrible mistake. I think you've controlled here for long enough.'

'I always loved you. I did everything for you,' she said.

'I wonder.'

'Right, I'll be gone. Look after yourself over there ... war breaks most people, but with some it makes them. It's made you, Pierce, altered you and it's bringing you somewhere you would never have gone otherwise. Time will see if that's a good thing.'

Clara was sitting in the parlour when Prudence walked in and looked at her coldly.

'I'm off,' said Prudence.

'I believe Fennell is helping you move?'

360

'I think Fennell has done quite enough, don't you? Don't think you've got rid of me, Clara. I'm still running the estate and I'll be just down the road. Keeping a close eye on you for when you fail and I will personally throw you out of this house.'

Prudence turned and marched away.

That night Clara was in bed and she stirred and reached out for Pierce but the bed was empty. She sat up and saw him standing staring into the fire burning in the hearth.

'Darling, come back to bed,' she said.

He turned and looked at her. 'Tell me – what makes you so sure I love you?'

She smiled at him. 'Because you married me.'

'People can marry for many reasons, love not always being one of them.'

'But it was in this case.'

'Why do you think so?'

'Well, what other reason was there?' She pulled her knees up and hugged them as she smiled at him. 'I heard you speak to Prudence when I arrived here one day. She was asking how much money I was worth and you told her nothing. I know you went to London to marry a wealthy woman to secure all your futures. And I'm sure you could have married a wealthy woman. But you didn't ... you married *me*.'

'Maybe I just fancied you. Couldn't quench my lust for you.'

She smiled at him. 'I heard you tell Prudence you had your reasons for marrying me. What other reason could you possibly have but you loved me?'

'I see!' Pierce nodded to himself as if everything had fallen into place. He walked slowly to the bed and sat on the edge of it and took her hand.

'You see, Clara, I could let you continue to believe that, but it really wouldn't be fair. I married you really because everyone else wanted to marry you.'

'I don't understand.'

'You were this Clara Charter that everyone was talking about. You brushed everyone off and yet here you were ... falling at my feet. Ready to do anything I wanted. I just had to marry you, to get on everyone else's nerves.'

'Don't play games with me, Pierce.'

'I'm not.' He lowered his voice to a whisper. 'And then when everyone said you were to be married to Cosmo Wellesley, well, that was the icing on the cake. Cosmo who I despised from school. Cosmo who took everything I loved in school away from me. My position, my friends, my place. And here was I in a position to take what he loved away. Without even a fight.' He lifted up her hand and kissed it.

She pulled back her hand.

He went over to his dressing room and emerged a minute later holding a bundle of letters and threw them on the bed at her.

She picked them up and saw her own handwriting on the envelopes and, as she looked through them, she saw they were all her letters to Pierce at the front. They were all unopened, and she realised he hadn't even bothered to open and read them.

'Do you need any more evidence?' he asked.

Clara drove Pierce to the station in silence, staring ahead. She pulled up in front of the station and he got out and took his bag from the back.

A group of soldiers marched to the train singing, '*Pack up your troubles in your old kit-bag...*'

She made no move to leave the car.

'Aren't you going to come on to the platform to prolong the goodbye?' he asked.

'No.' She turned to look at him. 'I'll say goodbye here.'

'Cheerio then,' he said.

'Will you be back for Christmas?'

He looked at her condescendingly. 'It's not boarding school, Clara.'

He turned and walked to the train.

When Clara got back to the house she sat staring at her unopened letters to Pierce for ages. Then she took them and went down to the guest bedroom and took up the floorboard that she had put her other letters under. She threw her letters to Pierce down with the rest of them and fixed the floorboard, covering it with a rug. She had thought about burning them, but decided she needed them in case she ever needed reminding of her feelings about Pierce.

72

The snowfall was coming to an end, leaving a thick coat across the entire countryside. Clara was stretched out on the couch in the parlour, a thick blanket over her, the fire roaring in the fireplace. She lay gazing out the window at the snow falling onto the white countryside and the lake. She reached forward for her sherry glass and finished the drink.

The doorbell rang and a minute later Fennell came in.

'Excuse me, ma'am, Johnny Seymour is here,' he said, looking a little concerned.

'Johnny Seymour!' She was shocked.

'Hello there!' said Johnny, walking into the room past Fennell. 'Thank you, Fennell. We'll let you know when we want tea.' He ushered the manservant out of the room and closed the door.

She sat up quickly. 'Johnny! How did you get here? I didn't hear any car.'

'I'm afraid I have another driving ban. This very nice fellow gave me a ride. He had converted his carriage into a sleigh. Very innovative. *Hmmm,* sherry, just what I need on a day like today.' He went over to the decanter on the round table beside her and poured himself a large glass.

'What are you doing here?' she asked.

'I've come to do work on that damned portrait I'm commissioned for. I've left lots of messages for you and you haven't got back once.'

'I know. I'm sorry. I've had a lot on my mind.'

He stood studying her. 'I can see that. You look awful!'

'Thanks! You know how to make a girl feel good about herself.'

'Well, I'm just saying. We don't want to capture you for posterity looking like shit, do we?'

'It's all about that bloody painting with you, isn't it?' She was annoyed.

He sat down on the armchair opposite her and crossed his legs, looking at her as she lay there, half covered by the blanket. 'Are you ill?'

'No.'

He looked concerned. 'Not bad news from the front?'

'No,' she sighed. 'No news from the front at all! As per usual.'

'Good then! We can get to work this afternoon.'

'No, I don't want to, Johnny. I don't want to continue with the portrait. You'll get your commission of course.'

'Not continue with the portrait! Out of the question.'

'And I don't want to argue about it. I've too much on my mind.'

'Has Prudence been a bitch to you?'

'No... We sent her to live at Hunter's Farm for bad behaviour.'

Johnny roared with the laughter. 'Best place for her.'

'So we can't continue with the portrait as we'd be unchaperoned in the house.'

'We won't be unchaperoned. You've a household of servants here.'

'Half a household. The other half is off getting killed in France.' She leaned forward and filled her glass with sherry from the decanter.

'Looks like you've been drinking a lot of that.'

'Why shouldn't I? Sherry– "Mother's Ruin", as we used to say.'

'Whatever would London society say? Clara Charter, of the Charter Chocolate family, belle of the ball 1910, 1911, 1912 and 1913!'

She viewed him suspiciously. 'You forgot 1909, I was a debutante for five years in total. Longest ever, or so I've been told. You've been doing your homework on me.'

'Just made a few enquiries, that's all.'

She sighed and gulped down her drink. 'Charter Chocolates! Anyway, liqueurs were always my favourite chocolate. And London society has a lot more to concern itself about now than my marital status. I'm just a distant memory there.' She gazed into her drink. 'The only person concerned about my marital status now is – me!'

He leaned forward with a smile on his face. 'Trouble in paradise?'

She put down her glass and sighed. 'I'll get Mrs Fennell to fix you something to eat, and Fennell can drop you back to your house or the station if you want to head back to Dublin.'

'*Pah!* Dublin! It'll take a long time to rebuild. You know, I couldn't find one city-centre venue still standing for my exhibition after the Easter Rising.'

'Is that all you care about?' She was suddenly crying.

He got up quickly and sat beside her. 'What's wrong?' he said, taking her hand. 'Tell me!'

'I can't tell you, I can't tell anybody!' She pulled back her hand, threw off the blanket, got up quickly and went to stand beside the fireplace.

'I'm a good listener, and it looks like you can't confide in anyone else.'

'I don't even know you, not really.'

'Yes, you do. We're old friends, well, in my dictionary definition we are.'

She started pacing quickly up and down. 'I think I've made the most terrible mistake with my life... I now realise I should never have married Pierce... I loved him so much I didn't care how he felt about me. Or I deceived myself he loved me. That he just wasn't very demonstrative. But now I know he has no feelings for me. None at all. I'm not even a nuisance to him. He just doesn't care.' She stopped pacing and put her hands to her face. 'And now I'm trapped.' Her voice cracked. 'Utterly trapped. I can't leave the marriage or this house. I'd be ruined. Utterly ruined and it would destroy my family. I have to put up with it. And then this terrible war and so many of my friends being killed. I can hardly believe it. All the people we used to party with and have friendships with suddenly disappearing, not even a funeral to give them. I remember an acquaintance of my father was once killed by an automobile. We were all shocked by it, talked about it for months. And now friends are being picked off like that children's song "Ten Green Bottles". What has happened to the world? To me?'

She started to cry. He got up quickly and came

to her and put his arms around her, holding her tightly. He swayed her slightly as he soothed her. 'It's all right. Let it go. Have a good cry, you need one.'

She dissolved into his embrace and started to heave with sobs, the comfort of a caring person letting her emotions flood out.

Eventually her sobs dissipated as she rested her head against him. She gently pulled back.

He smiled at her, took out his handkerchief and wiped her face. 'Don't worry – it's a clean one,' he said.

'I'm sorry. I hope the servants haven't heard me.'

He laughed. 'Who cares if they have?'

'I do!' She pulled away from him. 'I apologise. I've just been a bit emotional, as you can imagine.'

'Indeed I can. Where did you spend Christmas?'

'Here on my own. Pierce, of course, didn't get back. And I was too miserable to travel to London. I didn't even have Prudence – she went off to cousins in Dublin.'

'So you stayed here feeling sorry for yourself?'

'There certainly wasn't much to celebrate.' She sat down.

'Well, there might be now.' He smiled and sat beside her. 'I showed your work to several art critics in Dublin.'

'What are you talking about?'

'I nabbed some of your paintings from the library and showed them to a few people. They were very impressed, as I was. So much so, we decided to include you in my exhibition.'

She glared at him. 'Johnny, you had no right to show those to anybody. Or take them! It's stealing!'

'Borrowing, I would prefer to say.'

'Well, you can tell your gallery I won't be included in your damned exhibition or anything else.'

'Clara.' He grabbed her hand. 'Do you know what this means? There's so many artists would kill for this opportunity. And you're being handed it.'

'Well, give it to them then!' She stood up and began to pace again. 'Exhibition indeed! That's my private work for my own enjoyment, not to be gawped at by strangers.'

He sat back, looking bored. 'You're fooling nobody with this act incidentally. Pretending you don't want it.'

'Of course I don't want it! Even if I did, I couldn't. Lady Armstrong in an art exhibition while her husband fights the Germans! I'd be the talk of the place.'

She turned around, went to the window and looked out at the snow.

He got up and stood behind her very close.

'This same husband who doesn't love you?'

'That's irrelevant. I still have my position and reputation to consider.'

'It would mean you being up in Dublin a whole week.'

'Unthinkable.'

'You'd get to go to the theatre every night.'

'Ridiculous.'

'And eat out in fancy restaurants, well, the ones that weren't blown up in the Rising.'

'In times of war! Such bad taste.'

'And of course meet all the literati.'

'I'm overseeing a series of sale works for the war effort in the town hall, I couldn't spare the time.'

'It's only a week... Oh and the exhibition will probably be attended by people like WB Yeats.'

There was a silence.

'When did you say the exhibition was due?'

Johnny was such a force that he took over, and marched Clara back to posing for the portrait. She sat there while he painted her, trying not to laugh when he made jokes, trying not to cry when she thought of Pierce. He was continually going back up to Dublin to organise the exhibition and she began to dread those absences when he was away, as she slipped back into her unhappy life.

'Everything's ready,' beamed Johnny in the early summer. 'Are you?'

And then she found herself on a train, going with him to Dublin.

'I'll never understand how you talked me into this,' she said, looking at him accusingly.

He smirked at her. 'With surprising ease.'

73

Clara booked into the Shelbourne Hotel and had barely time to unpack and change when reception rang up and said Johnny was waiting for her in the foyer. Assuming he planned to go for dinner and might want to go out, she hurriedly got ready and went down to meet him.

'I only left you an hour ago!' she said.

'I know, but the play starts in half an hour,' he said, taking her arm and propelling her to the doorway.

'Play? What play?'

'We're off to see a play this evening, didn't I tell you?'

'No, you didn't. I'd planned to have an early night after all the travel.'

'Early night, *pah!*' he dismissed as he pushed her through the revolving doors and out to the waiting cab.

Clara had nearly forgotten what it was like to be in a theatre as she took her seat in The Gaiety. Looking around at the glamorous crowd, she cursed Johnny for rushing her out of her hotel in her comparatively plain attire.

'Hello, Johnny!' called a man waving from across the aisle.

Johnny waved back.

'Johnny, you're back! Good to see you!' said a

woman turning around from a few rows down.

'You seem to be quite well known,' said Clara.

'Of course I am.' He looked around the theatre. 'They're all wondering who you are. Wondering if we are lovers.'

Clara looked at him, shocked. 'Johnny!'

'I'm only saying what they're thinking.'

'Well, don't! You'll make me feel guilty.'

'Sorry – couldn't have that!' He smiled at her.

Soon the curtain rose. Countess Alice Kavinsky was the lead and Clara had to admit she found her performance in *The Taming of the Shrew* mesmerising.

Afterwards, when they were in the crowded foyer, Alice shouted over to them, 'Johnny, we're all going to Jammet's. See you there!'

Clara enjoyed every minute of her time in Dublin. But there was a feverish atmosphere there as the city was still being rebuilt after the Rising. It had been under martial law during the Rising and there was so much resentment that it felt to Clara like a furnace about to explode. Johnny had a huge list of things for her to do and he rushed her from event to event. One minute she was having lunch in one of Dublin's fine hotels with the intelligentsia, the next she was attending a political talk in a draughty hall.

Clara and Johnny were in a taxi cab back to Johnny's Dublin flat.

'It's like I've never heard people talk like that before,' she was saying. 'Not with such passion and vigour. I mean, before I married, before the war, all we talked about was which party to go to and how much everyone was worth. And after I got married, well, my husband's set seemed only to care about country pursuits.'

'And how does Dublin make you feel?'

'It makes me feel alive.'

He smiled at her as he studied her face.

Johnny's home in Dublin was a top-floor flat in Leeson Street in Dublin. The cab left them off outside and they climbed the steps to the front door and made their way up the stairs to his flat.

The flat was large and doubled as a studio.

He made her a cup of coffee and handed it to her.

'They make it all sound so exciting,' she said. 'That anything is possible. When I was beginning to think that nothing was possible.'

'The world can emerge from this war better than before. And this country can have a glorious future ahead of it.'

'Well, my time in Dublin has been wonderful. It was lovely to see and experience your world.'

'It can be your world as well.'

'No, it can't. Next week I will go home to my house and wait for my husband to return from war and then continue with our marriage and our life in whatever way it takes shape.' She looked into her coffee sadly.

He walked over to her and sat beside her. Taking the cup from her, he put it on the floor.

'You don't have to do that, Clara,' he said. He reached forward and put his lips on her mouth.

She pulled back quickly and stood up, shocked. 'I'd better go.'

'I've offended you.'

'No – it's just... I can't.'

He stood up and held her shoulders. 'I thought there was something between us?'

'I'm married, Johnny.'

'Unhappily.'

'I've made my decision.'

'People divorce all the time!'

'In your world, not in mine. I'm not one of your intellectual friends. I'm a woman who was brought up to fulfil a role. And the role I chose was Lady Armstrong.'

He grabbed her and kissed her again. 'Tell me you don't feel the same. That you don't have feelings.'

She pushed him aside. 'I'll see you at the exhibition tonight.'

She walked quickly from the room.

'I won't give up trying!' he shouted after her.

The gallery was full of people for the exhibition. She nearly hadn't gone, nervous of seeing Johnny again, scared of what he was beginning to mean to her. She wasn't stupid – she had felt the chemistry between them. So different from the relationship she had with Pierce. She had wondered would it be awkward for them that night, but he took control and with his forceful and jovial personality made sure she was comfortable.

She was one of a small select group of artists being exhibited and as she made her way through the gallery she was infused with a sense of pride to see her paintings hanging on the wall, her painting of Mrs Fennell at work in the kitchen being her main exhibit.

'It's getting a very positive reaction,' said Johnny.

'Really?' Clara was overjoyed.

'The critic from *The Times* said you were most promising.'

'Story of my life!' She smiled cynically at him.

He laughed and, taking her by the arm, led her around to introduce her to people.

Countess Alice sidled up beside her. 'I have to say I love your paintings.'

'Oh thank you!'

'I love the concept of it all. Lady Armstrong drawing her cook slaving in the kitchen for her.'

'It's not meant like that!' Clara said, shocked.

Alice was studying her intently. 'So you're Johnny's new muse. Let me take a good look at you... Yes, my memory serves me right – you are very beautiful, my dear.' She leaned closer to her. 'Have you slept with him yet?'

Clara's face clouded with concern. 'How dare you say such a thing!'

'I'll take that as a no then? Which explains why he is still so attentive to you. The problem with Johnny is, once he sleeps with you he tends to move on to his next muse.' Alice looked smug as she put her hand to her chest. 'I should know! I'm one of his conquests.'

Clara's eyes widened in horror, causing Alice to laugh nastily.

'Oh Clara! You poor thing! Did you think you might be special to him?' She laughed again. 'You're just his latest muse. As soon as he's finished your portrait and bedded you, he'll be off to his next well-heeled beauty. It's funny that for all his socialist talk, he only ever shares his bed with aristocrats. A case of "do as I say, rather than do as I do", I imagine.'

'Excuse me, please,' said Clara as she moved away from her.

Clara walked through the crowd quickly and suddenly felt an arm around her waist.

'There you are!' said Johnny. 'Come on. I need to introduce you to a critic.'

Back in her hotel room Clara rang down to reception.

'It's Lady Armstrong here. Please book me a cab for the train station first thing in the morning.'

Johnny bounded up the steps of the Shelbourne with a bouquet of flowers in one hand and a copy of *The Times* with a review of Clara's paintings in the other.

'Could you ring up to Clara Armstrong and tell her Johnny Seymour awaits her,' he said to man behind the reception with a big grin.

'I'm afraid Lady Armstrong left the hotel for the train station early this morning,' answered the receptionist.

'*What?* Did she leave any message?'

'No message,' said the man as he continued with his work.

Johnny turned away crestfallen and walked out, still holding the flowers and the newspaper.

74

Clara stood in the ballroom of the house looking at the unfinished portrait on the easel.

'You stupid woman!' she said to the image of herself on the canvas. 'Stupid, stupid woman!' She covered the painting with a sheet and went out into the hallway where she passed Fennell holding a tray with a teapot on it.

'Fennell, the portrait of me in the ballroom. Put it away somewhere, will you? An attic or somewhere out of the way.'

'Very good, ma'am. Mr Seymour will not be returning to finish the portrait?'

'No, Mr Seymour will not.'

And Johnny, who had obviously got the message, was staying clear.

As Clara drove through the little village she decided to stop and go into the church. She pulled up outside and walked through the summer sunshine into the small building. She was surprised to see Emily Foxe there at the top aisle, head down. She walked up to her.

'Emily?' she asked.

When Emily looked up, Clara got a fright to see her face white and her eyes red from heavy crying.

'What is it, Emily?' Clara asked, sitting quickly beside her and putting an arm around her.

'It's Felix. He was killed in that last ... battle,' she just managed to say the word.

'Oh no, Emily!' Clara pulled her close and hugged her tightly as she dissolved in tears. As she held the sobbing woman she thought of young Felix's innocent face, good nature and endearing stammer.

That night Clara was awoken by a loud bang. She sat up quickly in her bed. A minute later there was another bang and she realised it was a stone being thrown at her window. She jumped out of bed and hurried to the window, looking down at the forecourt below. She couldn't see anything, so she opened the window and peered nervously out.

'Clara!' said a voice from the shadows.

'Who is it?' she demanded.

'It's Johnny!'

'Johnny! What do you want at this hour?'

'I need to see you. Come to the front door and don't alert the servants.'

'I will not! This is ridiculous!'

'*Please!* It's an emergency.'

Clara hesitated and then quickly closed the window. She wrapped her silk dressing gown around her and left the room, hurrying down the stairs and across the hall to the front door which she unlocked and unbolted.

Johnny was standing there with his poet friend Thomas Geraghty beside him, Johnny propping him up.

'What in God's name is going on?' demanded Clara.

Johnny pushed past her and half-carried Thomas

across the hall and through into the drawing room.

Clara shut the front door and followed them quickly. Closing the drawing-room door behind her and turning on the light, she demanded again, 'What are you doing here?'

Johnny carefully placed his friend down on a chair and it was only then that she realised Thomas was wounded.

'What happened to him?' she asked, rushing over and looking at him.

Johnny said nothing but carefully pulled back Thomas's coat and Clara gasped as she saw the bloodstained shirt.

'He's been shot,' said Johnny.

'*Shot!*' Clara nearly screamed.

'It's okay. He's over the worst. We got him to a doctor who fixed him up and bandaged the wound.'

'But Johnny, he needs to go straight to a hospital.'

Johnny turned around and faced her. 'He can't go to a hospital, because he would be arrested, tried for treason and then shot again for good.'

Clara knelt down beside Thomas as realisation dawned on her. 'He was in the Rising?'

Johnny nodded. 'He managed to escape but they are looking for him everywhere. He was hiding in Longford, but they got wind of where he was. He managed to escape but they shot him in the process.'

Just then they heard a door open and close in the hallway.

'It's someone coming out of the servants'

quarters! Probably Fennell!' said Clara, panicked.

'Get rid of him!' ordered Johnny.

'If I don't say something now, I'll be an accessory.'

'If you say something now, you're condemning him to death. Do you want that?'

Clara looked down at Thomas, then dashed to the door and went into the hallway.

It was Fennell in his dressing gown, looking alarmed. Only then did it occur to Clara that he might have looked out of one of the attic windows and seen the two men.

'My lady! Is everything all right? I thought I heard somebody outside – some noises.'

'No, no, Fennell. It's just me. I couldn't sleep so needed a drink of sherry to help me on my way!' She smiled at him.

'I see.' Fennell still looked puzzled.

'Oh, I opened my window to get some air and slammed it shut – that might have woken you,' Clara improvised.

His face cleared. 'Aah, yes – that was it. Very well, my lady. But let me make you some hot milk – it may be more advisable.'

'Not at all. I'm happy with my sherry. You toddle back to bed.'

Fennell nodded and retreated back to the servants' quarters.

Clara waited until he was well gone, then returned to the drawing room and closed the door, locking it behind her.

'He heard you throwing the stones,' she said, 'but I told him it was me shutting my window.'

Johnny was pouring himself a large glass of

whiskey. 'Want one?'

She nodded and walked quickly over to him.

She kept her voice low so Thomas couldn't hear, though in fact he seemed to be only semi-conscious now, presumably from medication the doctor had given him.

'What on earth did you bring him here for?' she muttered angrily, grabbing the whiskey glass from him and taking a gulp.

'I couldn't think of anywhere safe to hide him,' said Johnny.

'How about your own house?' she snapped.

'It wouldn't be safe. They're searching all the houses in the area looking for him. My place will definitely be searched because of all the political people I know.'

'And what makes you so sure this house won't be?' she asked, half-panicked, half-incredulous.

'They'll never search here. Lord and Lady Armstrong's house? And your husband a high-ranking officer in the army?'

'You have it all thought out!' She was amazed and angry. 'You've put me in a terrible position, Johnny! You're asking me to harbour a criminal.'

'A freedom fighter.'

'I don't care what you call him! He's illegal and he's in my drawing room, in my house.'

Johnny went over to the front windows and looked out from behind the curtains.

'It's only for a couple of days until we can arrange for him to be transported down to the south. They'll never find him there.'

She hurried over to him. 'And where do you propose I hide him? Don't you think Fennell and the other servants will see him?'

'We'll put him up in one of the guest bedrooms and lock the door. They'll never know he's there.'

'No, Johnny! You have to leave immediately and take him with you. Take him to the south tonight.'

'I can't – there are too many road blocks.'

'Well, I don't care where you take him as long as it's nothing to do with me. He can't stay here. I'm sorry.' She turned and folded her arms.

'In that case you're sentencing him to death. He won't survive without your protection for a couple of days.'

She looked over at Thomas who was now asleep and thought of Felix Foxe and all the others who had been killed.

'All right, two days but no more. He has to be gone by then, do you understand me?'

Johnny smiled down at her and nodded.

75

For the next couple of days Clara's nerves were fraught. Her main concern was not alerting the servants' suspicions. She had breakfast delivered to her room in the morning, which she promptly brought down the corridors to the far end of the house where Thomas was hiding and brought whatever food she could to him at night. There was a real risk a servant might hear him move around or cough or moan from pain in his sleep.

'How are you today?' she asked on the third day as she brought in the silver tray of food to him.

He was at the window, peeping out from behind a curtain.

'Has the army been round?' he asked.

'Nobody has been round.'

'Johnny told you what to say to them if they come?'

'Yes,' she sighed. 'He's versed me well.'

'Good.'

Thomas came over to the small table she had put the food on and sat down, looking at her.

'I never thought when I met you before I'd owe you my life,' he said as he started to eat.

'Neither did I, I assure you.'

He nodded. 'Thank you.'

'There's no need to thank me. I was put in a hopeless situation where I was told your life was in my hands. I couldn't have your death on my conscience. But I don't approve of what you've done and I'll never forgive Johnny for putting me in this situation.' She sat down on the bed.

Thomas drank his coffee and smiled at her. 'Yes, you will. Everyone always forgives Johnny in the end.'

'I think you'll find his charms will be lost on me.'

'Too bad. That'll devastate him. He thinks very highly of you, you know. He has a soft spot for you.'

'I'm sure he has a soft spot for many.'

'A soft spot for many, but he's in love with you,' Thomas said matter of factly.

Clara went bright red and she stood up. 'I think

you're forgetting yourself, Mr Geraghty. Just because I've been forced to hide you gives you no permission to speak impertinently to me.' She walked towards the door. 'I'll be back for the tray shortly.'

She stepped out and closed the door after her, locking it. She walked quickly down the corridor, but suddenly stopped and leaned against the wall, Thomas's words whirling around her head.

'Mr Seymour here to see you, ma'am,' said Fennell.

She tried to look mildly surprised. 'Mr Seymour? Oh, show him in, Fennell.'

A few seconds later Johnny came bounding into the drawing room, followed by Fennell.

'My dear Lady Armstrong!' He bent down, kissing her on the cheek.

'Mr Seymour, to what do we owe the pleasure?'

'I'm afraid I've been neglecting my duties, Lady Armstrong,' he said in a loud jovial voice.

'How so?' Clara smiled back at him but her eyes were venomous.

'The portrait, Lady Armstrong, the portrait! I've come back to finish it.'

'How thoughtful of you, Mr Seymour. We'd given up hope of it ever been finished and we have exiled it to–' She looked at Fennell, 'Where exactly have we put the unfinished portrait, Fennell?'

'In the pantry, my lady.'

'The pantry!' Johnny exclaimed in mock horror.

'There you have it, Mr Seymour. All art finds its correct resting place, and yours has found its own – in the pantry.'

'Shall I fetch the portrait, my lady?' enquired Fennell.

'No, thank you, Fennell,' said Clara.

'By all means, Fennell,' exclaimed Johnny. 'And perhaps tea while you're at it.'

'Will I place it on the easel in the ballroom where it was before?' asked Fennell.

'What would we do without you, Fennell?' said Johnny with a wink at Clara.

Fennell nodded and left the room, closing the door.

'So now my servants obey you rather than me!' said Clara.

Johnny came and sat down quickly beside her. 'How is he?'

'Recovering and resting. And anxious to be gone as much as I am anxious for him to be gone.'

'The arrangements are made for tomorrow night. Bring him out through the French windows to the side of the house at two in the morning when the servants are safely out of the way.'

Clara sat on the chair, posing as Johnny painted.

'Well, if anything good has come out of this it's brought me back to finish your portrait. I thought when you walked out of the Shelbourne without saying goodbye I wouldn't see you again.'

'I had decided I wouldn't see you again, apart from events like tea or tennis parties that you deigned to come to while in these parts.'

'And why, may I ask, did you leave without saying goodbye?'

'Because I do not like being made a fool of.'

'And how was I making a fool of you?' Johnny

continued to paint and his voice remained calm.

'By playing with me.'

'What?'

'Come off it, Johnny. I'm wise to you now. You're a bed-hopping bastard with a short attention-span who thought it would be amusing to bed a colonel's neglected wife while he was off at the front.'

'Whatever gave you that impression?' He looked over at her, shocked.

'I heard about your reputation.'

'From whom?'

'It doesn't matter.'

'Well, I think that's very unfair, I really do.'

'And if all that wasn't bad enough, you arrive on my doorstep with a rebel, putting me in danger. I really never want to see you again after this.'

'You don't mean that.'

'Oh yes, I do!'

'What about the portrait?'

'To hell with the portrait! You've never been honest with me. At least I know where I am with Pierce, even if I don't like it. But you! You never even hinted to me you were a revolutionary.'

'I'm not a revolutionary. I've strong links with them, but that's where it stops.'

'And if you're not a revolutionary, why do I have a wanted man hiding upstairs in a guest bedroom?'

'I'm linked with them politically. I'm a politician.'

'Ha!' Clara laughed dismissively. 'What kind of country are you aiming to build with poets pretending to be revolutionaries and painters masquerading as politicians?'

'A better one than the one we are in now where youngsters get used as cannon fodder and farmers masquerade as officers.'

'An insult to my husband, no doubt.'

Johnny shouted, 'Yes, your husband! In your sham of a marriage!'

'Well, it certainly would be a sham if I continued seeing you. Tell me, when you had your affair with Countess Kavinsky was the Count already dead? But then, a little matter like that does not concern you, does it?'

'So it was Alice who opened her big mouth?'

'Why, how many others could have opened theirs? Count Kavinsky, he killed himself, didn't he? Were you the cause of it?'

Johnny glared at her, threw down his paints and then stormed over to one of the French windows and stood there staring out at the gardens.

She sighed and walked over to him.

'I'm sorry.' Her voice became gentle. 'Did he kill himself over your affair with Alice?'

'It was gambling debts that finished him off, everyone said it,' Johnny said quietly.

'I'm sure it was.'

He turned. 'We used to be friends – how did we end up hurting each other like this?'

'Because I'm not like you, Johnny. You want me to live the life that you do. And I can't. I can't flit around like you, not worrying about conventions.'

He reached forward and grabbed her, forcing his mouth down on hers.

'You're not like the others. I've fallen for you.'

She pushed him away and walked into the

centre of the room.

'And how do you propose we make it work? Snatched meetings wherever we can?'

'You could leave him.'

'Don't be ridiculous. I'd be ruined.'

Fennell walked into the room.

'Pardon me, my lady, will Mr Seymour be staying for dinner?'

'No, Fennell, Mr Seymour will be leaving now.'

When Fennell had left she said, 'I'll bring Geraghty to the french windows at two tomorrow night. You can take him from there.'

Clara unlocked the french windows and they went outside.

Johnny and two other men appeared from the shadows.

'Quickly, let's go!' said one of the men and, supporting Geraghty, they started to move quickly across the lawns. Johnny stood there, staring at Clara.

'Seymour, will you come on!' called one of the men softly.

'Will I stay or do you want me to go?' he asked.

'Stay,' she said quietly.

He turned around and called softly, 'You go on! You don't need me from here. Good luck.'

They stepped inside.

He closed the french windows, drew the curtains and slowly walked towards her.

'Are you sure?' he asked quietly as he put his arms around her.

'No,' she whispered back as she reached forward to kiss him.

76

Clara stirred in her sleep and woke. She saw Johnny sleeping beside her. She looked at the clock on the bedroom wall and saw it was seven in the morning.

She gently woke him.

He opened his eyes.

'You'd better go – the servants will be up and about already,' she said.

He smiled at her. 'Do they come in here unannounced?'

'No.'

'Then to hell with them!' He reached out for her. 'I can just sneak downstairs to the ballroom in a while and say I just arrived to paint.'

'Johnny, you enjoy taking risks far too much.'

'That's what life is for.'

She suddenly started laughing.

'What's funny?'

'I'm just thinking of what my grandmother would say if she knew.'

They spent nearly every day together, some time with her posing for him, the rest going for long walks through the woods or down to the lake, or driving out to the sea.

As they walked along the lake one evening, his arm around her, she said, 'I don't know what I was looking for. I was running around London like a mad thing, searching frantically for something. I thought I found it when I met Pierce. I thought it was a blinding love that would fulfil me.'

'I wish I met you first, before you met him.'

She smiled at him 'Why – do you think we would have married and lived happily ever after?'

'Maybe.'

'It was hard enough to get my family to accept Lord Armstrong, let alone an artist with dubious connections,' she said, smiling mockingly at him.

'You had the world at your feet before you married. You could have had it all if you had made other choices.'

'I don't think the world would have satisfied me... What about you? Is that all you want from life? Flitting between women like Dors, Countess Alice and me? A series of sheath-protected relationships.'

'Excuse me! I want to be a world-renowned artist and have a revolution!'

'But for yourself? For your personal life, don't you want something solid, long-lasting?'

'I never thought along those lines. I thought life was for enjoying and taking what you wanted. Until now.'

They had to be very careful not to arouse the servants' suspicions. Luckily there were few left in the house since the war started and the Fennells were very early-to-bed people.

'Goodnight, Fennell,' said Johnny happily as he threw on his hat and Fennell opened the front door of the house for him.

'Goodnight, Mr Johnny, and have a good one.'

'Oh, I will!'

The door was closed after Johnny and he paused and lit a cigarette before walking down the steps and along the forecourt, then making his way to the terrace at the side of the house where he knocked on the french windows. A few seconds later Clara opened the windows and he stepped inside and into her arms.

She had begun to sketch and paint under his supervision.

She had spent the afternoon painting the view down by the lake as he sat reading. After an hour he rose and came to check her work.

'Oh Clara!' he said. 'That's not good.'

She was taken aback by the insult. 'In your opinion, and I haven't asked for it.'

He reached forward, took the painting and tore it in half.

'Johnny!' she shouted angrily. 'That was mine and you had no right!'

'I had every right – it's bad!'

She turned and stormed away from him. He ran and caught up with her and grabbed her.

'Let me go, Johnny! I'm sick of you.'

He looked at her and smiled. 'You don't understand. You could be a great artist, the talent is there. But you need to know the difference between good and bad work, and you don't yet. That was bad, and you can do much better.'

Clara made journeys up to Dublin and would stay with Johnny in his flat there. She got to know all his friends and she found them exciting and full of fun and yet so political and dedicated to their beliefs. She felt she was part of something big and exciting. And they seemed to accept her without questioning. They didn't seem curious or concerned about her relationship with Johnny. She thought some of them must guess they were lovers, but they never made her feel awkward or even seemed to care. The crowd would often come down to the west and she began to invite them to stay at the house. It was a perfect disguise to excuse why Johnny was staying there.

She sat beside Johnny in front of the fire in the drawing room as a group of about twenty sat debating furiously about Irish independence.

Clara suddenly giggled.

'Stop it!' chastised Johnny, trying to look annoyed but smiling. 'You're supposed to be taking this seriously.'

'I am!' she whispered back.

'So why are you laughing?'

'I'm just thinking this room was never designed to be a talking salon for Irish republicanism!'

77

Prudence called up to the house to discuss the running of the farm as they moved into winter. Clara found Prudence's talk of farming tiresome and could hardly concentrate as she went on about the price of animal feed.

'Am I boring you?' asked Prudence eventually,

noting the glazed look that had come over Clara's eyes.

'No – it's just that Pierce left you to run the farm, so do you need me to sanction every little detail?'

Prudence snapped her ledger shut. 'In other words, yes – I am boring you. I suppose you'd much prefer to be off gallivanting with Johnny Seymour's set than listening to me.'

'Am I not allowed friends?'

'Oh, I'm sure it doesn't matter what I think one way or another around here any more. I don't know what Pierce will think about it all when he returns from the war. The company you keep is quite shocking.'

'I'm sure Pierce will think as he always has when it concerns me – nothing.'

As Christmas 1917 approached Clara gave all the servants two weeks off to go to stay with their families.

'Are you sure, Lady Armstrong?' Fennell said as he watched Clara decorate the Christmas tree happily in the drawing room.

'Quite sure, Fennell.'

'But you'll be here on your own. It's highly unusual. How will you feed yourself?'

'Oh, I'm a big girl now, Fennell, I'm sure I can manage.'

'But you will be going into the kitchen?' Fennell was incredulous.

'Fennell, with all my friends and Lord Armstrong spending Christmas in the trenches I'm sure I can put up with venturing into the kitchen to put a bit of cold turkey on a plate, don't you?'

Later, the Fennells looked at each other in amazement in the kitchen.

'I'm very fond of her, but she's highly unusual. That's what she said – that she'll make do herself over Christmas,' he said.

'It's all those new-fangled ideas she's picked up since she's been hanging around Johnny Seymour's set.' Mrs Fennell sighed heavily as she looked at the front of the newspaper whose headlines were mass killings in battles in France and Republican attacks on British army barracks in Ireland. 'The world is turning upside down, I can tell you that.'

With Prudence gone to Dublin to spend Christmas with cousins, Clara waited anxiously for Johnny to arrive on Christmas Eve. As he drove up to the front door she ran out to greet him.

'Two whole weeks,' he shouted as he hugged her tightly and they went in and closed the door behind them.

They lay out on the floor in front of the crackling fire, the candles on the Christmas tree twinkling.

'It's so strange just the two of us here, cut off from the world. This house wasn't meant for this. It was meant to be filled with people and servants.'

Johnny drew from his cigarette. 'Not just for a wife and her lover?' He handed her the cigarette and she smoked it.

'I often look up at those portraits of Pierce's ancestors looking down at me, judging me for what we're doing.'

'Can you judge happiness?'

'Many do.'

'Then let them.'

'We don't have a right to be this happy when so many people are suffering on the front... It will be 1918 next week. Will this war ever end?'

'I don't want to think about that.'

'Why?'

'Because Pierce will be coming home,' he said.

He leaned across and took a wrapped present from under the Christmas tree.

'Open this now,' he said.

She unwrapped the prettily wrapped parcel and found a little box. She opened it and saw a glittering brooch inside, an elaborate cluster of rhinestones.

'It's only costume jewellery, but I had it especially made for you by the costume department in the Gaiety theatre,' he said, pinning it to her dress.

'I love it,' she said as she held it tightly.

Clara stood at the open window of the bedroom. Johnny was still asleep. Snow had piled up high on the window ledge and the whole countryside was covered in it as far as she could see. It had begun to snow heavily again and it blew into the room, melting as soon as it touched the warm floorboards inside. She imagined there would be snow in France where Pierce was as well. And as she looked at the sleeping form of Johnny, she wondered how it had all come to this.

The next few days passed quickly in their own

little world. The heavy snow stayed and they wrapped up and went walking for miles along the lakeshore and through the countryside.

Johnny stepped back from the painting and said nothing for a while before looking over at Clara and declaring, 'It's finished.'

She came over and stood beside him as she looked at the canvas.

The painting was brilliant with colour, and was a close-up image of her sitting staring dreamily towards the viewer, her facial expression an unusual combination of hope and disappointment.

'Johnny – that's not me. You've let your feelings for me get in the way of your work. I don't look that good.'

He put his arms around her. 'It doesn't even do you justice.'

78

It was the spring and Prudence came marching through the front door carrying a stack of papers.

'Hello! Clara?' she shouted out. There was no response and she marched through the hall. 'Fennell?'

She walked to the back of the main stairs and through the door that led down to the servants' work quarters. She walked in to see Fennell sitting reading the newspaper at the fire and Mrs Fennell having a cup of tea.

'Well, I see this place has gone to pot since I left,' said Prudence as Fennell stood up quickly and put down the newspaper.

'Where's Clara?' demanded Prudence.

'Em – she has gone to the town to get some new paintbrushes with Mr Seymour.'

Prudence raised her eyes to heaven. 'Have they still not finished that damned painting? The Mona Lisa took half the time, I'm sure.'

'Mr Seymour seems to be a great perfectionist,' said Fennell.

'My arse!' She sighed loudly. 'When her ladyship gets back, tell her I need this paperwork signed by her urgently for the running of the farm. I'll leave it on the desk in the library.'

She gave them both a condescending look and turned and walked out. She was about to go into the library when she paused in thought and then crossed over to the doors leading into the ballroom. She went in and saw the large stand holding the canvas covered by a sheet. She walked over to it and pulled off the sheet and stared at the finished painting.

79

It was a Saturday night in April and a gang of Johnny's friends were down staying at the house. There was a great buzz because an American friend of his who was a Hollywood director called Paul Tierney was over from the States visiting and was staying as well. He had brought his latest movie with him and a screen and projector to show it.

'I'm just fascinated by all this movie stuff,' Clara said as Fennell put out the chairs in the ballroom for the guests to sit and Johnny and Paul Tierney set up the screen and the projector. 'I loved the theatre, but this is even more exciting.' Everyone took their seats.

'I'm going to show you a show reel from the war front first,' Paul informed them as the lights were turned off and the moving pictures began to flicker on the screen.

Clara sat at the front with Johnny and watched, fascinated at the black-and-white images of the soldiers in the front.

'Oh, Johnny, look at them. I could only imagine what it might be like from reading my friends' letters, but here it's like we're with them.'

Johnny looked at Clara's sad face. 'Come on, Paul, enough of all that! We want to be cheered up not fed up! Put on your movie!'

'You guys got no patience,' said Paul as he changed the film reel and his latest movie came to life on the screen.

Clara held Johnny's arm tightly as they laughed at the comedy.

'That's the first movie I've ever seen,' said Clara as it came to an end. 'I loved it!'

Everyone stood up and Clara took Paul's arm as they made their way to the drawing room.

'Now you can show us how to make all those new cocktails from New York you promised us,' said Clara.

'I can't promise you they will be perfect, but I can promise you a bad head in the morning,' said Paul.

'Excellent. Fennell, bring in the new cocktail shaker Mr Tierney brought us.'

'Oh, I think this is my favourite!' said Clara as she drank a Manhattan.

Johnny had put music on the gramophone and it was playing loudly in the drawing room as couples danced. Suddenly the door opened and Paul Tierney came in holding a film camera.

'Everyone just keep on going as normal! I'm making a movie of you all that I can take back to New York with me.'

He moved through the room filming the dancing but when he approached Clara she protested.

'Oh, don't film me!' she begged, putting a hand up to the camera.

'Why not?'

'I don't want it!' she squealed.

'Come on! The camera loves you! You could be my next discovery,' he said.

'Oh shut up!' she said. She walked away from the camera but he continued to follow her, filming her. She turned around and stuck her tongue out at the camera and then started to strike funny poses while everyone laughed.

Johnny came over to her and they started dancing in an exaggerated fashion, swooping around the room as Paul continued to film them.

Finally Clara collapsed on the floor laughing hysterically as the camera continued to roll.

'Oh stop!' she gasped. 'You're not to show that

film to anybody!'

She stood up, still giggling.

Then she turned and saw Pierce standing in the doorway.

'Pierce!' she said loudly.

Johnny turned off the gramophone and the crowd quietened down as everyone stared at Pierce in his officer's uniform.

'Please – don't let me be the cause of stopping the party,' said Pierce.

'Who's this guy?' Paul drawled as he turned off the camera.

'This – *guy* – happens to own this house,' said Pierce.

Clara walked slowly over to him. 'You never said you were coming back on leave,' she said, hardly believing he was there.

'Well, I was never much of a letter-writer, as you know,' Pierce said as he observed the glamorous crowd.

Johnny stared in silence.

Fennell walked into the room with a silver tray of cocktail glasses.

'Lord Armstrong!' he shouted in shock as he dropped the tray to the ground, shattering all the glasses.

Pierce looked down at the broken glass. 'I seem to be creating a bit of a stir.'

Clara quickly spoke to everybody. 'I'm sorry, if you could maybe go to your rooms, those of you staying here – and, those who aren't, if I could ask you to go home?'

Clara turned and looked frantically at Johnny who nodded. The crowd left the room, Johnny with them.

'Leave that, Fennell,' ordered Pierce as Fennell began to sweep up the smashed glass anxiously.

'Very good, sir,' said Fennell as he backed out of the room and closed the door.

Clara sat down on the couch and put her hand to her head. 'You've given me a terrible shock.'

'So it would seem.'

Pierce crossed over to a table and picked up one of the cocktail glasses and took a drink. 'Can't say I really like that,' he said, putting down the glass and making a face. He looked at her. 'You look like you've seen a ghost. Aren't you glad to see your returning husband?'

'I haven't seen you in a year and a half and then you just arrive without warning ... how do you expect me to react?'

'One thing I learned from war was the element of surprise.'

'I thought we had a marriage not a war.'

'Well, by the looks of tonight you haven't exactly been sitting at home pining for me.'

'How long can you stay?'

'I'm back for good. The war on the continent should be wrapped up soon enough now the Americans are there. I've been given an important government role here in Ireland and I'm more needed here with the present state of affairs.' He looked around at all the cocktail glasses. 'In every sense.'

80

Clara stood at the front door the next morning, saying goodbye to her guests.

'Thank you for coming,' Clara said to Paul Tierney.

'A little gift for you, the film I shot of you last night.' He handed her the film reel.

She smiled uncomfortably at him, desperate for all the guests to be quickly gone.

Johnny whispered to her as he stopped at the door. 'What's happening?'

'Please just go.'

'But what about us?' he demanded.

'Just go! I'll be in contact soon,' she whispered.

He nodded and left and she closed the door and leaned against it.

Pierce walked down the stairs. 'I hope you didn't get rid of them on my account? They looked like a spirited bunch.'

'They were going anyway,' she said.

He nodded and went into the dining room for breakfast.

Pierce came out of the bathroom, buttoning his shirt, as Clara sat at the dressing table combing her hair.

'You've lost weight,' he said.

'Have I?'

'Yes, it suits you.'

'Thank you.' She continued to comb her hair.

'I suppose we'd better invest in a new wardrobe of clothes for you. There's a lot of new fashions I saw in London. It's all gone very modern.'

She wondered how long he had been in London, and what he had been doing there.

'Why the sudden interest in my wardrobe?'

'Well, with my new government post, we'll be meeting a lot of dignitaries, military men. Have to put the best foot forward.'

'What exactly is this new role of yours?'

'A government advisory role for the military here in Ireland. Quite senior.'

'I don't think the British will be here long enough for you to be advising them on anything,' she said.

He sat down on the bed and looked over at her. 'A political view picked up from your new friends through Johnny Seymour, I suppose? I think you can say goodbye to that lot now I'm back. I don't think they are suitable company for you.'

She turned around and looked at him. 'They are very nice people, mostly actresses, writers and political thinkers.'

'You see actresses, writers and political thinkers. I see prostitutes, degenerates and anarchists.'

'That's unkind and untrue.'

'They're not our type and bid them farewell, please. Oh, Johnny Seymour is harmless enough I suppose, a bit of a fool, let's face it. And if he wants to keep such company that's his choice. But not ours.'

She turned around and started to brush her hair again, looking in the mirror.

'Besides, I think it's time you had a baby.'

Her forehead creased. 'A baby?'

'You're thirty next year. What are we waiting for?'

'A marriage, perhaps?'

'It's been hard on young married couples, the war coming when it did, forcing separation. We only had had three months together before I had to go to war.' He stood up and walked slowly over to her and put his hands on her shoulders. 'But we need to get on with life now.'

'I thought you made it clear you never loved me.'

'You don't need to be in love to procreate.'

81

Clara answered the ringing phone in the hall.

'It's me,' said Johnny. 'We need to talk.'

She quickly glanced around to see if there was anybody about. 'Yes. Where?'

'Cassidy's bar. Tomorrow at three.'

She put down the phone and quickly made her way to the drawing room.

Clara was sitting in the back of Cassidy's bar at a small table in a private alcove when Johnny came in and sat down. They looked at each other and smiled.

'Well – that was a turn-up for the books,' he said eventually.

'For one awful moment I thought you were going to tell Pierce about us.'

'Come on,' he smirked. 'I may be spontaneous but I know my social manners. It would be the height of rudeness to tell a returning war hero I had been knocking off his wife while he fought for King and country.'

'Oh Johnny!' she chastised but couldn't help from laughing.

'So – where do we go from here?'

'Well, we don't, do we? This is where we part,' she sighed.

He studied her for a long while.

'We could always elope,' he said then.

'Be serious!'

'I am,' he spoke in a casual way. 'You could divorce him.'

'And face the scandal?'

'It's becoming all the rage in certain quarters, you know.'

'Well, not mine.'

'Your parents wouldn't approve?'

'They would probably forgive me anything, but I'm not putting them through it and it would destroy my grandmother... You see, Johnny, marrying Pierce was the biggest mistake of my life. And I'm not willing or able to take any more risks with my life. Marrying Pierce was a leap into the unknown but running away with you would be – a jump off a cliff!'

'Thank you!'

'You know it's true. Besides you don't want to be lumbered with a divorced woman – married women are more your thing. Why don't you put me down as another notch on your bedpost and find another muse.'

'It was never like that.'

She reached out and held his hand.

82

As Pierce predicted, the war did end soon. The Germans surrendered. Armistice Day came and went at Armstrong House and Clara didn't feel there was much to celebrate as she thought of all her lost friends. There were riots in Dublin on Armistice Day as the population's opposition to British rule intensified. As for Pierce, he seemed to be unconcerned by the war's end as they sat that evening in the drawing room. As usual he had spent the day in the library on the phone he had installed there for his new job.

'Well, at least that was the war to end all wars. The world will never have to go through anything like that again,' she said.

He started laughing. 'Don't be so bloody naïve. That war is only the start of it. It's heralding the age of war.'

'Don't say that!'

'Why not? It's true! And the next one will be very close to home.' He put a cigar in his mouth and lit it. 'Well, now it's over, we can at least try to get back to normal.'

'Whatever that is.'

'Well, we can start the hunt season again. I'm

planning a December date for the reinstatement of the Armstrong Hunt – and the Hunt Ball of course.'

She made a sarcastic face. 'Can't wait! There will be a lot of young ladies with no one to dance with since half the young men were slaughtered.'

'No, because I'm going to invite my new colleagues from the government and military to attend as well. It will be an opportunity for you to shine as the society hostess you were brought up to be.' His voice was heavy with sarcasm, but she realised he also meant it.

'I'm of some use to you now at last then, am I? To impress all your new high-powered friends?' She reached into her handbag, took out her cigarette box and placing a cigarette in her mouth lit it.

He casually got up, walked over to her, yanked the cigarette out of her mouth and threw it into the fire.

'Disgusting habit in a woman.'

'Oh, it is so exciting, Lady Armstrong, having a hunt ball again here after all these years of war!' said Mrs Fennell. 'And I don't know where the money is coming from after all these years of frugality but Lord Armstrong said no expense is to be spared with the ball. It'll be just like the old days back when Lord Lawrence was in charge!'

Clara sat at the dining-room table with Mrs Fennell as they went through menus for food for the ball.

'Yes, the frugality was when Prudence was in charge of the purse strings, now it's Pierce. Though I imagine we still can't afford it, Mrs Fennell, unless Lord Armstrong's new government role is paying him a fortune, which I somehow doubt.'

Mrs Fennell stared at Clara, still surprised with the freeness of how she spoke in front of servants.

'These all look perfect, Mrs Fennell,' Clara said, handing back the menus. 'Expensive but perfect. Obviously Lord Pierce thinks his new friends are worth the money to impress.'

An array of expensive cars paraded up to the house the night before the hunt. As Clara put on her earrings and looked at herself in her silk cocktail dress, she realised she should be happy. She had everything she thought she wanted. The war was over, Pierce was back and needing her, if only for his own ends, and they would be the perfect society couple over the next couple of days. But she wasn't happy.

Pierce came in dressed in a tuxedo. 'The guests are arriving. Are you ready?'

She smiled briefly at him and took his arm. They walked along the corridor in silence and down the stairs. She could see the well-dressed guests from London and Dublin were gathered chatting amicably in the drawing room, being served drinks by Fennell and the new footmen. A lot of the men were wearing officer uniforms.

They began to mingle.

'Major Dorkley, this is my wife Lady Armstrong.'

'Ah. Lady Armstrong, enchanted.'

Clara smiled at him. 'I hope your room is to your satisfaction, Major Dorkley?'

'Couldn't be better. I know your uncle, Rupert Charter.'

She took his arm, ready to play the perfect hostess.

The next morning Clara stood at their bedroom window looking out at the forecourt which was filled with men and women dressed in their hunt costumes and being served drinks on their horses as the pack of fox hounds swarmed around.

Pierce came in dressed in the red tunic and white breeches of the hunt.

'Come on, the hunt is about to begin in half an hour.'

She looked at him. 'I'll see you back here when it's over then.'

'No, you're coming too of course.'

'No, I'm not. I hate hunts.'

'The stable boys inform me you've become an adequate rider. Your role as Lady Armstrong means you must attend the hunt.'

'I will not take part in it, Pierce! You know I abhor blood sports.'

'I don't care.'

'I don't even have a riding costume!'

He marched into his dressing room and emerged with one. 'I took the liberty of having one made for you.' He flung the outfit on the bed. 'See you downstairs in twenty minutes.'

Clara walked down the main steps of the house onto the forecourt in her riding clothes.

'Well, there's something I never thought I'd see. You on a hunt!' said Prudence as she rode past.

A stable boy brought over a horse and helped her to mount. She looked around and saw the familiar faces of the gentry mixing with Pierce's new military friends.

'You're certainly one of us now, dear,' said Mr Foxe as he rode by.

Suddenly she saw Johnny Seymour approaching her on horseback, smiling at her.

'Lady Armstrong, good morning to you!' he said cheerily.

'Mr Seymour, I didn't expect to see you here.'

'Oh, the Seymours have been attending the Armstrong hunts for centuries.'

'I see,' she said, wondering what he was up to.

'Your bourbon, Mr Johnny,' said Fennell, handing up a silver tray with a tumbler of bourbon on it.

'Oh, thank you, Fennell, couldn't face a frosty morning on horseback without one of these.' He drank it back in one go and placed the tumbler back on the tray. He rode up close beside her. 'How have you been?'

'Getting on with life,' she said.

Their eyes locked and his smile dropped.

As the horses raced across the countryside after the pack of hounds, Clara struggled to keep up with them. Johnny deliberately stayed back and rode alongside her.

'I thought about ringing you a thousand times,' he said.

'I'm glad you didn't.'

'I keep going into Cassidy's hoping to find you there with a glass of Guinness.'

'I don't go there any more. It wouldn't be right for Lady Armstrong to be seen there.'

He stared over at her. 'It never bothered you before. How long can you keep this up? Pretending to be something you're not. Even on bloody hunts now! Doing everything he wants you to do.'

'He needs a supportive wife, he's been through hell over there... And at least I have his attention now.'

'I only came today so I could see you.'

'Well, I wish you hadn't.' She kicked the horse's flanks and galloped off to join the others.

Clara was relieved when the hunt was over and everyone returned to the house for the Hunt Ball. She came out of her dressing room that evening to find Pierce was waiting for her.

'Try and spend a little more time with Lord Harrington, will you? He's going to be the next foreign minister, so Lloyd George has hinted. So worth keeping in with.'

She looked at him curiously. 'Where did all this ambition suddenly come from?'

He held out his arm to her. 'The trenches, Clara, the trenches.'

The ballroom and drawing room were filled with guests. Clara circulated making sure everyone was enjoying themselves.

Suddenly Johnny was beside her. 'I have to talk to you!' he whispered.

'Impossible.'

His eyes were pleading. 'Please!'

She sighed. 'I'll see you in the gardens to the

411

left of the second terrace in fifteen minutes.'

He nodded and walked off.

Prudence sidled up beside her, holding a glass of sherry. 'Enjoying yourself?'

'Just mingling.'

Prudence glanced over at Johnny who was looking their way. 'Well, just be careful you don't mingle too much.'

Clara put a fur coat around her and slipped out the front door and made her way across the forecourt and down the steps to the terraces and gardens.

'I wasn't sure you'd come,' said Johnny as he put his arms around her and kissed her.

'Johnny – this is stupid,' she said, kissing him before pulling back.

'I've been looking at you all day. You look miserable.'

'I didn't enjoy the hunt.'

'It's more than that. It's Pierce and this marriage.'

'I don't want to talk about it.' She moved away from him.

'Well, there's a few things you need to know about Pierce. There's going to be a war here, Clara. The British are not going to give independence. And the people want it. It's going to erupt and Pierce's new job is going to place him in the middle of it.' He came and put his arms around her. 'We can be gone from here. I can organise tickets to set sail for New York. We can start again. I've been in contact with Paul Tierney, and he said he'll help us with a new start over there. This country is going to explode – let's get out before we go down with it.'

'So typical of you, Johnny. Running away when the going gets tough. You spent four years here partying to escape the war in Europe and now when one starts here you're ready to run off from here as well.'

He tightened his grip on her. 'Don't you understand – I love you. I want to be with you any way I can.'

She pulled herself free of him. 'I'm going back to the ball. We shouldn't talk again.'

Prudence came up to Clara in the ballroom, shaking her head.

'I don't know what's got into Pierce. This is all costing a fortune that we can ill afford.'

'For goodness sake, Prudence, is it all about money with you? He's spent four years in hell ... he deserves to splash out this once and celebrate being alive, doesn't he? He survived, many didn't.'

'*Hmmm,* if the last four years were hell, why would he be planning another war then?'

'What are you talking about?'

'He's in the library as we speak, having a counsel for war meeting with his new military and political friends.'

'What are you talking about?'

'The war with the natives, darling! There's going to be a war here to stop them getting independence. I believe Pierce is going to be a driving force in it.'

Clara pushed through the crowd and crossed to the dining room, then tiptoed over to the connecting door to the library. She gently opened it a crack and peeped in. She could see Pierce's friends sitting around on the Chesterfield couches or standing nearby. Pierce himself was half-sitting on the desk, his arms folded.

'The last thing we really need is another war after we just finished on the continent,' said Lord Harrington.

'Yes, but war is inevitable,' said Pierce. 'The situation is growing worse by the day. Attacks on military personnel by the republicans. They want their independence and we don't want to give it. So we need to fight them. We've been trying to appease them long enough. And now we must fight back.'

'He's right,' said Major Dorkley.

'If we don't stand strong now and stamp out this rebellion it will lead to revolution,' said Pierce. 'Look what's happened in Russia. There will be anarchy if we don't stamp it out now. And not just here, it could spread from Ireland to Britain. There's so much unrest.'

'And where do we raise an army to crush this revolution?' asked Lord Harrington.

'There's an army of unemployed soldiers just waiting for another war, isn't there?' said Pierce.

Clara slipped away and returned to the ball.

Pierce came into the bedroom at three in the morning and found Clara sitting up in the bed reading a book.

'The party is still going on downstairs. I thought you were the last of the great party girls – why aren't you down with them?'

414

'I have a headache.'

'I went to a lot of expense and trouble for this weekend. You could at least look as if you enjoyed it.'

She snapped the book shut. 'You went to a lot of expense and trouble for yourself! It's a cover for you to plan your bloody war! I thought you'd have had enough of bloodshed out there in France rather than starting another one here!'

'Quite the little spy, aren't you?' He smirked at her. 'Well, I'm going back to the ball. There's a redhead down there eying me up. It might be her lucky night. Enjoy your read. Don't wait up.' He turned and walked out.

'I bloody well won't!' she shouted after him, and flung the book at the door.

Johnny was back at Seymour Hall that night listening to a recording of 'Women of Ireland' on the gramophone. The song came to an end and he went and opened a window. There was a cold breeze sweeping the countryside and a full moon turned the night sky into dark blue. The clouds were drifting quickly past a sole star. It was completely silent but for the wind rustling through the trees and a curlew calling in the distance. In the distance across the lake he could see the lights of Armstrong House, the hunt ball still in full swing.

83

The Anglo-Irish war of Independence exploded in January 1919 as the British sent over troops en masse to suppress the armed insurrection.

It was a guerrilla war and quite unlike the one Pierce had fought in France. Stories of tit-for-tat and retaliation came daily. An attack on a British army barracks, a burning of a town by the army looking for the culprits, as great swathes of the country were put under martial law.

Clara walked down the main street of Castlewest. Gone was the happy friendly feel to the place as British soldiers manned street corners. She passed the publican Mr Cassidy in the street.

'Oh good day, Mr Cassidy, how are you?' she said but Cassidy ignored her and walked past her. She looked to the ground, embarrassed, and headed quickly back to the house. Pierce's position as a military commander in the war had made them very unpopular with the townspeople.

Clara parked the car in front of the house and got out.

Major Dorkley was coming down the steps after attending a meeting with Pierce. Pierce had a steady stream of military personnel coming to the house to attend meetings.

'Good day, Lady Armstrong, how are you?' the major greeted her happily.

'I'm fine.'

The major looked concerned. 'Did you drive yourself into the town?'

'Yes, I always do. Ever since the chauffeur went to France and got killed,' she said.

'Not really advisable with everything going on. I think we'd better assign you an armed driver from now on, as your husband has.'

'Oh no, I'd hate that!' Clara was horrified. She looked over at the armed driver sitting in Pierce's official car which had been assigned to him by the government.

'Better safe than sorry! They shot a magistrate the other day. Cheerio!' said Dorkley as he headed to his own car.

'I'm afraid another kitchen maid walked out on me this morning, Lady Armstrong,' sighed Mrs Fennell in the dining room as she served Clara breakfast.

'Oh dear!'

'They just won't work here with all this fighting going on and Lord Armstrong's role in it all. I can't get any staff from Castlewest to work here any more.'

'I see. I believe my husband is going to recruit some domestic staff through an agency in London.'

'An agency! Has it come to that? The locals have worked here since the house was built.'

'It seems to be the way, Mrs Fennell.'

'Well, I don't know what to say,' Mrs Fennell sighed. 'If only Lord Pierce would keep his head down like the rest of the gentry and not draw attention to himself, but he won't! It was on his orders houses in Castlewest were searched and ransacked by those Black and Tan soldiers last week.'

'I'm sure Lord Armstrong didn't order the ransacking, Mrs Fennell.'

'Maybe he didn't, but it's what ended up happening anyway!'

Pierce walked in the room. 'Just toast for me, Mrs Fennell.'

Mrs Fennell nodded and left.

Pierce sat down and poured himself coffee.

'She can't get any staff to work here, Pierce. And with all the tea and refreshments to be served to your officer friends all the time, the Fennells are run off their feet.'

'I'll contact the agency again.'

'I don't know why you have to have all your meetings here anyway.'

'Because the military barracks in the town was burned down by the rebels.'

'I don't like my home becoming a military headquarters.'

Pierce picked up the paper and read about some atrocity that had happened in Tipperary.

'Too bad ... I'm having some armed soldiers placed at the entrances to the estate.'

'*What?* This is getting ridiculous, Pierce. Mrs Fennell was saying half the shops in Castlewest won't deliver to us any more. We're making ourselves isolated – we won't be able to live here any more.'

'Don't you understand, this is a war! If we don't win it, we won't be able to live here anyway.

It's a fight to the end. The rebels are burning down the Big Houses all around the country. We have to defend our way of life.'

'You're fighting for something that's over, Pierce, and I can't live like this any more.'

'Well, don't then. Go!' he said, smirking at her.

'You're so confident I won't, aren't you? You think no matter what I'll stay because I won't risk the scandal of leaving you, even though we despise each other.'

He stood up, finished his coffee and smirked again at her. 'Despise? A strong description, I think? But if it's the truth as you see it, then who am I to argue?'

Pierce had got word there were suspected rebels in the wooded hills high above the lake. He had brought some of his men and they were quietly making their way through the trees to search for them. Pierce gave a signal and the men separated out to cover more area. Pierce found himself on his own, holding his revolver in his hand as he moved through the trees. All he could hear was the birds singing loudly. He stopped and looked up through the tall fir trees to the blue sky above.

'Drop the gun,' a voice suddenly said.

One of the rebels was standing there with a gun pointing straight at him.

Pierce realised he had no choice and carefully placed the gun on the ground. The rebel kicked it out of the way. The rebel took aim, finger on the trigger. Pierce stared at him, his dark eyes boring into him. The man paused for a moment and then steadied his aim again. But Pierce's eyes continued to stare. The silence was suddenly disrupted by gunfire in the distance. The rebel glanced away, took a final look at Pierce and then ran, disappearing into the woods. Pierce sat down on a log and held his head in his hands as he began to shake.

'Sir, are you all right?' said one of his men finding him there.

'Yes, quite all right – let's get back to base.' Pierce picked up his gun and quickly retreated.

84

Clara hardly dared breathe as she drove into Johnny's drive and felt relieved to see his car parked there. She got out, walked up to the door and pulled on the doorbell. A minute later Johnny appeared, looking shocked to see her.

'I'm sorry to just appear like this, I should have warned you,' she said.

'No! Not at all! Come in.' He put his arm round her shoulders and brought her inside.

He led her into the sitting room.

'What's wrong?' he asked as they sat down on the couch.

'Everything. I can't go on, Johnny. Living with him. I can't stand it any more.' She became distressed and her voice cracked. 'You've no idea. He's like one of those machines they sent into battle against the Germans. There's no feeling with him, towards me – towards anything!'

'It's all right,' he soothed as he rubbed her back. 'I'm here. We can get through this.'

'I don't want to get through it – I want to get away from it, from him. As far as possible.'

'Do you mean it?'

'I've never meant anything more in my life.'

'But what about the scandal, the talk?'

'Bugger it! I don't care.'

He held her shoulders tightly and looked into her eyes. 'Are you saying ... you want to be with me?'

She nodded and smiled. 'If you still want me?'

'Of course I do.' He pulled her to him.

They spent the afternoon curled up on his couch, his arms around her.

'I forgot what this felt like,' she said as he stroked her hair. 'To have this closeness, this understanding.'

'Well, we'll be like this all the time from now on. Are we agreed on what we're going to do?'

'Yes – we'll leave for Dublin and then go on to London and explain everything to my family. Then we'll go to New York until the scandal dies down.'

'I can make a mint painting portraits for all those American millionaires.'

'A dreamer as ever,' she smiled at him. 'Don't ever lose that.'

'We need to do it quickly. There's no point hanging around.'

She looked at her watch. It was four in the afternoon. 'I'll go back and tell Pierce now. Then I'll pack what I can and you come and collect me at nine this evening and we'll drive straight for Dublin.'

'Do you want me to go with you to talk to Pierce?'

'No, I'm better off on my own.'

'How do you think he'll take it?'

'I don't think he'll care that much, to be honest. He'll be glad to see the back of me.'

She got up and he walked her to the door and held her.

'I'll see you at nine,' she said and kissed him before walking to her car.

Fennell opened the front door for Clara.

'Where is Lord Armstrong?'

'He's in the drawing room.'

'Alone?'

'Indeed.'

'See that we're not disturbed, please,' she said, handing Fennell her hat, coat and gloves. She steadied herself as she neared the door and then went into the drawing room. Pierce was sitting on the couch, legs crossed, having a whiskey.

'There you are,' he said. 'Mrs Fennell has been going on about no potatoes or some such nonsense. Deal with her, will you?'

She walked around the room for a while before sitting opposite him. 'Pierce, there's no easy way to say this so I'll just come out with it – I'm leaving you.'

He lit a cigar. 'I see! You're heading back to London?'

'At first. We hope to then go on to New York.'

'We?'

'Yes,' she sighed. 'I've been seeing Johnny Seymour. I'm sorry.'

He stared at her. 'So you're one of Johnny's girls now, are you? You seldom fail to surprise.'

'I hope to be his only girl from now on, not part of a club.'

'*Hmmm,* I wonder if he hopes the same? What about the scandal? You'll be swimming in it.'

'I don't care any more. It's better than what we have here.'

He put out the cigar, knocked back his drink, and coughed. He then got up and walked over to the drink decanters on the cabinet and poured himself another glass.

'When are you leaving?'

'Tonight. Johnny's collecting me at nine.'

Pierce's body suddenly shook. His hand dropped the glass he was holding and he let out a low gasp.

'Oh Pierce!' She got up quickly and walked over to him, put her arms around him and leaned her face against his back. 'I'm sorry, but this is for the best – for both of us.'

He had regained his composure and he moved away from her.

'And you think Johnny Seymour, the court jester, can make you happy?'

'He does make me happy, Pierce. That's the difference between you and him. Before we married I thought only you could make me happy. But I've never been actually happy with you. At the beginning I could live with your coldness and you being removed from everything. But since you've come back from the war your coldness has

423

developed into cruelty and I can't take that. Not just with me, but with everyone. The way you enjoy this war as you do. It's like you need to be at war, you survive on it. And I think the only thing you're really fighting is what's in your head.'

'Yes – well – there's probably nothing left to be said if you've made up your mind. Goodbye, Clara.'

'Goodbye,' she nodded and left the room.

She felt an incredible sense of relief and freedom as she walked through the hall to the stairs. She ran up the stairs and into the bedroom. She found her suitcases in her dressing room, opened it on the bed and began quickly to pack. She would be able to take only the minimum but it couldn't be helped. She could get the Fennells to pack up the rest of her things and hopefully Pierce would agree to send them after her.

She heard the front door bang and she went to look out the window. She saw Pierce walk across the forecourt to his open-topped car. The driver saluted him and opened the back door. Pierce sat in and the driver drove them away.

She had left her suitcases by the front door and called Mr and Mrs Fennell in to see her in the drawing room.

'Leaving? But leaving for where?' asked Fennell.

'You'll hear it soon enough so I may as well be honest with you. I'm leaving with Johnny Seymour.'

'Johnny Seymour!' they exclaimed together.

'Yes. We're starting a new life together.'

The Fennells looked at each other in amazement.

'I'm only taking a few suitcases now and I'd appreciate it if you could pack up the rest of my clothes and personal possessions into a few trunks. I hope to arrange with Lord Armstrong to have them sent after me.'

'Of course, my lady,' said Fennell.

'So I just want to thank you for all the service and support and friendship through the years.'

'Well, em, it's been a pleasure to serve you,' said Mrs Fennell, nodding. 'You were a complete lady.' Then she thought about the elopement with Johnny Seymour. 'Almost to the end.'

Clara tried not to laugh but got up and went to them both and kissed them on the cheeks. 'Goodbye – friends.'

Mrs Fennell wiped away tears as she and Fennell left the room.

'"Friends"?' said Mrs Fennell in astonishment.

'Always was the most unusual young woman,' said Fennell.

Looking at her watch, Clara saw it was nearly nine. She sat on the couch in the drawing room which gave her a view out to the front, waiting for Johnny to arrive. She smiled to herself, thinking how Johnny had never been early for anything in his life, and that night was obviously to be no different.

Time crawled by and she began to pace up and down the room, smoking, too nervous to do anything else to distract herself.

Pierce had not returned.

She lit up another cigarette and walked over to the window to see if she could see the lights of his car coming. She bit her lower lip and started to pace again as she saw it was a quarter past ten. She quickly walked out to the hall, lifted the phone and tried to get through to Johnny's house, but there was no answer. She walked back into the drawing room and resumed her pacing.

As the clock struck eleven o'clock, she could hear a car pull up outside and she excitedly jumped up and raced to the window. But it was Pierce returning. She turned quickly and sat down in an armchair. Lighting up another cigarette, she crossed her legs.

A minute later Pierce walked in.

'Oh hello! I'd thought you'd be gone by now,' he said.

'Johnny's running a bit late.'

'Story of Johnny's life!' Pierce looked down at his watch. 'But it's after eleven! I thought you said he'd be here at nine for you.'

'As I said, he's running late.'

'Has he rung you to tell you that?' He waited for her answer. 'From your non-answer, I'll take that as a no.' Pierce walked slowly to the couch and sat down shaking his head. 'I know it was never your strength to face facts, but I think in this case you're going to have to. I think your lover boy isn't going to show up, my darling.'

Clara blinked a few times as her eyes filled with tears.

'I think your lover boy got one whiff of you wanting to make a permanent arrangement and has done a runner, Clara. Fled up to Dublin to find his next *paramour.* Oh, the words I picked up in France. It was an education.'

He viewed Clara as her eyes continued to well up.

'No – I must put you out of your misery and not be cruel, as you were accusing me of being earlier. The truth is Johnny boy has been locked up.'

'*Locked up!'*

'Yes, his car was intercepted by my military personnel on his way over here to collect you – on my orders.'

'But you can't just arrest somebody like that!'

'I think you'll find I can. There's martial law and internment in place. I can have anybody I see as a threat arrested and detained for as long as I want.'

'As a threat to the country's security – *not to your marriage!'* she screamed at him.

'Oh, let's not get bogged down on the details,' he said in a blasé fashion.

His face became serious as he lit up a cigarette. 'Actually, Johnny Seymour *is* a threat to national security as well though, isn't he?'

'No, he's not!'

'All those shady characters he knows, hanging around with subversives. And then of course there is the fact he hid and helped Thomas Geraghty to escape, didn't he?'

Clara went pale.

'With you as his accomplice. Hiding him here in the house.'

She looked down at the ground. 'How did you know?'

'Prudence, of course. She was sending me blow-by-blow accounts of your activities with Johnny Seymour. Out rowing across the lake, long nights in front of the fire here, romantic Christmases together. All under the guise of the longest time ever known to the art world to paint a damned portrait.'

'You knew about me and Johnny all along?'

'Of course. Oh I didn't care, I can assure you. But when she reported it was getting serious, I thought I'd better get back and stop it. Good old Pru. She used to race up here whenever she heard a car, turning up here at night to spy through windows or use her key to come in and look through keyholes. And that's how she saw you were hiding Thomas Geraghty here. Oh, Clara – the things we do for love!'

'You've just said yourself you don't care, so why have you arrested Johnny?'

'Oh, I don't care what you do, but I do care what people think – even if you don't any more. I'm not ruining my reputation and the family name because my wife ran off with a circus performer! I want you to listen carefully, because this is how it is going to be. You will not contact Johnny Seymour again. To be honest he will not want to contact you anyway because I told him it was you who had betrayed him to me about Thomas Geraghty and set him up this evening to be cornered and arrested.'

'He'll never believe that!'

'Oh he did, I can assure you.'

'You bastard!'

'That's as may be. However, from now on, when

you leave the house you will be driven by an army chauffeur. If you try to leave me – get a train to Dublin, for example – you will be immediately arrested and charged with hiding Thomas Geraghty and interned in a women's prison. The term is treason, I believe.'

'You wouldn't dare!'

'Of course I would! I'd have nothing to lose in that situation. In fact I would be obliged to arrest you lest you go off and engage in other subversive activities. I am taking a risk as it is by not arresting you right now. So, yes, I'd have you thrown into prison and throw away the keys, tried for treason even. You might have thought your family would forgive you a divorce, but I can't see them forgiving you being found guilty of being a traitor to the Crown.'

'What else?' she said quietly.

'You will speak to nobody of this. You will not mention it in letters or over the phone. If I discover you have done so, the same penalty will apply. You will remain in this house and in this marriage for ever.'

'So I am to be a prisoner here?'

'I think we understand each other,' he said.

They sat in silence for a long time. She eventually got up and walked quietly from the room. Leaving her suitcases standing by the door, she climbed the stairs, stumbling once before pulling herself together and continuing. She went to their room, collapsed on the bed and cried.

The next morning Pierce was having breakfast and reading the newspaper while Fennell poured him coffee. Suddenly the door opened and Clara walked in and went and sat in her normal place, looking composed.

Fennell nearly dropped the coffee pot as he looked at her in astonishment.

Pierce watched her.

'I'll just have a light breakfast, please, Fennell,' she said. 'And pour me some coffee.'

Fennell nodded and walked over and filled her cup.

Pierce coughed loudly. 'Lord Harrington and some others will be having dinner here tonight – will you be joining us?'

'Yes,' said Clara. 'Perhaps if Mrs Fennell sends up some dinner suggestions, I'll select what to prepare, Fennell.'

'Very good, my lady,' nodded Fennell before quickly leaving the room.

Pierce took up his paper again and continued to read, while Clara drank her coffee in silence.

85

As the months went by, Clara got used to her house arrest. She had ventured down to the town a few times, under the scrutiny of her army chauffeur as Pierce had threatened, but she didn't feel welcome there any more as the locals shunned her, so preferred to stay in the house or gardens.

Clara and Pierce never made reference to Johnny Seymour again. To onlookers their marriage seemed the same as ever. To Pierce it seemed the same as ever. Clara disguised her hatred of him, just maintaining a cool distance. She had waited for Johnny to make contact, but he never did. Even if he had been released, she imagined he believed she had betrayed him to Pierce about Thomas Geraghty and hated her for it. Besides, Pierce went through her post every morning before she was allowed access to it. She wondered if Pierce would really have her arrested if she tried to leave him. After all, it would be the greatest possible disgrace for him to have his wife convicted of treason. But she daren't call his bluff.

The War of Independence was continuing and Pierce continued with his active role in it. Until finally a truce was called. After the truce came the treaty and then Home Rule was given and the British withdrew their political and army presence. At that point Pierce was advised that they should all leave the house for fear of reprisals.

Prudence marched through the house, giving orders. 'Yes, put that in the second car along with the rest of the silverware... No you can leave that here... Put that in the trunk with the china.'

Clara came down the stairs and saw the Fennells and the other servants rushing around following Prudence's orders.

Clara walked into the library where she found Pierce filling his briefcase up with papers.

He looked up at her. 'When you're packing try to only bring essentials and valuables. Leave everything else here. We'll secure the house and hopefully it won't be attacked when we're gone.'

'There's little chance of that!' snapped Prudence, walking in. 'I hear they burned down Grangly Hall in Roscommon last night. The poor owners, the Hilgards, weren't in any way involved with the Anglo-Irish war. They are just targeting Big Houses to burn down as a symbol of British rule. But with your bloody involvement this house is bound to be a target.'

'That's why we have to get a move on,' said Pierce.

'I've contacted our cousins in Dublin and we are welcome to stay as long as possible. Hopefully when things calm down we can come back here,' said Prudence.

Clara laughed harshly. 'After what Pierce did, you'll never be able to return here!'

Prudence looked at Pierce accusingly. 'You did nail your colours to the wrong mast. There are plenty of gentry families who endorsed independence and they are even being given jobs with the new government in Dublin.'

'You've changed your tune,' snapped Pierce.

'Well, we're all going to have to sing to a different tune now.'

'Enough of this talk, let's keep packing and be on the road for Dublin by this afternoon.'

Clara sat down casually on a Chesterfield couch and lit up a cigarette.

'*Clara!*' shouted Pierce. 'Let's get a move on and pack!'

'Oh, I'm not going anywhere, husband dear,' said Clara, smiling.

'What are you talking about?'

'I don't want to go and stay with your cousins in Dublin. I've met quite enough Armstrongs in

432

you two, thank you very much.'

'Don't be so stupid and get moving. I've no time for your silly antics.'

'And if I don't – what will you do, Pierce? Have me arrested, or interned like you have been threatening? Oh, but you can't any more, can you? The army is leaving and so is your power. There's an independent government in Dublin and I'm a free person again.'

Pierce stood staring at her in shock.

'All this time being locked up at your command is over. I'm a free woman. I even have the vote now.'

Prudence looked at Pierce's pale face and then looked to Clara. 'So what are you going to do, Clara? Going to London?'

'Finding your lover Johnny, now he's been released?' Pierce asked cynically.

'I'm not going to do anything. I'm going to stay right here – in my house, my home.'

'But we're all leaving!' snapped Prudence. 'Even all the servants.'

'Off you go. I'll be fine on my own.' She looked at Pierce and smiled but her eyes were accusing. 'You forced me to stay and that's what I agreed to do. I'm staying put.'

'But you can't, Clara!' shouted Prudence. 'It's too dangerous.'

'I've made up my mind.'

Pierce looked at her. 'I won't ask you again to join us.'

She stared at him bitterly. He grabbed his briefcase and walked out past her.

Clara looked out the french windows of the ballroom as she saw the cars drive speedily away. Then she walked to the front door and bolted it and leaned against the door, closing her eyes, before walking through the empty house.

'Lady Armstrong! Lady Armstrong!' came voices shouting from outside the house. Clara was upstairs in her bedroom writing at her bureau and she went to the window and looked out. Down in the forecourt she saw a British army car and two British officers in it.

She opened the window. 'Yes?'

'Lady Armstrong, I'm Captain Jones from the local regiment.'

'How can I help you, Captain Jones?'

'We are literally the last of the regiment left and we are leaving the country. We're driving to Dublin now, you can accompany us – please come with us.'

'No, thank you, Captain. I'm not leaving my house.'

'But, Lady Armstrong – don't you understand? – we cannot guarantee your safety once we have left.'

'Thank you for your concern, but I'm quite all right.' She closed over the window.

Captain Jones looked at his colleague. 'Well, we tried. It's as the locals say – she's not leaving.'

'They say she's waiting for her lover to return, the artist.'

'They also say she's gone mad – driven to madness by her marriage to Pierce Armstrong.'

He looked up at the house. 'Come on – let's get out of here.'

That night like every night, Clara sat at her bedroom window looking out across the lake to where Seymour Hall was. She had been doing it every night since Johnny had been arrested. If a light came on, he would be home and she would rush there and try to explain everything to him. She couldn't bear to think of him being behind bars for all this time. But now all the political prisoners were being released, he was bound to come home sooner or later. And they could continue where they left off and start their new life together. All she ever thought about was him and being back together with him. She lit up a cigarette and continued to look for a light to come on at Johnny's, but the house remained in darkness.

86

The loud banging at the door woke her in the middle of the night. She sat up in the bed. Her heart beat quickly as the loud knocking echoed through the house again.

'Johnny!' she gasped. She jumped out of bed and ran to one of the windows and looked out. But it wasn't Johnny – there was a group of men standing there holding burning torches.

She opened the window. 'What do you want?' she demanded.

'Could you open the front door and let us in,' said the leader of the men.

'No, I most certainly can't. Now you're on private property – so clear off!'

'If you don't open the door, we'll smash it down.'

'What do you want?' she demanded.

'We're burning this house down as a reprisal for actions during the War of Independence.'

Clara slammed the window shut and ran into her dressing room where she quickly changed into a dress. Panicked, she ran from the room and down the corridor. As she came racing down the stairs she heard a shattering of glass at the back of the house. By the time she reached the hallway a group of men came rushing up from the servants' quarters.

'Get out! Get out of my house!' she shouted.

'I'm afraid we can't do that, Lady Armstrong. We ask you to leave the house now with us.'

She was aghast as the men ran through all the rooms downstairs.

Two of the men took her by the arms and led her to the front door which they unbolted. She saw one of the men set light to the curtains in the drawing room.

'Oh, please let me get some of my items from the house,' she begged as they led her out and down the steps to the forecourt.

'I'm afraid we can't do that. When houses in Castlewest were burned down, that request went unheeded by your husband's guards.'

One of the men brought one of the ornate armchairs out and placed it in the middle of the forecourt.

'Take a seat, please,' said the leader.

She sat down and looked at the house. She could see flames dancing inside the windows of the drawing room and spreading quickly.

'I don't want to see this!' she shouted.

'Again, you have no choice. The people in the town were made to watch their houses burn down, and now you can watch yours.'

As she watched the flames shoot through the house, all she could do was stare in horror. She remembered Velma, the Frenchwoman who was staying in Hunter's Farm when she first arrived, telling her fortune and saying she would one day save the House of Armstrong. As she watched the house go up in flames, she realised that was not to be.

Clara got on the train and found a quiet compartment in which to sit. She was wearing a hat with a net that covered her face.

She looked out at the platform that was busy with people getting on and off the train.

The ticket master came down to her.

'Ticket, please,' he said.

She handed him her ticket and he read it out. 'A single to Dublin?'

She nodded. 'That's right – no return.'

Book 3

2007–Present

87

Kate and Tony Fallon were seated at a round table with three suited men in the restaurant in the Plaza Hotel in New York. Kate was a striking woman in her late thirties with long golden hair. Tony, aged forty-six, was a big man with black slightly curled hair, dressed casually in a suit and open-necked shirt.

'When Steve suggested meeting you to discuss the deal we were delighted to take the opportunity,' said Kate Fallon as she smiled around the table.

'We could of course have our pick and choose of investors – but Steve said you were the guys for us,' smiled Tony Fallon.

'Well, eh, when Steve first mentioned your project we got kinda excited,' said Mulrooney. 'We thought we'd better get a bit of the action going on in Ireland before we miss the show altogether.'

'And what a show is going on there!' said Steve.

'I just got a couple of questions,' said Mulrooney. 'The size and scope of this shopping mall you're building in Dublin – it will be one of the biggest luxury malls in Europe – you're sure the demand will be there?'

Kate gave a little laugh. 'Oh, the demand is there, gentlemen, I can assure you. The conspicuous consumption of the Irish has become notorious.' She lightly fingered the dazzling diamond

441

necklace around her neck.

'Some of those suburbs in Dublin put Beverly Hills to shame,' said Tony with a laugh. 'It's the second richest country in the world, you know.'

'And Dublin is the third most expensive city in Europe,' added Kate.

'It's come a long way from the Famine!' said Mulrooney with a laugh.

'The demand is there, rest assured,' said Kate. 'And that's why we are securing all the right anchor tenants – Tiffany's, Armani, Gucci. We're even hoping to get Harrods and Bloomingdales on board.' She flashed another smile at the men.

'And any project with Tony and Kate's name attached in Ireland will be a success,' said Steve. 'They have the Midas touch.' Steve Shaw was the Chief Executive of Eiremerica Bank, and Tony Fallon's company Fallon Enterprises was his biggest client.

'I saw a couple of films you were in, Kate,' said Mulrooney. 'You don't act any more?'

'No, I gave up acting when I married Tony.' She placed a loving hand on Tony's and smiled at him.

'You miss Hollywood?'

'I only ever made a couple of American films before I retired, so not really,' smiled Kate.

'How long have you two been married?' asked Mulrooney.

'Seven years,' said Tony as he held Kate's hand and smiled.

'You'll have to visit us in Ireland,' suggested Kate.

'Well, I hope to see you guys there some day

soon. I've always wanted to go to Ireland,' said Mulrooney.

'Of course you do! Everyone wants to go to Ireland,' smiled Kate.

'So – eh, gentlemen, are you in or are you out?' questioned Steve Shaw, looking slightly nervous.

Mulrooney looked at the handsome, smiling, confident Fallons.

'We're in,' said Mulrooney.

'Excellent!' said Steve loudly and snapped his fingers at the waiter, who arrived a minute later with a bottle of champagne. He opened it and filled their glasses.

'So,' said Kate, raising her glass. 'To a successful partnership!'

They all clinked glasses in the centre of the table and repeated. 'A successful partnership!'

Kate walked into their suite in the hotel and riffled her hands through her hair.

'Whoo! We did it!' Tony yelled loudly.

She sighed loudly. 'I thought at one point they were going to opt out.'

He came over and put his arms around her. 'You had them eating out of your hand. I couldn't have done it without you.'

She smiled. 'Yes, you could. I was just the window dressing.'

There was a knock on the door and Tony went to open it. Two bellboys entered carrying two huge bouquets of flowers.

'These ones are from Mulrooney,' Tony said, checking the attached cards, 'and these are from Steve Shaw and Eiremerica Bank.'

'Thank you,' said Kate to the bellboys. 'You can leave them over on the table.'

Tony's mobile started ringing and he answered it as the bellboys left.

'Hey – hi, Steve – yep, a great result ... sure...' Tony covered his phone and whispered over to Kate. 'They loved you!'

They loved the idea of making lots of money, that's all, thought Kate as she went to sit at the bureau and turned on the laptop.

'Okay, thanks again, Steve – let's meet for breakfast before we leave for Dublin.'

Tony hung up and threw off his jacket.

'Steve is thrilled.'

'So he should be. He and his bank will make another fortune out of you,' she said as she studied the laptop screen.

'Any emails?' he asked as he went into the ensuite and ran the bath.

'I haven't checked yet,' she said, distracted by the screen.

He came out of the bathroom.

She cleared her throat and said, 'Have you given any more thought to what we were talking about – the house?'

'Oh – you're not still looking at that place, are you?' He came over behind her and looked at the auctioneer's website with the Armstrong House photo on it.

'The auction is next month,' she said.

'I thought we decided we weren't interested in it,' he said.

'No, you decided *you* weren't. But I am still very interested in it.' She went through the photos on

444

the screen.

'It's a dump!' he declared. 'A medieval ruin. It's even fire-damaged. It's miles from Dublin, and doesn't suit our needs.'

She closed down the laptop and looked at him. 'All I'm asking is we go and take a look. Just to make an appointment with the auctioneer and see what it's like.'

'You already know what it's like. You grew up near there,' he pointed out.

'But I haven't been down there for years. I want to see what it's like now.'

'Oh Kate!' he moaned, annoyed.

'Please!' She looked at him pleadingly.

'Oh, how can I say no after that performance you put on over lunch?'

She leaned forward and kissed him. 'Thank you – oh, and Tony?'

'What?'

'Your bath is running over.'

'Damn!' he said as he raced over to the bathroom.

88

Nicholas Collins drove his Range Rover up to the front of Armstrong House and parked it in the overgrown forecourt. Janet Dolan's car was parked there and beyond it he saw Janet talking to a couple who were climbing into a very flashy car. Janet was from Dolans Auctioneers, the estate agents appointed to sell the house. Janet was a friend of his ex-wife Susan. Which was one of the reasons for her appointment as selling agent, as well as the fact that Janet specialised in large country houses.

The main source of conflict in his divorce from his ex-wife Susan had been Armstrong House. This house was his, inherited from his mother Jacqueline Armstrong Collins. He had wanted to keep it while Susan had wanted to sell it to set them up in comfortable new homes. He had felt it wasn't his to sell: it belonged to the long line of Armstrongs who had gone before him – and to his young daughter Alex who should inherit it from him.

In the end he was forced to sell and Nico knew it was the right decision. He had separated Hunter's Farm from the folio of property to be sold. He would hold on to that, at least so long as the Big House raised enough. Armstrong House would just continue to disintegrate – he certainly hadn't the money to do anything with it. And the money would set them up properly and secure Alex's future which was the main thing. But his heart still fought against his head.

He jumped out of his Range Rover and walked towards them. As he reached Janet she was waving the couple off.

'I'm putting them down as a definite maybe,' she said, making a note on her clipboard with her pen.

'Is that not a contradiction – putting the words "definite" and "maybe" together like that?'

Janet ignored him. 'All my appointments have

446

shown up today, ten so far.' She looked at her watch. 'I'm waiting for my eleventh now.' She peered down the driveway to watch for any approaching vehicle. 'I'm quite excited about the next viewing – it's Tony and Kate Fallon.' Janet had a cat-who-got-the-cream look about her. 'A bit of a coup to even get them to make a viewing – it will set tongues wagging.'

'Tony and Kate Fallon?' He looked unimpressed.

'Yes, you know, the shopping-centre magnate and his actress wife–'

'I know who they are!' he said quickly. 'They're very brash and flash, aren't they?'

'Brash and flash usually equals cash in my experience, so what's your problem with that?'

He looked up at the house. A lot of the windows on the front were boarded up. It was very rundown and dilapidated.

'I just didn't think they'd be the type to be interested in a house like this,' he said.

'They are just the type, Nico. All my clients in the country-house market are nouveau-riche businessmen intent on playing lord of the manor.'

'Tacky,' he said.

'Nico!' She was annoyed. 'Have you any idea how much money these kind of people are worth? They are the chance of you getting your asking price, paying off your debts, paying off your ex-wife and riding off into the sunset. If you're relying on the local farmers to pay your asking price, you'll be waiting a long time, I can tell you.'

He looked up at the house. 'It's been in my family for nearly a hundred and seventy years –

447

I'd like to see it go to a good home.'

'It's not an unwanted pet, Nico, it's a house –
and it will take somebody with the Fallons'
money to turn it into a good home.'

The peace of the countryside was suddenly disturbed by the thundering engine of a helicopter.

'Oh, here we go!' moaned Nico as he looked up
at the helicopter circulating in the air above the
house and he saw the words *Fallon Enterprises*
printed on the side of it.

'What an entrance!' declared Janet excitedly.

Kate and Tony peered down at the house as the
pilot continued to circle above it.

'It's fabulous!' squealed Kate.

'It's a fucking dump!' declared Tony. 'One of
the fucking chimneys is collapsed, from what I
can see.'

'Fabulous!' repeated Kate excitedly.

Nico and Janet looked on as the helicopter
descended and landed in what used to be the
gardens of the house.

'Come on,' said Janet as she rushed towards
them. 'You can meet them, and help show them
around.'

'I don't really want to,' he objected. 'I just
wanted to have a look – possibly a last look – at
the house.'

She grabbed the sleeve of his Barbour coat and
pulled him along with her. 'Yes, you do! There's
nothing like the personal touch.'

As the blades of the helicopter slowed to a halt,
the doors opened and the Fallons climbed out

and walked quickly towards Janet and Nico.

'Mr and Mrs Fallon, a pleasure!' Janet put out her hand and they both shook it. Nico thought for a second that Janet might make a curtsey.

'Sorry, I think we're a bit late,' apologised Kate.

'Not at all! Not at all!' gushed Janet.

'Was the traffic a bit heavy coming out of Dublin then?' smirked Nico as he nodded over to the helicopter.

'Well, it was a bit heavy getting to the heliport,' said Tony.

'You should get him to put one in your back garden then,' smirked Nico to Kate.

'I'm working on it,' nodded Kate with a smile.

Janet looked at them, not enjoying the banter. 'May I introduce Nicholas Armstrong-Collins, the seller, who made the journey all the way from Dublin to help show you around.'

Nico threw Janet a disbelieving look at her usage of a nonexistent double-barrelled name and the fib about his presence, then shook both their hands. 'Please call me Nico.'

The four walked away from the helicopter and to the front of the house.

'The view is amazing!' said Kate as she looked down the hill to the lake.

'It is until you look that way,' said Tony, pointing up at the house.

'How much land is going with it?' asked Kate.

'Fifteen acres, a boutique farm!' said Janet. 'Including the land going down to the lake and the property has its own lake frontage.'

Kate walked over to the balustrade of the forecourt and looked down.

'Those used to be fabulous gardens, believe it or not,' said Nico as he followed her over.

Kate looked at the terrace walls that had collapsed in places, with the ornamental bowls and statues knocked over.

'Sad how it was left to get into this state,' she said.

Nico looked at her, somewhat affronted. 'Well, no doubt somebody like you will manage to restore it.'

'Will we go inside?' Kate glanced at him momentarily as she walked past him.

They all walked up the steps to the metal door that had been placed there.

Tony knocked on the metal door. 'I'm guessing early Victorian?' he said and laughed mockingly.

'The original door was destroyed as were most of the front windows in the fire,' explained Nico.

'And when was that?' asked Kate.

'Ninety odd years ago. The War of Independence or the Civil War, I can't remember which,' said Nico.

'Yes, there was a small fire,' said Janet as she pushed the door open.

'Small fire! That's a bit of an understatement, isn't it?' said Tony as they walked through the hallway, seeing the rooms at the front of the house were badly burned.

'The fire damage is only to the front of the house, the rest is fine,' said Janet quickly. 'Luckily the fire went out or was put out before it gutted the place, as was often the case in those days. The arsonists must have been stopped or had to leave for some reason before they finished the job.'

Janet was improvising. She had no idea what had actually happened, nor had Nico as there had been no family lore on the matter.

Tony looked up and saw a part of the floor above his head was missing and he could see through to the sky through the missing roof. He looked at Kate and shook his head in dismay.

'Nico has owned the house for nearly a hundred and seventy years,' said Janet as they walked into the drawing room which again was burnt out.

'Not personally, may I say,' said Nico.

'I was going to say – you're wearing well!' said Kate with smirk.

They moved to the back of the house and went into the ballroom. All the French windows were boarded up apart from the arches at the top that let in the light.

The room was filled with old furniture and boxes.

'As you can see most of this room escaped any fire damage, and the attention to detail is amazing,' said Janet as she pointed out the elaborate carved roof.

'The trouble is – the ceiling looks as if it's about to fall down,' said Tony.

'No, I'm an architect, and I can assure you that ceiling is quite safe. Can't say the same for the rest of the house though,' said Nico and Janet gave him a warning look.

Kate started examining the furniture and boxes.

'That's family stuff and is not included in the sale,' said Nico.

'Thank heaven for that!' said Tony.

'I have to sift through it. But I'll have it all removed before I do.'

'I mean, if there's anything that takes your eye, I'm sure Nico will include it in the sale,' said Janet quickly. 'It would be nice to have some original furniture in the house when it's restored. It could be a treasure trove!'

Tony looked at the furniture in disgust. 'One man's treasure is another man's junk. No, thanks! And no offence, Nico.'

Nico shrugged.

'Shall we move on?' suggested Janet.

They looked around the rest of the rooms downstairs.

Then, as Kate went to walk up the main staircase Janet shouted, 'Stop! I'm sorry, but it's not safe. We have to use the servants' stairs around the back.'

She led them around to the back of the stairs and through a door that led down a passageway to the kitchens and sculleries. These were in a semi-basement with only the top halves of their windows on a level with the back yard and what used to be the walled kitchen gardens. Kate frowned when she realised the room was half below ground level. Tony spent a lot of his leisure time in the kitchen as he loved to cook and entertain while he did so. Yes, this room would need serious renovation ... perhaps the level of the back yard could be lowered ... then it could form a patio outside...

'A lot of the servants' quarters is remarkably well preserved,' said Janet, startling Kate out of her reverie.

'Pity it's just basic rooms though, isn't it? All the ornate detail was obviously in the main part of the house,' said Kate.

Janet then led them outside to the back yard and showed them the stables and carriage houses which she presented as an exciting extra opportunity for renovation. Tony looked incredulous but Kate was enthusiastic.

Back inside, they went up the servants' stairs and exited onto the first floor of the house. As they viewed some of the rooms at that end of the house they observed they were smoke-damaged and in a dilapidated state.

'I'm sorry we can't go any further,' said Janet. 'Health and Safety. The floors to the front of the house are fragile and might not take the weight.'

'You trying to say I'm fat?' said Tony accusingly.

'No, Mr Fallon! Of course not!'

Tony roared with the laughter. 'I'm only joking ya!'

'I see!' Janet smiled and tried to laugh. 'Very funny!'

They came out of the front door and looked up at the house.

'Well, thank you for showing us around,' said Kate.

'So what do you think?' asked Janet.

'It's certainly interesting,' said Tony, looking unimpressed.

'Will we see you at the auction next week?' pushed Janet.

'We've a lot to discuss,' said Kate, smiling at Tony. She looked at Nico. 'You'll miss the house when it's gone?'

'I guess. I still own Hunter's Farm – it's a small house down the road. The family has always used it as a holiday home since the main house was fire-damaged.'

'So there will still be an Armstrong presence in the area,' said Kate.

'We'd better fly! Literally!' said Tony. 'I've a shopping centre to build. Thanks for everything!' He shook their hands quickly. Then he and Kate held hands and headed back to the helicopter.

They climbed in, the pilot started the engine and the blades began to swirl.

'"I've a shopping centre to build"!' Nico mimicked Tony's voice.

'I don't know if you were more of a hindrance than a help with the house viewing,' said Janet as they watched the helicopter take off.

'Come on, Janet! They aren't serious buyers. He hated the place.'

'*Hmmm,* but she didn't,' said Janet.

Nico had got back to Dublin by the early evening and had just opened the door to his rented apartment in the Docklands when the intercom rang. He knew it was his ex-wife Susan dropping in their daughter Alex for the weekend. He pressed the button and let them in.

A minute later, eleven-year-old Alex came bounding in and gave him a hug, followed by Susan.

'Janet told me you met her down at the house,' said Susan.

'She's quite the little spy, isn't she? She was

454

busy showing lots of prospective buyers around, you'll be glad to know.' He couldn't leave the bitterness out of his voice.

Alex had gone running off to her room.

'Janet said Tony and Kate Fallon were down looking at it,' she said brightly.

'*Hmmm*, my mother would be turning in her grave at the thought of that type living in Armstrong House.'

'Jacqueline would be turning in her grave twice as fast at the thought of what would happen to her precious son and granddaughter if we didn't sell it – rented flat for you, selling Alex's home–'

'I know, I know, we've been through all this before,' he said crossly. 'You've got what you want – we're selling it, aren't we?'

She sighed, looking at his upset face. 'I thought you agreed this was the best thing for us all.'

'I have. Doesn't mean I'm happy about it though.'

Alex came out of the bedroom and Susan gave her a kiss and a hug. 'Right, I'll leave you to it. See you Sunday.'

89

It was approaching midnight when Tony pulled into the gateway of their house in Dublin. He pressed a zapper and the electric gates opened. He drove in and parked outside the white modern house. He glanced at Kate beside him. They had been at a function all night.

They both got out of the car and walked in silence to the front door and let themselves in. Tony pressed the code into the alarm panel to turn it off while Kate walked upstairs to their bedroom where she changed into a silk night-dress, got into bed and started leafing through a magazine. She stopped to scrutinise a photo of herself in the society pages. A few minutes later, Tony came in.

'You were quiet tonight,' he said as he took off his tie.

'Was I?' she said.

'Anything the matter?' He sat down on the bed beside her.

'No.'

'I thought you said if I went to see that house you'd be happy?'

She put down the magazine. 'I would have been happy if you hadn't made up your mind you disliked it before you had even seen it.'

'Disliked it? I hated it! I'd like to take a big sweeping brush and sweep it into the lake!'

'Well, I love it!'

'But why?'

'I just do!' She jumped out of the bed and started to pace the floor. 'Look, we need a place like that.'

'Why? We have a beautiful house here that has almost everything we need.'

'No, Tony, everything *you* need. I've been trying to tell you for a long time. I want a fresh start somewhere.'

He looked at her as if she were mad. 'A fresh

start! What more do you want? Most people would kill for the life you have.'

'Oh, yes, we have all the material things we could ever want. And our life is a whirl of parties and travel. But I want more than just that... I feel life is passing us by. Monday, New York. Friday, London. Sunday, Rome. We've no time for ourselves any more. You're always in meetings. I'm always following you around to meetings. I want somewhere for us, just us. Somewhere that can be our home, just for us.'

'This is our home!'

'This is a place we pass through on our way to the next meeting or event. It's no better than a hotel.'

He sat in silence for a while. 'I didn't realise you felt so strongly about that damned house.'

She sat down beside him. 'I feel that strongly about our lives. There has to be more to life than the next deal, the next shopping centre. We're living our lives for other people, not for us. I want us to find a place where we can just relax and get to know each other again.'

'I thought we did know each other.'

'When was the last time we talked? I mean really talked about anything else other than business and what party we're going to? And there are always so many people around. Every time I come back the house is filled with your work people. We need somewhere like that house. Somewhere we can be alone and see where we really want to go in life.'

'And why that house? Out of all the houses we could buy?'

'I grew up in the town near there, Castlewest,

457

before we emigrated to New York. I spent a lot of time playing around that house growing up. We used to cycle there. We weren't supposed to be on the property, but we went in anyway. Nobody was there to spot us. I've always loved it, and I would love to own it and restore it.'

He looked at her for a long while. 'Okay – you can buy it. Go to the auction next week and buy the house, doesn't matter how much it costs.'

Kate suddenly screamed with delight and jumped on top of him.

'Will you stop!' he said laughing loudly as she hugged him tightly. 'Now listen to me! This is on condition that you take care of the whole rebuilding. Do you understand me?'

'Yes! Yes!' Kate agreed excitedly.

'I want nothing to do with it – I'll be too busy with the shopping centre. So don't come to me if you have any problems with it. Okay?'

'Deal!'

Nico looked around the packed auction room at the Shelbourne Hotel.

'There's been a huge amount of interest,' Janet informed him. 'I think we may get the asking price.'

'Hopefully,' nodded Nico.

'Or maybe even more! Look who's just arrived in!' squealed Janet as Kate Fallon walked into the room, dressed immaculately in a cream suit, her hair beautifully styled, diamonds sparkling at her neck and wrist.

'And she's without him, that's a good sign,' said Janet as Kate walked to the top of the room and sat down.

'But he's the one with the money,' said Nico.

'Yes, but women are much better at auctions than men. She'll always follow her heart when push comes to shove, but he'd get scared and follow his head. Anyway, I'd better get going. Wish me luck!'

'Indeed!' said Nico as Janet walked to the auctioneer's stand at the top of the room.

'Ladies and gentlemen, welcome to the Shelbourne and today's auction with Dolans Auctioneers. Today we are opening the auction with Armstrong House. This stunning period property in need of refurbishment is a unique sale to the discerning eye. I'm starting the bidding today for this property at a cool one million. Who bids me one million? Thank you, sir.'

As the bidding got under way Nico could only watch as one hundred and seventy years of his family history were auctioned away. What amazed him was how quick it was and it seemed no time until a now overexcited Janet was practically screaming, 'Sold! To Mrs Kate Fallon, ladies and gentlemen!'

Kate was swamped with people wishing her congratulations in the Shelbourne after the auction. Nico looked on as a couple of journalists descended on her for an interview about her latest purchase. He watched her as she laughed with them and delivered witty lines to the journalists, like the seasoned actress she was. When the press photographer asked for a photo, Kate hopped up on the grand piano, crossed her legs, struck a pose and flashed a smile for him. Nico raised his eyes to heaven as he went to seek out Janet.

Kate escaped to the restrooms and grinned at herself in the mirror, thrilled she had got what she wanted. She left the restrooms and walked towards the bar where she had organised to celebrate with a few friends. Suddenly she heard the unmistakable voice of Janet Dolan speaking to Nico on the other side of a pillar, and she stopped to listen in.

'You must be delighted, Nico! One and a half million! It got even more than I expected.'

'Yes, not that I'll be seeing any of it. It'll all be going to pay off those Armstrong debts that have been passed on through the generations, not to mention my ex-wife's mortgage, not to mention her lawyer, not to mention my lawyer.'

'Well, at least you can be free of it all now,' said Janet.

'Yeah, but I'm the one who sold the family seat, aren't I? No matter how hard things were in the past, they always hung on to it. I just sold out!'

'You'd have been mad not to in this market. Besides, Nico, the house is falling down and you don't have the cash to save it. At least the Fallons will do something with it now.'

'Yes, I dread to think what though. They will turn it into a veritable Disneyland of tackiness. I can see it all now – they'll turn the old ballroom into an indoor heated swimming pool complete with naked Grecian statutes. And there will be marble everywhere and Jacuzzis and ... oh, I shudder to think!'

Janet giggled. 'You don't know that.'

'Oh, I do! Did you see those chunky diamonds she's wearing today. It's all about money and nothing about taste with them.'

Kate fingered the diamond necklace around her neck before she continued to the bar.

'Tony?' asked Kate as they ate out that night.

'Yes, darling?'

'I was just thinking. Nico Collins is an architect, isn't he?'

'So he claimed.'

'Why don't we employ him to renovate the house? He knows it more than anyone else?'

'You can employ whoever you want. I made it clear that's your baby, and I don't want anything to do with rebuilding it.'

'Yes – sorry – I forgot,' Kate nodded.

90

Nico's architect's firm, Collins & Darcy, was a small company he had set up with a college friend, Darrell, a number of years before. It was based in a small Georgian building in Baggot Street.

Kate walked into the building for her appointment. She had made sure to wear extra diamonds for the meeting.

'Good afternoon, Kate, good to see you,' said Nico as the secretary showed her into his office.

She shook his hand and smiled broadly before

sitting down.

'I was surprised to hear from you again,' he said, looking a little concerned. 'I thought all the contracts had been signed and the money paid and it was all done and dusted.'

'Yes, it is. I wanted to speak to you about another matter.'

'Oh really?' said Nico, sitting forward and looking interested.

'Yes, I was going to enquire about engaging your services as an architect.'

He smiled broadly. 'Of course! I would be delighted.'

'You know my husband is in the process of building a gigantic shopping mall?'

Nico's eyes widened and his mouth dropped. 'Yes, I'm aware of it ... and you would like to employ us to d-d-design it?' he stuttered in amazement at the magnitude of the contract.

'Oh no, don't be silly!' She waved her hand in a dismissive fashion. 'A little practice like yours couldn't possibly cope with a project of that size.' She gave a jingle-jangle laugh.

Nico's mouth closed firmly as he looked at her, annoyed.

'No – I merely mention the mall because my husband is so busy that he has entrusted me with the house and I was going to suggest you handle the renovation.'

'The house? You mean my house? I mean your house?' He shook his head, irritated with himself. 'The house you bought from me?'

'Yes – what other house would I mean?'

'Well, thank you for thinking of me. I'd love to

462

do the job.'

'Good! Then if you could submit a quote to me? By Monday? I'm anxious to get on with it.' She stood up and put out her hand which was dripping in diamond rings and bracelets.

He took her hand and shook it.

'Ta ta!' she said as she turned and strode out.

Nico sat looking after her, surprised, delighted and for some reason frightened by the offer of work.

Kate had arranged to meet Nico at the house and as she neared Castlewest in her red Ferrari she was amazed how much it had changed since her family had emigrated in the eighties. As she passed housing estate after housing estate, and pharmaceutical plant after information-technology centre, she realised the town was buzzing with prosperity. As she drove through the main street all the memories of growing up there came flooding back, and she realised she had probably changed more than the town. The town's proximity to the lake and beautiful countryside and nearby sea had also made it a tourist destination and there were many tourists wandering around.

She put her foot down and headed out on the new motorway that led towards the house. She turned off it and drove through the local little picture-postcard village that she remembered was near the house. Most of the houses in the village were now bought as holiday homes for professionals living in Dublin. She sped through the village and continued around the lake towards her destination.

Kate drove through the gateway and up the overgrown driveway, screeching to a halt in front of the house. Nico was already there waiting for her. Stepping out of the car, she walked across to him.

'You decided to travel by more conventional means this time?' he said.

'It's Tony tends to use the helicopter not me. Besides, I needed my car. I'm staying down for a few days while I organise things.'

'You staying in Castlewest?'

'No, Ashford Castle.'

'Where else?' He didn't hide the note of cynicism in his voice.

She reached into her bag and took out the keys, then walked up the steps and unlocked the metal door.

'I've been working on some sketches and designs for you to look at...' He went to unzip his folder as he followed her through the hall.

She dismissed him with a wave of a hand. 'Yes – later.'

He looked at her, affronted at her rejection. 'I thought if we kept to as much of the original design and lay-out of the house...' He trailed off as she darted into a nearby room.

Before he could follow her in, she marched back out into the hall and looked at the staircase.

'That stairs are going to take a lot of restoring, it's in a dangerous state as Janet said,' advised Nico.

'Well, I was planning on ripping the whole thing out!'

'What?' He looked at her, amazed.

'And instead of a staircase put in a glass elevator, what do you think of that?'

'But–'

She marched into what had been the dining room. 'And I was thinking of turning this room into a gym.'

'Into a gym?' he checked, in case he was hearing things.

'This figure doesn't keep itself, you know. Then the small sitting room–' she looked to be deep in thought, 'into a sauna.'

'A sauna!'

She walked across the hall and into the large drawing room.

'*Hmmm,* that fireplace has to go!' she declared.

'But it's the original fireplace from the 1840s! It's the one thing that survived the fire in this room.'

'That's my point – so old-fashioned and damaged! In fact, I want all the fireplaces re-placed. All those old-fashioned ones in the bed-rooms, *yuk!* I want underground heating put in instead!'

'Into a Victorian house?' He was incredulous.

'With marble floors.'

'Marble!'

'Marble floors – everywhere!' She marched out and down the hall. He hurried after her. 'Except here in the hall, of course. I want tiles here which light up and change colours as you walk on them. I saw it once in a shop in Rome, amazing!' They entered the ballroom. 'And here! I want this turned into an indoor heated swimming pool.' She marched around the room.

He raised his eyes to heaven, as his face turned red.

'But not just any indoor swimming pool. I want statues – Grecian and Roman and every other type we can think of. And swings hanging from that ceiling! So we can swing – over the pool – while we sip Pina Coladas!' She had a satisfied dreamy look on her face.

'I think – *ahem* – Kate, I think we have very different ideas of how this renovation should be done.'

She looked at him, full of concern. 'Oh dear – do you think my plans wouldn't be in keeping with the house?'

'Yes, I do!' he said angrily.

'Oh my – do you think it's all in bad taste?'

'Yes, I do!'

'A veritable Disneyland of tackiness even?' Her face changed and she looked knowingly at him.

His mouth dropped as he realised she had overheard what he had said to Janet in the Shelbourne on the day of the auction.

'You've been having me on?' he realised, his face going even redder, this time from embarrassment.

She nodded.

'You're quite an actress!'

'That *was* my profession.'

'You shouldn't have been listening in to other people's conversations.'

'Well, then, you shouldn't have been speaking out loud in public.' She walked around the room, inspecting it. 'Not a very nice way to speak about the people who had just handed you one and half million bucks, was it?'

'I just had reservations about how you would develop the house.'

'Based on what exactly? You don't know us, you don't know anything about us. If you had wanted to do the house up a certain way, why didn't you do it yourself?'

'Because I didn't have the money to do it.'

'Exactly! So why would you think you were superior to the people who have that money and made it themselves?' She walked past him. 'Good day, Mr Armstrong! Close the door after you, will you?' She walked out of the room. A couple of minutes later he could hear her Ferrari speeding off down the drive.

Nico was driving back to Dublin when the phone rang.

'How did the meeting with Kate Fallon go?' It was his business partner Darrell Darcy.

'Not so good. I think I got fired.'

'How?' Darrell was aghast.

'By being an ass. She's a fairly ruthless business-woman behind all that charm and diamonds.'

'Pity you didn't realise that before you pissed her off then,' said Darrell.

'I know,' he sighed. 'Talk to you later.'

Nico continued to drive for a while, deep in thought. Then he suddenly turned and headed to Ashford Castle.

It was late in the evening as Nico parked outside Ashford Castle and walked in through the front doors. He walked over to reception and asked the receptionist to ring up to Kate Fallon's suite.

'She's having dinner in the dining room,' said the receptionist.

Nico went there and hovered at the entrance, looking around at the full restaurant. He spotted Kate immediately, sitting at a table with four others. She was talking happily, causing her fellow diners to laugh.

Suddenly she spotted him and her face creased in confusion as she saw him smile and wave over at her.

'If you could excuse me a minute, please,' she excused herself with a smile, then put her napkin on the table and walked over to him.

'What are you doing here?' she asked, her eyes wide with puzzlement.

'Look, I know we've got off to a bad start. And I shouldn't have judged you the way I did. But … I really want this job! It means a lot to me. I would love to be involved in the renovation of this house. I feel I owe it to the house – and I will work round the clock to give you what you want.'

'I see!' she said.

'And to show you how committed I am, I will even reduce my fee by twenty per cent if you allow me to continue working for you.'

'Right!' She studied him intently. 'Well, I accept your twenty-per-cent discount, and now if you could allow me to get back to my dinner?'

'Of course, and thank you, you won't regret it.'

She turned to go before stopping and looking back at him. 'Incidentally, I never said anything about firing you from the job today – but your offer of a twenty-per-cent discount is accepted and much appreciated anyway.'

His mouth dropped open as she walked back to her table.

91

Nico pulled into the gateway of the Fallons' house in Dublin, looking up at the high electric gates and high wall around it. He opened his window and, reaching out, pressed the intercom on the pillars.

'Hello?' It was Kate herself.

'Nico Armstrong for our meeting.'

The heavy iron electric gates suddenly started to part and he drove in and up the short drive. He looked up at the new white building with pillars at the front and long windows and it was as he had imagined it would be. He grabbed his folders and walked towards the door.

The front door opened and there stood Kate, in a white flared satin trouser suit.

'You found the place all right?' she asked, as she moved back to let him in, and closed the door after him.

'Yes, your directions were easy to follow.'

He followed her through a round hall which had a spiral staircase. They walked down some steps into an oversized sitting room. As he expected the house was all cream sofas, glass tables, cream carpets, spacious, with double doors leading into other rooms.

She fitted into her movie-star surroundings as she poured them both a drink and sat down opposite him. His ancestral home wasn't going to know what hit it, he thought.

He unzipped his folders and started handing her his drawings.

'These are the plans we're submitting to the Council for the rebuilding for planning permission. It's everything you asked for, and we just need final approval from you before we submit them.'

She quickly looked through the plans. 'These all look in order. So where do we go from here?'

'As soon as we get planning we can get the building work done straight away. I've already tendered the building firms. After that we will be renovating the interiors, which will need a big input from you on how exactly you want your house to be.' He looked around at the room, taking it all in. 'You mentioned this was going to be a main residence for you and Tony?'

She stood up, lit up a cigarette and started walking around.

'Yes, we are going to relocate there. So it's going to be a home for us. Tony likes his parties and to entertain, so it will have to be a show place as well. That house, I believe, used to have a reputation of being one of the best houses in the country for balls and parties.'

'That's right.'

'We want it to have that reputation again. I want it to regain its reputation for glamour and beauty.'

As he looked at her he thought that if anyone

could do it, she could.

'I've a clear idea of how I wish the house to be. I want it restored as much as possible to the original interiors that were there.'

He nodded approvingly.

'With, of course, a modern feel. Tony hates antiques – he says you never know who's had them before you!' She gave a light laugh. 'So we'll have very chic modern furniture but with the walls, ceiling, features to be as close to the original as possible.'

'I see. I can't find any good records in libraries of what the inside of the house was like, only the outside. And of course it was so long ago nobody who lived then is around to tell us... There may be something in the artwork stored in the ballroom. I can take a look and see.'

'Yes, if you could.'

The front door opened and they could hear two men talking loudly and jovially.

'Here's Tony now,' said Kate.

Nico began to tidy away the drawings as Tony came in with another man who Nico immediately recognised from the press as Steve Shaw, the head of Eiremerica Bank.

'Hello there, again,' said Tony as he shook Nico's hand before going over and kissing Kate.

'Nico was going through the plans with me,' explained Kate.

'Very good. Are you joining us for dinner, Nico?' asked Tony.

'No, he was just leaving,' Kate said.

'Nonsense, I'm making meatballs – you'll love them!' said Tony.

'No, I really should be going,' said Nico.

'I insist,' smiled Tony.

Nico realised when Tony Fallon insisted, it wasn't wise to resist, even if his wife looked displeased that Nico had overstayed his welcome.

It was all very informal. They were ushered into a giant kitchen and all had to sit around an island while Tony cooked. As if being in the company of the head of Eiremerica Bank wasn't enough, they were soon joined by several other guests who were captains of industry or well-known faces from the entertainment industry. Nico felt out of his depth, and nobody seemed that much interested in him anyway, as they fawned over Tony and Kate.

'When you're redesigning that house we've just bought make sure you renovate that kitchen into a super-duper one for me, Nico,' said Tony as he served meatballs on to everyone's plates.

'Tony does all the cooking in our home,' Kate said. 'He says the kitchen is the main room in any house and he practically lives here.'

'I've done some of my best business deals over my kitchen table,' said Tony as he continued to serve.

'Yes, we plan to do a total overhaul of the semi-basement,' said Nico. 'The kitchen was designed as a working room for cooks and kitchen maids – on strictly utilitarian principles.'

'What house is this?' asked Steve, suddenly alert, looking at Nico as if he had seen him for the first time.

'We've bought an old country pile and Nico is rebuilding it for us,' said Kate.

'How very exciting,' said a woman called Melanie who Nico recognised as a television presenter. 'I hear that's all the rage. I know one friend who is a developer who bought an old manor and got an underground car park put in and a car elevator, so his wife can bring the car up into the kitchen to unpack the groceries!'

'Well, I'm afraid Nico has banned us from installing anything vulgar, haven't you, Nico?' Kate looked at him teasingly.

'Where's the house and who did you buy it off?' questioned Steve.

'Typical banker – you only stopped short from asking how much we paid for it,' Kate mocked him, causing Steve to look embarrassed.

'The house is down the country, and we actually bought it from this man here,' said Tony, placing his two hands firmly on Nico's shoulders.

Everyone looked at Nico.

'And how did you come to own the house?' questioned Melanie curiously, studying Nico.

'It's been in my family for generations,' said Nico, made uncomfortable by all the sudden attention.

'It's in a terrible state though. It hasn't been lived in for–' Tony stopped and looked at Nico. 'Well, when was it last lived in?'

'Not for nearly ninety years. The last person who lived there was my grandfather, Pierce Armstrong,' said Nico.

'That was Lord Pierce Armstrong, wasn't it?' asked Kate.

He looked at her, surprised. 'You certainly have done your homework, haven't you?'

'I always do when I'm buying something.' She

473

held his look.

'Lord Armstrong? That sounds intriguing – are you a lord, Nico?' questioned Melanie, getting excited.

'I'm afraid not – the title went one way and the money the other. There's some distant cousin in England who got the title – my mother had no brothers, you see, to inherit it. All I got was the draughty, dilapidated house – and I don't even own that any more!'

'What a shame!' Melanie immediately lost interest in him again.

'So – you will soon all be having weekends with us at our country estate,' said Tony, bemused at the thought as he sat down to join them to eat.

Later, everyone had gone and Kate was stacking the dishwasher in the kitchen.

'I wish you hadn't asked Nico to join us tonight,' she said.

'Why? He's seems a nice enough fella,' said Tony.

'I just don't want to blur the lines with him. We employ him to do a job for us. I don't want him thinking he's our friend.'

'Ah, will you come on! Most of those people there tonight depend on us for their living in one way or another.'

'He's just a bit pompous sometimes.'

'Is he? Hadn't noticed. In what way?'

'I just think he looks down on us a little,' she said.

'What?' Tony was incredulous. 'Why would a tuppenny-ha'penny architect look down on us?'

474

Kate closed up the dishwasher. 'Oh, for reasons you'll never understand.'

Kate looked at Tony's puzzled and confused face. Going over to him, she put her arms around him and smiled. 'Oh, it doesn't matter. Who cares what Nicholas Armstrong-Collins thinks anyway?'

You seemingly, thought Tony.

92

As the months went by, planning permission was granted and work began on the house. Nico was busy overseeing the work and made the trip down regularly from Dublin. He was busy in his own life as well as the divorce became final. They had paid off the mortgage on his former home with Susan and he'd bought a house for himself in Ranelagh. By the time they had paid off the Armstrong debts and legal fees, there was only loose change left.

'At least you're not saddled with any debt any more,' Susan had pointed out. 'You're free now.' She had looked at him wryly. 'Free to concentrate on your work – without *any* distractions.'

He didn't mind being away from Dublin for a while after the long-drawn-out divorce. So he spent a lot of time at Hunter's Farm. The beauty of being an architect was he didn't always need to be in the office and could work from the farm, which also allowed him to be near Armstrong

House to supervise the work there. The drawback to the whole situation was the constant interfering presence of Kate Fallon. He quickly discovered she was a hard taskmaster who wanted to be involved in every aspect along the way.

'With the money she's paying, even with that stupid twenty-percent discount you threw at her, if she wants you dancing to *Swan Lake* around that house down there, then you do it!' insisted Darrell when Nico complained of her interference. It was easy for Darrell to say that, he wasn't the one who had to put up with her, thought Nico.

He was in the house inspecting the work as the team of builders were busy renovating around him. The house was beginning to take shape. The rooms that had been destroyed by fire had been rebuilt and plastered, the roof had been replaced. Even the stairs were being lovingly restored.

'Oh, here's trouble,' said one of the electricians as the familiar red Ferrari roared up to the front.

'Not again!' Nico said out loud. 'She must be keeping Ashford Castle going with the amount of business she's giving them staying there.'

A minute later, Kate came striding in, moment-arily examining the new front door which she had sourced in Italy.

'You know, you really should not be in here without a hard hat and protective clothing,' Nico said as she walked over to him in high heels and a business suit. She gave him a withering look and ignored him.

'I could get into trouble with you swanning around here like that,' he continued.

'Your problem, Nico, is you worry too much

476

about things that will never happen.' She continued with her inspection.

He seethed as he followed her through the rooms while she examined the work.

'You're way behind schedule,' she pointed out.

'No, we would be on target,' he said evenly. 'But you'll find we are simply working to a new schedule caused by your own interruptions.'

She swung around to face him. 'I hope you remember there's a clause in our contract saying that *you* have to compensate us, if you go a certain time past the schedule.'

'I think you'll find that does not stand because *you* caused the delays.'

She turned and kept on walking briskly. 'I think you'll find it does.'

She somehow enjoyed winding him up. It was so easily done. Seeing he was getting more annoyed, she pushed a little further. 'Why not get it checked out by a lawyer ... if you can still afford one after that divorce you had.'

He became incensed. 'Excuse me, do you think that's an appropriate thing to say?'

'Is it not? Why not have it checked out by the lawyer while you're checking the contract.' She stopped and ran a hand over a plastered wall. 'Look at this, Nico – this is a bad job.'

He ran a hand over it. 'Actually – no, it isn't.' He looked dismissively at her. 'What would you know about plastering, to be fair?'

His attitude angered her. 'I think I've been involved in enough construction of shopping centres to know a bad plastering job when I see one,' she said.

'Who's the architect around here?' he demanded.

She made a sarcastic face and raised her hands. 'Oh, I'm sorry, *is* there an architect around here? I didn't realise there was!'

'You know something?' He took off his hard hat and flung it on the ground in front of her. 'You're so fucking clever? You finish the building of your damned house yourself!'

He turned and stormed off, causing all the builders to cheer loudly.

Kate turned around to the men and said, 'What an exit! I thought *I* was supposed to be the Diva around here!'

The builders clapped and cheered even louder.

'Excuse me, Mrs Fallon, we've found something – could you come and take a look?' asked the foreman.

'Certainly,' she said and she followed him upstairs to one of the bedrooms where they were removing the old floorboards. She peered into the crevice where there were stacks of old letters, some in bags.

'Get them out,' she said.

He pulled the bags out and brushed the dust off them. Kate took out a couple of the bundles. She saw they were addressed to Lady Clara Armstrong, Armstrong House.

'Do you want me to place them in the ballroom with all the other crap?' asked the builder.

As an actress she loved reading through scripts and old books, and she would love to delve through these letters to an actual person who lived in the house.

'No, it's fine, I'll take these with me, thanks,' she said, putting the bundles of letters back in the bags. She picked them up and headed back to her car.

Nico parked outside Hunter's Farm, marched up to the front door and let himself in. He strode down the corridor and into the sitting room where he poured himself a drink.

'Damned woman!' he said out loud.

His mobile rang and he saw it was Darrell.

'Yes?' he snapped.

'Oh – you sound in a bad mood.'

'I am. I've just walked off the Fallon job.'

'Ah, Nicholas!' Darrell was irate. 'What's the problem this time?'

'The same as the last time – Kate Fallon! She's impossible to work with. She's parading around all the time giving orders, undermining me, no respect. She prances around that building site as if it's a movie set, in glitzy frocks, delivering witty one-liners – usually at my expense!'

Darrell chuckled. 'You'll kiss and make up tomorrow. You always do.'

'Not this time. I'm not going back. I'm way behind with all my other work because of her demands. I'm staying down here a couple of weeks to try and catch up, which means I won't have Alex this weekend.' He walked over to the leather-top desk and turned on his computer.

'Right – I'll talk to you later,' Darrell said, deciding to finish the conversation rather than to listen to any more of Nico's moans.

Nico poured himself another drink and rested

against a sideboard while he drank it. He looked at the framed photo of his ex-wife Susan smiling from a silver frame on the sideboard.

'And you can piss off too!' he said, grabbing the photo and turning it face down.

Kate carefully laid the stacks of old letters on the glass table in their house in Dublin. Most of them seemed to be letters to Clara. But what intrigued her was a group of letters addressed to Lord Pierce Armstrong at a military headquarters in France. But these letters were unopened.

She turned on her laptop and started to do an internet search through hereditary peers of Britain and Ireland.

The front door slammed and Tony came bounding in.

'Hi, love.' He bent down and kissed her. 'What are *they?*' he said with a note of disgust, pointing down at the old letters.

'We found them today hidden under floorboards in the house. They are letters to Lady Clara Armstrong mostly dated 1915 and 1916 – isn't that exciting?'

He peered down at them. 'Hmmm – and who was Clara Armstrong when she was at home?'

'I'm just checking on a hereditary peer site. Here she is – she married Lord Pierce Armstrong, who was Nico's grandfather, in 1914 – that's all it says about her. She must be Nico's grandmother.'

'Does he know you have them?'

'No.'

'Don't you think you should give them to him, in that case?'

'Perhaps. I want to take a look through them first.'

'But why would you want to?' He stared at the letters in puzzlement.

'I want to know about the people who lived in our house before us, that's why.'

'I see!' He raised his eyes upwards. 'Always the actress – researching for your new role as mistress of the house?'

'Besides, Nico walked out on the job today.'

'Oh no – why?'

'He can't take direction.'

'And you can't take a back seat!' he accused her.

'Don't worry – he'll be back in a couple of days – with another twenty-per-cent discount no doubt!'

He bent down and kissed her approvingly. 'I trained you well! I'd better quickly change into my tuxedo. We're running late for tonight's charity ball. Why aren't you changed yet?'

'Oh Tony, I've got a terrible headache. I think I might have to miss it,' she pleaded.

'But they'll all be expecting you!'

'I know! I'm sorry!'

He looked at her with the letters spread around her. 'You just want to spend the night reading through those silly letters, don't you?'

'Do you mind?' She looked guilty.

'I guess not,' he sighed, smiling. 'I'll see you later.'

93

Kate was lying out on their bed reading a magazine. Tony came out of the bathroom and joined her. Her mobile started ringing and she answered it.

'Mrs Fallon, it's Jeff Maguire here, foreman at the building of your house here.'

'Oh yes, Mr Maguire, how is everything?'

'You tell me, Mrs Fallon! Nico Collins hasn't turned up for the past three days and we've gone as far as we can go without Mr Collins signing off on the work.'

'Damn! Can't you just keep on working until he arrives?'

'No! It has to go on his insurance if there's a problem, so he has to sign off. Or you replace Collins with a new architect and it goes on the new firm's insurance. But at the moment you're paying men for sitting around doing nothing.'

'Bugger!' Her face creased with worry. 'All right, I'll take care of it, Mr Maguire.'

'Trouble?' asked Tony.

'Bloody Collins is playing hard-ball and not turning up to work. Cheek of him!'

Tony studied his wife. 'What is the problem between you and Nico? It's been nonstop clashing since he started working for us.'

'Whatever problem there is, it's his problem!' she said, exasperated.

'Nothing to do with you, of course?' he said knowingly.

'He just gets on my nerves!'

He put his arms around her and used a soothing voice. 'Tell Tony – why don't you like him? What's he done?'

'Oh nothing! I'm being stupid.'

'Kate?' he said, with a warning face.

She sighed loudly. 'When I was growing up in Castlewest near the house, we were poor. Before my family left for New York we had nothing.'

'I know. Same as my own background. We're self-made. But what's that got to do with Nico Collins?'

'I remember him growing up.'

'Do you? I thought you didn't know him.'

'Oh, I didn't, I can assure you. We lived in different worlds. He and his family would come down to their holiday home for the summers. You know Hunter's Farm, down the road from where we've bought?'

'Uh huh,' nodded Tony, interested.

'His father was an architect and his mother was this very beautiful woman called Jacqueline. Everyone knew of them, because they seemed quite glamorous to us back then. I remember watching them, Nico and his brothers and sisters when they came into town or were playing by the lake. I mean, they were nobody compared to the Armstrongs in the past, but they just seemed so confident and classy. I guess I was envious of them. They seemed a million miles from my family, my life.'

'That's a long time ago. Why is that interfering

with your relationship with Nico now?'

'We've fought for everything we have. Both of us, fought from the bottom up. And I just feel Nico is resentful of us because of what we have – and he's arrogant. When I say something, or make a suggestion, he makes me feel ... he makes me feel like I'm not that important.'

'Come on, Kate, you're on top of the world, everyone wants to be your friend, be with you. You're letting insecurities from the past get the better of you. You're no longer that girl in that town looking on at the Armstrongs enviously. You have more and have achieved more than they ever could. We've done it together.'

She sighed. 'You're right of course.'

'So you've two choices: either get rid of him, or forget all this nonsense and let him get on with rebuilding our new house. Our new home.'

She looked at him and kissed him. 'Thanks, Tony.'

Nico answered the door at Hunter's Farm and was taken aback to see Kate standing there.

'I think we need to talk,' she said, taking off her sunglasses.

He sighed and moved out of the way to allow her to enter. She stepped in and followed him down the corridor and into the lounge. She was impressed by the interiors which were antique and elegant and obviously hadn't been touched for decades.

He leaned against a sideboard in the lounge. 'So?'

'I'm not going to beat around the bush. I need

an architect and you need a job.'

'Actually, no, I don't. I was snowed under with work. I'm burying myself here in Hunter's Farm to try and catch up with it.'

She dismissed him with a wave of her hand, that gesture she had that really irritated him. 'Yes, but this job is special to you. It's your ancestral home – you want to have a part in its restoration.'

'Cut the shit and tell me what you want.'

She lit up a cigarette. 'Here's the deal – I'll stay out of your way while you complete construction and only come back when you are ready to renovate the interiors and need my input. Say – in three months?'

'Four months,' he corrected.

She made a face. 'Four months then. Until then I'll stay out of your way.' She put out her hand. 'Deal?'

He thought for a second and then shook her hand. 'Deal.'

'Great. Now we can all get back to work. You're worse than a trade union, Nico.'

'And less of the wisecracks,' he warned.

She laughed. 'That's not part of the deal. Go on – make me a cup of tea to seal the pact.'

He nodded and walked off to the kitchen. She walked around the room and took in the ambience, liking it. She looked at the photos on the wall, mainly happy family photos of the Collins family growing up. She stopped and studied the photo of his parents, Jacqueline smiling happily as she walked along the lakeshore. She walked to the sideboard and saw a photo frame turned over. She picked it up and studied it.

And the ex-wife, I presume, she said to herself.

Nico was back in Dublin and was in the video rental shop with Alex while she selected some DVDs. Kate had taken him by surprise with her offer of a truce. He thought she was uncompromising, one who would never give in. As they had sat and chatted that evening in Hunter's Farm over tea, she had even managed to be charming – talking about day-to-day things in a relaxed way he would never have thought possible of the Fallons. She had chatted about her acting career and he was intrigued to find out how good an actress she apparently was. She had said she was a varied actress running the gamut from comedy to serious drama.

Nico was peering up and down the video rental shop.

'May I assist you?' the guy who worked in the store finally asked.

'Em, yeah – I'm looking for a Kate Fallon DVD?'

'Kate Fallon?' The man was confused. 'Ah, you mean Kate Donovan who married Tony Fallon. Yeah, we've got some of her stuff here all right. What are you looking for? Her early stuff is on the end of that shelf, while her later stuff is on the end of that one.'

'Well, what's the difference?'

The man laughed. 'Well, her early stuff is pretty trash, to be honest, but her later stuff ain't so bad – she even won a couple of awards.'

'Er,' Nico scratched his head, 'I think I'll take one from either end of her career.'

'She cut her career short when she married Tony Fallon – you know, the magnate?'

'Was she a loss to the film world?'

'I guess we'll never know. She was only getting into her stride when she retired.'

Alex placed three DVDs on the counter and announced, 'I'll take these.'

After Alex had gone to bed, Nico put on one of the DVDs and settled back to watch Kate Fallon for the night. He was intrigued as he watched her grace the screen. He found the characters she was playing hard to associate with the Kate he knew.

'So, are you acting in the movies, or acting in real life?' Nico questioned her image on the screen as he knocked back his brandy.

94

Kate had spent the day curled up in front of the fire in their lounge, reading Clara's letters. From what she could see they were all from soldiers fighting on the front in the First World War. She was fascinated as they described their daily lives. But more intrigued by how they spoke to Clara. They held her in such high esteem, almost as if they were in love with her.

Dearest Clara,
I was so overjoyed to get your letter today. You don't

know what it means to me to know I'm in your thoughts at this horrible time. I think of the past here all the time, it stops me dwelling on the present. I remember the fun times we had in London before all this started, before you left for Ireland. Remember that funny incident at the Charlemont Ball...

Soon she found herself lost in his words as he described the night and Clara's fairytale life. She was dying to open the unopened letters addressed to Pierce Armstrong, but was putting off doing so. She was curious to know how they had found their way back to Armstrong House unopened and who were they from. Maybe they had never reached him with the war, she reasoned. She had a feeling looking at the elegant writing they were from Clara writing to her husband at war. Somehow she was reluctant to open them – as if it would be an intrusion into something private and even sacred.

The front door banged. Tony came in looking hassled and went straight to the drinks cabinet where he poured himself a large whiskey.

'Have you not left that position all day?' he asked, seeing her stretched out in front of the fire with the letters:

'Only to get some chocolate! These letters are so intriguing, Tony!'

He walked over and knelt down beside her.

'How can you even read that scrawl?'

'I think he had beautiful handwriting!'

'He?'

'A Captain Hugo Arbuthnot, who was a great friend of Clara's, and was in love with her from

488

what I can read. Isn't that amazing? To read his words about her?'

'*Hmmm,* truly amazing,' he said sarcastically. 'Wasn't she supposed to be married to Nico's grandfather?'

'Yes, but there's none from him. I guess she hid these in the floorboards so he wouldn't get jealous.'

He looked at her, puzzled, then jumped up and went to turn on the television.

'I can't wait to see how the house is coming along,' she said.

As the news came on the television Tony raised the volume loudly and said '*Shhh* – I want to hear this. Lehman Brothers has collapsed.'

'What?' asked Kate, jumping up and coming over to sit beside him as she listened attentively to the report.

Tony swigged back his drink. 'Unbelievable!'

'What does it mean?' Kate said concerned.

'Who knows? It's not just Lehman Brothers – all the banks seem to be in terrible trouble.'

'Ours included?' Her face creased with worry.

He smiled at her. 'I'll give Steve a call tomorrow. Should be nothing to worry about.'

95

Kate kept to her bargain and kept out of Nico's way until she finally received a call from him one day to come and meet him at the house. When Kate and Nico met, they each felt they harboured new revelations about the other. Nico had curiously sat through Kate's movies, and now felt he was an expert on her acting skills. After watching her weep, laugh, fall in love and murder on screen, he now felt there was more to her than the tycoon's wisecracking wife. As for Kate, addictively reading Clara's letters made her feel she had a link to Nico's past.

Nico turned the key in the front door of the house and she held her breath as she walked in after him.

As she walked through the hallway she loved the freshly finished feel and aroma. She excitedly walked from room to room, and up the stairs where everywhere had been replaced and made safe.

'It's marvellous!' she said as she quickly came down the stairs. 'It's like a proper house again.'

'I'm delighted you're delighted,' he said with a smile, surprised there wasn't one criticism or piece of sarcasm. 'Come and see the basement.'

She followed him eagerly and was overwhelmed to see the change. As planned, the level of the big back yard had been dropped and the old flagstones replaced. The kitchen was now full of light and the back yard formed an attractive patio outside.

'So – where do we go from here?' she queried.

'The next step is where you come in. We now have to create the interiors, so you need to direct me as to what you want. The house before was a damaged canvas, and we've repaired it, but it's still a blank canvas, and now we need to paint our picture on it.'

As Kate listened she thought it was such an interesting way of describing it.

'You had some ideas of how you wanted it,' said Nico.

'Yes, indoor swimming pools aside.' She looked mockingly at him.

They walked into the ballroom and Kate circled around all the boxes and items of furniture stored there belonging to Nico.

'Sorry this stuff is still here. I'll order a truck and get it brought down to a stable I've cleared at Hunter's Farm.'

Kate traced a finger along a broken sideboard. 'Is there anything of value here?'

'Doubtful. Anything of value not destroyed by the fire was removed by my grandfather Pierce soon after and sold to help pay the mounting debts,' he said, picking up a box of chipped crockery. 'Nothing of monetary value here, but I still need to go through it and throw out what I don't want. Anyway, it'll be gone tomorrow and no longer your problem. But what I was thinking is that there are a lot of old paintings and photos here, so I might pick up some pictures of what the rooms looked like before the fire, which would greatly assist us in the restoration.'

'Oh, that would be great, thanks, Nico.' She began to examine a broken gramophone with intense curiosity. 'Nico, if you want you can go through the items here. There's more light and room here than in a stable at Hunter's Farm, I imagine.'

'It would make it easier. I can order a skip and discard stuff as I go through. You don't mind?'

'Of course not, and if you find anything to help with the restoration, great!' She picked up a jewellery box and examined it. She had been so intrigued reading Clara's letters, she was burning with a curiosity to see what was amongst the items in the ballroom. 'If you want – I can help you sort through things.'

'You?' he asked derisorily.

'What's so unbelievable about that?'

'You with your manicured hands and your Karl Lagerfield dress?'

'It's Chanel actually.'

He gave her a condescending look. 'I don't think it's really your scene rummaging through cardboard boxes. I wouldn't want to keep you from some photo-call or film premiere for a charity somewhere.'

'Nico!' Kate snapped angrily. 'Will you stop suggesting I'm nothing but a trophy wife who has no interest in anything but having my photo in the magazines!'

'I'm sorry, but that's what I thought you were!'

'Well, like most things you think you're an expert on, Nico, you're wrong! Anyway, sort it out on your own. Call me during the week.' She turned to leave.

'Hold on!' he said quickly. 'I'm sorry. I would very much appreciate your help in sorting things out.'

Kate was amazed at the ruthlessness with which Nico went through the items. She feared that instead of being a help to him, she was more of a hindrance as she stopped him every time he went to throw away something in the skip he had ordered. She would take the item, study it, point out any merits it might have, and fight for its survival before Nico insisted on its demise.

'It's a useless jug! It's cracked and the handle is missing!' His voice rose as she physically stopped him from throwing it into the skip outside the open French window.

'But it might be an antique, I can have a friend of mine check it out,' she argued.

He laughed. 'You obviously have no idea about the world of antiques. But I do! And this is value-less!' He chucked it into the skip and it broke asunder, then he walked back inside the ball-room.

She followed him, intensely irritated, aware he did know about antiques, and fully aware her knowledge was limited. And she hated that fact. Like everything she envied, this knowledge would have been just handed to him with the world he was brought up in.

He opened a box and there was a brooch inside it.

'I wonder whose breast this adorned?' he said,

studying it.

'I wonder?' She took the box from his hands and looked at it intently.

'Now don't try and tell me that's worth something?' He looked at her knowingly.

'No, Nico, one thing I do know is jewellery. It's a piece of worthless costume jewellery.'

'My sentiments exactly!' He snatched it back out of her hands and went to fire it into the skip.

'No! Wait!' She grabbed it back out of his hand. 'But it's very pretty!'

'Kate! I don't have storage room to be cluttered by this kind of junk!'

'Well, can I have it then?'

He looked at her and shrugged. 'If you want.'

'Thank you.' She went and put the brooch box into her handbag. 'It's just very nice to possess something that belonged to a former resident of the house, whoever she was.'

'You'd never make an antiques dealer. There's no room for sentiment in the antiques business.'

They continued to rummage through the items. Suddenly Nico found a large photograph in a box and sat down on a chair, staring at the photo with curiosity.

'What's that?' asked Kate.

'It's a photo of my grandfather Pierce ... on his wedding day,' said Nico.

'Really?' Kate walked over excitedly and peered at the photo of the beautiful couple walking out of the church.

'You don't really look like him,' Kate observed. 'Or your grandmother,' she added as she studied the stunning bride.

'Oh, she's not my grandmother,' said Nico quickly.

'No?' Kate was intrigued and, pulling up a chair, sat down beside him and took the photo from his hand to study it further. 'Who is she then?'

'It must be his first wife Clara. I've never seen a photo of her before.'

'Clara,' she said the word gently, putting a face to the letters she was reading.

He took the photo back from her. 'She was a society beauty from London. She would have been the last lady of the house here.'

'I see... But what happened to her?' Kate was mesmerized by Clara's face.

'She and Pierce divorced. They had no children. In fact, she was a complete bitch to him.'

'She doesn't look like a bitch,' said Kate, surprised by his words.

'Looks can be deceiving. He fought in the First World War, and rose very high in the ranks. While he was off fighting in the trenches, she was having an affair behind his back.'

'You're joking me!' She took the photo from him again and peered at it.

'Yes, she had an affair here in this very house – *his house.*' He looked around the room.

'How awful!'

'Aha – she was renowned for having wild parties here while my poor old grandfather Pierce fought for his life... I believe she ended up having an affair with Jonathan Seymour.'

'The artist?' Kate asked.

'He wasn't so famous then. But, yes, that's the one.'

He reached down further into the box, scooped up a dozen other photos and started looking through them. They were all photos of Clara, taken with her posing in different rooms of the house.

'Ah! Now these could be useful!' said Nico. 'Look at these!'

He started handing the photos one by one to Kate.

'Some of them are taken in the rooms that were destroyed by the fire. These can give us an actual record of what the rooms were like so we can restore them. Brilliant!'

But instead of concentrating on the décor of the rooms, Kate was drawn to Clara in the photos, this ethereal beauty from another time looking back at her.

'And since they are all of Clara, this is how the house looked just before the fire.'

'What happened to her? To Clara?' questioned Kate.

'After the fire here in the house, Pierce divorced her on grounds of adultery. He went to live in Dublin, where he worked in the diplomatic corp for the British embassy. He eventually married my grandmother, Joan. They had a daughter, my mother Jacqueline. But that was a short-lived marriage as well.'

'Another divorce?' asked Kate.

'No... The Second World War broke out, and he re-enlisted as an officer and went to fight in France even though he was in his fifties by then. He was killed in his first week there. Shot.'

Kate went back and looked at Pierce and

Clara's wedding photo again.

'My grandmother married again after Pierce died – a Dublin businessman – and went on to have more children. My mother Jacqueline, although she never knew Pierce as she was only a baby when he died, had a very happy upbringing. This place came to her on Pierce's death.'

'And what about Clara? What happened to her?'

'I don't know what happened to her. And after how she treated my grandfather, I'm not really interested either.' He got up and started to work again.

'Can I borrow the photos, just to study the rooms?' she asked.

'Sure... I wonder what this is?' he said, lifting up a round silver canister and going to open it.

'Wait!' she ordered, hurrying over to him. 'That's an old reel of film, don't expose it to the light!' She studied it. 'Very old from what I can tell.'

'I wonder what it's of?' he asked.

'I've a friend who specialises in adapting these – want me to get him to take a look?'

He shrugged and handed it to her.

Hours later they were still sorting through the stuff.

'Now look at this!' said Nico excitedly and Kate rushed over. He had uncovered a large portrait, the bottom half of which was covered in dust and smoke damage. But Kate immediately recognised the face in the portrait as that of Clara from the photos.

'It's impossible to see the signature on the painting,' said Nico, peering at the bottom of the portrait.

497

Kate stared at the painting of Clara. 'Are you going to throw it out?' she asked, half hoping he would say yes, so she could lay claim to it.

'No. I've a friend who restores paintings, so I'll get him to take a look at it.'

He carried the painting out to his Range Rover.

96

Back in Dublin, Kate couldn't stop studying the photos of Clara. She was fascinated with the beauty who had been the last mistress of their house. She almost felt a connection with her. She suddenly spotted a brooch Clara was wearing in one of the photos and hurried to her handbag and took out the one Nico had said she could have. As she compared her brooch to the one in the photo she realised it was the same.

'Thank you, Clara!' she said, amazed by the discovery. 'It's almost as if you've handed it to me through time.'

'Are you beginning to talk to yourself? First sign of madness, you know,' said Tony walking into their bedroom. He was wearing a tuxedo as they were going to a dinner party.

Kate tidied away the photos and went to sit at her dressing table to pin the brooch on to her evening gown.

He came over to her and placed his hands on her shoulders while standing behind her.

'New piece of jewellery?' he asked.

'No, a very old piece. We found it in the house and Nico said I could keep it. It used to belong to the last woman who lived there, Lady Clara Armstrong.'

He bent down and examined it. 'Is it expensive?'

'No, it's only costume jewellery.'

'The way this banking crisis is going, there's going to be a lot of ladies around Dublin swapping their diamonds for costume jewellery.'

She took his hand and they walked out of the room and down the spiral staircase.

'This financial crisis seems to be getting worse. I was watching it all on the news,' she said.

'Yeah, the bottom seems to be dropping out of the country, maybe even the world.'

She looked at him with a smirk. 'Do we need to economise?'

He smiled back. 'No, I think we're fine.'

Kate rode into the forecourt at the stud farm outside Dublin, dismounted and handed the reins to one of the grooms.

'You're a natural, Mrs Fallon,' said the head groom as he walked over to her. 'Hard to believe you only started riding a few months ago. And, as you've asked, I've got some fine horses set up for you to buy when you move into your new country house.'

'Excellent. Thank you! We expect to be moved in over the next couple of months, so be ready to go with them.'

She strode out of the yard and as she got into her car her phone rang.

'Kate, I've managed to sort out that film for

you. It was very old, but very good quality considering. It's of a party – I would say in the 1920s or earlier. I've transferred it on to a DVD for you.'

'Wonderful! Thanks, Marty! Send it over by courier to me, will you?' She started the engine and drove off.

Kate pulled up alongside Nico's Range Rover and jumped out, carrying her laptop with her. The landscape gardeners were busy restoring the gardens and rebuilding the pillared walls, garden steps and Victorian ornaments. She rushed up the steps and into the house.

'Nico?' she called loudly as she walked quickly past the craftsmen who were busy carving the ceilings and decorating the walls.

'He's in the kitchen, Mrs Fallon,' said one of the men.

She hurried to the back of the main stairs and down the steps to the kitchen which now had an automatic glass door that slid open to allow her to enter.

Nico was overseeing the final touches to the kitchen's renovation. As Tony had expressly ordered, the kitchen had been transformed into a Mecca for the modern chef. A beautiful cream Clive Christian kitchen had been installed with cream porcelain tiles and a round island. There were various glass frosted doors around the kitchen that led into separate small rooms including the wine room, the chocolatier room, cigar boutique, the bakery and the refrigerated fruit room.

'Nico, quick, I've got to show you something,' she said, placing the laptop on the island counter and turning it on.

He sat up beside her.

'This is the roll of film we found that my friend put on to DVD,' she explained.

The film started playing on the screen and Nico peered closely. He recognised the woman on the screen as Clara from her photos. The film was taken in the house and there was what looked like a party going on. The film was concentrating on her as she played up to the camera and danced around the room. The camera was focusing on her face as she smiled, before she fell to the ground laughing.

'It's Clara!' stated Kate.

'I can see that,' said Nico as he peered at the grainy black-and-white footage.

'Look at them, all so elegant at a party here at the house!' Kate was thrilled.

'*Hmmm*, yeah, there's some good detail of the room we can work with.'

As Nico pointed out different aspects of the detail to be observed, he realised after a while that Kate wasn't paying him attention. She was far too busy focusing in on Clara. He spotted Kate was wearing the brooch they had found, and her normal array of diamonds were absent.

All the workers had gone as Nico and Kate walked out the front door and he locked it behind them.

'Are you heading back to Dublin?' he asked as they made their way to their vehicles.

'No, it's a bit late,' she said.

'Back to the hotel for the night?'

'Yes.'

'You are meeting friends there?'

'No, nothing planned ... why?'

He looked awkward. 'You haven't had dinner.'

'No.'

'I thought if you were free we might have something to eat, while we continued to discuss the next steps for the house?'

'Oh!' She hesitated for a second before nodding and smiling.

They managed to get a last-minute cancellation at The Ice House restaurant in Ballina, and they were shown to a table at the window with the river below it.

'So how is all this banking collapse affecting you?' asked Nico.

'Oh, I've tried not paying attention to it. It's all very worrying, isn't it?' She smirked at him. 'Why, frightened you won't get paid? Is this dinner a polite excuse to check our cash flow?'

'No!' He was suddenly embarrassed.

'I'm joking!' she said.

'I find your sense of humour very annoying at times.'

'Oh, you'll get used to me in time.'

'Not really. The house is nearly finished, so I imagine we won't be in contact from then on.'

'Well, you'll still be a neighbour of ours in Hunter's Farm. I'm sure we'll be friendly neighbours.'

He looked at her sceptically. 'Come on, I'm hardly going to be invited up to your soirees. I've seen the level of people you socialise with.'

'It really bothers you, doesn't it? Our wealth?' She was irritated but curious. 'Why exactly? Is it because you don't like self-made people like me and Tony having what you don't have? Are we a bad reminder of what your family once had and no longer do?'

'No, I'm not a jealous person.'

'We all have to adapt to changing circumstance in life. You and your family have had to adapt to becoming normal, me and Tony have had to adapt to becoming not normal.'

'I doubt you and Tony were ever – normal – in the kindest sense of the word.'

'I used to be incredibly normal.' Kate took up her glass of wine and took a sip. 'Do you ever wonder why we chose to buy your house? Out of all the country houses in the country, why yours?'

He shrugged. 'The views? The price?'

'In a country full of views, and a bank balance as large as ours, those are not major considerations.'

'Why then?'

'I grew up in the local town.'

'Did you? Castlewest?' He sounded disbelieving as he looked at her.

'Oh yes. In the Heevenmore area of the town, are you familiar with it?'

He made a face. 'Yeah, but that's...' He paused trying to find the right word.

'Rough,' she said. 'Very rough. The Alsatians go around in pairs there.'

'But you have an American accent.'

'Yes. My parents moved to New York in the

eighties when I was a teenager. Trying to get a new life. A better life.'

'And you obviously did.'

'Eventually I did. My family settled in Queens, in an area that was even rougher than where we came from. And we struggled – oh, how we struggled day in day out. Never enough money to pay the rent or the bills. It was tough. But I wanted more, and I didn't care how I got it. I had a voice and the camera liked me, I had that going for me, I knew. So I became a singer. Started off in clubs and bars. Moved up to singing in nicer clubs in Manhattan. Eventually started getting a name for myself.'

'And how did you start acting?'

'Oh, that was easy. I dated a film director.'

'I see!' He raised an eyebrow.

'It wasn't like that. I was in a long-term relationship with him. And then I started becoming quite famous, especially in Ireland. They love a "local girl made good" story in Ireland.'

'I saw some of your films,' he admitted.

'Really?' She was surprised.

'Em – yeah, they were showing on one of the movie channels.'

'How did you like them?'

'Very good actually. I enjoyed them. Why did you give up acting? You'd could have gone on and become a big star.'

She sat back and sighed. '*Might* have gone on to become a big star. And then again – might not have. I had a good break, and a good run, but who knows when that would have stopped. And as I got older, they might not have wanted me any more, and I would be struggling to get parts, and always trying to be younger, prettier – no, thank you. When something better came along, I knew when to quit.'

'The something better being Tony?'

She nodded and sat forward. 'I met Tony at a function in Dublin. Of course I knew of him – who hadn't heard of Tony Fallon? He was like me – he had come from nowhere and made something of himself. We were kindred spirits. And he loved me, and I loved him. And I trusted him. I admire his drive – if Tony wants to do something, anything, he does it. Nothing gets in his way. I like being with him. It wasn't a tough decision to leave acting behind. Not tough at all. We knew straight off we were meant to be together. He proposed to me after one month.'

'A month!'

'Well, there was no point in hanging around. We were in San Francisco when he proposed. We got a plane straight to Vegas and got married the next day. You probably think that's tacky, do you?'

'Not at all. Who am I to criticise a marriage as successful as yours? But you still haven't answered your own question – why did you buy this house?'

'Because I've always loved it. We used to cycle out from the town and play in the grounds when we were kids. Even broke in a couple of times. And I promised one day I'd own it and live in it. I didn't even believe the promise myself. But here I am – doing exactly that.'

He held up his glass in a toast. 'To fulfilling promises then!'

She chinked her glass against his as the food arrived.

'Tell me about your daughter Alex,' she said.

'Alex?' he smiled. 'Alex would buy and sell you before you've sat down to your breakfast. She's got all her mother's determination and all my cynicism.'

'Quite a combination,' she said.

'Not a great combination in a marriage though.'

Kate tried to tread carefully but her curiosity was too strong. 'So you had an amicable divorce?'

He looked at her, surprised.

'It's just I spotted her photo still at Hunter's Farm. Most divorced people I know use their ex's photos for dart practice.'

'It came as a shock when Susan asked for a divorce. I just always imagined we would always be together, and of course there was Alex, which was a glue. But she said we weren't actually happy together. She said we weren't unhappy either, but she wanted more than that. And she wanted to try and find it before it was too late. We were going through the motions, she said.'

'You disagreed with her?'

'Looking back, I suppose she was right. But we still get on very well. We have to, for Alex's sake. She's the most important thing in both our lives. Do you and Tony want children?'

She was surprised that he was being as direct as her. 'Yes, I guess. We always planned to anyway. It's just finding the time ... our lives are so busy. That's why it was important for us to find this house and get something back for us, to give us the time to be a family, start a family.'

'It's funny with families, isn't it? One wonders who we take after, who we are like.'

'It must be interesting with your family as you can trace your family tree so easily, being descended from peers.'

'I know, but I don't know what they were like – what they were really like.'

'Well, the man who built the house, Lord Edward Armstrong, your great-great-great-grandfather must have been a very ambitious man to build a house like this for his bride Anna. You know he imported stone from Germany and there was a handcrafted oak fireplace in the master bedroom.'

'Where did you find all that out?'

'Oh, I've been researching on the internet about the building of the 'Big Houses' and the families who built them. I found some entries about the building of our house. You can see Edward had wonderful vision – maybe he would be an architect if he was alive today, like you!'

'*Hmmm,* and I imagine he would be much richer than me if he was alive today as well.'

'He was very rich then. He had an estate of eight thousand acres. Imagine that!'

'I guess.' Nico was thinking that, despite Kate's extravagant lifestyle, she might have too much time on her hands if she was preoccupying herself with pursuing particulars of the Armstrongs' history.

'I wish we could find out more about Clara.'

'Why Clara?' He looked puzzled.

'I've done internet searches on her, but all I can find is she married Pierce, your grandfather–'

'I know who he is,' said Nico, irritated that she seemed to be hijacking his family history as well as taking over his ancestral home.

'–in 1914. I found it on an aristocratic records website. So he would have been sent off to war just after they got married. Isn't that tragic?'

'Tragic for him when she was screwing around behind his back, I think,' said Nico.

'Don't you know anything about her? About her family?' she pushed.

'For goodness sake, it's nearly a hundred years ago, Kate! Who knows – who cares?' He saw the very disappointed look on her face and said, 'I believe she was a member of the Charter Chocolate family in England. That's all I know.'

'Well, that's something to go on,' said Kate, excited.

'Go on to where? What do you care?' He was perplexed.

'Oh, I don't!' Kate sat back with a nonchalant air. 'Just interested in the people who lived in my house, that's all. Who happen to be your ancestors, the Armstrongs.'

'Clara wasn't. And anyway nobody knows who the Armstrongs are any more, and nobody really cares.' Except you, Kate, he added mentally.

'I think if I had your family tree I'd be intrigued by it,' she said as she looked dreamily into her aperitif.

97

Kate was dropping some plans down to Hunter's Farm and she was surprised to see a young girl answer the door.

'Hello there!' smiled Kate. 'You must be Alex?'

'That's right, but how do you know?'

'Oh, I've heard all about you,' Kate smiled.

'Who is it, Alex?' shouted Nico from the lounge.

'It's me – Kate!'

'Oh, come on in, Kate,' said Nico, popping his head around the corner.

'Nice meeting you,' said Alex with a grin and she ran up the stairs.

'Yes, you too,' smiled Kate.

She joined Nico in the lounge.

'She looks like you,' she said.

'Don't let her hear that, I think she would prefer to look like her mother,' said Nico with a wry smile.

'I just wanted to deliver these drawings I got from an interior designer to you.' As she handed over rolls of drawings, she spotted the painting of Clara in a corner. 'You still haven't done anything with Clara's portrait.'

'No, I've been too busy. I keep meaning to bring it up to Dublin for my friend to work on it. I'll do it this weekend.'

Alex came bounding into the room.

'Alex, do you like horses?' asked Kate.

'Oh, yes, I love them,' said Alex.

'Well, I'm having a delivery of horses to the stables up at the house today. Why don't you come up and I'll show them to you. If it's all right with your father?' Kate looked to Nico for approval.

'Yes, fine, Kate,' said Nico, surprised by her offer.

Kate and Nico worked hard over the following weeks. But it didn't seem like work as both of them loved the house and wanted it to be restored to its very best. The walls and ceilings were meticulously refurbished, shining polished wooden floors reinstated, cream tiles in the hallway, thick carpet in the drawing room, chandeliers hung. Kate had scoured modern furniture designers, the auction rooms at Christie's and Sotheby's, to assemble the right furnishings. Nico was surprised that her decisions were always the correct ones.

Landscapers worked around the clock to restore the broken walls and ornaments and the gardens were brought back to life under their attentive care.

Finally the curtains and drapes were hung and the house was complete.

Nico let out the last of the workers and walked across the exquisite new hallway and into the opulent drawing room where he found Kate opening a bottle of champagne.

'What's this?' he asked.

'A celebration. We did it!' She was delighted.

She poured them both a glass and they went walking through the house, admiring the work.

510

As he looked around at the rooms he decided the house had been given a modern twist but still retained all of its old-fashioned charm.

They walked into the library which had been turned into a state-of-the-art office.

'And I guess here is where Tony will run his empire,' said Nico as he sat down on one of the elongated sofas there.

'Yes,' she said, sitting beside him.

'What are you doing about staff for the house?'

'I've arranged housekeepers from the local village, and a part-time cook. As you know Tony likes to do most of the cooking and when we entertain a large group we'll use caterers.'

'You're not having any live-in staff?'

'No. Tony would hate that, somebody under his feet. I suggested it and he said he was frightened he'd end up getting drunk one night and get into the wrong bed!'

'Sounds like he's getting used to the idea of moving down here?'

'He was only saying this week he can't wait for the move, can't wait to get away from Dublin.'

'He's changed his tune about the house then? He's come around to your way of thinking?'

'Work is very pressurised for him. Building this shopping mall. And everyone is so worried in Dublin these days after the economic crash, so many businesses are closing down. We bought the house for me, but I think it's going to do him more good. He'll be able to switch off, as much as Tony can ever switch off.'

'Well,' he said, leaning forward to chink her glass, 'to your new house!'

'Thank you for all your help. I couldn't have done it without you.' Reaching forward she kissed his cheek.

She drew back and smiled at him, their eyes locked and they stared at each other for a while.

Kate jumped up from the sofa awkwardly. 'So when are you going back to Dublin?' She quickly walked over to the fireplace and took a drink of her champagne.

'Tomorrow!' He jumped up as well and walked to the other side of the room. 'Half my clients seem to have gone broke, so I need to see where we stand.'

'Yes, yes.' Kate spoke in a fast and furious way, almost to distract both of them from the strange feeling that had just passed between them. 'Tony said some of the retail stores are trying to get out of their contracts to open up in the shopping centre with the change in the economy.'

'Really, can they do that?'

'Who knows? Tony always says you should never let the other person be able to get out of a contract, but always ensure you have some hidden clause that lets you out!'

'Clever man!' Nico said awkwardly.

She nodded and managed to look Nico in the eyes. 'He's a wonderful man.'

'Anyway, I'd better go.' He put his empty champagne glass on the coffee table.

She smiled quickly at him as he walked from the room and she heard the front door slam. She turned around and looked at the worried expression on her face in the mirror over the fireplace and quickly drank back her champagne.

98

Nico had heard the helicopter fly over Hunter's Farm on its way to Armstrong House. He had felt very uncomfortable about the moment on the couch with Kate. There was some boundary crossed and he didn't want the feeling to linger. He decided the best course of action was to meet Tony and her together and pretend it had never happened.

He went out and drove up to the gateway to Armstrong House. An electric gate had been put in and he reached forward and pressed the buzzer.

A few seconds later the CCTV cameras on the gateway turned and focused on him. He waved and pulled a sarcastic face. The gates opened and Nico drove up the long avenue to the house.

'I didn't think we'd be seeing you so soon,' said Kate as she opened the door.

'I heard the helicopter and thought I'd just check how Tony liked the work.'

'That was him flying, he's just got his pilot's licence,' said Kate as he followed her into the drawing room. She was smoking a long thin cigar and dressed in one of her glamorous outfits. 'Tony's delighted with the work on the house.'

'That's what I like to hear – a satisfied cus-
tomer.'

'He's on the phone in the library.'

Suddenly they could hear Tony shouting at the

top of his voice, the sound echoing around the house.

Kate's face clouded in concern.

Nico was surprised. He didn't imagine the charming Tony Fallon capable of the anger he seemed to be expressing in the other room.

'Drink?' asked Kate.

'No, thanks,' said Nico.

Tony suddenly came into the room, looking hassled.

'Fucking idiots!' he said.

'Eh, Nico dropped by to say hello, darling.'

'Oh hello,' said Tony.

'Just checking you were settling in all right?'

'Yes. I wish everybody did a job as well as you, Nico,' Tony said, marching over to the drinks table and pouring himself a large vodka. He turned around and looked at Nico. 'Actually, I never spoke a truer word. You did a bloody great job here. I've just sacked the architects working on my shopping centre, and I'm going to employ you to take over.'

'*What?*' Kate and Nico exclaimed in unison.

'Makes perfect sense. You're easy to deal with, you're good at what you do, and you get on with Kate – always a bonus. You're hired!'

'For your shopping centre?' Nico was incredulous.

'Tony, you need to think this through,' cautioned Kate.

'What's there to think? I need an architect and he's an architect.'

'But Tony, you need to ask him to tender for the job, and come up with proposals and–'

514

'Bullshit! I'm sick of talk and I want action. When can you start, Nico?'

'Well, I – em–' Nico was flabbergasted.

'Tony, you're being ridiculous. Nico runs a tiny little firm and wouldn't have the resources for what we need for the mall,' Kate argued.

'Actually that's not true.' Nico found himself becoming angry. 'We are well positioned to accept any employment, including Tony's.'

'They do houses, not commercial work,' Kate said.

'Actually, that is not correct either.' Nico became even more annoyed. 'We do a lot of commercial work.'

'You don't have the commitment we need,' Kate snapped.

'We do!' he snapped back.

She turned to Tony. 'I don't think it's advisable to hire Nico when he is now our neighbour. If things go sour, I don't want bad feelings.'

'It's an advantage I live close by. I can be available for meetings here when you're here, and in Dublin when you're there.'

'That's settled then. Hired!' Tony marched over to Nico, pulled him up by the arm and slapped an arm around his back as he walked him to the library.

Kate sat down and frowned as she dragged on her cigar.

Kate came down the main staircase in the house that evening having changed into evening wear. She and Tony were going to the Mount Falcon Hotel for dinner to meet some business associates including Steve Shaw.

'Come on, Kate! We're running late!'

They quickly made their way to the car outside and set off. 'Tony, will you relax! The whole point in moving here is so we aren't in a rush to everywhere,' she chastised.

They pulled out of the gateway and Tony put his foot down and sped down the road.

'I wish you had checked with me before you hired Nico Collins,' said Kate.

'Why? You don't usually concern yourself with who I hire and fire?'

'Well, this is different. Nico is my contact.'

'Oh, is he indeed?' Tony didn't hide the sarcasm. 'I thought you'd be delighted I hired him. It's been Nico thinks this and Nico thinks that for months.'

She glanced nervously at him. 'And I valued his opinion when it came to rebuilding the house. I just have reservations about his opinion on shopping malls.'

'So you made obviously clear today. You were quite rude. Try not to be so tonight?'

'Tonight?'

'Yes. I invited Nico along.'

'Oh Tony!' She sighed loudly and sat back, annoyed.

'Why not? He's part of the team now and should get to know people.'

'Part of the team? You see, this is what I'm trying to say to you. You don't normally hire people at a whim like you did today. You interview them again and again and consult with everyone. It's just so unlike you!'

'Exactly! Look, what has my way in the past got me? A load of hassle building the mall. It's time I took some quick decisive action.'

She studied him carefully. He'd looked terribly stressed-out recently.

'Besides, I do know Nico,' he went on. 'We've known him for quite a while now, and he seems great. And we can see from the house that his work is great, too.'

She sat back, resigned to the decision but angry.

Tony glanced at her and saw the brooch from the house was the only jewellery she was wearing.

'Where are all your diamonds? Your Rolex? Why are you just wearing that daft brooch?'

She rubbed Clara's brooch gently. 'I felt like just wearing this.'

'Well, don't in future! We need you with all your diamonds on as usual. To give the right impression we are not affected by the credit crunch. We don't want people to think we're in financial trouble and had to hock your jewels.' He put his foot down and sped even quicker.

'Tony! Please slow down!' demanded Kate, but he ignored her.

As Nico drove up the long avenue to the Mount Falcon Hotel he rang Darrell.

'You are not going to believe this – I have great news! Tony Fallon has appointed us as architects of his shopping centre!'

'You're right – I don't believe it, and it's not such good news.'

'Sorry?'

'Nico, I don't know if it's a good idea to get any more involved with the Fallons.'

'And why not?'

'I don't know if they're our sort of people. They are too demanding. Since they employed us to redo their house it's all you've been working on. All our other clients and work has suffered and we're way behind with everything. Imagine what it would be like if we took on this job? We couldn't cope.'

'We'll hire more people. Expand.'

'I don't think that's a good idea in today's crashing economy. I think we should concentrate on what we have and try to keep it safe.'

'I disagree. This is a once-in-a-lifetime opportunity. Your problem is, Darrell, you don't know how to grow. How to think big.'

'You've definitely been spending too much time with Kate Fallon!'

'Who said anything about Kate? It's Tony that hired us.'

'Sure it was!' Darrell sounded cynical.

'I have to go! I'm at the restaurant.'

'What restaurant?'

'Mount Falcon. I've a business dinner with the Fallons and their partners.'

'Say hi to Kate!' Darrell said sarcastically and hung up.

They had a large round table in the corner of the restaurant overlooking the parklands around the hotel. Nico observed Kate holding court throughout the evening. She had everyone eating out of her hand, as she charmed her way with an array of witty stories and anecdotes. Charmed everyone, that is, with the exception of Nico who she steadfastly ignored and spoke around, leaving him feeling decidedly uncomfortable. After dessert, she excused herself from the table and Nico watched as she walked elegantly through the restaurant and out to the foyer. He waited for his moment and then followed her out. He saw her through the windows, strolling along the drive smoking as she gazed out over the countryside.

'Well, thanks a bunch for today!' he said as he walked up beside her, startling her.

'For what?'

'Exactly! You purposely went out of your way to try and stop Tony from giving me that job.'

'No, I didn't.'

'Of course you did. And I want to know why?' He was angry.

'I don't have to explain myself to you.'

'With your money you feel you don't have to explain yourself to anybody, but I deserve to know why. You set out to sabotage Tony employing us.'

'Sabotage?' she repeated mockingly. 'Get over yourself, Nico.'

'I thought you were happy with the work I did on the house. I also thought after our initial problems we managed to get along very well and were friends now. Why were you trying to stop Tony from giving me the job?'

'For all the reasons I listed to both of you this afternoon!' she said.

He shook his head and said, 'I just don't get you.'

'Good! You're not supposed to!' She flung her cigarette into a bin and walked back into the restaurant.

99

Kate had read and re-read all the letters to Clara from her friends at the front. She was enthralled by them, thinking of how Clara had received them and read them in the same house, only separated from her by time. They were like a window on the past of the previous owner.

But she still hadn't opened the letters addressed to Pierce. She had been severely tempted but she felt it wasn't her place to open these letters that had never been opened by the person they were written for. She wondered whether it wasn't Nico's right to open them as a descendent of Pierce Armstrong. Time had gone by while she pondered these ethical issues. But she was intensely curious about what they contained, who had written them, and why they remained unopened.

Then one evening, almost on impulse, she reached for one and carefully opened it.

Armstrong House
1st of December 1914

My Darling Pierce,
I'm desperately worried about you. I still haven't

received any letter from you and I'm not sure if you are getting my post. Prudence says she is receiving letters from you all the time, so there can't be a problem with the post getting through to you.

Is it something I have done? I feel so lonely here without you. I think about you all the time. If you could just drop me a line. I know you must have more on your mind than me, with the war to fight. I imagine you reading my letters and getting comfort from what I say to you...

Tony walked into the room. 'Are you still reading those damned letters?'

'Yes... I opened some of the closed ones. They are from Clara to her husband begging him to write to her. They mustn't have got to him and were returned to her. It's very sad. She doesn't sound like the woman Nico described at all, running off having an affair behind Pierce's back. She's longing for his attention here.'

'Never mind all that. What have you done about organising our housewarming party?'

'Oh, yes – well, nothing to be honest. I didn't think you were in the mood with all the trouble at work.'

'Of course I'm in the mood for it. What's the point in spending all this money doing up this pile if we can't show it off?' He went over and looked out the front windows. 'Besides, I think we need to throw a ball here, to show everyone the Fallons are still on top, even if the world is turning upside down in this recession.'

'I'll meet caterers and party planners during the week when I get back from London.'

'London?'

'Yes, I've seen a mirror going for auction at Sotheby's which would be perfect for the dining room.'

He nodded and smiled. He'd often seen Kate at an auction and she pursued her goal with ruthlessness. 'We need this party to be a big affair. No expense spared. We need to show everyone that the recession is not affecting us.'

'Leave it to me. It will be a party to remember,' she affirmed.

He bent down and kissed her. 'You never let me down.'

In London, having safely acquired the mirror at Sotheby's, Kate had met some old friends from her acting days for a quick lunch at the Fifth Floor Restaurant in Harvey Nichols. She was mindful of time and kept one eye on her watch as the mirror was a mask for her real visit to London.

'I'd better rush, I need to fit in a bit of shopping,' she said.

She quickly kissed them goodbye and rushed out to get a taxi. An hour later she was turning into the headquarters of Charter Chocolates plc which was housed in a Victorian redbrick building. She had done her research and discovered the factory had a museum and visitor centre and she made her way there. A busload of children and another busload of Japanese tourists were just reboarding their transport after completing their tour, and by the time she entered the museum it was relatively empty.

She wandered around looking at the displays of

everything from replicas of the merchandise they had made over the years, to antique brass machines from the 1800s that had made the chocolates and sweets, and mannequins of workers dressed in their different work-clothes over the centuries. It was the photographs on the walls that most interested her, most of them taken within the factory in bygone years, of visits by dignitaries and royalty.

'Good afternoon,' said a kindly-looking man in his sixties, who she took to be the museum's curator.

'Oh hello... It's quite fascinating, isn't it? I feel as if I've been allowed into Wonka's chocolate factory.'

'Yes. I'm always surprised by the interest people have in the history of the place.'

'The Charter family no longer own it, I take it?'

'No,' he smiled. 'They sold it in the 1920s. It's been publicly owned on the stock market since.'

'Are any of the family still involved here?'

'I'm afraid not.'

'Oh dear,' she sighed. 'I think I might have had a wasted trip.'

'I'm sorry?'

'I'm trying to locate one of them, you see. Well, she's dead now, but maybe a relative of hers. I've some items belonging to her and would love to return them to her family.' Seeing the man's face being overcome with confusion, she said, 'I bought a house that a member of the Charter family lived in and found photos and some other items.'

'I see!' He was obviously intrigued.

'Have you ever heard of her? Clara Charter, she

married Lord Armstrong.'

'I've worked here forty years, and my father worked here before me,' said the man. 'The Charter family was quite a large family. I don't really know anything about Clara though the name seems familiar. But come and let's see if we can find anything.'

He brought her into an archive room and started taking out photo albums and flicking through pages of photos. 'Aha! I thought I remembered her name. There she is!' He pointed to a photo marked 1913 with the caption–

'Mrs Louisa Charter, her son Terence and granddaughter Clara on a visit to the factory May 1913.'

'Yes, that's her!' Kate became excited.

'Right, she was Louisa's granddaughter then. Louisa's husband and his brothers owned the factory, though her son Terence wasn't involved. From what I know he was a banker, a very successful one. I do recall now hearing that one of his daughters married an Irish Lord. There was a nasty divorce case, but that's the last we heard.'

'Oh dear!' Kate was disappointed.

'I do believe one of the Charter family is on a charity board for the Red Cross. I could get her details for you, if you want?'

'Thank you – that would be wonderful. I'll be returning home to Ireland though so may I leave you my card?'

'Certainly. I'll send the details on.'

100

Kate was very busy planning the ball at the house over the next few weeks. There was a constant stream of event organisers and caterers visiting the house and going through details for the night.

'Tony wants the night to be spectacular, so we have to put everything into it,' she advised Chloe, a public relations woman she had used for several parties in the past.

'I'm thinking ice statues inside the house, I'm thinking the ballroom being the centre of the party obviously, I'm thinking all the gardens lit up!' gushed Chloe delighted with the commission as half her clients had gone broke over the previous year.

'Good, I'm working on the guest list and will get it to you shortly,' said Kate as Tony walked into the drawing room.

'How's it all going?' he enquired.

'Very good, Mr Fallon, it's going to be a wonderful event,' said Chloe, packing away her files into her briefcase.

'Glad to hear it,' said Tony as he went to pour himself a glass of wine. 'Drink?'

'No, thanks. I'm just leaving, have to get back to Dublin for meetings.'

Kate stood up to show her out.

'Don't worry, Kate, I'll show myself out,' smiled Chloe as she exited the room.

Kate started to clear away the paperwork from the coffee table.

'Nico is on his way up for a meeting,' said Tony.

'Lovely.' Kate didn't hide the sarcasm in her voice.

Tony picked up the guest list from the coffee table. 'This is the guest list for the party?'

'Uh huh,' answered Kate.

'Speaking of Nico, make sure he gets invited, won't you?'

Kate looked up at him. 'Nico? Why would we invite him?'

'Because he's our colleague,' said Tony.

Kate found herself becoming angry. 'He's not our colleague, Tony, he's one of your employees. I can't see any reason why we should invite him. I thought you wanted this party to be for the movers and shakers?'

'I do!'

'Then leave Nico off the guest list. He's hardly a mover or a shaker, is he? He's a second-rate architect from a second-rate architectural firm who has no business being at our party. He won't fit in, and nobody will know who he is, and he will be like a spare part walking around.'

She looked up to see Nico standing in the doorway of the room. There was an awkward and uncomfortable silence. Nico looked incensed and Kate was mortified.

'The PR woman let me in as she was leaving. Sorry, I should have knocked,' said Nico.

Kate coughed loudly as she quickly tidied away the rest of the paperwork.

'Oh, there you are, Nico,' said Tony, taking

charge of the situation. 'Drink?'

'No, thank you,' said Nico evenly.

'Right!' Tony put down his glass and quickly walked over to him. 'Let's have our meeting!' He clapped Nico on the back and led him into the hall. As the atmosphere could be cut with a knife, he decided it was best if they left the house. 'I hate having meetings in offices all the time, don't you? I must bring you down to the pier at the lake to see my new power-boat I just got delivered.'

The two men went outside and walked down the steps to the forecourt. Tony talked incessantly about the shopping mall as they crossed the fore-court and walked down the first flight of steps onto the terrace and from there into the gardens. They continued down through the gardens until they reached the lakeshore. Nico couldn't concen-trate on what Tony was saying, he was so angry with Kate.

'What do you think?' asked Tony as they walked down the pier and came to the two-seater power-boat moored there.

'Very nice. You have all the toys,' said Nico, hardly looking at it.

'Jump in and I'll take you for a spin,' said Tony, taking the keys out of his pocket.

'Now?' asked Nico, as he watched Tony get into the boat and start it up.

'Come on!' ordered Tony.

Nico got into the boat and sat down beside Tony. Tony revved up the engine and the boat took off across the lake at high speed.

'It's great, isn't it?' laughed Tony.

Nico looked around him and saw the house

disappear into the distance. He tried not to show any nerves at the high speed. Suddenly Tony brought the boat to a halt in the middle of the lake and with the motor off the lake was returned to a complete silence.

'You know, I had my reservations when Kate wanted to buy here, but it was the best thing I ever did,' said Tony. 'I love it here.'

'I'm glad it was the right move for you.'

'She's a wonderful woman, Kate. I always listen to her advice, she's always right.' He turned and looked at Nico. 'Don't mind what you overheard back there in the house, she didn't mean it.'

'No?' Nico looked at him sceptically.

'I know she's very fond of you. She was always singing your praises when you were working together on the house. You could do no wrong in her eyes. She has a lot of respect for you, honestly. And for your family. She's always going on about the Armstrong family. She's reading those letters found in the house all the time – totally fascinated by them.'

Nico looked at him in confusion.

'And when she was over in London recently she tried to make contact with relatives of Clara Armstrong to give back the photos, the letters and the brooch.'

'She did?' Nico's mouth dropped open.

'So you see, she wouldn't bother with all that if she meant what she said.'

Nico stared back at the shore where the house was a distant dot. Tony started up the boat again and powered back to shore.

Nico left the house and was walking across the forecourt to his Range Rover when he saw Kate on horseback trotting up the avenue. He went to meet her.

'Did you enjoy your boat trip?' she called out.

'Oh yeah, between the speed boats and helicopters you've turned this place into a James Bond movie set!'

'A bit of life in the place has done it wonders.'

She dismounted and started to lead the horse by the reins up the avenue.

'Well, look at you – you might as well be to the manor born! Tell me what's next – when are you hiring a butler and under house parlour maids?' His voice dripped sarcasm.

'Can I help you, Nico?' she asked coldly as he walked quickly alongside her.

'I just wonder how far you are going to go to research this new lady of the manor role you've chosen.'

'What are you talking about?'

'Well, you've bought the manor, learned how to ride a horse – and now you're trying to take over my family history.'

She stopped and faced him. 'I haven't a clue what you're going on about.'

'What's all this about reading Clara's letters? Where did you get them and why didn't you tell me?'

She silently cursed Tony's big mouth. 'The builders found them under floorboards in a bedroom.'

'A bedroom? Are you sure you didn't take them from the items belonging to me stored in the ball-

529

room? Not that it matters – they are still personal effects from the house and you have no right to them.'

She let go of the horse's reins and it wandered off as her voice rose. 'Are you accusing me of being a liar – as well as a thief?'

'Well, you tell me – are you?'

'I don't believe this! How dare you! Ask any of the builders and they will verify my story – not that I should have to ever answer to you.'

'Well, why didn't you tell me about them then?'

'I was going to after I had read them.'

'Well, how bloody long does it take to read them? And they are not yours, they belong to my family!'

Her temper rose. 'Well, if you want to investigate that legally – go ahead! There's an argument they belong to us as they were part of the sale of the house.'

'It's all about "legally" with you lot, isn't it? You think you can get anything you want by just hiring a hot-shot lawyer. Whatever about "legally", and that argument is nonsense anyway, they are documents from my family's past, so belong to my family. And that's what you're after, isn't it? A past – a history like my family's?'

'I didn't realise you could patent history,' she snapped back.

'And what's all this about you trying to track down Clara's relatives?'

She doubly cursed Tony's big mouth. 'Why not? It's a free world. I can do what I want. As you say, Clara's things belong back with her family, but you're not her family. You have no respect for her items, you'll just throw them away like you did her other stuff and that's why I didn't hand them to you. You're not descended from her, and I want to return them to the Charter family.'

He shook his head. 'I think it's a bit more than that, isn't it? You're researching for your new role, actress that you are. What is it – do you want to be Clara?'

'Oh shut up, Nico,' she snapped, mounted the horse and trotted off to the stables.

From the upstairs bedroom window in the house Tony had observed them arguing.

A little while later, he was walking down the stairs as Kate came storming in.

'You can fire that Nico Armstrong-Collins, or whatever he calls himself, first thing in the morning!' she said.

'I can't! I've signed a contract with him.'

'You always said you leave in a secret clause to be able to get out of any contract – now use it and get rid of him!'

'What's wrong now?'

'Why did you tell him about Clara's letters and me looking up the Charter family?' she demanded.

'Didn't realise it was a state secret.' He looked at her, amused.

'*Ahhh!*' she shouted in frustration and pushed past him up the stairs.

Nico slammed the door of Hunter's Farm behind him and marched into the sitting room. Damn that Kate Fallon! He poured himself a drink and

531

sat down. Who did she think she was? Parading around the place as she did. Grabbing letters not belonging to her, looking up distant relatives of his. It was none of her damned business. As he calmed down he realised what had really upset him was overhearing how she had described him earlier. She had dismissed him as being insignificant. And that had hurt. He didn't want to be insignificant to her. But to retaliate by calling her a thief and a liar was going too far, he realised. He had just wanted to hurt her back. He knew he had handled the situation disastrously.

101

The public relations company had mailed out all the invitations to the ball, and Kate had collected the post and was going through it in the drawing room, sorting out the RSVPs. Amongst the mail, she found an impressive white envelope with an English postage stamp, addressed to her. She opened it and read:

156 Nell Gwynn Apartments
Sloane Street
Kensington
London SW 1

Tel. 0207 8761462

Dear Mrs Fallon,

Your details were given to me by a cousin who in turn had been contacted by the curator of the museum at Charters Chocolates. I believe you have come into the possession of some items once belonging to my relative Clara Charter, the former Lady Armstrong. I would very much be grateful if you contacted me at the above. I look forward to hearing from you.
Dr Amanda Charter

Kate felt excited as she reread the letter. She had been giving up hope of making contact with any relative of Clara's. She immediately reached for her phone and dialled the number.

The taxi pulled up outside the Nell Gwynn apartments in Chelsea. Kate got out, and entered the mansion block. It looks like the Charter family still have plenty of money, she thought as she looked around the opulent building.

'I'm here to see Dr Amanda Charter,' she informed the concierge.

'Mrs Fallon?' asked the concierge, checking his appointments book.

'That's right,' confirmed Kate.

'She's expecting you. The fifth floor, Number 156.'

'Thank you,' said Kate and headed over to the lift.

She reached the apartment and rang the bell. A few moments later a middle-aged woman answered.

'Dr Charter is expecting you – if you care to follow me?'

She led Kate down a hallway and into a large

expensively furnished living room with fine views across the city. A woman was waiting there, aged in her sixties, expensively dressed with a neat blonde bob and a slim neat figure.

'Mrs Fallon, nice to meet you,' said Amanda as she stood up and shook hands.

'Thank you for meeting me,' said Kate.

'Please take a seat,' said Amanda as she sat down and lifted a silver teapot. 'Tea?'

'Please,' Kate answered.

Amanda filled two cups. 'I was intrigued to hear about you, Mrs Fallon, from the Charter museum.' She handed over the cup of tea. 'You're the actress, aren't you?'

'That's right. Myself and my husband bought Armstrong House in Ireland and, well, we found some old photos, letters and a brooch belonging to Clara, and wanted to return them to her family.'

Kate observed Amanda to be a shrewd woman, self-composed and confident, and although her looks were faded somewhat she still cut a striking figure.

'Armstrong House – that is a name I haven't heard in a long time. I thought it had burned down?'

'Parts of it, but we managed to restore it.'

Amanda sat forward expectantly. 'Could I see what you have?'

'Of course!' Kate quickly opened her briefcase and, taking out a large envelope, she pulled out the photos it contained and handed them over.

Amanda put on her glasses and began to study the photos.

'They are taken inside Armstrong House,' said

Kate. 'In various rooms.'

Amanda smiled. 'They didn't exaggerate her beauty, did they?'

'They?'

'People who knew her when she was young, relatives of mine... I only knew her later in her life when I was a child, but she had changed by then.'

Kate then handed over the letters. 'Most of the letters are from friends of hers fighting in the First World War. The rest are letters from Clara to her husband Pierce. They were returned to her unopened, I don't know why.'

'You opened them?' Amanda asked, looking up.

'Well, yes–'

'And read them of course?'

'I did, yes.' Kate suddenly felt intrusive.

Amanda sat back and crossed her legs. 'How can I help you, Mrs Fallon? You didn't come to London just to hand me a few photos and letters. You could have sent them in the post if you were that anxious for them to be repatriated to her family.'

Kate sensed there was a no-nonsense toughness in Amanda.

'I – I confess I was curious to find out what had happened to Clara after she left the house.'

'You are just being a bit nosy then, are you?'

'I hope I'm not coming across like that.'

'Perhaps you're researching an idea for a new movie project you're working on?' Amanda raised an eyebrow cynically.

'I haven't worked in film for years, Dr Charter, and have no intention of returning to that business,' Kate said sharply.

Amanda studied her. 'No, and I guess with a

husband as wealthy as yours you have no reason to.' There was a silence before she spoke again. 'I'm sorry if I was rude. It's just hearing again about Armstrong House and Clara – it's brought back a lot of difficult memories for my family. Clara, you see, had a very difficult time there, especially towards the end. When Clara met Pierce Armstrong, she fell head over heels in love with him. She could have had anybody but chose to have him. The trouble was, he didn't particularly want her, but took her anyway – because he could, I imagine. She endured a terrible cold and unloving marriage, that was when he was there, which wasn't often because he was fighting in the war. She tried everything to make her marriage work with him, but he basically told her he had never had any feelings for her.' Amanda picked up the letters to Pierce from Clara. 'He didn't even open and read the letters she sent him at the front. He returned them to her unopened. Clara had really no options. There was little or no opportunity to exit an unhappy marriage. She finally found solace with a member of their circle, a neighbour, the artist Jonathan Seymour. They had a relationship and fell in love and were to elope. Pierce was in a high command position and Ireland was under martial law at the time with the War of Independence raging. When her husband Pierce found out they planned to elope, he had Seymour arrested and interned...' Amanda's voice trailed off as she picked up the photos of Clara again.

'And Clara?'

'Clara was held prisoner in Armstrong House.

He told her if she tried to escape he would have her put in prison as well on some charge to do with subversive activities Seymour had involved her in.'

'Oh!' Kate got a shock at the thought of this beautiful woman so unhappy and unable to leave the house.

'Jonathan Seymour spent some months held in isolation in prison as ordered by Pierce. When the war in Ireland was over and Pierce's power gone, Clara expected Jonathan to come for her. But he never did. I believe prison changed him considerably. He had some sort of breakdown and left for America as soon as he was released where he concentrated on his art, and as we know went on to find considerable success.'

'And what happened to Clara?'

'After Ireland was given independence the Armstrongs evacuated from the house, fearing reprisal. But this was her opportunity to break free of Pierce and she refused to leave with them. She intended to wait in the house for Jonathan to come for her. Then the republicans came, removed her forcibly and burned the house down. She never spoke of what happened that night fully. She returned to London in disgrace. When Pierce discovered she was leaving him for good and there was nothing he could do about it, he immediately filed for divorce, citing her adultery. For a woman to be divorced on those grounds back then was a scandal. She didn't contest it. She was thirty-three when she arrived back in London. If she had been born ten years later and never met Pierce she might have been one of those bright young things of the twenties you hear about. From what I know that era would have suited her perfectly. But she was born just ahead of her time, and broke all the conventions of her time. Her family, my family, were horrified by the scandal of the divorce. Their connections managed to keep it out of the papers, but everyone in society knew about it and her affair with Seymour. She became persona non grata. She was sent down to her grandmother's estate in the countryside and that's where she lived quietly for the rest of her life.'

'I see.' Kate picked up one of the photos and stared at it.

'You look disappointed,' Amanda said.

'I'm very disappointed for her.'

'Were you hoping she would have gone on and done something dramatic with her life? We don't expect people like her to drift into ordinariness, do we? We expect people like her to be as glamorous and exciting all their lives. But people break, and then if they are allowed to be ordinary that's the best they can hope for. I just remember everyone saying it was a shame what became of her – that she had been a great beauty, the centre of everyone's attention, had married into the aristocracy. I suppose she was quietly destroyed by her experiences.'

'Well, I'm very sorry to hear that. I thought – I don't know what I thought.'

'She followed her heart, and that was her undoing. But then we can't help where our heart takes us, can we, Mrs Fallon?'

'No – no, we can't,' sighed Kate.

538

Amanda studied her. 'What troubles you, Mrs Fallon?'

'Sorry?'

'Women don't go around chasing fantasies from a hundred years ago when they are happy with their own lives.'

'I wasn't chasing a fantasy. I was just–'

'Returning photos and letters of Clara to her family. I know and thank you. Well, you found out what happened to her, but I don't think it's given you any answers.'

'I don't know what I was looking to find out. I felt I had some bond with her. Maybe in the same way I always bonded with the characters I played. I felt I knew her and could feel her in the house. Maybe I wanted to be her. We bought the house from Pierce's grandson, Nicholas – Nico – Collins. And he told me about her, about her affair with Jonathan Seymour. We employed him to renovate our house and got to know him very well.'

'Yes, Pierce did get married again much later, to a lovely young Dublin socialite. He seemed to have attracted the same type as Clara again. They were married only a short while before he was killed in the Second World War, before he had a chance to destroy that girl's life like he had with Clara. They had a daughter, I believe?'

'Yes, Jacqueline, who was Nico's mother.'

'She has passed away?'

'Yes, a few years ago, I believe.'

Amanda nodded and looked at the floor.

'And what's Pierce's grandson, Nicholas Collins, like?' Amanda asked.

'Oh, he's – he's a little bit arrogant, takes himself quite seriously, cynical. Can be sarcastic at times, but amusing.' Kate smiled.

Amanda studied her. 'And does Nico Collins know you've fallen in love with him?'

Kate looked at her and blinked a few times.

'Oh,' nodded Amanda knowingly. 'It's that serious, is it?'

Kate said nothing.

Amanda sat forward. 'If you felt Clara was somehow communicating with you, maybe she was warning you. Warning you not to let your emotions run away with you. Not to ruin your life over thinking you want someone, that the reality is very different from what you might think it is.'

Kate wordlessly picked up the brooch and gave it to Amanda.

Amanda glanced at it briefly and handed it back to Kate. 'You keep this. I think it will mean more to you than to me.'

'Thank you.' Kate took it and put it in the briefcase and then took out a DVD.

'There's a film also. We found an old film roll taken of Clara at a party in the house.' She handed it to Amanda.

The front door of the apartment opened and closed, and a tall distinguished man came into the lounge.

'Oh, hello there,' he said.

Amanda and Kate stood up.

'Mrs Fallon, this is my husband, Harry Beaumont – I use my maiden name, Charter, in my professional life.'

'Ah, you're the lady who was bringing the

photos over from Ireland.'

'Yes,' said Kate.

'Very kind of her to track us down, don't you think?' said Amanda. 'Is there anything else we can do for you, Mrs Fallon?'

Kate picked up her briefcase. 'I'd better be going. I have to get to the airport.'

'I'll show you to the door,' said Amanda as she led her down the corridor.

'Nice meeting you,' said Kate to Harry and she followed Amanda.

Harry walked over to the coffee table, picked up the photos and began to look through them.

Amanda came back into the room.

'Strange woman,' she said.

'Did you find out what she wanted?' asked Harry.

'She wanted to know what happened to Clara.'

'And did you tell her?'

'No, Harry, I'm not in the habit of discussing personal family business and secrets with strangers. Besides, she's friends with Pierce Armstrong's grandson Nico. We certainly don't want the Armstrongs finding out the truth at this stage. Let sleeping dogs lie.'

He studied the photo of Clara. 'Do you ever regret what Clara chose to do?'

'No, she made the right choice.'

She crossed over to the DVD player and placed the tape in it.

The film of Clara at the party came on the screen. Amanda watched it intently. It was only then that Harry saw Amanda's ice-cool exterior crack as her eyes filled with tears.

'Seeing her there in her youth, so full of life. I heard what she was like but to actually see it...' She trailed off.

Harry smiled and put an arm around her.

102

Kate was seated at the island in the kitchen on a Sunday morning, thinking about her visit to Amanda Charter. Ever since the meeting, she'd had a strange empty and sad feeling. She had felt this way before. When she had been making a movie, she gave it her all and then when it was finished she felt somehow dissatisfied. And now as she looked around the house she had put so much into, she had that same dissatisfied feeling, made all the more acute after hearing the fate of Clara.

Tony came down the old servants' stairs that led directly there from upstairs, in his dressing gown.

He bent over and kissed her. 'I'm heading to Dublin this afternoon.'

'On a Sunday?' Kate was surprised.

'I'm afraid so. I've a couple of people to meet, and I have to be out on site at the mall first thing in the morning.'

She looked at his tired and hassled face and went over to him and hugged him. 'Aren't you overdoing it a bit?'

He laughed dismissively. 'I live my life over-doing it!'

'It's just I thought when we bought this place and moved here you would be able to take it a little easier.'

'I will do once I get over the hurdles with the mall. Promise.'

'But will there always be another shopping mall to build?' She looked at him with a resigned air.

'Will you be all right here on your own?'

'Of course I will.' She smiled at him.

They had breakfast in the kitchen and went for a walk down by the lake, before she waved him off in the early afternoon. Then she took out her favourite horse and rode down to the local village and back. She liked the village at the weekends because everyone was down from Dublin to their holiday homes there. She managed to just get back to the house before it started to rain.

She had a bath in the evening and the rain started to become heavier and soon was pelting against the window as she relaxed in the bath. Afterwards, she came downstairs dressed in jeans and shirt and, opening the security panel on the wall, activated the security system. As she tried to snap out of the deflated feeling she had, she realised she'd had this restlessness for the past few months and it was like she was directing it into Clara and the effort to try to find out what had happened to her. But maybe it was as Amanda Charter had said, she wasn't happy in her own life. As the rain became heavier and turned into a storm, she closed over the long glamorous drapes in the drawing room and threw some wood and turf on to the fire, watching it turn into a blaze. She then settled back on the sofa.

The rain was lashing down outside and the wind was howling as she looked around the room. As she thought about all she had learned about Clara, she imagined her there in that room, the exact same room just separated by time. The loneliness and despair she must have felt trapped in her loveless marriage. The horror she must have felt at being told she would never be allowed to leave him or the house. And suddenly the house seemed very different to her. It wasn't a home lovingly restored, an echo from another era, a kinder more elegant era.

The echo was in fact not a nice one. It was an echo of a woman's misery. And the house had known Clara's secrets and had kept her secrets. And what other secrets did the house have from other people who had lived there at different times? What else had happened in the house? As she heard thunder outside she suddenly felt herself becoming nervous and wished Tony was there.

Suddenly the lights went out and she was plunged into darkness. She jumped up, scared, and tried to figure out the silhouettes in the darkness. She moved quickly to the door but tripped over something and went flying to the floor. She pulled herself up and carefully felt her way to the door. Opening it, she walked into the hall and tried the light switches there several times before she realised the electricity was gone throughout the house. She looked around the darkness of the hallway and could make out the arched window at the top of the stairs and just about see the rain against it. She thought about going to the kitchen and looking for a torch, but she didn't want to make her way through the dark corridors that led down there. She could hear a banging somewhere outside like an unbolted stable door. But as she realised the security system would be down, she wondered if it could be somebody trying to break in. She made her way to the sideboard and felt her way around until she found her car keys. Then she went to the front door and unbolted it, and raced out into the night. The rain pelted down on her as she raced across the forecourt to her car and jumped in. She started it up and raced down the avenue.

Minutes later she swung into the driveway of Hunter's Farm. She jumped out of the car, and ran through the rain and started ringing the doorbell incessantly.

'Who the fuck is it?' demanded Nico as he swung the door open.

Kate jumped into his arms, holding him tightly, looking terrified.

Kate had changed out of her wet clothes and came into the sitting room, wearing a bathrobe.

Nico had a pot of tea waiting and poured her a cup, handing it to her as she sat on the couch.

'Are you all right?' he asked, concerned, sitting opposite her.

'Yes ... I'm sorry for just barging in on you like this.' She felt embarrassed. 'I got so frightened.'

'Frightened of what?'

'The house, I guess. I suppose there's a reason these big old houses used to have so many servants living in them. It's not like a normal house where you just run into the kitchen to find a candle. I didn't fancy that maze of corridors in the darkness to get there.' She sipped her tea.

As he looked at the indomitable Kate, he couldn't imagine she scared easily, and seeing this new vulnerable side to her was a revelation.

She looked at him. 'I managed to track down a relative of Clara Charter's in London and met her to give her back the letters and photos.'

'You did?' His eyes widened with amazement.

'Yes, eventually. Houses are permanent, people aren't. The people who live there come and go, but the houses remain, a witness to the lives unfolding there. To the secrets. From what I heard Clara's life was very difficult in our house. I've been dwelling a lot on what she went through and I just caught a fear tonight in the house. A fear of the house bearing testimony to what went on there. And not just Clara, but everyone else who lived there from Lord Edward and Lady Anna onwards. You like to think your house, your home, has only good memories, but that's not always true.'

'Maybe you're better off not knowing, Kate.'

She shook her head.

'Look, it's probably just a fuse blown in the house,' he said. 'We can check it in the morning... You can stay here tonight.'

'No! Thanks, but no, I'll go to a hotel in Castle-west,' she said quickly.

'Don't be stupid, Kate, it's after midnight now. The hotel receptions will be closed for the night. I won't have you going off at this time to town to try and find a room to stay in – Tony would never forgive me!'

She looked at him quizzically. 'Would you not be

546

more worried if he found out I stayed the night here?'

Nico looked puzzled. 'No – why would I be?'

She didn't say anything for a while before saying, 'What do you think of me and Tony, Nico?'

'What do I think of you?'

'Yes, now you've got to know us.'

'Well – eh,' he smiled. 'I think you've got it made. You're the dream couple. You have it all.'

'So we seem happy to you?'

'Of course you do. What have you got not to be happy about?'

'A lot. I don't love Tony any more. I haven't for a long time. I've tried to convince myself I do, but I don't. I've tried everything to make our marriage work, more for Tony's sake than mine. You see, he does still love me.'

'I had no idea.'

'I've been going through the motions for a long time. Our life was this merry-go-round and I thought at first we had just lost sight of each other. That if we could get rid of everything else, the parties, the meetings, the business, and there was just us, I could get the feelings I once had for him back. Then I saw the house for sale, your house. And I remembered it so well from growing up. And I thought this was a chance to put our lives on the right track. That we could start again almost. We could move down here away from all the distractions of Dublin and the jet-set life we live and it would be just me and Tony and I could be the wife he deserves. We could have an easier pace of life and find each other again. Remember what it was like when we fell in love with each other at the beginning. I'd hoped then we could start a family here, have children and live happily ever after in our house.'

'But Tony adores you.'

'I know he does. But I'm only deceiving myself and him. I keep thinking what you said once about your marriage, that you were still in love, just couldn't live together any more. Whereas the way I feel with Tony is that I'm so comfortable with him I could live with him forever, I just don't think I'm in love with him any more. When I heard about your grandfather's first wife, Clara, I thought somehow I could identify with her. Especially when I found out about her affair with Jonathan Seymour. I thought maybe she was like me – trapped. And then I met with the relative, Amanda Charter, in London. Clara was trapped all right. But not the way I was. She was in love with her husband Pierce but he made her life hell.'

'That's not true!'

'It's what her relative told me in London.'

'Well, she would, wouldn't she?'

'Yes – in the same way you'll defend your grandfather. The truth is you both only know what you've been told. But I'm not relying on other people's testimonies about my life. I'm here and I'm living it. Tony tries his best to make me happy, but he knows, deep down, that I'm not.'

Nico shook his head. 'And what are you going to do?'

'That I don't know, Nico. Since it's a night for confessions, when I met you, something happened to me that I didn't understand, and I've been fighting it ever since. I found myself falling

548

for you. And by the time I realised that, I was in too deep. You were a threat, Nico. A real threat to me facing up to myself and my marriage and my life. And that's why I wanted you away from me. That's why I pleaded with Tony not to employ you. My feelings for you were too dangerous.'

Nico stared at her. 'You're being very honest with me ... you're very brave.'

'I'm only being brave because it's over, Nico. I've finished with those feelings for you. I've forced myself to put you out of my mind.'

'For you to concentrate on Tony?'

'For me to concentrate on getting my life right.'

They sat in silence for a long while before she stood up. 'I'm very tired. Can you show me to my room?'

He nodded then led her up the stairs and opened a door.

'Thanks,' she said, closing the door quickly.

Outside, the rain continued to pour down. Across the road in a lay-by, Tony sat in his car watching the lights go off in Hunter's Farm.

There was an awkwardness the next morning between Kate and Nico as she came downstairs into the kitchen, dressed in her dried clothes.

'Perhaps you could take a look at that fuse box for me this morning? I don't fancy the day without electricity.'

'Of course. I'll drive up after you to the house. Oh, I forgot to tell you, I got the portrait of Clara back from the restorer.'

'Really?'

He walked out and came back a minute later holding the portrait which had been magnificently restored.

She stared at Clara's image.

'And it turns out the portrait was painted by Jonathan Seymour. I thought that should interest you.' He pointed to Johnny's signature, now plain to see at the corner of the portrait.

'A portrait of Clara by her lover. But I think I've left Clara in the past now, where she belongs,' she said with a sigh. 'Anyway, I'd better get going, I've a ball to organise.'

He hesitated. 'Kate, what you said last night...'

She walked quickly to the window. 'The rain has gone – it looks like it's going to be a good day.'

103

Kate walked through the house the evening before the ball. The event organisers and the caterers had just left after their day's work. The ballroom had been set out in rows of tables, dressed with white linen and table decorations. Walking out to the hall, she saw it had been decorated with a beautiful array of garlands. She walked out the front door and across the forecourt to the row of steps leading down to the terraces. She sat on the first step and gazed out at the view. It was a warm summer's evening, and the sun was beginning to go down over the lake. Tony spotted her from the drawing room and walked out to her.

'It looks like we're all set for tomorrow?' he said.

'Yes.' She looked up at him. 'It will be an amazing night.'

'With you hosting it, how could it not be?'

'Tony ... I've been thinking ... maybe we should sell the house and move back to Dublin.'

'Sell the house! Are you mad? With the property crash it's only worth about half of what we paid for it and that's before all the money we spent renovating it!'

'Well, rent it out then or something. I just think we might be better off away from here.'

He stared at her incredulously. 'But I thought you loved living here. It was your dream!'

'I know it was! I just think it might be time to move on. I miss our old house and—'

'Our old house that you compared to a hotel? Oh no!' He shook his head disbelievingly. 'I don't buy that. What's the matter Kate, trouble in paradise between you and Nico?'

Her eyes widened, shocked. 'I'm sorry?'

'You and Nico had a lovers' tiff?'

'I don't like your idea of a joke.'

'No – and I don't like your relationship with Nico.' He turned and walked quickly back across the forecourt and into the house.

'Tony?' she shouted after him.

She got up and raced after him.

'What are you talking about, Tony?' she demanded as she followed him into the drawing room.

He turned and faced her. 'I think you know exactly what I'm talking about. All that time spent together doing this place up. Lunches together, business dinners together – nights together!'

'Nights together? What are you going on about?'

'I know about the night you spent down in Hunter's Farm when I was away in Dublin.'

'And how do you know about that?' She became angry. 'You were having me watched?'

'It doesn't matter how I know, I just know!'

'So what? I spent a night down in Hunter's Farm because I got frightened up in the house on my own when the lights failed.'

'You, frightened?' He laughed dismissively. 'Just so handy his bed was down the road for you to fall into!'

'You bastard! I slept in the spare room.'

'Yeah – sure you did!'

'Ask Nico if you don't believe me, although you'll only succeed in embarrassing both him and yourself.' She took out a cigarette, lit it up and started smoking.

'Don't take me for a fool, Kate. I know you! I know you better than you know yourself. You've fallen in love with him! I know you have!'

She stared at him, startled, and they lapsed into silence. He walked over to the window and stared out.

She went and sat down on the couch and spoke quietly. 'I admit I have feelings for him.'

'Oh Kate!' he exclaimed as he put his face into his hands.

'I couldn't help how I felt, Tony. I've fought it every step of the way and I have not been with him, I swear.'

He turned and faced her. 'So you were just emotionally unfaithful to me then? I think that's even worse.'

She put out the cigarette and stood up. 'I'm sorry – I really am! As soon as I realised how I felt I kept away from him, and tried to get him out of our lives. But then you employed him and I couldn't get away from him. I begged you not to employ him.'

'And why do you think I employed him? It wasn't because of his super architectural skills, I can assure you.'

'So it was a ploy to try and catch us together?' She shook her head in bewilderment.

'I knew you had fallen for him, and so I wanted to see what you would do. Give you the opportunity to go with him and leave me, if that's what you wanted.'

'If you knew this was happening why didn't you fight for me? Instead of testing me?'

'I love you, Kate, but you don't love me any more.'

'I just don't know what's been happening to me lately. I got so caught up in the house here, and the people who lived here and Nico was part of that. He's part of them and I ended up having these feelings that I couldn't understand.'

'If you weren't happy with me and your life you would never have had your head turned by him! And now you want to sell the house! And run again! Where will you run to this time? More importantly – what are you running away from? Because wherever you run the same problem will be there, just in different surroundings. Because, let's face it Kate, what you really are running away from is – me.'

She looked at his distraught face. 'I just wanted to get back to the way we were, Tony.'

'Turn back the clock?' He smiled cynically. 'You can never do that, Kate.' He went and sat down opposite her. 'Even if I wanted to, we can't.'

'What do you mean?'

'It's all falling down like a pack of cards, Kate. The business – there's no money left, only mountains of debt.'

'What?' She went to him and sat beside him.

'The banks are calling in the debt. The shopping centre is doomed and we put everything up as collateral. There's no way out, Kate.'

She put her arms around him. 'Why didn't you tell me? I could have helped.'

'I didn't want to worry you.'

'Oh Tony!' She hugged him tightly.

'A lot of the people we owe money to will be at this ball tomorrow and they'll be demanding their money back, Kate. I don't know what to do.'

'We'll handle them together, Tony. We'll put on a show tomorrow and let them see the Fallons are still in charge.'

'I don't care about losing everything, Kate. But I couldn't cope if I lost you.'

'You haven't lost me. You never will. We can sort this out together. Like we always used to.' She hugged him tightly.

104

The next day an army of caterers were busy setting the tables in the dining room with an array of cutlery and delph, while the band set up their stage. The kitchen had been taken over by the cooks. The event organisers were rushing around checking all details.

Kate walked through the organised chaos into the drawing room and over to the window where she could see Tony doing manoeuvres out in his power-boat on the lake. Chloe the PR woman came in looking hassled and carrying the morning newspapers.

'Right, I think we have everything under control, Kate,' she announced.

Kate turned and looked at her. 'Good. I see the classical quartet has just arrived.'

'Have they? I'd better go and meet them.' She looked a little embarrassed as she held out the papers. 'I thought you might want to see these.'

Kate took the newspapers from her and read the first headline.

'Building Work Stops at Fallon Shopping Centre.'

As Kate quickly looked through the other papers, she saw they shared the same headlines.

'Can you make sure Tony doesn't see any other papers lying around?' she said. 'I'll keep these.'

Chloe nodded and exited the room.

Kate sat down slowly on the couch as she began

to read the article. The phone rang on the table beside her and she reached out and answered it.

'Kate Fallon speaking.'

'Kate, it's Peter O'Brien here at *The Times,* can you confirm that the ball you've arranged for tonight is going ahead in light of the revelations concerning your husband's business?'

Kate steadied herself and tried to sound cheery. 'Of course the ball is going ahead. It's business as usual, thank you.' She hung up the phone and bit her lower lip.

Later Kate walked into their bedroom and saw Tony at the dressing table staring at his image in the mirror.

'There you are!' she smiled. 'I've been looking for you everywhere. Everything is nearly set up downstairs so I'm going to start getting ready. My beauticians are arriving shortly.'

He didn't say anything.

She walked over to him and placed her hands gently on his shoulders and said softly, 'It might be a good idea if you started to get ready as well. You don't want to be rushing last minute.'

'I don't know if I can face them all, Kate.'

She bent down and whispered in his ear, 'Of course you can. We have to face them. We have to show them that we're still on top.'

He reached up for her hand and held it tightly.

The quartet was positioned at the bottom of the stairs playing classical music. Waiters were positioned around the hall holding aloft silver trays of champagne flutes to greet the guests.

Kate and Tony walked down the stairs holding hands. Tony was dressed in a tuxedo while Kate wore a long red gown and her best diamonds, with her hair loose down her back.

As they positioned themselves near the front door to greet their guests, she whispered to him: 'Remember, big smiles.'

Tony nodded and squeezed her hand while he forced himself to smile happily.

'Kate! Tony! I just love what you've done to this house,' said two friends as they came through the front door.

Kate smiled broadly as she kissed both of them on the cheeks. 'I'm very much looking forward to giving you the grand tour a little later. In the meantime – champagne?'

Nearly all the two hundred guests had arrived and the downstairs of the house was crowded with laughing, talking people. The quartet had finished and the band had taken over and were playing a version of 'Mack the Knife'.

Kate was mixing and mingling, playing the perfect hostess, keeping a watchful eye on Tony all the time.

Suddenly she came face to face with Nico.

'Kate! I've been trying to ring you all day!' he said, his face a mask of concern.

'I've had a lot on,' she said.

'What the fuck has been going on? I read the papers, everyone is talking about it. Has Tony gone bust?'

Kate looked over at Tony who was watching them together.

'Nico, I really can't speak now. I have to go.' She moved quickly away from him and hurried over to Tony and put an arm around him.

At that moment Steve Shaw came through the front door with four other men. Kate recognised the other men as investors in Tony's business. Although they were all dressed in tuxedos, only Steve had been on the guest list.

The men came straight over to Kate and Tony.

'Steve, good to see you,' smiled Kate as she bent forward and kissed him on the cheek.

Steve ignored her. 'Tony – we need to talk.'

Kate saw Tony visibly pale.

'Steve, we have two hundred guests here who need our attention,' Kate said in a determined voice. 'We are not speaking about business tonight – whatever needs to be spoken about can be spoken about tomorrow.'

Steve gave her a filthy look. Kate smiled at the four men with Steve.

'Good evening, gentlemen, nice to see you all again. I must have missed seeing your names on the guest list, but you are very welcome regardless.'

She saw Chloe busily rushing around and called over to her.

'Chloe, I wonder if we can make a quick arrangement with the caterers to set four extra places. These gentlemen are unexpectedly joining us for dinner.'

'I'll see what I can do.' Chloe frowned and rushed off.

A loud bell sounded throughout the house.

'Ladies and gentlemen, dinner is now being

served in the ballroom,' said the head waiter loudly and the crowd started making their way in to dinner.

'If you could excuse us?' Kate smiled at Steve and the other men and led Tony away.

'Thank you,' whispered Tony. 'I couldn't face them tonight.'

'You don't have to. And when you face them, I'll be there with you – every step of the way.'

He managed to smile at her. 'For better and for worse?'

'For richer and for poorer.' And she kissed his cheek.

She held his arm tightly as they walked down the centre of the ballroom towards their table at the top. She felt everyone's eyes on them as they walked. Some eyes sympathetic, some curious, others gleeful. At one stage in the middle of the room, Kate felt Tony falter slightly and she was frightened he would fall. She gripped his arm tightly and they continued to their table and took their seats.

All the French windows along the side of the room were open to allow some air to circulate. The band had relocated to the stage and were playing the jazz version of 'Mad About The Boy'. Kate was glad she had placed some of their closest friends at their table – they were working overtime to pretend everything was normal.

The guests had finished the starters of goat's cheese tartlets or warm chicken salad, and now a multitude of caterers were serving barons of lamb for main course with a mushroom stroganoff for vegetarians.

Kate saw Nico seated in the middle of the ballroom staring at her. She saw him take out his mobile phone and send a text. A few seconds later she heard her mobile phone bleep and she discreetly took it out of her handbag and read it:

Meet me after dinner in the forecourt – please.

She put away her phone and tried to concentrate on the conversation around her.

Dinner lasted for over an hour, and as the guests retired to the drawing room for drinks the caterers quickly got to work removing the tables to clear the ballroom for the dancing later. As Kate mingled, she saw that Tony was in safe hands with old friends. She walked through the hallway and slipped out the front door. She walked down the steps and manoeuvred through the array of Bentleys, Mercedes and Range Rovers parked there, looking for Nico. She spotted him over by the steps down to the terraces and went over to him.

'I can't stay long,' she said. 'Tony will be looking for me.'

'Is it true what they are writing in the papers – that Tony is finished?'

She nodded and sighed loudly. 'I'm afraid it is. I only found out yesterday myself.'

'But I thought Tony was indestructible.'

She put her hands in the air and said cynically, 'Well – there you go!'

'So what are you going to do now?'

'The bankers and investors are already in there baying for blood. We'll have to meet them and see what can be done.'

'We?'

'Me and Tony.'

'Kate, I've been thinking a lot since that night in Hunter's Farm. About what you were saying about me and you?'

She looked at him and shook her head. 'I shouldn't have put all that on you, Nico, I'm sorry. I'm fine now.'

'But what you said about us?'

'There is no "us", Nico. You were just a distraction for a bored wealthy socialite with nothing better to do. And as I will no longer be bored, wealthy or a socialite, my little ... infatuation has now ended, you'll be glad to know.'

'Kate!'

'I know I've allowed myself to have silly thoughts and been living in fantasy land instead of concentrating on what is real – my life. Tony needs me now more than ever. I can't let him down now. Please forget everything I said.'

'So you're letting duty come before your real feelings?'

'I'm putting my husband before anything else – and that includes you.' She looked at the determined look on his face. 'Especially you! Don't you get it, Nico? Are you still so high and mighty, thinking you are an Armstrong, that you can't believe you were just a distraction to me? Something to occupy me and entertain me when I was bored?'

'You said it started off like that – but the feelings became real.'

'I say lots of things for whatever audience I'm speaking to.'

'Kate, I feel the same way about you. I haven't

admitted it to myself, because it seemed so stupid. You seemed so happy with Tony and how could I ever compare to somebody like the great Tony Fallon?'

'Nico, don't say any more. I should never have told you those things and I'm sorry I did. You were part of the whole fantasy of buying the house. That's over now. I have to get back to Tony and my guests. Goodbye, Nico.'

She turned to walk away but he grabbed her arm. 'Nico! Tony needs me. Don't you get it – he *needs me.*'

She broke free from his grip and walked back to the house as her eyes welled with tears.

Kate walked through the guests in the hallway and into the ballroom where the band was playing, the saxophonist filling the room with his music as the people danced. The song came to an end and the saxophonist came to the microphone.

'We're having a lot of requests for our hostess, Mrs Kate Fallon, to sing a song. We all know she is a lady of many talents. Could we have a song please, Mrs Fallon?'

The crowd cheered as Kate shook her head and tried to back away but she found herself being pressurised into going up on the stage. She took the microphone and smiled to everyone.

'I hope you're enjoying the night?'

There was a cheer from the audience.

'It's been a while since I sang in public, but here goes!'

She started to sing 'Summer Wind'.

As she sang, she saw Nico come into the room and stand staring at her, hurt on his face. She tried not to stare back as she sang.

She spotted Tony on the other side of the room. She smiled over at him just as Steve Shaw and the four men encircled Tony. It looked like an argument was developing between them and then she saw Tony nodding and following them out of the ballroom. As the song came to an end, she accepted their applause before she quickly got down from the stage and hurried out to the hall.

She saw Chloe and rushed over to her demanding, 'Chloe, did you see Tony anywhere?'

'He went into the library with those gate-crashers!' she sniffed.

Kate swiftly made her way across the hall through the crowd and went into the library. Tony was there sitting behind his desk as Steve Shaw and the other men talked loudly and aggressively.

'What's going on here?' demanded Kate as she walked across to them.

'We have things to discuss,' said Steve.

'And I told you we were not discussing anything tonight. Not with the ball going on.'

'Oh yes – the ball!' Steve quipped sarcastically. 'You're like Nero fiddling while Rome burns. And how much did this little extravaganza cost you tonight?'

'That's nothing to do with you – it's our private business!' shouted Tony.

'That's where you're wrong, Fallon, because you owe us millions since your empire has just collapsed. We now own you.'

'We will meet you with our accountants and go through everything with you tomorrow,' said Kate.

'Until then I'd like you all to leave my house.'

'Your house!' snapped Steve with a derisory laugh. 'You don't own this house any more. You don't own anything.'

'Leave now!' demanded Kate.

Steve approached her. 'Your days of giving orders are over, you stupid slut!'

'Don't you dare speak to her like that!' shouted Tony, jumping up from his chair.

'Or what? What can you do? You've no power any more, Tony. You're finished.'

Tony suddenly ran from behind the desk, across the room and out the door. Kate hurried after him. In the crowded hallway, she pushed her way through the people, shouting 'Tony!' as she saw him run out the front door.

She managed to get to the front door and raced down the steps.

Outside Kate saw Tony flee across the forecourt and down the flight of steps to the terraces. She ran after him.

'Tony – please wait for me!' she begged as she reached the steps.

She could see him running down the flight of steps to the next level. She chased after him, her hair and gown flowing behind her. She rushed down the series of steps and terraces until she finally reached the lakeshore. She saw Tony run down the pier and jump into his power-boat and she heard him starting it up. As she ran down the pier she knew it was too late.

He sped into the night at top speed.

'Tony!' she shouted after him.

Suddenly Nico appeared beside her. 'What is

going on?' he demanded.

'It's Tony! He's beside himself. He's not thinking straight. He's–'

There was suddenly a loud bang, followed by an explosion out in the lake.

'*Tony!*' she screamed into the night as the fire from the explosion lit up the lake. She turned and fell into Nico's arms, sobbing loudly.

105

ONE YEAR LATER

As Kate looked around the board table of accountants, bankers and investors, in Eiremerica Bank's headquarters in Dublin, she steadied herself. The meeting was the latest in a long line of meetings held to try and resolve the tangled web that was Tony's financial affairs. As she looked at the uneasy and concerned faces all focused on her, she reminded herself she had been through far worse since Tony's death. As if dealing with the shock and grief hadn't consumed her enough, she then had to relive it publicly with the coroner's inquest. Then there had been the headlines and constant press intrusion. And finally the realisation that as Tony's wife who had signed certain documents she was responsible for the millions in debt he had left behind. And when she had a quiet moment, if she got a quiet moment, she had to deal with her own grief over Tony.

Steve Shaw had been speaking for a considerable time, outlining to everyone the seriousness of the situation, as if anybody needed reminding.

'So, Mrs Fallon, what are you going to do to pay back all this money?' demanded Steve.

Kate's lawyer Michael Delaney sat beside her. He had been one of the few who had stood by her and shown himself to be a true friend.

'As you all know,' began Michael. 'Kate was not involved in Tony's business affairs directly and so this has all come as a considerable shock to her.'

'So what? I saw her being around when business was discussed!' snapped Steve.

'As you well know I never attended any boardroom meetings, Steve,' said Kate. 'I accompanied him when he and colleagues were having dinner or to social occasions to support him. In fact, you used to practically insist I attend them to charm your investors.'

Steve scowled at her. 'Regardless, you were his wife and as his wife you co-signed contracts, leaving you responsible for the debt.'

'Mrs Fallon is selling all assets at the moment to try and pay back everything,' said Michael. 'You've taken all business assets including the shopping centres. The house in Dublin is already sold, all jewellery gone. The house in the country is presently on the market. She will be left penniless.'

'There are still millions owing on personal guarantees,' said Steve.

'I know!' Kate raised her voice. 'You've said it enough times! I'm starting my acting career again. I've met with all my contacts and I hope to be earning money to start paying this debt off.'

'Well, let's just hope you are still a popular enough actress with the public to start earning big money!'

Kate hoped so too.

Kate and Michael walked out of the Eiremerica headquarters.

'When I think how they used to fawn over Tony!' said Kate, in despair at how she was being treated.

'People are false,' said Michael. 'Will you be able to get big-paying roles in films at this stage?'

Kate pulled a doubtful face. 'I have to believe I can, otherwise I'm finished. I have to go down today to the house in the country and close it up before the auctioneers take it over. Then I fly to New York to try and start working.' She leaned forward and kissed his cheek. 'Thanks for all your help.'

He watched her walk over to a taxi rank and get into a cab. She waved to him as the taxi drove away.

Kate put the last of her clothes into her suitcase and closed it. She picked up the suitcase and walked out of the bedroom, along the corridor and down the stairs.

As she reached the hall, the front doorbell rang. Putting down the suitcase, she went over and opened the door.

Nico was standing there.

'Hi – how are you?' He stepped inside and hugged her.

'Just finished packing,' she said, hugging him back.

They walked into the drawing room.

'I see Dolans Auctioneers have already put the "For Sale" sign up at the gateway,' said Nico.

'Have they? They must have done it this morning. They don't hang around, do they? In fact, one thing I've learned over the past few months is that nobody hangs around, regardless of what has happened.'

He held her hand tightly.

'When are you leaving for New York?' he asked.

'My flight is tomorrow evening. All the meetings with the accountants, auditors, banks are over. At least I don't have to go through that any more.'

'What's the outcome?'

'Well, as I feared. Not only have I nothing left, but I am responsible for a multi-million-euro debt as Tony's wife. I signed documents during our marriage that hold me responsible in the, quote, "untimely demise" of Tony. Let's face it, it was very untimely.' She crossed over to the window and looked out at the lake.

Nico had been wanting to ask Kate a question for a long time but hadn't wanted to upset her. He decided to ask it now.

'Do you think he meant to do it?'

'You read the coroner's report like everyone else: death by misadventure. It's kind of apt that they used that word – Tony lived life so adventurously, it's little wonder a misadventure did him in.'

'And you believe the report?'

'I don't know what I believe, Nico. I don't think he meant to kill himself. But he wasn't himself that night with everything going on. I don't know what was going on in his mind. I don't know if he saw the rocks in the lake, if he could have avoided them. Or if he was travelling so fast he couldn't stop when he did see them. Misadventure sounds as good an explanation as any.'

'So what will you do now, once you get back to New York?'

'I have to figure out a way to pay back these debts I'm saddled with. I've been in contact with all my old friends from the film industry to see if I can start acting again. But in all honesty, I don't believe I'll ever be able to pay this money back. It will be hanging over me forever, stopping me from moving ahead with my life.'

'Can I do anything to help?'

'I think you've been enough help already, Nico.' She smiled at him as she thought back to how he had given her so much support. How she wouldn't have been able to get through Tony's funeral or the months after without him.

'There is one thing you can do for me, I'd arranged to meet Janet from Dolans Auctioneers to give her the keys to the house today. I don't feel like waiting around to meet her. Will you give them to her?'

'Sure.'

'Thanks, I'll text her to say to drop in to you at Hunter's Farm then.' She paused, gazing at the floor. 'I should have known in the months leading up to Tony's death that he was in trouble. His life was falling down around him. I should have known, I should have seen something was wrong. Too busy with this house, with daydreams from the past – with you even.'

'How were you to know?'

'I should have. I'd better get going.' She walked out into the hall.

Nico picked up her suitcase and they walked to the front door and opened it. Kate took a final look around before walking out with Nico and locking the door behind them.

They walked to her car and he put her suitcase inside. She looked up at the house.

'You'd think this place would have bad memories for me after what happened with Tony. But it doesn't. I just think this was where we spent our last time together. And it's been my refuge from the world over the past year. I could close that door and just not care about the rest of the world. Now I have to face it.'

She hugged him tightly and got into the car. Looking up at the house, she started the engine and drove off down the avenue as Nico stood there looking after her.

Nico answered the door at Hunter's Farm and Janet Dolan stood there.

'Hello again,' she said brightly.

'Hi, Janet,' he said, gesturing to her to come in.

'Well, I never expected to be back here selling that house again,' she said, following him into the lounge. 'Especially under such tragic circumstances.'

'I can imagine,' said Nico, handing over the keys.

'Awful business, and they were such nice people, Kate and Tony.'

'Yes, they were.'

'Well, when you fly too close to the flame you can get burned,' she said in a jaded seen-it-all-before way. 'They were just living the high life too much.'

'I thought you liked all that flash behaviour,' he said irritably.

'Well, I don't know about that. It's all very excessive looking back on it, isn't it?' she tutted. 'I don't know who I'm going to get to buy the house now since the receiver appointed me. I explained to them the country-house market is all but dead at the moment. We've had to diversify into becoming an auction house for antiques as well as property to survive even.' She surveyed the antiques in the sitting room. 'Anything good you want to sell?'

She spotted the painting of Clara and went up to examine it.

'Where did you get this?'

'It's mine. It's been in the family for years. It's of my grandfather's first wife, Clara.'

Janet peered closely at the painting, examining it intently. 'But this is a Jonathan Seymour!'

'That's correct, he knew Clara.'

Janet turned around excitedly. 'But Nico, do you know how much Seymour paintings are going for? They've shot through the roof. Especially now everyone is worried where to put their money safely! They are investing in fine art.'

'Really?' said Nico, coming closer and staring at the painting.

Kate answered the phone in her hotel room in Dublin.

'Kate, it's Michael Delaney here,' said the voice on the other end.

Kate fretted at hearing her solicitor's voice, hoping another issue hadn't arisen.

'Hi, Michael.'

'Kate, I was wondering if you could come into the office to meet me today?'

'Today! Oh Michael, I'm flying to New York this evening and don't really have the time.'

'It is very important.'

'But what is it about?'

'I'll explain when I see you.'

She sighed. 'Oh all right, I'll see you at two.' She hung up the phone.

'Thanks for seeing me at such short notice,' said Michael, opening up a file as Kate sat down opposite him. He studied her. 'Kate, you got married to Tony in a Las Vegas ceremony.'

Kate nodded. 'Yes, we made the decision to get married quite quickly and just went and did it. You know how impulsive Tony could be.'

'Indeed.' Michael looked rueful. 'Kate, going through Tony's papers I found one on your marriage, and... I don't know how to say this, but it's appears you were never actually married, in the legal sense anyway.'

'*What?* But that's ridiculous!'

'I'm afraid it's not ridiculous. After you got married and returned to Ireland, Tony was informed that the establishment you got married in did not have the correct licence to officiate a marriage ceremony.'

'But why didn't he tell me?' Kate was amazed.

'According to the file, he didn't want to upset you – and,' Michael looked a bit embarrassed, 'well, you did get married in such haste, after knowing each other such a short space of time, and he wanted to make sure the marriage was successful before recommitting. As it stood, it wasn't a valid wedding – well, you know Tony – he always liked to have a hidden clause in any contract–'

'–to let him get out of it if he so wished,' Kate finished the much-repeated expression of Tony's for him. 'Including our marriage, seemingly!'

'Oh, I'm sure Tony meant to fix the situation when he got round to doing it. He left everything to you in his will ... that was when he had anything to leave.'

'But what does this mean? Other than the fact our marriage was a lie.'

'Your marriage might have been, but your relationship wasn't. But this means that you are not responsible for all that debt. Anything you signed as his spouse is invalid as you were not his wife.'

'But will they not accuse me of fraud?'

'How can they? You were an innocent party. Oh, I'm sure they will try and fight it, but I'm confident they won't get anywhere. The signatures are for Kate Fallon, and as we've just discovered Kate Fallon does not exist, legally anyway. You've always still been Kate Donovan. You're free, Kate.'

'Maybe that's why he didn't get around to marrying me again for real,' said Kate as she started to cry. 'He couldn't get himself a hidden clause to get out of the debt, but he managed to get me one. Oh Tony!' She looked up to the ceiling and started to laugh through her tears. 'You clever – stupid – *brilliant* man.'

106

The auction rooms at Dolans was packed as Nico hovered at the back. The portrait of Clara was positioned at the top of the room beside Janet who stood at the auctioneer's podium. Nico was still stunned after Janet's revelation that the painting was very valuable, and she seemed confident she could acquire several hundred thousand euros for it. He hardly dared believe it.

'Ladies and gentlemen,' began Janet causing a hush to fall across the room, 'Dolan auctioneers are delighted to bring a Jonathan Seymour painting to the market today. The portrait is of Clara, Lady Armstrong. The portrait has remained in the Armstrong family since it was painted. The renowned artist Seymour has acquired international acclaim...'

Nico drifted off as Janet continued to sing the portrait's merits. This was different from when he was forced to sell the house. This sale would have no liabilities waiting to snare the money. Janet started the bidding, and the offers came fast and furiously until he heard Janet shout 'Sold!' The painting was sold to a London art gallery for seven hundred and fifty thousand euros and Nico was glad it was going to be exhibited as opposed to being held in a private collection.

As everyone departed the auction room Nico went up to Janet and the portrait.

'It got even more than I was expecting!' said Janet delighted.

'Or I! Thank you, Janet. I didn't think there would be that much demand with the economy the way it is.'

'There's always money, Nico, it just ebbs and flows to different people, that's all. And it looks like it's about to flow back to the Armstrong-Collins family. Any plans what to do with it?'

He looked at her and nodded. 'Yes, I want to make an offer for the house.'

'The Fallon house?' said Janet, licking her lips at the prospect of a second big sale on the same day.

'Yes – Armstrong House. I would like to offer seven hundred and fifty thousand for it.'

'Seven hundred and fifty thousand!' Janet exclaimed. 'But that's only half of what the Fallons paid for it when it was a wreck, and before they spent all that money doing it up.'

'I know, but as you know it's a crashed market and it's all I have to offer.'

'Well, I know but–'

'Come on, Janet, you could be sitting on that house for years in this market and then not get what I'm offering today.'

'Well, I'll have to check it with the receivers. It's their decision obviously.' She took out her mobile and went off to make a phone call. She arrived back a few minutes later.

'It looks like we have ourselves a deal. They

accepted your offer.'

Nico smiled happily.

'You're just a speculator, Nico,' snapped Janet huffily.

'No – I'm just bringing the house back into the family – where it belongs.'

107

Kate was back in Dublin having managed to secure a role in a film being shot on location in the city. She had just finished filming a scene and was in her dressing room waiting for a journalist to interview her about the movie. There was a knock on the door.

'Come in,' said Kate and the door opened and in walked the woman journalist. Kate immediately recognised her from the photo in Hunter's Farm as being Nico's wife Susan.

'Hi, Kate, I'm Susan Collins from *The Times*.'

They shook hands.

Kate nodded and smiled at her. 'I just want to make sure my agent made it clear I won't talk about my deceased husband Tony or his business, only the film I'm making.'

'Yes,' said Susan with a chuckle, sitting down. 'Your agent made that very clear indeed.'

'Sorry,' apologised Kate. 'I'm just asked so much about it, and I don't want to talk about it at all.'

'Understandable,' said Susan, taking out her

miniature tape recorder and turning it on.

They spent half an hour talking about the film and then Susan concluded the interview and turned off the recorder.

Kate looked at her curiously. 'You're Nico's ex-wife, aren't you?'

'That's right. You bought the house in the country from us,' stated Susan, surprised Kate knew who she was.

'How is he?' asked Kate.

'Very well actually. You know Nico – never gets too excited about anything, or never gets too down either. Always on an even keel.' She pulled a humorous face.

'That's a good way to be. I've learned to be more like that myself... I always felt he hoped you two would get back together?'

'Well, there's no chance of that. I'm getting married again.' Susan flashed her engagement ring.

'Oh, congratulations!'

'I haven't told Nico yet.'

'I wonder how he'll take it?'

'Our daughter Alex was always singing your praises when she met you,' said Susan. 'Thank you for being so kind to her.'

'It was no trouble. She's lovely ... like her father. Some woman will be very lucky to have Nico.'

Susan looked at her, suddenly aware. 'Yes, she will... I hope he finds what he's looking for someday. Why don't you ring him up now you're back in Ireland? I'm sure he'd be delighted to hear from you.'

'Just tell him I was asking after him when you speak to him next.'

Alex was on her school holidays and Nico was driving them down to Armstrong House to spend the vacation there. It was the first time Alex had been at the house since he'd bought it, and he was excited about showing it to her. Since buying the house he hadn't spent that much time there. He had been too busy in Dublin, working hard on the architect business.

Alex was now fifteen and as she wisecracked all the way down he couldn't help but marvel at how grown-up she had become.

'Well – what do you think?' Nico asked as he put on the kettle in the kitchen to make them a cup of tea.

She sat up at the island. 'I feel sorry for the Fallons,' she said. 'All the work they put into this place, only to lose it.'

'I'd say that was the least of their problems.'

'Kate Fallon is back in the country.'

'Is she?' Nico was surprised.

'Yep – Mum interviewed her for the news-paper.'

'Really?' Nico was shocked.

'Yes – she's making some film on location here. You were really friendly with her, weren't you?'

'We – knew each other well, yes.'

'I remember her being very nice.'

'Well, she's a very nice woman.'

'She goes by her acting name Kate Donovan again now.'

'Does she?'

'Well, I suppose there's too much negativity attached to the Fallon name after everything that happened.'

'You read too many newspapers, Alex.'

'Mum said all Kate did was talk about you, singing your praises.'

'Did she really?' Nico was surprised.

'She must miss this house terribly.'

'I don't know if all her memories here were good ones.'

'Mum really liked her. Said she was very interesting.'

'Kate is a very remarkable woman. I learned a lot about this house from her. I always took it and our family history for granted. But she didn't. She was intrigued by it all... Now I'm more aware. Generations of our family lived here and now, one day, it will be yours as well – and you'll keep the family line going here.'

'Such a big responsibility for my little shoulders,' she sighed dramatically.

'You'll understand it one day,' he said, putting the tea in front of her and sitting opposite her.

'Dad – I've something to tell you... Mum's getting married again.'

'Oh!' He was shocked.

'To an editor at the paper.'

'Right!'

'He's very nice, and she's very happy. And I really like him.'

'Well, I suppose that's the main thing!' He nodded.

'Mum's going to phone you this week to tell

you herself. But I thought I'd tip you off.'

'Very thoughtful of you.'

'So what are you going to do now?' she quizzed.

He looked startled. 'About Mum?'

'No, with your life!'

'What do you mean – what am I going to do now? Nothing!'

'*Hmmm*, I was afraid of that. The fact is I don't think you've really moved on from the marriage. I think you felt the bond was still there, through me and everything.'

'Is that a fact?' he said sarcastically.

'And I suppose you're both so fond of each other, you might have even thought you might get back together again one day.'

'That's rubbish, Alex – you don't know anything about it.' Nico was getting annoyed.

'Anyway, I think you need to get on with your life.'

'When I need advice from you, Alex, I'll ask for it.'

'Well, I mean, what are you going to do with the rest of your life? Spend it rattling around this house all on your own?'

'I hadn't given it much thought.'

'Well, maybe you should.'

'Thank you! Now what do you want to do this evening?'

'Kate's very cool. All my friends love her. They couldn't believe it when I told them you were friends with her.'

'I used to be a friend of hers, Alex. I don't know her any more.'

'Well – you could change that. She's at the same

phone number incidentally.'

'Alex–'

'No need to say another word! By the way, Mum wants you to attend her wedding.'

'Great! I really can't wait for that day!' said Nico sarcastically.

108

Alex walked down the aisle after the bride. The church was filled with guests. She saw her father and smiled at him. He smiled back at her. Alex had been worried he might become emotional on the day, but he seemed happy.

The bride reached the top of the aisle and Alex quickly got to her post, straightening out the bride's long wedding train. The groom winked at his bride and took his position beside her.

'You're all very welcome here today,' began the priest, 'to celebrate the marriage of Kate and Nico.'

'It's not too late to back out,' Nico whispered to Kate as the priest continued.

'You're not getting rid of me that easy. Besides, I never believe in walking off until a scene is finished,' Kate whispered back and squeezed his hand.

In the congregation two of the guests were having a whispered conversation.

'Let's hope this husband has a luckier time of it than her last one,' said one of the women.

'They seem in love though,' said the other woman.

'Don't forget she's an actress by profession! I think it's a rebound job myself. Him getting over the ex-wife remarrying and her getting over Tony's death. I mean they've only known each other five minutes.'

'No – he's known Kate for years. He renovated the house for herself and Tony.'

'Well, I don't know – the ownership of that house has been passed back and forth between the two of them like a game of tennis – and now they are both ending up living in it together! Deuce! It's more a love affair with the house than each other, if you ask me. Neither could bear to leave it!'

The priest pronounced them husband and wife and Nico leaned forward and kissed Kate. They made their way down the aisle quickly and confetti was thrown as they left the small church in the little village near Armstrong House.

Outside, the wedding party was gathered in the sunshine as Kate and Nico accepted congratulations and posed for photos.

'Well, I have to hand it to Kate – you could shove her in a tub of shit and she'd still come up smelling of roses!' said one male guest to another outside the church.

'What do you mean?' asked the other man.

'Well, let's face it – a couple of years ago she'd lost her Tony, lost her house, lost her career and owed millions. Now look at her – she somehow managed to weasel out of all that debt, her career is back on track, married to a lovely new husband, and even got her house back!'

'Ah well, Kate's been through a terrible time with everything. It would have broken a lesser person. She deserves a bit of happiness now. And besides she's changed a lot. She doesn't go to premieres and parties any more. She told me she was happy just being with Nico here at home in the house.'

The two men looked at Alex as she moved from guest to guest, chatting happily.

'Nico's daughter seems to be quite a character.'

'Ah,' said the other man smiling, 'my family have known the Armstrongs for generations. Alex's surname might be Collins, but she's an Armstrong through and through. Come on, it looks like we're off back to the house for the reception.'

Kate and Nico's car led the caravan of vehicles around by the lake and up to the house. As their car stopped, they both got out and the photographer arranged them in a pose in front of the house.

Nico started laughing. 'I was just thinking of a wedding I was at recently and somebody commented the bride was something new, to the groom, something old due to her advancing age, something borrowed as she had been married to the groom's best friend previously, and something blue – she had a rather morose nature!'

Kate started laughing with him. 'I never thought about that when I was getting ready.' She touched Clara's brooch she was wearing. 'I suppose this brooch fills all the requirements for the day too – something new, to me ... something old ... and something borrowed, from Clara ... and something blue, a relic from an unhappy marriage. But now it's going to be a symbol of a happy one.'

And as the other guests arrived, Nico and Kate led them up the red carpet through the front door and into the house.

Epilogue

1940

Pierce and his wife Joan walked out on to the airfield at Dublin airport where the small passenger plane was waiting. Joan was holding their twelve-month-old daughter Jacqueline. He was dressed in his officer's uniform. It felt strange but somehow right to be back in uniform.

'I don't know why you have to go to this war,' Joan said in a final protest. 'You've done your part in the last war. This isn't your fight, it's the next generation's. And Ireland is neutral and isn't even in the war!'

'I've told you before, I have invaluable experience to offer them,' he said.

If the truth be known, Pierce was excited by the prospect. It was as if he had been waiting for the last twenty years for this to happen again. He had spent nearly two decades pen-pushing at the British embassy in Dublin. Twenty years seeing his role in life ebbing away. No longer a respected peer in this new country. His beloved house in the country practically destroyed. His looks gradually

584

fading, and the attention they brought and which he took for granted lost. Years of thinking about the past and what had gone wrong. And then he had met Joan at a ball two years ago. She was the daughter of a Dublin businessman and a renowned beauty. There was a restlessness about her that night as if she was searching for something in the same way Clara had been the night he had met her. And when they were introduced, it was like she had found what she was looking for in Pierce. She reminded him so much of Clara. And it was like he was being given his youth back, another chance. And with the war approaching, it was as if time was repeating itself.

Joan was determined not to cry. She knew Pierce hated scenes and tears. Everyone told her she was mad for marrying Pierce Armstrong. They said he was cold and selfish. And he was all those things, she had to admit. But with her, he struggled to be something else as well. Often not succeeding, but he did try.

'I've been to the solicitor and everything is taken care of if anything happens to me,' he said.

'Pierce, don't!' pleaded Joan.

'Yourself and Jacqueline will be looked after, everything goes to you. Such as it is, mainly the house in the country and what's left of the farm. You can call on Prudence if you need anything.'

Joan pulled a face. 'I'd rather not!'

He stared at her and then managed to smile and bent forward and kissed her.

'Will you phone me when you arrive in London later?' she asked.

'Yes.'

'Will you be home for Christmas?' she asked.

He thought of the rude response he had given Clara when she asked that in the last war. He nodded and said, 'I'll try.'

He kissed her again and then Jacqueline before quickly walking up the steps and into the plane. He took his seat by the window and looked out at his wife and child on the airfield, waving. He smiled at them and waved back as the plane's propellers started and the plane began to taxi down the airstrip. He would be stationed a few days in London and then next week he would be in France on active duty trying to stop the German advance. Life had given him a second chance.

Clara held the envelope nervously, looking at the neatly typed address on the front. She looked at her watch and saw it was nearly two in the afternoon. Slipping the envelope into the pocket of her cardigan, she walked over to the mirror in the sitting room and smoothed down her pale silvery-blonde hair, and checked her appearance. Her visitor was now nearly an hour late and she anxiously looked out the window down the parklands of the country house in Kent she had inherited from her grandmother, Louisa.

She picked up the newspaper on the coffee table with headlines about the war, and leafed through the pages. She stopped when she found the photo of Pierce with his young wife and a baby girl in the society pages and read the caption underneath: '*Lord Armstrong with his wife Joan and their daughter Jacqueline*'.

As she heard a car approach, she folded over the

newspaper. She went quickly to the front door, opened it and rushed to the man who approached her, smiling, and enveloped him in a hug.

'You look younger every day,' he said happily as they went into the sitting room.

'Everyone says you have become a charmer, but choose your audiences more carefully. I'm immune to flattery!' she said grinning, as they both sat down on the couch and she took the hand of her eighteen-year-old son James.

'Nobody is immune to flattery,' he said, grinning back.

'How were your final exams?'

'Not too bad. I think I scraped by.'

She reached into her pocket, took out the letter and nervously handed it over to him. 'This arrived for you in this morning's post.'

'I know what this is,' he said and he looked at her worried expression before adding, 'And so do you.'

She nodded and he quickly tore it open and read the letter inside, before looking at her and smiling. 'The Royal College of Surgeons ... accept me as a student!'

'James!' Clara hugged him tightly. 'I've been that worried all morning, such a relief!' She shook her head in delight. 'You'll make an excellent doctor, just like my brothers.'

He folded the letter away into the envelope. 'It might have to be delayed with the war. I might be drafted.'

'Oh James, don't say that!' All Clara's horrible memories of the last war were haunting her since this new war had started. 'You're far more use as a medic in the war than a soldier. Much better to try and save lives,' she said imploringly.

'We'll see,' he said.

'James ... I've been meaning to talk to you for a while. It's about your father.'

His face clouded over. 'What about him?'

'Pierce has married again and they have a baby daughter.'

'So?' He looked disinterested.

'So now you're an adult, it's your choice if you want to make yourself known to him. You know why I did what I did, why I kept you away from him. But now you're old enough to make your own decisions. If you want to make contact with him and claim your legacy, I won't blame you for it.'

'My legacy?'

'You are the rightful Lord Armstrong, heir to the house and land in Ireland. I don't want you to regret it in years to come.'

'I won't regret it. I don't want the title or that house. You made the right decision all those years back, the only decision. And I stick by what you did.' He reached out and took her hand. 'His life was the poorer for not having us in it.'

'Aren't you even – curious?'

He looked at her, thinking of the terrible times she had suffered in her marriage and how brave she was rearing him on her own when she had returned to London and discovered she was pregnant.

'Not in the least. This is my life, the only one I've known, and the only one I want,' confirmed James.

She squeezed his hand tightly. 'I'd hoped you would say that.'

'I don't want to invite my father back into our lives after you went to such great lengths keeping me a secret from him.'

'I had no choice ... Pierce was very damaged. He was a bad husband and he would have made a terrible father. And I knew he would have fought to take you from me.'

'I know, and you were very brave all these years bringing me up on your own.'

'I loved every minute of it. Besides, I had a lot of help from my family, they closed rank around me. Especially my grandmother. Sometimes it was hard to believe, but I was always Louisa's favourite.'

'Anyway, the house in Ireland is uninhabitable, isn't it?'

'It suffered a terrible fire, yes,' she said, as she thought about that dreadful night.

'Well, I don't want the responsibility of that, thank you very much.'

James pointed up at the painting Clara had done of Armstrong House which hung on the wall and said, 'It's very sad. It used to be such a beautiful house.'

Clara smiled as she looked at the painting of the house and said, 'Maybe it will be again, some day.'

The publishers hope that this book has given you enjoyable reading. Large Print Books are especially designed to be as easy to see and hold as possible. If you wish a complete list of our books please ask at your local library or write directly to:

Magna Large Print Books
Magna House, Long Preston,
Skipton, North Yorkshire.
BD23 4ND

This Large Print Book for the partially sighted, who cannot read normal print, is published under the auspices of

THE ULVERSCROFT FOUNDATION